Happily
Ever After

Happily Ever After

ANNETT HOLLIDAY

POOLBEG

This novel is entirely a work of fiction. The names,
characters and incidents portrayed in it are the work of the
author's imagination. Any resemblance to actual persons,
living or dead, events or localities is entirely coincidental.

Published 2004
by Poolbeg Press Ltd
123 Grange Hill, Baldoyle
Dublin 13, Ireland
E-mail: poolbeg@poolbeg.com

Typesetting, layout, design © Poolbeg Group Services Ltd.

1 3 5 7 9 10 8 6 4 2

A catalogue record for this book is available from the British Library.

ISBN 1-84223-118-9

Typeset by Patricia Hope in Palatino 9.6/13.5
Printed by
Litografia Rosés S.A., Spain

www.poolbeg.com

About the Author

Annett Holliday is from Dublin and has always loved writing, often giving herself the starring role in her self-penned school plays.

She met her 'surfer dude' husband Pete in Australia in the 1980s and after a decade of sunny climes brought him home to Ireland – they now live in Co Meath with their two sons. With encouragement from family and friends Annett started to follow her dream of writing a novel and just made the deadline for the Poolbeg/Open House Write A Bestseller Competition in {insert date} in which she came second.

She is currently taking a three-year career break from her job and has almost finished her second novel.

Acknowledgements

I have always read the acknowledgement pages of other authors avidly – they provide a fascinating glimpse into their personal lives – so here's a glimpse into mine.

Firstly, I want to thank God, for without him nothing else would be possible.

Secondly I wish to thank my mother, Angela, for instilling in me a love of reading, which in turn inspired my imagination. So all those trips to the library weren't in vain after all, Mum!

I'd also like to thank my sisters and brothers for being themselves and keeping my feet on the ground, even though my head is always in the clouds.

Thanks too are due to my friends and cheering squad, especially the brilliant Lisa Harvey, who has been like my personal assistant and a one-woman IT support team. Lisa, thanks for all your hard work and encouragement and the occasional shove in the right direction that I so needed, and it spurred me on. Also, Sharon, Clare, Cliona, Marie and Audrey, who all read the manuscript and voiced their approval.

Thanks also to Michelle Browne, who loved the book too and sent me my first-ever fan letter and made me feel like a real writer.

Thanks too to all my work colleagues at NSAI, who encouraged me to write more after my many articles in the staff magazine – giving me the impetus to continue writing my novel.

Thank you Wendy Nolan for all your help too and Bernard McEvoy of Dundalk Book Binding who made me my own copy of *Happily Ever After* for free.

Thanks also goes to all my extended Holliday family out in Australia who are all very supportive. They hope eventually to have the book in print there!

Thank you so much to Paula Campbell and all the wonderful staff of Poolbeg for giving me this opportunity. I was on cloud nine for days after I discovered I was going to be in print. And many thanks too to Lucy Taylor who edited the book and for saying so many kind things about it – it meant a lot.

And last but not least to my dear husband, Peter, and sons, Alex and Finn, who had to endure a cranky and preoccupied partner and Mum, whose head was full of characters and not much else for the longest time. This is for you, guys.

And to you, dear reader, I thank you for choosing *Happily Ever After* – I hope you enjoy it.

*To my mother Angela – who taught me
the importance of never giving up*

Prologue

June 1986

"Quickly, Ali! The wedding cars are here," Trisha yelled up the stairs.

Ali's heart leapt.

"Coming," she cried through gritted teeth. "Hold still Emma, till I get these bloody flowers back into your hair!"

Emma squirmed. Her dark eyes flashed with annoyance.

At eighteen months old she wasn't quite flower-girl material, although she looked heavenly in a swathe of cream silk.

At last the hairgrip clicked into her dark shiny curls as Emma wriggled free from Ali's grasp and tottered from the room, as fast as her little chubby legs would carry her.

Ali took a minute to check her appearance and finally allowed herself a satisfied smile.

She looked in the mirror to find a girl that didn't look anything remotely like her. This girl was an elegant vision, with upswept hair piled high in a classic chignon, held in place by four baby cream roses. A far cry from her usual mass of wayward auburn curls that normally tossed about her head with abandon. Her dress, a simple sheath in pale gold chiffon, felt like gossamer and draped its way elegantly to her ankles and flattered her slender figure.

Trisha had worked wonders with Ali's makeup. Ali normally got by on a touch of mascara and some pale lip-gloss. Today she hardly recognised the glamorous polished creature that looked back at her and for once she was happy with her own reflection. She believed it when Trisha had told her that she looked divine.

This was such a special day . . . it was a beautiful wedding day.

She couldn't help thinking how far she had come and then spent a moment reminiscing on all that had gone before . . . one thing was for sure, life would never be the same for either of them.

An unexpected tear sprang to her eye. She blinked furiously. Now wouldn't be the best time for her mascara to run. She never thought she'd make it to here, right now, when she couldn't be happier. Well, maybe just a little bit happier.

She took a deep breath at last.

"Calm down Ali. In a few hours your life will be altered forever, if things go according to plan . . ."

She thought of all that had gone before. Suddenly her beloved mother's face appeared in her mind and she felt a deep pang of loneliness for her. If only she could have been here today. Still, it wasn't a day for sadness. Not this day.

Ali then smiled brightly and gave her reflection one last look before she heard Trisha yell once more.

"Ali, are you ready yet? I've nearly drunk half a bottle of Baileys for me nerves. Will you please hurry up!"

Ali grinned. "Good old Trisha, she never stands on ceremony," she thought. "She is the best friend anyone could wish for. I owe her so much. So I'd better go now, before she's three sheets to the wind going up the aisle."

"Ready!" Ali yelled back and gathered her bouquet. And boy, was Ali ready . . . She'd been ready for years . . .

Chapter 1

1975

It was after five by the time Ali made her way home from school. She and her best friend Trisha had been kept late in detention by Sister Ambrose, who couldn't abide giggling in her maths class and Ali and Trish had been caught redhanded, so an extra hour of logs and theorems ensued for the unfortunate pair. As a result she had to run home as fast as her skinny legs would allow her. If she wanted to get out for the disco tonight, everything must work out perfect.

She rushed straight into the tiny kitchen of her two-up, two-down redbricked house, where her mother was anxiously cooking a steak for her father's dinner. Ali suddenly felt a mixture of pity and anger emerge, looking at her mother sweating in the steamy little kitchenette. She was darting to and fro, juggling pots and pans, anxious for everything to be just perfect. Within seconds they heard the key turn in the lock of the front door.

4

"Here he is," whispered Joan, in a resigned tone that was mixed with anxiety and irritation.

Ali stood beside her mother. She always did on a Friday evening.

For that was when her father would arrive home drunk and usually belligerent, half of his wages already spent.

Suddenly her father appeared in the kitchen, bleary-eyed, unsmiling and smelling of beer.

Ali's stomach turned. God, she almost hated him.

He gave a false little smile.

"Well, if it isn't the little women!" he smirked as he stumbled, weaving haphazardly towards his chair. "Where's me tea?"

He looked at Joan menacingly, the green eyes bleary and bloodshot.

"Here," she said meekly, placing a prime piece of sirloin before him. "Watch the plate. It's piping hot," Joan announced smiling, proud of her creation.

"Hmm," her father replied, eyeing the production.

He shrugged off his jacket and rolled up his sleeves, surveying the table. Everything had to be perfect. The matching steak knife and fork, side plate and napkin. The table had to be set every day in a precise manner, complete with silver milk and sugar bowls.

He was quite the lord of the manor, Ali mused. It was far from that he was reared, as her mother sometimes said.

She watched her mum, who was nervously washing the pots while occasionally stealing glances over to her husband for a reaction to the meal.

She looked at her father.

He was a small man.

Small in every way, she thought, especially heart. He was slim and wiry like herself and had the same auburn hair, which was a likeness that bitterly irked her, but most striking was the permanent scowl he wore. It was the scowl of a bitter and disappointed man.

He was busy carving into his steak silently. He was pretty drunk. Ali could tell by his glazed eyes and the slack-jawed expression. She hoped he was so drunk that he would fall asleep soon so she could sneak out with Trish to the disco. He simply had to. There was no way she could miss it, especially tonight. Trish had promised her a loan of her new 'elephant' flares.

Joan wiped a wayward curl from her eye. The kitchen was very hot and steamy, but she still looked beautiful, Ali thought. Tall and slim, with olive skin, huge brown eyes and black curly hair.

Joan still hovered while her father still chewed. Obviously the jury was still out on this one. Just then her father pushed his plate away.

"Call this steak?" he said quietly. Menacingly. "This is a piece of rubbish I wouldn't give to the dog!"

His voice got louder. He stood up and wobbled slightly.

"You're bloody useless, you are!" He pointed at Joan, jabbing a finger in her face. "I'm sick and tired of working my arse off all day for you bunch of layabouts. And then, to get served a lump of fat and gristle at the end of it!"

He then lifted the table up and with both hands toppled over its entire contents. Plates and cutlery flew everywhere.

Joan didn't move.

Ali's father then staggered out of the kitchen and left all the debris behind him. Neither Ali nor Joan was shocked.

This happened at least once a month.

When drunk her father was a bully, throwing furniture over either by accident or design. They had kind of got used to it.

The tense knotted feeling whenever he was around was the worst part, however. Somehow you never got quite used to that.

As long as she could remember he had been cold and distant. Ali couldn't recall a single hug from him, which saddened her deeply.

But right now she felt a mixture of pity and hate.

She helped her mother pick up the mess of food and broken crockery.

"Bastard!" she hissed vehemently.

"Now, Ali," said her mum half-heartedly, tears were dancing in her eyes.

"No!" said Ali fiercely. "It's just not good enough, Mum. He barely brings home enough money for any of us to eat – let alone steak. You eat burger while he refuses prime beef. You'll have to stand up to him, sooner or later."

Then she immediately regretted the statement. But she was just so frustrated by her mother being cowed by her bullying father.

She swore many times she would never be like that whenever or if ever she got married.

Her three younger brothers slowly appeared in the kitchen, white-faced and wide eyed. They had heard the fracas.

7

"When I grow up," glowered Damien, who was eleven, "I'm gonna bash him up 'til he cries. Then he'll soon find out what it feels like."

He angrily wiped a tear from his eye with his sleeve.

"Damien, you must respect your father . . ." began Joan.

"Respect?" spat Ali. "Respect is something you earn, Mum, and I'm afraid he hasn't."

Louie, who was just nine, stared at the mound of broken glass, his lips quivering with fear, but Kevin, who at twelve was the oldest, set about fetching a dustpan and brush to clear away the evidence of his father's temper, anxious to prove he was the man of the house and unafraid.

After that they all tidied up the kitchen in silence. Her mother would have to sleep in with little Louie tonight. It would always be the case after one of her father's outbursts. An uneasy quiet would fall over the house for the rest of the evening.

"I won't go out, Mum, just in case you need me," Ali said, feeling she was abandoning Joan if she went to the disco.

"You will not," Joan insisted. "He's gone to bed now, and you need to get out and enjoy yourself. Here's a fiver. Now slip across quietly to Trisha's and get ready, there's a good girl. Just make sure Mr Costello collects you both at eleven o'clock, OK?"

"Fine, Mum – thanks."

Ali took the five pounds knowing full well it was hard for her mother to come by. "I'll bring you back the change."

8

She grabbed her bag and slipped out quietly into the cold October air. The house was quiet and still, as it always was after one of her father's outbursts.

When her father occupied the house it seemed an entirely different place. During the day there was boisterous laughter and warmth but as soon as he darkened the doorway the happy mood evaporated. Everyone crept around as if on eggshells awaiting an eruption.

Too often he obliged.

Ali often wished he'd either have an accident or suffer a stroke and be immobilised or lose his memory; anything that would make him more docile. Anything to force a change, to make him nice like Trisha's dad but of course nothing ever happened. Nothing ever changed. Each week he was as miserable as the last.

Gerry O'Neill was a frustrated and bitterly disappointed man.

Life had let him down – or at least that was according to him. He had had delusions of a grand career on the stage and had been heavily involved in amateur dramatics in his youth. He had hoped to be a great Abbey actor. But ambition was no substitute for talent and his best achievement had been bit parts in local productions.

Giving up his dream, he ended up getting a job as a bus conductor with CIE and over the years his disappointment festered and he began to drink. Now he was a bus inspector, which was hardly the most loved of professions. He drank daily and was bitter and twisted. He never expressed any joy at the blessings he had been given, like a lovely family and a gorgeous wife, but seemed intent to focus on the negative and tried his best to drag them all down to his dark bitter world.

Ali hated him.

She could admit it only to herself and felt interminable guilt over it, but there it was. She hated the fact that he drank most of the money he earned while Joan had to become a cleaner to make ends meet. Her mother cleaned the rich houses on Clontarf's seafront, houses only a couple of miles from where she was reared. She cycled hail, rain or snow, sometimes with Louie on the back of her old bike, worked like a slave (as far as Ali could see) and then cycled home to Drumcondra to clean her own house. Yet Joan never uttered a word of complaint – even though Ali knew she felt demeaned having to clean up after many of her peers. Ali wondered how she had ever fallen for the dour little man that was her father and Joan never discussed it. She had come from a good family and was so beautiful; it just didn't seem to fit.

"He used to make me laugh," her Mother would say wistfully when Ali would ask her about him. "He was the kindest, sweetest and funniest man you could meet. That was the man I fell in love with, but then the drink took hold of him, just like his father before him. It's not his fault really." Then she would swiftly change the subject. Ali couldn't fathom it except to decide she'd never fall in love and definitely never marry – especially not beneath herself . . .

But right now Ali wanted to forget all about her unhappy family life. She just lived for Friday nights when Trisha and she went to the Grove, only the coolest disco on the northside. Trisha was the total opposite of her friend Ali, and if Ali hadn't loved her so much she'd have hated her. Trisha was the proud owner of a 36c chest, a curvy 'Marilyn Monroe' figure as her mother termed it and long thick blonde hair that hung like satin down her back. She had bright blue eyes and a wide confident smile, whereas Ali was a complex pile of insecurities. She was freckle-faced and had a flat chest, and simply hated her curly auburn hair. She longed to have Trisha's sallow skin that tanned easily, and her confidence. Trisha in return envied Ali's twiggy-like figure and quick mind. They had almost been like sisters ever since Trisha had moved into the tiny redbricked terraced house when she was little more than a toddler. Ali could never remember a time when Trisha wasn't around.

Now Ali found Trisha alone in her tiny bedroom that she shared with her elder sister, Anne. Anne had copious makeup bags filled with hidden treasures of Rimmel, Miners and Biba. Glittery eyeshadows and lip-gloss lay stacked beside kohl eyeliner and purple mascara. Anne was into glam rock and it showed.

"Do you think this purple lip-gloss is a bit too much?" enquired Ali, as they plastered themselves in Miners make-up and Biba sky-blue eyeshadow.

"No. You look deadly. I want to look just like yer woman outta ABBA," sighed Trisha. "The blonde one, of course, seeing as I'm blonde too and we share the same thunder thighs."

She looked down disdainfully at her legs.

"Hey, do I look fat in these 'elephant' flares?"

They both spluttered out laughing.

"Derek better be there after all this effort," said Trisha pointedly, almost de-lashing herself with an eyelash curler.

Derek was Trisha's main squeeze at the Grove, although lots of fellas liked her. Ali was shy and hadn't had a boyfriend yet. Mainly in Ali's opinion, this was due to a lack of cleavage but she lived in hope.

Ali frowned at her reflection in the mirror comparing herself to her beautiful friend who was smiling at her own reflection – naturally.

Finally they were ready and descended into the hallway where Mr Costello was waiting to drive them. Mrs Costello came into the hall, pronounced both girls stunning, and gave Mr Costello a peck on the cheek. Ali was transfixed. Displays of affection between her mum and dad were non- existent. It always surprised her to see it with other people.

The Grove disco was packed solid and Mud's 'Tiger Feet' blared out from the scratchy sound system. Ali just loved it. It was so exciting to enter that hall. It had a unique smell, which was a heady mix of musk cigarette smoke and sweating bodies. Trisha searched the vast crowd for Derek and, suddenly spotting him, made her way through the throng.

Derek Mooney was easy to spot – he was over six feet tall at only sixteen and built big with it. Due to his size Derek had a lot of friends. There were two guys with him tonight and one of them appeared to be smiling at Ali. She almost looked behind her to make sure, but Yes! He had actually smiled at her.

She blushed furiously and thanked God for the awful

blue flashing lights that concealed her crimson face.

He was tall, blond, and skinny, with a rangy frame not unlike her own and he had a lovely smile.

"Do you want to dance?" he asked immediately much to her surprise.

She nodded vigorously as her heart pounded. "God," she prayed silently. "Please don't let me stand on his feet!"

The DJ announced a slow set and Errol Brown's velvet vocals belted out 'Emmaline'. As they swirled around effortlessly, somehow they just seemed to fit and all Ali's nervousness fell away.

He smelled so good.

"I'm Ben," he offered at last, after a silent three minutes.

"Ali," she replied, smiling shyly. "It's short for Alison." ("What an idiot! Of course he knew that," she berated herself).

"C'mon, I'll buy you a Coke," Ben grinned, and they went outside to the cool hallway and talked for ages. He told Ali he was from Sandymount, attended Mt Temple, the only co-ed and coolest school in Dublin and knew Derek from the rugby team.

She studied him while he chatted away. He had that easy confidence just like Trisha. Ali envied that. She was always tongue-tied or blushing. Ben had cornflower-blue eyes, curly blond hair and white even teeth. She noticed them just before he kissed her. A kiss so soft she felt she would melt. Her very first real kiss ever.

Her heart pounded so loud she felt he surely heard it. Her head was swirling. She couldn't believe it. At long last at fifteen someone liked her enough to kiss her. This had to be the best day of her life.

And she never wanted it to end.

The rest of the night flew by in a short pleasurable blur but that feeling she felt inside when Ben first brushed her lips with his would always be imprinted in her memory.

Hasty kisses and phone numbers were exchanged at eleven o'clock and Ali and Trish hurried out the door, in case they were spotted by Trisha's father, Jim. Boyfriends were still frowned upon, so they made sure their exit from the door was solo and innocent-looking. If Mr Costello knew Trisha had been kissing a six-foot tall rugby player all night, he'd have hit the roof.

Ali simply floated to the car park where Jim Costello was waiting.

Trisha's dad was his usual jovial self and chatted all the way home with the girls. Ali couldn't help but compare him to her own father most times, but tonight she was enveloped in a warm fuzzy feeling and couldn't wait to clamber into her cosy bed and relive the whole night in all its delicious glory.

Tomorrow at school she'd give Trisha all the gory details.

Tonight she had to make it to bed quietly in case her father caught her. Nothing could spoil this. Luckily there was no sound in the house when she turned the key in the door and she soon climbed into bed and drifted off to sleep with thoughts of Ben filling her mind.

The following day Trisha got the full story and also told her some background details that she had gleaned from Derek about Ben.

"Derek says his folks are rich, but he does tend to

exaggerate. His father's a doctor, though. So, are you seeing him again?"

"Well, he said he'd phone on Tuesday," said Ali doubtfully, all the old insecurities re-emerging.

'Then, he will," insisted Trisha. "You'll see."

Chapter 2

The important first-ever 'boyfriend' phone call happened as promised the following Tuesday and Ali made a date with Ben for the Grove the following Friday. She confided in her mother and they both agreed to keep it from her father, who would totally forbid any liaison. His alcoholism had its advantages in that at weekends he was missing a great deal of the time and semi-comatose the rest of it, so she had a little more freedom, and Joan was strict but sensible about Ali's maturity. Successive Fridays followed and Ali and Ben met in semi-secret.

Ben was so sweet. Ali was tipsy with affection. Sometimes they would meet after school when Ben caught a bus down to Drumcondra and would wait for Ali outside St Mary's and soon Ali took him to meet Joan, who was immediately smitten by his tall good looks and impeccable manners. He charmed her entirely.

"Yes, Mrs O'Neill, that's a beautiful apple tart, Mrs O'Neill. My mother only has shop-bought ones."

Ben was a complete natural. Ali longed for his easy

confidence. It was a confidence bred from class and comfort. Ali was aware of his comfortable middle-class background. She hadn't been to Sandymount where he lived but had gleaned that the house was on the Coast Road, that his father was a doctor and his sister was studying law at Trinity. His older sister was married to a barrister. When he spoke of his future it seemed pre-ordained that university was a foregone conclusion, as was a medical career like his father's. She often listened to him plan his future while staring at the well-worn carpet in her little house wondering how she would ever fit into his world.

University was not an option for Ali in 70's Ireland. Only the rich or occasionally a poor scholarship recipient went to university. The lucky ones got to do their Leaving Certificate. Ali hadn't planned a career for herself; she just wanted a nice job in a travel agency or in an advertising firm. She was scared to aim any higher. But she stayed silent when Ben asked of her career plans and feigned indifference. She never wanted him to see what she really was, a plain ordinary girl from Drumcondra. He saw something special in her and she liked that, however much of a fraud that made her.

She dreaded the day he'd invite her to Sandymount and she'd have to meet his posh parents. But she decided to cross that bridge when she came to it, if she came to it. It might never happen. He'd probably tire of her long before then . . .

3 months later . . .

"Jeez, Trisha, what the hell am I going to wear?"

Ali threw herself onto her narrow bed, which was covered in tonnes of both their clothes. Almost every stitch they both possessed had been tried on, discarded and eyed over twice.

"Look," said Trisha exasperated, "you're only going to Sandymount ye know, not bloody Balmoral."

"I know!" wailed Ali, "but all my stuff is so old or even worse, tacky and cheap. I don't want to look cheap. Not today of all days. I'm meeting his parents and I know it's a test to see if they like me."

"OK. What about that cream dress your mother got you from Etam's? That's nice and I have a lovely angora peach cardi that'll go over it."

"Let's see!" said Ali excitedly, as she foraged among the sorry jumble to retrieve the hopeful dress.

"Yeah, this looks ok. Where's the peach cardigan?"

She found it trampled on the floor.

"Yes, this could work," she smiled for the first time that day.

"Ye'll look deadly!" declared Trisha, glad to see the worst was over. "Here. Try on my cork platform sandals. You're gonna knock 'em dead!"

"Hope so," wished Ali, half to herself.

Somehow she doubted it.

The moment she'd dreaded had finally arrived. She'd received an official invite to Sandymount for tea to meet Ben's parents, well ostensibly to spend some time studying – but it amounted to the same thing. She was to be given the once-over by his family.

She so wanted their approval.

Ben had become very important to her, but she felt a

little out of her depth. Still, she had to face the music and meet them – sooner or later.

Two hours later, she stepped off the number sixteen at Dame Street and walked over to College Green where Ben was waiting for her, smiling in the sunshine as he spotted her approach.

Her heart leapt when she saw him as it always did. He quickly kissed her and grabbed her hand.

"C' mon, we'd better get a move on. Mum doesn't like anyone being late for her little soirées."

Ali guessed he was a little nervous too.

Ben felt like telling her that she looked really pretty in the cream dress and peach short cardi, but he somehow didn't.

Ali's only make-up was a slather of peach lip-gloss, and kohl on her green cat's eyes. She looked every bit of the fresh innocent girl that she was.

They made a mad dash for the bus and then sat in silence for the whole trip. Ben clasped her hand tightly as if afraid if he let go she'd bolt. She had considered it. She looked out the window at the watery late spring sun. The tide was out at Sandymount and seagulls dived screaming onto the mud for food.

"Our stop is next," Ben suddenly announced and they clambered off the bus and almost ran up the road like a couple of kids, laughing all the way.

Ben's house shocked Ali. It was large, detached and was surrounded by a huge granite wall, a winding gravel drive and large mature trees. A pale green Audi sat neatly beneath the large bay windows and gabled roof.

Ali's heart sank as a tall reed-thin blonde woman,

immaculately dressed in Hermes, opened the door. She was unsmiling and looked at Ali like she was something unpleasant that she had found under her shoe.

"Benjamin, you are late!" she said frostily and turned on her heel.

They meekly followed her into the large wide hallway and on into the dining room. Ben squeezed her hand, not noticing Ali's face, which was now a deep crimson. A man who she presumed to be Ben's father was sitting at the head of a hugely ornate dining table complete with fresh cut flowers and fine silverware.

"There you are!" blustered Ben's father in a booming yet warm voice and smilingly stood up to greet them. "Isabel was a little worried about the soufflé."

He rolled his eyes at Ben knowingly.

"Sit down, sit down, the pair of you. Alison, it's simply lovely to finally meet you."

Ali liked him straight away as he winked conspiratorially at her. "We can't have the damn soufflé fall flat, can we now?" he laughed heartily.

Mr Murphy was very tall, he must have been six feet four at least, and had a shock of grey curly hair and twinkling blue eyes. He was immaculately dressed like his wife and was well tanned.

Ben flopped into his chair leaving Ali standing awkwardly.

"Sit down beside me, dear," smiled his father at Ali. "I'm John by the way."

Isabel was fussing over the dishes with another woman who had brought them on a large silver tray into the room.

"Good God, they have a maid!" thought Ali incredulously.

"Yes," said Mrs Murphy eventually, allowing herself a small smile, "it's very nice to meet you, dear. Ben mentioned he'd met a new friend."

Isabel Murphy's tones were cordial but her eyes were icy. Ali noticed Isabel was eyeing up her clothes.

Obviously they didn't pass muster.

Then Isabel's eyes became fixed on Ali's borrowed cork-sole sandals.

"I never should have worn these!" Ali thought furiously and tried to sit demurely clasping her hands in her lap. Just then she noticed with despair that her hem was becoming undone in her dress. She felt so self-conscious in this rich house with these rich people. She didn't feel she belonged and apparently for that matter neither did Isabel Murphy.

The meal passed in a stressful blur. Ali ate little, while Isabel asked all the pertinent questions, i.e. where did Ali live and go to school and what did her father do for a living. Ali wished the ground would open up and swallow her. Ben's mother had wrinkled up her nose with distaste at every insufficient reply. Ali could practically feel the woman's barely concealed dislike, but Ben appeared blissfully unaware. He just smiled and chatted away animatedly about medicine to his father, whilst she was being grilled. She willed him to excuse them both but he didn't stir.

Ali looked at Isabel Murphy and couldn't help but compare her to her own mother. Isabel was immaculately coifed with long elegant hands and perfectly manicured nails. Her jewellery was heavy and copious and her darkly tanned skin was deeply lined. Crow's feet surrounded the icy cornflower-blue eyes. Ben's eyes, Ali noticed with some discomfort.

Ben's mother was rake-thin and brittle in nature. She was the complete opposite to soft youthful dark-eyed Joan, whose nails hadn't seen polish in years. Ali hated her, for making her feel so small and cheap.

After what seemed a lifetime Ben eventually rescued her.

"Guess we better do some studying, I suppose," he offered in mock dismay, fooling no one.

"Not in your bedroom Benjamin," insisted Isabel with a look that said it all. "After all, the study is the most appropriate place."

She glared at Ali.

The implication was obvious. Isabel thought they were going to get up to something.

Ali was here to steal her precious little son away like some common little tart.

"Rotten oul cow!" thought Ali angrily, while smiling at her through gritted teeth.

"That went rather well," breezed Ben, when they were finally alone. "They really seem to like you."

Ali was incredulous.

"What planet were you on, Ben? Your mother hates my guts!"

Ben grinned.

"Oh that's just Mum. She's a little stand-offish at first – in fact she's a bit of a snob, but she's really nice once you get beyond that."

"Yeah, right!" snapped Ali. "And we're never going to get beyond that, are we? Because I'll never be good enough."

Ben was silent.

"Your father's nice," she added now, dimly trying to change the subject.

"He is the best," enthused Ben. "He's a really good mate too. I can tell him everything. It's always been that way as long as I can remember, you know."

Ali winced slightly. She, in fact, didn't know. It always hit home when people spoke glowingly about their fathers; it almost seemed alien to her. She couldn't relate to anyone having a close relationship to their father as her own role model was so skewed.

"Guess we better do some study, seeing as we're in the bloody study," she blurted out angrily.

Just then Ben kissed her, gently at first and then more passionately.

She felt weak. Almost light-headed. It suddenly felt dangerous, here in his house with his mother seething beyond the study walls. She kissed him back just as passionately, partly to say up yours to his awful mother.

A noise outside the door of clattering pots and pans brought them both back to reality.

"That'll be Mrs Mulvanney," half-whispered Ben. "She's always banging about after a large meal. Doesn't much like cleaning up!"

"Does she cook for you?" enquired Ali, as if it was a normal everyday occurrence in one's life to have a cook.

"Yes," he replied. "She comes in three times a week to

23

cook and clean while Mum is off on a charity bash or whatever. The old dear has terrorised us for years."

"Oh," said Ali in a small voice, trying to imagine a cook squashing into her tiny kitchen in Drumcondra, with her mother. These people live in a different world to me, she realised.

Not for the first time today she was made painfully aware of her class difference, and she didn't like it one bit. Then she looked at Ben again and her heart melted. It was too late. She couldn't help herself.

She was in love with him.

On the way home Ali was quiet, remembering how many times Ben had been in her tiny worn-out little home and never appeared to notice how poor they were. He obviously wasn't a snob so why should she let it affect her?

As they walked up her little street with all the tiny redbrick terraced houses, she decided to broach the subject.

"Why didn't you tell me you were so posh?" she ventured, hoping she sounded light-hearted.

"Am I?" laughed Ben.

He seemed a little confused and embarrassed.

"Yep," she said grabbing him by the collar and pulling him towards her to kiss him. "Very southside!"

"Look, Ali, I can't help where I'm from, no more than you can. But it seems to me you have everything you need here, doesn't it? Except of course, we have Mrs Mulvanney, but I wouldn't call her an asset at the best of times."

"Yes," she laughed. "She did bash a lot of pots about, didn't she?"

They both grinned.

"Don't hold it against me, Ali. I doubt if I could get Dad to sell the Audi." He kissed her nose gently. "See ya Wednesday, OK?"

She kissed him back long and hard.

"You betcha!"

She went to the door and looked back. He hadn't moved.

"Will you come over to the house again sometime?" he asked anxiously.

"Yeah, sure," she lied.

"Great! OK, then," he smiled happily.

Ben sauntered off down the street to catch the two buses home again.

She watched him for a minute and then went inside to tell her mother about the debacle of an evening.

Joan was in the kitchen, hand-washing school shirts.

"Oh, Ali love, how did it all go?"

Her mother looked up, all excited. There she was, her hair all askew, crimson-faced and up to her elbows in sudsy water. She had never looked more beautiful to Ali than she did right now.

She almost came to tears. But instead she bit her lip and regaled the whole sorry tale of smug Isabel Murphy and how cheap she had felt by the end of it all.

"Alison O'Neill," said her mother, when at last she had finished her sorry tale, "there is nothing cheap or common about my daughter. Your family may not have a lot of money but you are not poor. A BMW does not make you a better person. I have been well off and I have been poor, and some of the nicest people I have ever met live right here on this street and not in Clontarf Villas where I grew up. Just remember you are as good as anyone else, and that mother of Ben's must not have much breeding if she was as ignorant as you say she was. Ben is a lovely boy, but he is very lucky to have you."

"Ben's a lot poorer that me in one sense," replied Ali, giving her mum a huge hug, "having that old hag for a mother when I'm so lucky to have you. Thanks Mam."

"Right," said Joan. 'Now, we better get those kids in off the road and up to bed before himself gets in. He'll no doubt be late tonight so hopefully we'll all be in bed long before he falls up the street."

Over at Sandymount Isabel Murphy was pacing up and down impatiently, looking at the slow-ticking clock and willing her son's speedy return.

"It's half past nine for heaven's sake!" she muttered angrily, half to her husband John and half to herself.

"God, woman! Will you sit down and relax. You're wearing a hole in the carpet," boomed John Murphy, exasperated. "He'll be along soon. Don't be such a mother hen."

"It's not that," she snapped. "It's that awful girl. She's hardly what I had in mind for our only son."

John Murphy stood up and went over to the window where she was standing and peered out over her head.

A beautiful sunset was filling the horizon.

He put his hand on her shoulder.

"Well, I thought she was delightful," he said soothingly. "Anyway, how serious can it be? The boy is only sixteen."

"Her father works on the buses, for heaven's sake!" she retorted shrilly, pulling away.

"Oh Isabel," sighed John, in a low resigned voice. "When did you turn into such a snob?"

"When you brought me here to this big mausoleum!" she screeched angrily and turned on her heel and stormed from the room, slamming the large oak door behind her. Her husband went back to his *Irish Times*, but he read it uneasily for the rest of the evening.

He knew Isabel.

If this friendship lasted there would be trouble ahead.

Trouble indeed.

27

Chapter 3

The romance didn't fizzle out. The Inter Cert came and went and Ali and Ben's relationship grew stronger and closer. Both Ben and Ali did well, scoring six honours each, but Trisha scraped by with just two. You would never have known by the huge fuss her family displayed and the ensuing Costello hooley was the talk of the street. Ali couldn't help compare the utter silence in her household that greeted her joy at doing so well. Her mother was fretful, as her father was having a particularly hard week. She could only manage a half-hearted "Well done, love."

In fact, it almost went unnoticed until her father got tanked one night and berated her for thinking she was cleverer then the rest of them.

She simply couldn't believe the vitriol her father displayed towards her for doing so well. All her friends were parading around with gifts of watches and gold jewellery from their parents and she had narrowly escaped a black eye.

Ben said nothing but bought her a lovely silver ring from Kilkenny Design, which had almost made up for it. He'd received a hundred pounds cash from his parents.

Ben barely mentioned his parents these days. Ali hadn't been invited back to Sandymount since the first time, and she dared not broach the subject. Ben seemed to be a bit embarrassed by it all.

He never uttered a word about that night so she knew she hadn't won approval from his awful mother. But how could she berate him about his parents when she had her own alcoholic father to hide?

She knew Ben guessed something was amiss, the way he was always spirited out of her house by an anxious Joan and Ali, before Gerry O'Neill arrived home pissed and aggressive. He was the proverbial loose cannon. The O'Neill family had somehow always thought this terrible secret lay between their walls and avoided outside contact with the rest of Joan's family to protect the fiction of a happy family, but many had guessed the truth. Joan was a proud woman, however, and didn't want anyone's pity. So they continued to cover up and allude to Daddy 'not being well' to outsiders, which was a euphemism for him being stone drunk. Ali often wondered if Ben guessed or wondered why half the time the telephone was cut off or even a couple of times they had no electricity, because her father had drunk his entire wages and there was no money to pay the bills.

She felt so ashamed. She didn't want to draw attention to her shabby home and threadbare clothes to well-off

Ben, who simply wouldn't comprehend it. So she borrowed clothes from Trisha, limited Ben to the parlour, where at least there was an old but good carpet and the best furniture and just hoped for the best, that he wouldn't notice the reality of her life too much.

Joan had taken on more cleaning jobs in order for Ali to stay on in school until the Leaving Cert. Her father had insisted that she wasn't going to sponge off him any longer. She would 'pay for her own bloody books' or get a job. Ali knew he couldn't spare any of his drinking money for her education, so decided to help out by getting a weekend job. Joan's sister Evelyn worked in a high-class boutique off Grafton Street and suggested they would give Ali a try. Ali was cringing at the thought of having to deal with the public, as she was chronically shy, but knew she had to do it. Her mother was worn to a thread and she had to help out. So she went to work at Davinia's.

The owner of Davinia's was a lady called Davinia Carey. She seemed to be about fifty and to Ali, was impossibly glamorous. She was tall and sleek with a short black bob and was always impeccably dressed and made-up. She would waft into the boutique in clouds of Estee Lauder *'Youth Dew'* and was constantly laden with designer shopping bags crammed with *'just have to have its'* as she termed her copious purchases. She drove a mad yellow MG sports car and called everyone 'Lovey'. She would send Ali down to Wicklow Street every Saturday morning for cream-filled brandy snaps and coffees from O'Sullivan's and sometimes into Switzer's for a pricey lipstick. Ali noticed with some distaste that Davinia's designer lipsticks cost more than Ali's entire Saturday wages (a huge £5.00 of which £3.00 Ali gave direct to Joan). Still, even though she detested the job, most of the time Davinia was hilarious and she felt grown-up earning her own money at long last.

Ali would sit on the number sixteen bus at seven pm every Saturday after her slice of the glamorous life and gaze out into the muddy Dublin traffic and wonder what state her family would be in when she got home.

Would the contents of the table be strewn over the floor?

Or would her father have meekly gone to bed too drunk to care what sort of dinner lay before him, or would Joan be sitting half-perched on the chair biting her nails still awaiting his arrival and whatever devastation would ensue?

Ali just wished it would be different. She wished for a father like Trisha's. She just wanted to be happy.

Trisha was happy. Not because of her happy home life, that was just a fact of her existence, but happy because she had dumped the bold Derek and had met the love of her life, Mick O 'Toole, the man she knew she'd marry.

She hadn't told anyone this awesome fact, not even Ali, her closest friend; she just felt it deep in her bones.

Mick was an apprentice plumber, who went to college with her brother Jim. He had called around the house a number of times and she'd noticed him, all black curly hair and deep brown eyes and sallow skin. Then suddenly he seemed to be over every night calling for Jim until Jim told her in exasperation that Mick fancied her and would she please go out with him so Mick would give him a rest, going on and on about her so much he was boring the arse off him.

Jim was never big on romance.

They had gone to the pictures and he'd held her hand and lightly touched her hair and hadn't dived on her like most fellas did.

He didn't even talk to her chest.

Then he'd asked to see her again and when she agreed let out a little yell of *"Yes!"*, because he was so pleased.

They had double-dated with Ben and Ali and had gone bowling out to Stillorgan. Both of the lads had got on famously, much to the girls' delight.

Mick was nothing like any guy Trisha had ever met. He had direction and ambition and a clear plan of how his life was going to be. It surprised yet pleased her and she found herself getting caught up in his enthusiasm. She also felt a little guilty, because she hadn't even thought about what she wanted to do with her life. Basically, she just couldn't wait to jettison school and get a job earning money so she could start having fun.

She had approached her parents about leaving after the Inter Cert, but they had said to stick it out for another year and see how she felt. She knew she was no scholar, but had a flair for design.

However, in 70's Dublin that didn't amount to much. Especially in a convent like St Mary's where they basically educated you to get a nice little office job until you snagged a husband. Trisha never aimed high because little was expected of her. Right now she'd be happy with a proper leather handbag and a nice smart jacket from

Dunnes, not her old hand-me-down jacket that had belonged to her elder sister, Anne.

When she listened to Mick with all his plans and dreams, anything seemed possible. So she began to form an idea in her head, one she'd have to discuss with Ali.

She knew she wanted to do something different. She just didn't know quite what yet.

Chapter 4

"Jeez! It's the middle of September and it's still roasting! Will this summer ever end?" Trish complained as she threw off her heavy wool jumper.

1976 had been the warmest summer on record. The normally lush green grass was still a burnished copper in September and the natives had grown tired of the much longed-for nice summer and just wished for some cool rain. Especially Trish and Ali, who were still forced by the sadistic nuns to wear the full heavy serge uniform more suited to a cool winter in Slovakia than now tropical Dublin.

"Don't worry, Trisha," smiled Ali. "In a couple of months we'll be freezing our bums off and all of this will be a distant but beautiful memory."

They walked home slowly, discussing as usual their favourite topic, men. As they turned the corner into their street they noticed clusters of women gathered in doorways as they always did when something was amiss. Then

Ali noticed a police squad car parked outside her house.

"Oh, no," she thought in dismay. "I hope the old man hasn't got arrested for being drunk and disorderly and the cops have brought him home again."

Her cheeks burnt red as she neared the house. Then she noticed Trisha's mum, Mrs Costello, in her doorway. She was in tears and being comforted by another neighbour. A rising panic filled her.

Her own front door was wide open and she almost bumped into a young garda coming out, who just looked at his shoes as he passed her awkwardly.

The kitchen door was ajar and she could see her father sitting at the kitchen table with his head in his hands. He was weeping loudly. She somehow found her voice.

"Dad! What's wrong?"

"Oh, Alison!" he cried, his face contorted. "It's your mother . . ."

She could smell the drink on his breath.

"What?" she shouted. "What's the matter with her?" She was angry and terrified.

"There's be-been an acc-accident," he stammered, wiping his eyes. "Your mother and Louie were on her bike. A car hit them and she went under the wheels. There was nothing anyone could do –" He stood up and grabbed her by the shoulders. "Ali, your mother is dead!"

Ali felt her head swim and suddenly everything went black.

When she came to, she was in her bedroom. The room was dark and Ali sat bolt upright. Mrs Costello and Trish, who were both standing over her, immediately soothed her.

"Shh, now, love, you've had a terrible shock. Try and rest yourself."

"Louie, where's Louie? Is he all right?" Ali cried, bursting into hot tears all over again.

"He's in the Mater hospital, Ali," replied Mrs Costello quietly. "But he's going to be fine in a couple of weeks, just rest for now."

Trisha was smiling at her and holding her hand.

Tears streamed silently down her cheeks.

"Where is my father?" Ali asked, in a dead voice.

Her face was stone. Trisha knew that look.

"He's downstairs," replied Trisha hurriedly.

"He's being comforted by neighbours," added Mrs Costello pointedly, putting her hand on Ali's arm.

Ali didn't notice – she rose up out of the bed like a robot.

"I must see him," she said quietly, but her voice was steel.

She walked slowly downstairs. She could hear male voices from the kitchen. Her father was slumped over the kitchen table with several of his boozing buddies in tow. Empty bottles of whiskey lay strewn around. Ali marched right into the middle of them. Her father raised his head in surprise.

"Ali," he said. A look of fear crossed his face.

She didn't flinch.

"I see you're doing what you do best, " she said, in a deadly quiet voice. "Guess not even your wife's death could stop you. Come to think of it, it's the perfect excuse to go on an absolute bender. Party time for the poor devoted husband!"

Her voice dripped disgust. The whole place was deathly quiet.

"Now Ali . . ." he began and faltered.

"*Shut up!*" Ali roared. "I just want everyone to know here and you to know, that you *killed* my mother."

An audible gasp escaped from the neighbours.

Ali continued. "You killed your wife just as much as if you had driven that car yourself."

"That's not true!" Gerry O'Neill wailed drunkenly, looking about for pity. "I loved her. I loved your mother!"

"It was because of you," Ali shrieked, "that my mother had to scrub bloody floors – and all because you drank your entire wages every week. You bastard! If it wasn't for you, she never would have been on that bike and she'd be here right now. You ruined my mother's life the day you put that ring on her finger and I'll never forgive you for what you put her through. Never! I hate you!"

She burst into tears and fled the room into the hallway just as Kevin was answering a knock to the front door. Through her tears, Ali could see the face of Ben in the doorway.

"Ben, oh, Ben!" she wailed and flew into his arms and sobbed uncontrollably. Perhaps Ben could make her feel like she wanted to live again because right now she just wanted to die. He wrapped her up in his arms and carried her upstairs – and stayed with her until at last, exhausted, she finally slept.

The next few days passed in a blur. People came and went in the house, paying their respects. Ali felt hardly there. It was if a large fog had descended on her and she could only see things vaguely, through a deep mist. She and Ben went to see little Louie in hospital. He looked so small and vulnerable in the large hospital bed and kept tearfully asking for his mother. It was heartbreaking to see him all broken. Her father had finally told him the news with the doctor's permission and Louie cried for a solid day.

The funeral took place while he was still in hospital. It all just felt like a bad dream to Ali. It was surreal. There was her father, surrounded by his cronies, the perfect widower, with his white face and red eyes. Ali knew it was more due to alcohol than grief. Where had he ever been for her mother when she was alive?

Joan's sisters were there too, in all their finery with their fur coats and big cars. They had been of little help to her too, although Ali did know her mother hid a lot from them. She just hated them all. They were alive and her mother wasn't, and they had never been there for her mother when she was alive. Why did they do the big caring act now? She hated everyone, except for Ben and the Costellos. They had been wonderful and Ben had hardly left her side. They had been amazingly supportive.

But none of it helped.

Ali felt there was a hole in her life. A hole so wide she doubted that she would ever fill it, and she doubted she would ever be the same again.

Chapter 5

A few weeks had passed and finally Louie came home from hospital. He was still quite frail and was on crutches. Ali decided then that she would not return to school. She had already told her aunt to tell Davinia that she had quit her Saturday job, because she would now have to look after the boys. She had to. There was no one else and she owed it to her mother to look after them as her mother would have.

Her father was worse then useless. He drank more than ever, although his violent outbursts had ceased. Too late, thought Ali angrily, She still hated him, and took delight in serving him the paltriest of meals, which he ate in silence. She silently dared him to utter a single word of protest. He never did.

Ben tried to persuade her to carry on at school, trying to tell her she'd get a better job with a better education.

"I know all that!" she had retorted angrily. "But I'm all they have right now. I have to be their mother and I'll have to look after them properly and I can't do that and go to school too."

Ben then suggested maybe finishing her studies in night school.

She then told him everything. All about her father and his alcoholism and how she couldn't even consider the night-school option, because she couldn't depend on him to be home early or sober enough to look after her brothers.

"You poor darling," he had said, tears dancing in his eyes. "I had no idea how awful your life was."

Ben had then held her hand and stroked her hair and told her everything would be OK. But inside he really felt a little out of his depth, although he cared for Ali, even loved her, and knew he just had to be there for her now.

Even his mother had softened a bit when he had told her the awful news. He had always known something was amiss in Ali's family, but had never guessed at the truth. He felt something had been robbed from him too when Ali's mother had died as Ali had lost all her zest for life. Her innocence was gone.

Then he felt enormously guilty for feeling so selfish, worrying how this all had affected him, when Ali was experiencing the pain.

At seventeen he just felt a little unable to cope with such big issues.

Emotions swirled around inside him daily, but he kept his feelings to himself and tried to be upbeat for Ali's sake. She needed him now and he couldn't let her down.

Trisha was the same. She tried so hard to be cheerful and as bright as a light bulb, and largely ignored Ali's deep black moods. She wanted to make it all better for her friend but knew she couldn't. She also felt guilty for having her mother and father safe and happy and for being in school, when really Ali was the bright one who deserved to be there. Ali had turned into a mother hen overnight, coping with Louie's weepiness and slow-mending injuries, Kevin's silence and moods and Damien who was now getting into trouble at school.

Trish saw it all and wondered at a solution. She knew Ali would sacrifice herself for the kids now and become the parent.

It made her so mad to see Mr O'Neill carry on selfishly drinking himself into oblivion, when he could see Ali was not grown up enough for the responsibilities she had to shoulder. She talked to her mother about it.

"Surely there's something we can do," she had protested.

"Well, I've been cooking myself to death for them, sending over casseroles and stews almost every day. I can't approach Mr O' Neill. He wouldn't accept criticism, never could. But I might be able to talk to Sister Ambrose and we could sort something out regarding Ali's schooling. Other than that, well . . . I've got my hands full with my own six kids, love."

"I know," sighed Trisha and gave her mum a huge hug.

"Thanks, Mam. You've been great. I just feel so sorry for her."

"Yes, I know," replied her mother, sniffling back a tear. "Joan would turn in her grave, if she could see her poor kids suffering. That man ought to be ashamed of himself.

41

I'll go and see Sister Ambrose tomorrow and explain everything. Maybe she can come up with some ideas."

A few days later, Ali was outside the front door cleaning the windows, when she saw a flurry of black in the distance. She peered up the street and saw Sister Ambrose, her form teacher, striding towards her purposely.

"Oh no!" she grimaced to herself panic-stricken. "What does she want?"

"Hi, Sister Ambrose . . ." Ali smiled weakly, crimson with embarrassment.

"Hello, Alison," replied Sister Ambrose warmly. "And how are you, dear?"

Ali blushed to her fingertips.

"I'm fine, Sister. Why don't you come inside?"

She then led the nun into the only half-decent room in the house, praying the boys hadn't wrecked it since she'd tidied up last night. Thankfully, it was tidy and clean; the shabby appearance she could not help.

"The reason I'm here," said Sister Ambrose crisply, "is to try and find a way that we can get you back to school, young lady. You are far too good a student to just drop your studies in this way. I know, I know." She put up her hand to Ali's instant protests. "You have a family to look after to all intents and purposes. But I have a suggestion. The boys are in school until three pm is that correct?"

Ali nodded, confused.

"Well," she continued, "then perhaps we can arrange for you to leave at three pm also. The teachers have all agreed to give you study notes for any lessons you will miss."

Ali was unsure.

"But, Sister, there's so much more to do, the boys' homework, then housework and meals. I can't see how I'd fit it all in."

"I've thought of that too," smiled Sister Ambrose, who was now on a roll. "There are several ladies who help out at the convent every week and there's one particularly nice one, a Mrs Donovan, who said she'd love to come and clean up for you a couple of times a week. So that should ease up the pressure a bit."

She took Ali's hand in hers.

"Look, Alison. I know you've had a terrible time. Losing your mother, it was an awful tragedy. She was such a good woman. But I'm sure she would have wanted you to finish your schooling. Education was important to her. And you deserve a future of your own. Please. Think about it."

"I will," replied Ali, and smiled the first genuine smile since Joan died.

Perhaps there was a shaft of light at the end of the tunnel after all. She suddenly felt very old and weary, much older than her seventeen years. After Sister Ambrose left, she sat in the dreary front room and cried. She cried this time for herself and the loss of her innocence and when she was finished she got up and did the ironing. But she did so with a lighter heart.

People cared and would help her. She would get through this and survive. She'd do it not just for Joan but also for herself.

Two weeks later, Ali went back to school. Mrs Donovan came to tidy up twice a week and worked like a Trojan. She sang her way around the little house, cooking cleaning and ironing.

She was such a treasure, that Ali was much relieved. The boys liked her too, and often a warming casserole was tucked in the oven on a particularly cold day, the rich smell greeting them as they came through the door. It brought a little homeliness back into the house.

Her father hadn't been told of the new addition and didn't appear to notice. He was absent a lot and when around was paralysed with alcohol.

Ali decided to hurl herself deep into her studies so she wouldn't feel the raw pain of missing her mother. She wished to be a little girl again and clamber into her mother's big double bed as she used to do when she was sick, and Joan would read to her and pamper her. She wanted to feel safe and loved. She felt life would never be the same, but at least at school she could forget for a while and be just like everybody else – but she wasn't and there wasn't anyone who could change that.

Chapter 6

Christmas came all too soon. It was a time the family would dread. An invitation arrived by phone from Joan's sister, Evelyn. The family was invited for Christmas dinner.

Evelyn lived in Clontarf with her schoolteacher husband, who liked to be called Mr Clarke by all and sundry including his wife. Mr Clarke was a small self-important man, with an oily comb-over and a sleazy eye. But he was well-off and Evelyn, who didn't really like children either, was happy to fuss over him and give all her love to their two poodles instead.

Ali recalled having been to their house only once when she was little, so she was unsure how successful the day would be, but decided to accept, as they would all be miserable in their own home with painful reminders of their mother everywhere.

The day was a hilarious disaster. The boys were boisterous and wild with excitement at the toys they had received (Sister Ambrose had ensured that Ali was helped out financially by the nuns). Then Kevin stood on one of the dogs while Louie knocked over the Christmas tree while chasing the other. Her father, who looked incongruous in an ill-fitting second-hand suit, tried his best to appear sober, but almost couldn't find his mouth during the meal.

Ali was mortified.

Evelyn smiled frozenly while Mr Clarke fiddled with his gold cuff links impatiently and gave the boys daggers looks. Eventually, Ali gave up stressing over the impression they were making and allowed herself to laugh at the situation and even had a glass of champagne to celebrate the day.

Later, in the kitchen while she prepared the dessert, Evelyn gave Ali a huge hug and pressed a cheque for £50 into Ali's hand. Ali was overwhelmed.

"Now you get yourself something nice out of this," she whispered conspiratorially to Ali. "Get into Switzer's sale and get yourself a good winter coat. You look freezing in that old tatty thing."

"Oh, Auntie Evelyn, this is too much, really."

"Nonsense, I insist – this is just between us, mind. And don't spend it on anyone else."

"I won't," promised Ali, and pocketed the cheque quietly.

"Look," said Evelyn softly, as tears danced in her eyes. "I should probably take on you children, perhaps even Louie . . . but Mr Clarke, well he doesn't really like children, especially boys. I suppose it comes from being around them so much in school all day. But just know this, Alison. If you need me at any time for money or just a chat, you know where to come. I miss her too you know."

A tear splashed onto her cheek.

"I know," replied Ali, thankful that Evelyn wasn't offering to take them in permanently. A couple of hours were just about bearable with the insufferable Mister Clarke. But she wasn't such a bad old stick after all.

"We'll be fine, Evelyn, honestly. Just you wait and see."

Chapter 7

Summer of '78

It was the summer of 1978, and all too soon the Leaving Certificate examinations loomed. Ali and Trisha were petrified. The thought that this was finally it, and forever more they would be judged on these results was daunting. Trish, in particular, had reason to worry as she had spent far too many evenings canoodling with Mick rather than hugging her books. At the time it hadn't seemed so important, not nearly as much as it did now and it was too late.

"Jeez, I'm terrified of the maths exam," wailed Trisha. "I've approximately ten minutes to cram six months of revision in. I just know I'll fail. It's checkout chickdom for me, I'm afraid."

Ali laughed despite her growing nerves. She had studied as well as she could with all the awful events of the past year, but she feared it wouldn't be enough.

"Go away, ye big eejit. You'll be fine! As long as we pass, we'll be OK for our new jobs at Quinnsworth!"

"At least we can burn these yokes." Trisha grimaced as she pulled off her heavy woollen jumper. "It's absolutely pathetic that we have to wear all this heavy wintry shite in June. Isn't it just amazing how when the exams are on, the sun splits the trees and when it's over, we'll have another seven weeks of rain before autumn arrives. Ye know what, Ali, if this weather keeps up for the weekend we could go out to Dollymount, you, Ben, Mick and I. We'd have such a laugh."

"I can't, I'm afraid," sighed Ali, "unless of course, I take the boys along. I can't leave them alone all day, especially Louie."

Trish rolled her eyes towards heaven.

"God, Ali, you're no fun any more. You can never do anything on the spur of the moment."

"I know," replied Ali, irritated by her friend's impatience. "You think I like it this way? Every minute of every day I know I can't really be seventeen any more. I'm so tired trying to be everything to everybody. I'm trying to study, be a mum to the boys, make time for Ben, see you, do all my chores; it just gets on top of me sometimes. I just feel like running away from it all . . ." her voice quavered.

"Oh, I'm sorry!" apologised Trisha, contrite. "I'm a selfish cow, so I am, not seeing you're under so much pressure. Are you really serious about wanting to get away from it all?"

Ali nodded, blinking back salt tears.

"How about Australia then?"

"Australia?" gasped Ali. "Isn't that a bit drastic! I

thought you were going to say let's go off to London for a weekend or something . . . "

"Well, I know it's a wild idea, but our Dermot is planning to go over with a few of his mates next year. Apparently they're crying out for chefs in Sydney."

"He's hardly Egon Ronay!" laughed Ali. "He's an army cook."

"Yeah well," replied Trish indignantly, "he's still a chef all the same." She smiled then. "He still burns the toast, though." They both laughed. "Promise me, Ali." Trish was suddenly serious. "Promise me we will go off someday, somewhere out of dreary little backwater Dublin. I want to see a bit of the world before I settle down and get old."

"You're on, I promise," agreed Ali, and they shook on it. "Now, we'd better get to Saint Mary's and pass these bloody exams. If we don't, we won't be able to get a job to pay for the bloody trip, and we'll be stuck here forever. Let's get going, Costello. Just think, in two weeks' time, we are never going to have to look at another school book ever again!"

"Yeah!" hooted Trisha loudly as they ran down the road, half girls, half women, towards their futures, out of school and into the real world, not realising for one minute that life would never be quite as simple again.

Across the other side of the city, a nervous Ben was waiting on a lift from his father, to take him across town to Mt Temple for his exams. He simply had to do well to get into medicine. He had worked like a Trojan, but was still unsure if it was enough. He had hardly seen Ali over the past two months and knew she hadn't been pleased. They had had their first big argument over it.

"I can't see why we can't study together, Ben!" Ali had fumed. She had nearly said, "Like we used to" but stopped herself.

"Well . . . your house is a bit noisy," he offered weakly "and my mother hasn't relented on letting me study again with . . . em . . . friends at my place."

"Ye mean she hasn't relented about me studying over there. Honestly Ben, why don't you ever stand up to her! You act like you're seven years old around her, instead of seventeen."

"I will stand up for myself after the exams are over. She won't be able to rule me any more." he insisted.

"Oh yes, she will," retorted Ali, exasperated. "It'll be your precious medical career then."

"Oh, listen will you, for God's sake! I won't be at home any more then because I'm moving out. I'm getting my own place."

Ali was stunned. Most young people in Dublin stayed at home well into their twenties and the majority of them until they got married. It was quite unusual and she would never have expected it of Ben.

"Who with?" she managed, hoping it didn't sound like she was jealous, because that was how she felt.

"With Joey, Derek and Oliver," he replied casually. "We're getting a place in Rathmines."

Ali had even more mixed feelings on that score. Four guys in a bachelor pad, the place would be wall-to-wall women and pizza boxes. She didn't like the sound of it at all. It felt like he was moving on and away from her. She suddenly felt very insecure.

"Mum will hit the roof." He grinned.

"Yeah!" Ali laughed, suddenly brightening.

At least the old bag would hit the roof. That gave her some comfort.

"When was all this planned?" she asked testily.

He knew that tone.

"Only a few weeks ago – Oliver approached me. He knew I was having it tough at home with the old dear. He and Joey had already found a place. It belongs to Joe's uncle. The people living there now aren't moving out until September, so it'll be perfect. Just in time for starting college. Besides, it'll give you and me a lot more private time together."

"Yeah," replied Ali before she knew it. "That's what I'm afraid of."

"Thanks a lot!"

It was now Ben's turn to be annoyed. He had being applying subtle pressure for some time now for Ali to sleep with him, but she had always managed to resist, despite their dizzy passion. She was half-afraid of pregnancy and half-afraid of discovery. Her little house was always hectic, with her brothers or her father blundering about. It wasn't very private, but now with the flat looming, they would have somewhere private to go.

"Oh, you know what I mean, Ben. I'm worried about . . . "

"Yes, I know. You're worried about getting pregnant. I told you I could get condoms from the UK. I have a friend there."

"Just give me time, Ben. I won't be pushed into this, OK?"

And that was the end of the subject for the moment.

But she knew it wouldn't be for long. She simply didn't feel ready even though she loved Ben, but was afraid he'd eventually go off her if she didn't. She'd have to talk to Trisha about it.

Trisha had her own problems. She had done the deed with Mick one night after they'd had a few drinks and the house to themselves. She hadn't meant to. They were having a lovely time and just got carried away. It hadn't even seemed like real sex. It seemed to be over before it even got started. It had been damp and embarrassing and Trish had wondered what all the fuss was about. Mick was equally embarrassed and apologetic, taking full responsibility. It felt a little bit cheap and tawdry on the living room floor with *Minder* on the TV in the background. Trish resolved not to let it happen again any time soon and decided she wouldn't tell Ali, as it just didn't feel right, even to herself. Not as romantic as she'd pictured it. And Ali was such a puritan. Next time it will be different. I'll tell her then. It probably wasn't even proper sex anyhow. Later on in her little bed that night, she consoled herself with that thought and tried to push any scary ideas of pregnancy away. She blushed pink even at the word pregnancy. She just prayed she would be OK.

But panic set in, just the same.

She remembered Sarah Keogh at school had told her you couldn't get pregnant the first time, but then also remembered Josie O'Loughlin telling her that semen could travel up your leg and live outside your body for 48 hours.

"Jesus! I'm driving myself mental," she fumed as she

tossed and turned. Her little bunk bed was such a kiddie's bed really. And here she was now a woman. "I'll be grand," she told herself before dropping off into a fitful sleep.

Never having sex again anyhow. It's just not worth the worry.

Five weeks later . . .

"Ali, I have got to talk to you!"

It was Trish. Bleary-eyed and at the front door. It was seven am and it was Saturday.

"What? Are you for real, Trish? It's practically the middle of the night!"

Ali was still half-asleep, not noticing her friend's distress.

"Oh just let me in, will ya? It's freezing out here," she spat forcefully and Ali ushered her inside.

"What's so awful it gets you up at this ungodly hour?" said Ali as Trisha flounced onto Ali's bed.

"My periods are late," said Trish, in a small quiet voice, while twisting a well-worn hankie agitatedly between her fingers.

Her face was bright red and Ali could tell she had obviously been crying.

"Late?" echoed Ali, dimly unaware. "Why would that be?"

Then the penny dropped.

"Oh, Trish, you didn't, did you? You didn't sleep with Mick."

Ali sat down, gobsmacked.

"Well, sleep didn't actually come into it!" joked Trish, but her eyes were filled with tears. "Oh, Ali! It only happened once. I even sometimes imagined it never happened, y'know. But now my periods are two weeks late and I can't believe this is actually happening to me! I'm some stupid bitch!"

She burst into tears.

Ali was terrified for her friend, but felt she had to be strong and reassuring.

"Now, now," she soothed, patting Trisha's sobbing form. "Look, you're often late anyhow, aren't you, sometimes even up to two weeks? Maybe your dates are slightly wrong, and I know for a fact worrying about them makes them even later, you know."

"Does it?" sniffed Trisha, suddenly hopeful.

Ali was a brainbox. She was never wrong about these things.

"Yeah, it sure does," replied Ali, now on a roll. "You need to give it more time, a couple of weeks anyhow. Then we can go to the new Well Woman Clinic in Cathal Brugha Street. Lady doctors run it and they even give the Pill out, no questions asked."

"Who told you that?" asked Trisha, lifting a long wedge of blonde hair from her face.

"Ben," said Ali, sheepishly. "If you must know, he's been putting pressure on me to sleep with him for quite a while now. Although your story has just put me off for another year."

"Well, I never want to see another willy for the rest of me life!" said Trisha fiercely and they both burst out laughing, but really it didn't seem too funny.

The next week that followed was long and fruitless. Trisha had felt the odd twinge now and again, but as yet no period. She was becoming increasingly worried and found it hard to hide her unease. She was tetchy and irritable with everyone, and tearful while alone.

Then Sunday came and she awoke to the familiar dull cramp and rushed to the bathroom to see the crimson stain that she had often cursed.

She now almost wept for joy. She told her mother that her period had arrived and she wasn't up for Mass today and crawled back into bed with the latest Cosmo and two tablets. An hour later the cramps were almost unbearable, despite the painkillers and the blood flow was extremely heavy.

She felt incredibly weak as she barely made it into the loo and then felt something come away from her in a gush. She was petrified.

It felt so weird. She made herself look into the bowl and saw a small pink form that almost resembled a human ear. Her heart turned over. She stared at it for what seemed like forever, then summoned her courage and flushed it away. She hadn't learned too much about pregnancy and babies in life class but she knew deep within herself that she had just suffered a miscarriage.

She managed to get back to bed and just wept and wept.

Eventually she staggered up and managed to get her blood-soaked sheets into the washing machine get a fresh pair and get back into bed. The awful pain had subsided but she felt dreadfully weak.

But she simply had to try and act as normal as

possible when the family returned. They could never know.

When her mother came into to her room, she managed to convince her that her period was just heavier than usual and she felt a bit fluey too, and she wouldn't be up for dinner. After that she just lay in bed until the room became dark and then slept. But that image in the bathroom was imprinted in her memory and the little girl in Trish died that day. She never told a single soul what had occurred, not even Ali or Mick. She just told them that her periods had arrived and she was OK. They were none the wiser, but Trisha was. She was suddenly all grown up.

Chapter 8

Ali was worried. Ben was going off to the south of France for three weeks with his parents and without her. They weren't going alone but with some old family friends – friends that just happened to have a suitable daughter of about Ben's age. Ali could guess Isabel's plan.

Divide and conquer didn't just happen in the history books.

Ali knew she had to be careful how she reacted, as she knew Ben was blissfully ignorant of his mother's secret agenda. She knew he would never believe it anyway. But it all fitted a little bit too perfectly for her liking. Ali could read between the lines from what he had told her.

Karen was Isabel's best friend's daughter. Her father happened to be a producer at RTE and Karen also just happened to be reading politics at UCD.

Apparently she was pretty, rich and a perfect match for Ben.

Kate, Karen's mum, was one of Isabel's closest friends

from the Bridge Club and they lived in nearby upmarket Blackrock. She was entirely suitable and Ali wasn't. Ali knew a threat when she saw one.

"What, Karen?" laughed Ben when Ali tried to broach the subject that he might take a fancy to her. "She's good crack and as mad as a hatter, but she's not my type. Karen's a real man-eater. Anyway, I've known her since I was about seven. I used to put frogs down her back. We're more like cousins. And why are you feeling so insecure, Miss Sensitive. You know I love you, don't you?"

He nuzzled her neck. She stared out to sea. They were up on Howth Head.

It was a splendid summer's day with a bright blue sky and an azure sea. Dublin could look terrific when the sun shone.

"Yes, I do know that," she replied evenly. "But three weeks is a long time for you, lusty guts, and if she's such a man-eater, well maybe you'll get consumed."

"Well, you could always make me yours forever, you know," he whispered sexily, kissing her ear.

"Now, Ben," she grinned. "You know that's not fair. Remember we agreed no pressure. I'm just not —"

"I know," he said glumly. "You're not ready yet. It's OK kiddo, I'll wait. Just as well I love you, though."

Ali felt his disappointment but was still peeved at the pressure he always applied. She hadn't told him about Trisha's scare. She raged inwardly on the train journey home. It's not the guys who take the risks. It wasn't Mick that was the one who went crying to his mates with worry, when Trisha's periods were late. Ben wanted her to sleep with him, but it was Ali who had to worry about the consequences. He seemed so blasé, just go on the Pill and don't worry. But Ali knew it wasn't quite that simple.

She realised with a shock that she really didn't trust men and this was why she held back. She also knew that her first role model, her father, had constantly let her down and so she feared Ben would ultimately do the same.

She was cool with him when they said their goodbyes and later on regretted it.

She wouldn't see him for three weeks and the memory of her he was left with was Ali as the frozen Ice Queen. She poured out her heart to Trisha in Trisha's bedroom, where all their deep issues were discussed and mulled over amid cotton buds, nail varnish and teddy bears.

"If you want to sleep with Ben then go ahead, but just be sure that it's what you want, and not just what he wants. And if you do decide to go for it, don't be an idiot like me. Protect yourself."

"I do want to sleep with him, but, I'm afraid he'll just think I'm a tart afterwards. You know what men are like."

"Mick's not like that!" replied Trisha indignantly.

"Yeah, I know," sighed Ali. "Mick is really good. But, Trisha, you are so sure of him. He seems to have your whole lives planned out already."

"OK, you're right," agreed Trisha. "But it's a bit scary too. He's got that bit of land his uncle left him out past Swords and he's planning on building a home soon and then getting engaged . . ."

"Y' see," interrupted Ali. "You know that he wants you forever."

"And that's what scares me. I love Mick, I really do,

but if I'm not careful I'll end up married with a couple of kids on each hip, never having actually done anything or having been anywhere. And how will I know that he's the one for me if I don't date anyone else or do anything else? I just don't feel ready to settle down yet, though I'd hate to lose him, he's so wonderful."

Mick was wonderful. Ali had to agree. He simply couldn't see any further than Trish. He was straightforward and good, much like all of Trisha's life.

Ali had to be careful not to let envy take hold, but everything seemed to go so right for Trisha. It always had.

Isabel Murphy paced up and down her perfect pink bedroom.

Her husband John had said once that it was like sleeping in a huge pink trifle but Isabel prided herself on her impeccable taste (only the best Laura Ashley florals would do). She fluffed up a pink frilly cushion angrily. She simply couldn't believe the news.

Ben was actually moving out of home. She was horrified.

Obviously that little bitch has set him up to it. She just knew it.

Ben had said he was moving in with a few male friends from school. But Isabel had no doubt whatsoever that little floozy would be up there flaunting herself at him and in no time at all he'd be up to his neck in nappies and wedding bells.

That was not what she had planned for her only son. It had taken her years to polish off her own raw Dublin accent and shake off her own humble background, but she had done it. She had left the slums behind and married up in the world. She had no intention of ever going back there. No son of hers was going to drag her back to the northside for some slum bride!

No. Karen was ideal for Benjamin in every way. She had looks, brains, breeding. They had looked so perfect together on the trip to France. Kate, Karen's mother, had let her know in no uncertain terms that Karen was well smitten after the holiday even though Ben had seemed inured to her obvious charms. Kate confided in Isabel that Karen was endeavouring to cross Ben's path as often as possible. Isabel for her part said that she would do everything in her power to facilitate the pair of them getting together. She knew Ben liked Karen; he just felt bound to that awful O'Neill girl and her tragic family. She was his puppy love and he simply hadn't moved on. But he would, if she had anything to do with it.

Just then, Isabel looked accidentally into the mirror while deep in thought and she caught herself unprepared.

"God, I look ancient!" she blurted out, shocked by her appearance.

Deep frown-lines on her forehead and around her mouth made her look old and unpleasant.

"I'm checking into the New Blackrock Medical clinic for a mini face-lift," she decided. Several of her close friends had already done so. "Got refreshed" as they termed it.

Men were pretty loose among her set and often strayed from their frayed wives and found a younger model. Rich men encountered no difficulties acquiring young beauties – but it wasn't the same for women. She doubted if John would ever consider leaving her, though he may have had the odd fling. She wasn't sure and didn't want to know either. Still, it wouldn't do any harm to look a few years younger. She needed a confidence boost. She'd definitely have a lift. Must book it tomorrow, she reminded herself, making a mental note.

"Anyway, Ben is my immediate problem," she said aloud to her image.

He was a problem she would have to address, but she knew she must be careful. Her young son was headstrong and she mustn't endear him more to the O'Neill girl by appearing to be against her. No, she must box clever on this one. A plan began to form itself inside her brittle blonde head.

A plan that would put an end to her son's sorry relationship, once and for all.

She smiled at herself in the mirror before sweeping from the room.

Time for action. Just a couple of phone calls should do the trick.

Suddenly everything didn't seem so dark after all and her mood lifted so much she began to hum a little tune while walking downstairs.

Chapter 9

Ali was helping Ben move into his new flat. She didn't dare go to Sandymount to help him pack – though it would have been delicious to see his mother's face. Instead, she hung around the new flat, helping to unpack the myriad of cardboard boxes stuffed with inane rubbish that the boys had collected. Incongruous pots lay beside cricket bats and African death masks. Their taste was eclectic and the results would be interesting.

She had liked the house immediately. It was a nicely kept period house, with large airy rooms and huge bay windows and they had managed to get the entire downstairs floor. The upstairs was rented by a couple of sales reps that were almost never home.

The scullery had been converted into a tiny but well stocked kitchen and they each had a bedroom with an en suite. Ben's wasn't the biggest room, but it was at the back of the house and had a lovely view of the garden and caught the sun. It would be impossible to heat in winter, but during the summer time it would be great. The walls were painted a warm cream and Ben had a lot of Man Ray prints that would look great on the large space. The centrepiece of the room was a huge king-size bed, which took Ali aback for a couple of minutes. You couldn't miss it.

Ali flopped down into it and mused how Ben's mother would see it. She suppressed a giggle. Just then Ben arrived.

"Like it?" he beamed, throwing a bundle of clothes on top.

"Yeah, it's great," laughed Ali, " but I do think it's a bit small."

"Well," replied Ben sheepishly, "you know us tall lads need a big bed to sleep in. My feet were hanging out over all the single beds."

"Oh yeah," Ali smiled, "so that's your excuse and you're sticking to it, eh?"

"Yup," said Ben flopping onto the bed beside her. "So how's about you and me test driving it, then?"

With that he pounced on Ali and proceeded to tickle her half to death. She was screaming with laughter when there was a hard knock on the half-open bedroom door and there was Isabel Murphy, standing in the doorway looking aghast. She was holding a small casserole dish in her arms.

"Well, well. Getting rather cosy already aren't we?"

She fixed a fake smile.

Ali jumped up and fixed her skewed blouse. Ben just sat on the bed, nonplussed.

"Hi, Mum er . . . I didn't expect you so soon."

"Obviously," murmured Isabel ignoring Ali entirely. Her eyes were seemingly transfixed on the new bed. "Here, I brought you this."

She pushed the casserole dish into Ben's hands.

"Mrs Mulvanney made it. It's Irish stew. I know it's your favourite. There should be enough for everyone." She passed an icy glare to Ali, then composed herself and flashing a winning smile to Ben, said, "Well, darling, aren't you going to show me around?"

With that, she swept from the room. Ben meekly followed, but Ali stayed behind in the bedroom, well out of her way. A full forty minutes later she was still there, getting more agitated by the minute. Ali felt cross with Ben, for ignoring her. She could hear Isabel's fake high-pitched laughter in the distance. She obviously approved of Ben's other friends, all of whom Ali genuinely liked too, but they all just happened to be sons of doctors or bankers, men rich enough to subsidise their sons' first move away from home. They obviously fitted Isabel's criteria for Ben's companions.

Unlike Ali.

She had just tidied the last sweater away into the huge chest of drawers when Ben finally re-appeared.

"There you are! Why are you hiding yourself back here? Mum is about to leave and wondered if you wanted a lift home?"

Ali was aghast.

No way was she accepting a lift from Cruella de Ville. She thought quickly of a suitable excuse.

"That's great, but no thanks, I thought I'd hang out here with you for another couple of hours, if that's OK. I don't feel like going home just yet."

She flashed her brightest smile.

"OK," said Ben, placated. "Come and say goodbye then."

"What is she up to?" wondered Ali. "I know she can't stand me. She barely acknowledges my existence, and now she suddenly wants to drive across town with me. There has got to be an ulterior motive."

Ali couldn't imagine Isabel's sleek car turning up her ordinary little street. The boys could be out playing, scruffy and boisterous or worse still, her father could be in residence, obnoxiously drunk. An absolute nightmare scenario played in her head while Ben took her hand and led her down the long hallway towards the front door, where Isabel was holding court with Oliver and Joey.

"Ali's staying for a while, Mum," Ben said.

"Yes, thanks Mrs Murphy, but I'm not just ready to leave yet."

"No problem," Isabel gushed. "Well, boys, behave yourselves, won't you?" She spoke to the boys smilingly but was looking at Ali, getting the message across. "And Ben, I'll see you when your clean laundry runs out!"

Ben laughed as he kissed her tanned cheek.

"Thanks, Mum."

"Alison dear, you really must come back to San Etienne for lunch sometime. I'll have Ben arrange it, shall I?"

Ali was in shock.

"Y-Yes that'd be lovely, er thanks," she mumbled awkwardly, while Ben squeezed her hand.

"You'd better not stay out too late, dear," reminded Isabel malevolently. "I'm sure your father would be worried about you."

Her look spoke volumes.

"I won't," replied Ali breezily and turned around and went back inside, leaving the boys waving the wicked witch off as she flew off on her broomstick back to Sandymount and the relative safety of the middle classes.

"The rotten old cow!" thought Ali. "She thinks we're having sex. That's why she wanted to take me home." She sat on the bed glumly. "But why did she ask me to lunch, when she patently hates my guts?"

"I think she thinks we're having illicit carnal knowledge!" quipped Ben when he came back. He grabbed Ali tightly. "God, I wish we were."

Then he kissed her passionately.

Her head swam.

They fell back onto the soft candlewick bedspread. His hands were on her.

"No, Ben, no!" she almost shouted and sat bolt upright.

"Huh?" he retreated.

"I just can't. I feel your mother is going to burst in the door any minute with the morality police. Please, not now, eh?"

"Well . . . when then?" Ben said flatly. "You know I love you but all this waiting. It's kinda hard, y'know?"

"Yes," said Ali looking downwards. "Literally!"

They both laughed. Ali looked deep into his blue eyes. "Soon, Ben," she said softly, soothingly. "Really soon."

"Good," said Ben, his mood lifted. "That means I will now share with you my absolute favourite meal, Irish stew. That's if the other two dopes haven't already demolished it. C'mon, I'll race ya to the kitchen."

The four of them then sat in the tiny kitchen, while Ben shared out the steaming casserole. They all had a glass of red wine from the chipped earthenware mugs that Oliver had brought and had a laugh.

It was just so nice not to have to worry about the dinner or where the boys were (Trisha's mum was keeping an eye on them).

At least for one night she could relax. Be free, have a laugh and be eighteen.

Later on Oliver persuaded them to go and see a few friends of his who had formed a band at school. They were a support act for Revolver at the Celebrity Club on Abbey St.

The guys were all around Ali's age, eighteen and were spotty and intense but she liked their music, which Oliver had proudly told her was original. The drummer was quite cute though, Ali thought, with his long blond hair and their name was quite catchy. U2. Had a real ring to it. Oliver insisted they were so talented, that they would go far.

At 11 pm Ali headed home because she had a job interview. It was to be her first, and she didn't want a cloudy head. The job was in travel agency just off Grafton Street, and while it wasn't highbrow medicine in college, for her it was the next best thing. While she sat on the bus she wondered how the next year would go. They were all out of school now and sometimes with the best intentions people simply drifted off and went their own way. She desperately did not want that to happen, not to her and Ben. But she wondered how long it would last, him mixing with the uni crowd, needing to study while she worked full-time. That awful Karen one was in university too, though thankfully not on the same campus.

Deep down, Ali felt Karen was a hidden threat.

Ben had said little about the trip to France with Karen and her parents, just that they'd had fun and a few laughs. Karen, apparently, had pounced on every French guy she had met, some eligible but also a few that weren't.

Ben had thought it funny, because her mother and his thought she was a plaster saint when she was really quite wild.

Ali hadn't really seen the funny side but smiled idiotically when he regaled her with the tale of one incident when an errant guy's wife had appeared and poured a glass of wine over Karen. Ali felt insecure and jealous as hell that this vixen had been in close quarters with her boyfriend for three weeks. She trusted Ben a fair amount but reading through the lines realised that trusting Karen with your boyfriend was like trusting a Rottweiler with your budgie – it just didn't make sense.

Thank God the holiday was over and her relationship was intact.

She knew that time was running out however, for her to keep on playing the blushing virgin. She had been dating Ben for almost two years now and just because she had a deep fear of abandonment, it shouldn't stop her from showing him her love in a physical way. It was something she would just have to get over if this relationship was to survive.

She made a big decision as the empty sixteen bus trundled up the Drumcondra Road; she would tell Ben at the weekend that she had decided she was ready. She couldn't stop smiling when she pictured his lovely face when she told him, Ben loved her and this would bring them even closer.

"Yes!" she decided. "I'm going to do it!"

The next day was lashing rain and Ali who was running a bit late couldn't find her umbrella. She then got teemed on waiting for the ever-late number sixteen, which invariably arrived in pairs and this day was no exception, so when she got to the interview she looked like a drowned rat. Her hair dripped onto the plush carpet and had multiplied into a million damp curls, and the Penneys grey pinstripe suit she had carefully chosen looked as thin as paper when wet. Her CV which was nicely done, she had thought earlier, encased in a crisp new manila folder, was now damp and curled up at the edges. The girl at the reception desk had been nice however, and had fetched her a small hand towel so she could at least dry her face. She was too irritated to be nervous until she saw the previous applicant leave the Interview room. She was immaculately dressed in an expensively cut navy suit, perfect blonde bob and a leather briefcase in which no doubt sat a perfectly dry exciting CV.

Ali almost turned around and walked out but for a booming voice which emanated from the interview room. "Next!"

Ali jumped and almost ran into the room. The voice was commanding and belonged to a rather large well-tanned lady who wore a tropical pink flowered blouse and shorts, no less. The vision shocked Ali out of her nervousness.

"Maisie Carter," said the lady pushing a black curl from her eye.

Her hair was as wayward as Ali's; curls sprouting everywhere, except Maisie's hair was very short and very dark, much like herself.

"Sorry about the gear," she continued smilingly. "I'm just back this morning from a travel agents' trip to Cairo and the bloody 'plane was delayed. I don't normally dress like this for interviews, even though it's damned comfortable."

"And I don't dress like I usually bathe fully dressed either," quipped Ali, "but I was caught in the rain. So sorry about the state of me too!"

They both laughed, ice broken.

Maisie Carter turned out to be a real character.

Ali liked her immediately.

She was larger than life, ample both in frame and in personality.

She had a real mother-hen quality about her that drew Ali in. After fifteen minutes she offered Ali the job.

"Long hours, lousy pay but great perks," she explained and told Ali after a year in Maisie's full-time employ, she'd qualify for one long trip and a couple of short ones.

"You need a sense of humour to work here," smiled Maisie, "and I think you'll fit right in. Unlike the last interviewee who was a bit of a starchy pants!"

Ali laughed – she had felt so inferior to the classy blonde.

She was ecstatic as she left the building. Grafton Street had never looked so vibrant. The damp drizzle couldn't depress the dazzling flowers the dealers sold or her mood either.

She simply had to go down to Roche's and find Trisha, who had managed to get a job there. Perhaps they could have lunch. She was bursting with excitement and had to share it.

"You jammy bitch!" screeched Trisha, who was green with envy.

They were in Bewleys for lunch.

"I can't believe I'm selling tights, while you'll be selling holidays! Please say you'll take me first on one of your freebies."

"Of course," smiled Ali, "it goes without saying. We'll be able to meet for lunch most days too."

"Yeah," replied Trisha morosely, "if you like taking your lunch at three o'clock, we will. That's what's been happening. Old ratchett face lets everyone else go first. She hates my guts already. Jeez, my feet are killing me! I doubt if I can survive this, long-term."

"Oh, you'll get used to it," said Ali. "Just think of all the calories you're burning."

"You're right!" agreed Trish suddenly brightening at the thought. "I think I'll have to have this apple tart and cream, just to keep my strength up, mind."

She grabbed the dessert and headed for a seat.

"How's Ben's new place?" she asked after her food had been demolished.

"Oh, it's really nice and roomy. I think he and the lads are going to love it."

With that she told Trisha the entire story of the double bed and Isabel Murphy.

"She really is an oul battle-axe," confirmed Trish. "So you're not doing the old horizontal shuffle, then?"

"No," sniffed Ali. "I dunno why. I mean I love him. In fact I've decided to go for it. I feel he's getting a bit fed up waiting."

"Well, you've got to want to do it for yourself, Ali, not because you're being pressured. But if you are sure, then best of luck to you, but don't take any chances, OK?"

"Yes, Marjorie Proops. I won't. I'm not supposed to see him tonight, but I might give him a call and tell him the good news."

"What? That you're about to give him your cherry?"

"No, you goose, that I got the job. Honestly, you young ones have got a one-track mind."

Trish blushed. "Nuff said. Now, are you going to finish that cheesecake? I need some more fortification if I've to stand on these poor oul legs for another four hours. Give it over here; I'll have to be quick. Or Miss Ratchett will send me to granny's corsets if I'm late back."

Ali laughed herself silly. Trish was a tonic. She really was.

It would be fun working in town together. She couldn't wait.

That evening, the awful rain had passed and the sun shone in its Indian summer way. Derek and Joey were trying to persuade Ben to go out with them to Malahide for a few drinks.

"I can't, lads," insisted Ben, 'really, I can't."

"You mean you won't, Murphy," said Derek while stuffing his large face with pizza. "Honestly, you're like a married man, complete with ball and chain."

"Oh, come on. I've got to hit the books. Get a head

start. Anyway, why would I want to go anywhere with you two apes."

"Ben," said Joey evenly, "in five weeks' time you'll be up to your arse in medical books. This is the last bit of summery weather for the next nine months. You've got to come and enjoy yourself, man. Come on, just a few bevies and a bop. You don't have to go off on Ali if you don't want to. It'll mean all the more girls for myself and Derek."

"Anyway," interjected Derek, who was never long on tact, "there's hardly a stampede to your bedroom, if you catch my drift."

"Just because we're not all sluts like you, O'Malley," retorted Ben hotly. "OK, I'll go, just for you, Joey. I'll go to bloody Malahide. But only if you two bozos fork out for the taxi fare."

"Done," said Joey, triumphant.

Ben was an asset when girl-hunting. His looks attracted them over, then Joey moved in. And Derek, well, Derek blundered around a lot and generally put them off with his clumsy size twelve feet and penchant for belching. But with Ben on board it should be an excellent night.

Later on that evening Ali phoned Ben's flat. Oliver answered the phone and told her that Ben had gone out with the others. He hadn't said he was going anywhere so she was a little disappointed. She had really wanted to tell him her news and also mention that she'd come to a decision about them. But it would have to wait. She'd tell him in person, which would be much better.

Instead she headed over to Trisha for a chat and a lesson in the finer arts of male seduction.

Meanwhile Ben was getting pretty well oiled in Gibney's thanks to a Guinness promotion and a warm evening. Gibney's courtyard was packed to capacity and buzzing with atmosphere.

"You guys are sad," laughed Ben at his ogling friends.

"Now that's what I call talent," whistled Joey at an attractive tall blonde who had just walked past. She had a pair of white shorts and a killer tan on her long legs.

Ben turned around. It was Karen, his old friend, and she looked terrific.

Just then she spotted him and came straight over.

"Ben Murphy, how are you?" she yelled and draped her arms around him before planting a huge kiss on his lips.

"Hi," said Ben, aware of the admiring looks of his counterparts. Derek's large mouth hung open. "Have you been away again? You weren't that brown coming back from France."

"Oh, I've just been to Ibiza for a week with the girls from uni. Had a wild time," murmured Karen seductively. "And the tan goes all over."

Joe and Derek were now green with envy. Ben couldn't help himself. He was enjoying this immensely.

Just then Karen's friends called her and she sidled away sexily, every male eye in the place glued to her fabulous legs.

"She is a cracker!" enthused Derek.

"Yeah, shame you're already taken, Murphy, but she appears rather taken with you."

"We're just good mates," insisted Ben laughing despite himself. It felt good to have his friends envious.

"Well, she can be my mate any time," drooled Joey, eyeing Karen's rear appreciatively.

Karen wasn't short of attention for the rest of the night.

Almost every single guy in the place approached her at one stage or another. She appeared to be enjoying all the attention but spent a lot of time winking over at Ben.

"Are we going dancing?" asked Joey at midnight.

"Yeah, why not?" replied Ben. "I need to dance off some of this Guinness. I'm feeling a bit Brahms and Liszt."

"Right, the Big T it is!" said Derek as they stumbled out onto the street to get a cab.

Tamangos was packed full of luscious women and soon Derek and Joey hit the dance floor in search of romance. Ben spotted Karen by the DJ box, her fabulous tan accentuated by the fluorescent lights.

He went over to talk to her and she led him onto the dance floor where a slow set was just starting.

Ben felt a little light-headed and knew he had far too much to drink. But Karen smelled so good as she moved even closer to him and the next minute they were kissing.

"You know I'm dating someone," he said finally.

"I don't care if you don't," Karen replied silkily and kissed him again.

His head was swimming.

It was all a bit of a blur after that. They eventually all piled into a taxi back to Rathmines. Karen and Ben ended up in his bedroom in a mass of tangled limbs and sweaty passion.

Eventually they slept.

"God! Who turned all the lights on?"

Ben came to. He had a thumping headache.

Sun streamed into his bedroom, making his head thump even more.

He turned over and collided with a mass of blonde curls and a very tanned back.

He was horrified.

"Oh no! I didn't, did I?" he thought panicking.

Little bits of last night floated back to him, as if on film. Yes, he had. He had slept with Karen.

He then felt ashamed and angry with himself. How could he have done it?

How could he have done it on Ali? He had been dating the girl for two years and now he had gone and lost his virginity to someone else.

He groaned audibly and Karen turned around, wide-awake. She was grinning like a Cheshire cat.

"Morning, sexy."

She kissed his parched lips. He hurriedly backed away, sat upright and ran his hands through his hair maniacally. This was so awful.

He just wanted her to leave immediately. Then he felt guilty for being such a heel. Karen was a nice girl. It wasn't her fault.

He hadn't exactly pushed her off. But he loved Ali.

"You should have thought of that last night, you idiot!" he berated himself silently. Karen leaned up on one elbow.

"Look, it's all right, Ben. It's not like I was a virgin or anything. Though I do believe you were. But you were such an adventurous one. You did surprise me," she giggled. "Look, I won't tell anyone if you don't."

Ben looked at her hard.

"Karen, I'm really sorry, but I've been seeing Ali for two years and I really love her –" he trailed off.

"So you say," replied Karen tartly. "But it makes me wonder how much you do love her if you sleep with the first girl that comes along."

She had a point. He was a pushover. Right now, he just wanted Karen to get the hell out of here. He got up quickly and searched around for a pair of boxer shorts to cover his embarrassment – their clothes lay in tangles on the floor. He found his jeans and pulled them on rapidly.

"I'll just go get us a cup of tea," he blurted and escaped to the relative safety of the kitchen.

"Don't be too long," she sang out after him.

Oliver was in the kitchen eating muesli, looking bright-eyed and bushy-tailed. He obviously hadn't been anywhere.

"Who's been a naughty boy then?" he said sardonically.

Ben was aghast.

"How the hell do you know?"

"Ben," replied Oliver, rolling his green eyes in amazement, "the whole flat, no, probably the entire house, could hear you two, though I was the only coherent one, so the others won't remember anything." Oliver looked at Ben hard. He was a serious and sincere guy whom Ben had the utmost respect for. "What the hell are you at, man?" he asked Ben. "I thought you were serious about Ali?"

"I was! I mean, I am," Ben replied hotly. "Look, I got drunk, lost my wits. I don't know how it happened. It just did. I've just got to get Karen out of here pretty damn quick. Ali is due to come over today . . ."

"Oh yeah, she phoned last night," interjected Oliver, through mouthfuls of cereal.

"What did you say?" Ben was filled with guilt and panic. He wasn't sure what hurt more, his head or his conscience.

"I just said you were out with the other two stooges. Ben, I won't tell Ali anything, but you had better 'fess up. These things have a habit of revealing themselves, and if you don't tell her and she finds out, things could get a whole lot worse."

"No way!" said Ben emphatically. "This is one mistake Ali need never know about. It'll never happen again."

The kettle was boiling. Ben grabbed two mugs and hastily made the tea.

"I've got to get her dressed and out of here within an hour," he whined, looking at his watch.

Oliver looked at him in disgust.

"Ben, she wouldn't be here if it wasn't for you – you have to bear the responsibility for that."

"Yeah, I know," sighed Ben. "Jeez, Oliver, why do you have to be so bloody righteous all of the time?"

After plying her with copious mugs of tea, Ben managed to convince Karen he had to prepare himself for college and needed the day to himself. He didn't know why he hadn't just told her the truth – that his steady girlfriend of two years was coming round. He was annoyed at himself at the further deception, but obviously he'd have to become good at it if he were to keep the truth from Ali and manage to keep dopey Derek and Joey quiet too.

What he hadn't reckoned on was Karen herself, who

quietly slipped her gold bangle off her brown wrist and placed it deep underneath a pillow.

Karen smiled to herself as she got dressed. Once his little girlfriend found the bangle, Ben would be all hers. She really loved Ben. She always had, in one way or another. She knew he didn't feel the same.

But he would, eventually. She'd make him fall in love with her.

It was preordained. Both of their families agreed that they were perfect for one another. Even Isabel Murphy had practically told her to go after Ben. She had telephoned her and insisted if Karen popped up at all his local haunts eventually they'd get together and she had been right. She would win him over. She waved Ben goodbye and got the cab to drop her to Sandymount. She'd just pop in to Isabel before heading home and give her the good news.

Meanwhile Ali was en route to Rathmines, with a hopefully purchased carrot cake from Bewleys. It was Ben's favourite. She couldn't wait to see him, tell him the good news about the job and about them.

She just wished the bloody bus would go faster so she could get there quicker.

She arrived around noon. Oliver answered the large door.

Ben was in his room he informed her and then quickly disappeared.

That was strange, she mused. Oliver was usually full of chat when they met, but she didn't think too much of it as she strode towards Ben's room. Her heart was beating with anticipation.

Ben was lying on the bed looking more than a bit seedy.

"Hey! Are you feeling a bit human yet?"

She waved the Bewleys box in front of him tantalisingly.

"Ali, hi. God, I do feel a bit rough actually."

"Had a hard night on the rip, by the look of you. Oliver told me you went out with the macho men."

"Uh, yeah, we went to Malahide." He took the cake box and placed it on the locker.

"Any good?" she asked and without waiting for a reply planted a big kiss on his mouth. He smelt of stale beer and something else. "Or did you miss me too much?"

He pulled away quickly.

"Yes, course I did. Listen I feel a bit stale. I'll just hop into the shower and have a shave and I'll feel better, OK. Won't be long."

He jumped up, quickly grabbed a towel and was gone.

Ali sat on the bed. The room was a total mess. She decided to tidy it up a bit and make the bed. She pulled off the covers and then the pillows and saw a gold bangle on the sheet. She picked it up slowly and saw an inscription on the inside.

It read: "to Karen – love Mum & Dad Xmas 1977."

Ali just couldn't take it in. She sat on the bed and just kept looking at the bracelet and trying to figure out an innocent explanation for how it got there.

There was only one reason she could come up with and as the realisation dawned on her she felt her heart would break. Obviously Karen had been in Ben's bedroom, no, his bed and he hadn't told her so he must have something to hide.

She was still sitting there holding the bracelet when Ben came back dripping wet from the shower.

"Feel a lot better," he breezed, before he saw Ali's face. She was ashen with shock and anger.

"What's this?"

She shoved the bangle in front of his nose.

"Oh, it – em – it must be Karen's."

He looked shocked.

"Shit!!" he thought wildly. "Think of something!"

"That's what I thought," said Ali in a voice she didn't recognise. "Did you sleep with her, Ben?"

She was terrified to ask, but the voice came from somewhere. She felt like she wasn't really there. Like she was outside herself watching the nightmare unfold. Ben didn't answer her – he just looked out the window as if he was searching for a reply.

"Yes."

There it was, the answer that would change everything between them forever.

"But it was the biggest mistake I ever made," he said softly.

"Yes, It was."

Ali's eyes filled with tears. Her heart was truly broken.

She got up off of the bed. The bed that she had thought by now would have been filled with their passion. She placed the bangle on it and walked out. Ben followed her to the front door dripping wet in a towel but she couldn't hear him. She could only hear her heart break into a million pieces as she ran up the Rathmines Road in hot salt tears.

Chapter 10

A week later Ali still felt punch-drunk. She was inconsolable.

Ben had let her down so badly she felt ashamed. Ashamed and angry that she had put so much trust in him. He had always been her rock, her constant partner over the past two years and now she felt all at sea, like her left leg was missing.

Ben had got her through her mother's death and now she felt like she had endured another one. She missed her mother so badly now for some kind words and advice.

Ben called over to her house several times but she refused to see him. She simply couldn't.

"You're weird," said Kevin, her brother, who had answered the door to Ben. "He's dead nice and you're such a wagon to him."

"You don't understand, Kevin," she had replied wearily.

"Yeah, I do, "muttered Kevin. "I understand he was the

only one who played football with me, and now you've had some stupid row I can't see him any more!"

She felt sorry for the boys. They loved Ben too. He had become a big surrogate brother to them, seeing as their father was mainly absent.

They missed him too. She felt awful for them, but she simply couldn't look at his face right now without slapping it. She needed time.

Time to calm down, but it was over. If this was love they could keep it. Late at night while alone in bed, she'd sob uncontrollably when no one could hear, and when she slept, she dreamt of Ben, but it was always the same ending to the dream, when she found Karen locked in his arms. The pain she felt was physical. She actually ached all over.

Trish dragged her out one night with the Roche's Stores crowd. They were a really nice bunch and Ali made a good pretence of enjoying it all, but inside she really felt like running a mile.

Instead she threw herself into her new job at the travel agents.

She helped people plan trips all over the world and it somehow kept her sane. It gave her the travel bug just to listen to the names of the cities. Bombay, New York, Sydney. She would love to escape dreary Dublin right now and fly anywhere. Trouble is she'd have to take herself with her and she knew it didn't matter if she was in Dublin or Delhi – her misery was the same.

After a few weeks Ben called in to see Trisha in Roche's.

"You're such a eejit!" blurted out Trish in her usual no-nonsense manner.

"Don't you think I know that?" replied Ben miserably. "Trish you have got to help me. Please!"

"Yeah, well right now I have got to stock these hair dyes." (Oul ratchett face had promoted her to toiletries.)

Trisha was brusque. Ben now just irritated her.

"All right! Meet me in the Kylemore in fifteen minutes. It's my tea break then. Now scat."

He was morosely nursing two teas when she arrived.

"Trisha, I know I was incredibly stupid, but I was drunk and it all got out of hand. I never meant it to happen and she means nothing to me. I swear."

Trisha was unconvinced.

"Ben, that is such crap and you know it. Ali loved you so much and you let her down. You know she's had such a hard time lately and she had such a problem trusting men. She was totally mad about you but she was scared."

Ben was perplexed. "Scared?" he echoed.

"Yes scared – scared of giving herself to you and being rejected. I managed to convince her that you have the utmost love and respect for her and she rushes off to tell you she will sleep with you but then discovers you've already gone ahead and screwed around with some chinless wonder from Clontarf."

"She's not from Clontarf," corrected Ben. Now he was irritated.

"Whatever, does it matter? Look Ben. You'll get no sympathy from me. Ali is determined to forget you; you've blown it. It's over, period."

"Doesn't she love me any more?" asked Ben now in despair.

"Em, no," lied Trisha, looking over his shoulder.

She absolutely hated to do this but she had promised Ali.

"OK," said Ben and pushed his tea away. "That's all I wanted to know. Guess I'll see ya around, Trisha. Tell Mick I'll give him a call, OK? We'll go for a pint."

She could see the words were automatic, but there were real tears in his eyes. He rushed out of the door. Trisha sat for much longer that she should have after he had left, wondering if it was the right thing to do, to break his heart too. Still, it was what Ali had told her to say if he asked. Later that day, she phoned Ali at work.

"I did as you asked," she told Ali. "Are you sure that's what you want him to believe?"

"Absolutely," replied Ali vehemently and felt her heart close a little. No one would ever get the opportunity to hurt her like that again. "I'm perfectly sure."

"Oh, ducks," said Trisha sadly. "I hope you won't regret this."

"I don't care," said Ali, even though they both knew it not to be true. "I've got to forget him. I've got to move on."

Chapter 11

1983

It was ten past six before the last client left Carter Travel. Ali was exhausted. It was a wet and blustery November Friday and she was just dying to get home into a hot warm bath. Being the manager now was tough. It meant she had to stay late, work harder than ever and supervise three twittering juniors, three girls barely out of their teens that were short on the work ethic and long on gossip.

But Maisie Carter had the "utmost faith in Ali's abilities" as she described it before flitting off on a six-month world cruise with her husband.

Ali felt flattered by Maisie's confidence in her. Even though she knew she had outgrown her job and could do it blindfold, she felt an amazing loyalty to Maisie and also felt welded to Dublin. Even though the boys were grown up now, she still felt they needed her.

Her father too, had declined over the years. He lost his

job at CIE when he was found drunk on duty and had smashed eleven bus windows in at Phibsboro garage when they tried to get him to leave. After that he was suddenly at home all day drinking. He seldom ever changed out of his pyjamas, shuffling down to the off-licence in them, barely concealed in an overcoat, to replenish his supply of booze. He began to have blackouts, and was still moody and belligerent. He seldom even bothered to eat. His life was just revolving around alcohol and it had destroyed his mind. His presence in the house was still oppressive and miserable.

Ali tried everything to improve life for the boys herself but the house had no heart. She felt duty-bound to stay as long as possible and make it some kind of a home for them all, but it was almost impossible. They all depended on her money to keep them afloat. She felt so guilty but she often wished him dead to set them all free.

Kevin was twenty-one now. An apprentice welder, he had inherited his father's predisposition to alcohol dependence, something that he emphatically denied. He tried hard to hide it because it was a great shame to him that he was like his father. He had hated his father's drunkenness so much. But he was quiet and gentle at least and Ali's heart ached for him because he seemed so sad, so without hope for the future.

Damien was eighteen and trainee chef at technical college. He was a lot like Joan, tall and dark with handsome Latin looks. He also had his mother's smile and tolerant temperament. He supported Ali in everything she did, but found it hard to judge his father. He held no anger or bitterness towards him. He was accepting and placid, just like Joan. Ali felt sometimes like shaking him for it, as he got walked upon by all and sundry.

Louie was sixteen. Already six foot tall and dark too, but with a strong character and a ready wit. Louie succeeded at anything he tried. He was an accomplished sportsman and academically bright too. Everyone loved him and he was immensely popular. Ali was so glad for him because he had suffered so much the loss of his mother. He and Ali knew she was dear to his heart. He was of all the boys the strongest in character and the one Ali relied on the most. He was her confidante, and they had a special bond. It was almost like a parent-child relationship. After all she did all but raise him for the past six years.

"Go and live your own life, Ali," he had said to her. "Stop hanging around here wasting yourself on an old man who'll never appreciate it. I'm sixteen now, and as soon as I'm seventeen I'm off to join the Navy or the Air Corps. So I'll be out of here, and the other two gorillas are big old and ugly enough to look after themselves and the old man too, if it comes to it!"

"But Louie," she had replied smiling, "it is you who look after me!"

Despite Ali's assurances she desperately wanted to get away from Dublin, from Ireland, away from her family, but mostly away from Ben and his forthcoming wedding. It hurt to even contemplate the event. It had never been written in her script that he would be marrying someone else, least of all Karen Kennedy.

But there it had been for all to see. A large splashy

announcement in the *Irish Times* that Mr & Mrs Des Kennedy were delighted to announce the forthcoming wedding of their beloved daughter Karen to Benjamin Murphy etc. Not that she hadn't already heard the shocking news through Trisha a few days beforehand. Mick who was still friendly with Ben and often met for the odd pint had got Trisha to prepare Ali for the worst. But somehow seeing it in print made it all the more real.

Ali had heard soundbites on Ben's life over the intervening years. She knew that he had qualified as a doctor and was training in the Mater, for instance, and that he had not dated Karen for a full year after they had broken up. Apparently, according to Mick, Karen had gradually worn him down, made herself an indispensable friend to him after their split, was his shoulder to cry on when Ali could not forgive him and moved in for the kill from there. Ali had to admit Karen's ambition to land Ben was a campaign of military precision, and it had worked.

Ali was sure now that the bangle in Ben's bed was no accident. Even now, the thought of them in bed together made her feel violently angry. Time had not dissipated it. She blushed crimson even now with the very thought of herself going over there to his flat to apologise for being reticent about losing her virginity to him and all along her had leapt on the first trollop who offered herself. Really!

Anyway, it was all water under the bridge. He was lost to her. And it was his entire fault she thought bitterly as the wind swept her to the bus stop. It really was a cow of a night.

"God, how I wish Trisha wasn't engaged to Mick. I

really couldn't ask her to leave him now and go overseas for a year."

She wondered if Trisha had remembered their earlier plan to visit Australia.

Despite their earlier plans of travelling life had seemed to intervene.

Trisha's engagement a year previously had put paid to the old dream of the girls travelling the world. Ali was thrilled that Trisha was so happy with Mick and planning their future but she also felt sad for herself and a tad envious that her life hadn't gone so well. She had had various shallow relationships with other guys but they all got fed up with Ali's terseness and aloof manner. They never lasted long. And she couldn't care less. It just re-iterated her lack of belief in love anyway.

The rain dripped down onto her neck from her umbrella as she clambered onto the steamy number sixteen bus.

"God, what I wouldn't do to be in Sydney right now," she thought, "sunning myself on Bondi! Ben's bloody wedding would seem so far away."

She climbed upstairs and found a window seat, and wiping away the fogged-up windowpane she watched the unrelenting rain lash on the other poor unfortunates. She hoped her father would have passed out by the time she got home so she could have her long hot bath in peace. She tried not to think at all as the heavy bus staggered towards Drumcondra, lumbering with its heavy load of exhausted workers all wet and miserable, wishing to be anywhere else. Closing her eyes, the heavy lull of the engine made her drowsy and gradually Ali fell asleep.

Meanwhile, Trish was sitting in Fagan's with Mick, having a quiet drink. They were discussing the land Mick had inherited outside Swords. Mick was so excited he was just like a little boy with his hand in the sweet jar. His eyes lit up as he talked about it. Trish sat looking at him as he chatted away about his plans. She couldn't help smiling. The big arms encased in a check shirt and his mop of black curls that fell into his chocolate-brown sooty eyes. He was so strong and solid that she always felt safe with him. Maybe just a bit too safe. Now he was talking about the house he'd build on the land for them both. It would be the house of their dreams. It would have five bedrooms, theirs would be upstairs to have some privacy from the kids, and he'd make sure she had a laundry and a kitchen to die for.

Trisha felt he had her whole life mapped out in front of her – it was all a bit too predictable. She felt swamped. She loved Mick dearly and there would never be another man for her. But she felt she would die if she just married him without ever seeing any of the world. She had developed itchy feet some time ago but just couldn't face telling him, as she didn't want to lose him. She had always remembered the pact she and Ali had made years ago about going to Australia. Her brother had gone out there the previous year and was still there. He wrote glowing letters describing Sydney and begging her to come, promising free lodging if she did. Trish knew Ali was desperate to get away, now more then ever. She decided to broach the subject with Mick. It was now or never, before he picked the floor tiles and the children's names out.

"Mick, I have something to say."

She interrupted him mid-flow but decided her nerve wouldn't hold if she didn't speak now.

"What, love. What is it?"

His chocolate brown eyes were all full of love and concern.

"First of all, I love you and I still want to marry you. I still want the house, the kids, the whole kit and caboodle . . ." she then wavered.

"So what's the problem?" he grinned.

"I want to go travelling to Australia!"

There. She'd said it. She had thrown a hand grenade into their relationship and waited.

"What?" Shock had registered on his face and the smile had evaporated. "Australia, why? When? Why now for God's sake?"

"Because Mick, I'm 24 years old. I have been dating you since school. I haven't been any further then Bettystown and I just feel there's a whole wide world out there, and I haven't seen any of it. It wouldn't be fair to marry you and always regret not experiencing anything different. I doubt if I would be happy. But I still want to marry you and do everything we planned. Just a bit later, that's all."

She searched his face for some understanding. But all he looked was hurt.

"I don't want you to go," he said quietly. "How will I plan the house without you?"

"So don't plan it," she said taking his large gnarled hand in hers. "We've got the land. Just hold off on the building. It'll all still be there when I get back. Then I'm all yours."

"How long are you going for?"

She could see tears well up in his eyes. He blinked hard and looked at the floor.

"Well, I haven't even discussed it with Ali yet. I thought I'd talk to you first, but six months at least, maybe a year."

She hadn't thought that far ahead; she just wanted his approval.

"Just promise me you'll come back to me, Trish," he said at last and looked at her as if she was someone he wasn't quite sure he knew.

"Of course I will, ya big eejit!" she replied giving him a huge hug. "Sure, who else would have me?"

She felt so much better. He had given her his blessing. It meant so much to her although she would have gone anyhow. This just made life easier. She couldn't wait to get home and tell Ali the good news, but had to hold her excitement. She didn't want Mick to think that mentally she had already got on the plane, but in reality she had.

It was after 8 p.m by the time Ali got off the bus. The biting wind whipped her around the legs as she scurried around the corner towards her home. She said a silent prayer that her father would be asleep – she hadn't the energy or strength to deal with him tonight. Her feet were killing her and she was dog-tired. Lately he had become more agitated than usual and the violent rages he had displayed towards Joan had returned. It seemed to Ali that the boys could control him better than she could. He seemed to vent all his rage on Ali when she was alone. Often she would just lock herself in her room and wait for the anger to subside or until one of the boys arrived home.

She was deep in thought as she turned the key in the lock. Her father was standing in the hallway, a cigarette in one hand and a bottle of whiskey in the other. He eyed her darkly.

"Here she is," he sneered. "The jailer! The miserable daughter who would rather let her father rot than give him a few bob for his only comfort in life."

It was a familiar tune. Ali tried her best to ignore it. He blamed Ali for not supplying him with money for his alcohol. He hated her for it.

"How are you, Dad? And how was your day?" Her voice was ice.

She hung up her coat and walked wearily into the tiny kitchen.

On the table was a large container. It smelled of paraffin oil and it was placed on a bundle of newspapers. Ali guessed it might be for the old heater her father sometimes used.

She opened the fridge and got out some eggs to make an omelette. Her father rambled about the house muttering and ranting to himself. It was an old rambling diatribe he often bleated out when drunk about how they all robbed him of all he had and how they all lazed around his house and how he wanted them all the hell out.

Suddenly he was in the kitchen facing her.

"Well, little woman, I've been waiting all evening for ye to arrive. Y'see I been doing some thinking and I've decided I want you and those three good-for-nothing bastards out of my house!"

"Yes, Da," she said almost pleadingly. If she didn't answer him, his aggression just rose even higher.

"Now sit down. I'll make you your tea. OK?"

He swayed slightly and jabbed his finger in her direction.

"I want nothing from the likes of you except *peace* in me own home. Now are you going to get out or am I going to have to burn the lot of ye's out meself!"

He swayed even more. Then he lifted the oil container up.

Suddenly Ali paid full attention.

He looked almost comical. His hair askew, and she found herself focusing on his shabby stained pyjamas.

He was manic. Ali tried to remain calm but a deep rising panic overwhelmed her.

Suddenly, her father overturned the oilcan and the paraffin splashed onto the table then dripped in pools onto the floor.

'Dad!" she shrieked.

It was too late. Almost in slow motion he half toppled with the heavy can and the cigarette, which had been between his lips, fell to the floor right in the middle of the oil. A flame suddenly whooshed skywards and within seconds the kitchen was a fireball. Ali tried to grab her father but he was behind a ball of flames. The fire between them was just too high and too hot. She saw the back door was behind her and somehow got to it and opened it. The gust of wind fanned the flames even higher and she saw her father was now amidst a fireball. The flames were now leaping into the hallway.

Ali ran screaming for help. She scaled a six-foot wall in seconds and pounded on the Costellos' back door. Mr Costello was there in seconds. She managed to get some words out before almost collapsing in shock into Mrs Costello's arms. Trisha's brother, Darren, phoned for the fire brigade. Mrs Costello quickly immersed Ali's hands into a bucket of cold water. It was only then that Ali realised that her hands had been badly burned. She could hear the sound of broken glass next door as Mr Costello vainly tried to rescue her father. He and two of his sons tried to douse the flames with buckets of water and garden hoses but to no avail. It was futile. The house was a mass of flames.

Minutes later Mr Costello came back. His face was black with smoke and his eyes told her it was no use. He couldn't reach her father.

Ali felt numb.

"He just went crazy," she tried to explain. "He poured paraffin all over the place and before I knew it there were flames everywhere!"

"Now, now," soothed Mrs Costello who looked in shock herself. "Sure the poor man's mind had long since gone, love. It's not your fault. You did everything you could for him, poor soul. Isn't it lucky that it didn't all happen when ye were all asleep in your beds!"

She shivered herself at the thought and hoped fervently that the flames wouldn't catch fire onto her own roof. Just then the noise of the fire brigade startled them.

"Thank God!" Mrs Costello exclaimed.

It took two units of the fire brigade nearly an hour to put the fire out. Luckily enough they had managed to contain it from the other terraced homes, but the O'Neill house was completely gutted and they had lost everything.

They took her father's charred body out sometime later. By now a huge crowd had gathered and Louie and Kevin had arrived home to the awful news. They were ushered into the Costellos' front room where they were given large whiskeys while Ali told them the full story.

None of them could believe what had happened. Ali thought about all the times she wished her father dead and guilt fell over her like a fine mist. She felt somehow responsible. Surely she could have saved him? A paramedic arrived to attend to her hands and decided she needed further treatment in hospital. She was actually glad her hands were burnt.

It meant she hadn't just stood there – she had tried to save him at least.

Somehow it made her feel better. Better for feeling deep down a sense of release that he was gone and his and their torment was over.

In the ambulance the medic spoke to her quietly and gently as her tears fell. For the first time in years she actually felt safe at last.

Her tears were a mixture of sadness and relief.

She was finally free.

Chapter 12

The fire brigade and police decided to record the fire as an accidental spillage of the paraffin resulting in the accidental death of her father. This decision made it possible for Ali and the boys to collect a modest sum from the insurance. Enough to help them re-build their house: and their lives and bury their father.

The funeral was a quiet dismal affair with few friends and family.

Gerry O'Neill had only one brother in Mayo and a sister in Boston. The brother arrived on the day, spoke to no one and stayed only briefly.

A few drinking buddies that Ali was unfamiliar with arrived too but they made a small sorry bunch. Ali shed some tears for the sad ending her father had and the waste of a life that could have been happy but wasn't. She felt a mixture of shame and relief. She and her brothers had decided not to lay him next to their beloved mother but buried him in a plot with his own parents on the other side of Glasnevin Cemetery.

"I hope you find some peace, Dad," she murmured as they laid the coffin down. She looked briefly around for Ben but he wasn't there.

After the funeral the four of them went back to the guest-house they were temporarily staying in and discussed their futures.

Louie announced that he was joining the Navy, as he had indicated, after his seventeenth birthday in a couple of weeks. Ali was relieved. As Louie was the youngest, he was her biggest worry. Damien and Kevin had decided to get a flat together in the Drumcondra area and said that there'd always be a bed for Louie if he wanted one. They all had decided unanimously that after the insurance money rebuilt the Drumcondra house they would sell it and divide the proceeds equally. None of them wanted to return to the place that held so much unhappiness for them.

"Well, Ali," said Louie, "so far you've not said very much. Are you going to live with Trisha or what's on the cards?"

"Trisha has asked me to go to Australia with her and if it's OK with you guys I'd really love to go . . ."

"What are you waiting for?" said Kevin. "Go! It's time you lived your life, Alison. You've been a really great surrogate Mum to us all. But it's time for you to cut the apron strings and have fun. We'll keep an eye on the big fella." He slapped Louie on the back playfully.

Louie rolled his eyes in mock disgust.

"More like the other way around you mean! Anyway, Ali, when do you intend to head off?"

"Well, there's a lot of planning to do, but my boss is back from her cruise in a couple of weeks so perhaps a few weeks after that. The tickets should be no problem and Trisha's brother is already in Sydney."

Talking about it made it seem all the more real and she began to get excited. It was the first thing to make her happy in a very long time.

Ali began to feel like a young woman again, like the young woman she was and her heart lifted with a promise of happiness unknown.

Six weeks later

"Trish, stop fretting and relax. I have the passports, tickets and boarding passes right here. Just sit down and take it easy, will you? You're making me dizzy!"

Ali was trying to placate Trisha, who was a bundle of nerves. She had never been on a plane before and was hyperventilating at the thought. They were in Dublin Airport's new fancy lounge bar stiffening Trisha's departed nerve with a large whiskey before their flight. Mick had gone in search of some sandwiches and their respective families were milling about the bar.

Only Mrs Costello sat still in the corner, red-eyed and silent. She didn't quite approve of these two innocents heading off halfway around the world to hot heathen Australia. She was sure Trisha would be led astray, just when she had safely assumed Mick was about to take her off her hands.

"That young one," she thought to herself crossly, "just hasn't got a clue! A site in Swords with full planning permission and a fella who'd swim the Liffey for her and she throws it all away to swan off to shaggin' Sydney!"

It took her all her time not to drag her daughter off by the ear and talk some sense into her. But Jim Costello had refused.

"No, let her go. Sure won't it all be here for her when she gets back!" he had replied to his wife's complaints. Her husband rarely interfered, so she had taken his advice and had stayed quiet on the subject, hoping he would be right.

Fellas like Mick O'Toole weren't ten a penny.

Trish looked at her mother's stony face and gulped down a little more whiskey.

"Just don't let me cry, God," she pleaded skywards, "or she'll really go to pieces."

Just then Mick came back laden with a tray of sandwiches and steaming tea, which seemed to lift the collective mood.

Ali couldn't believe they were actually about to leave for Australia.

Just a few short weeks ago Maisie Carter had arrived back from her cruise to the news of Ali's impending departure, but considering all that Ali had been through was gracious enough to provide them with really cheap tickets.

"Just promise me when you get back you'll come back to work for me," Maisie said. "Sure, won't you be twice as knowledgeable for my long-haul clients with all your travelling experience?"

Ali had hugged the large lady fiercely. She had really been like a mother hen to Ali for the past few years and now even though Ali was leaving her in the lurch she still treated Ali more like a daughter than an employee.

Now it was almost time to board the plane and say their goodbyes.

Both shed copious tears despite the whiskey, and Mick seemed so forlorn that Trisha almost turned back. Ali was proud that Louie had arrived smartly dressed in his Navy uniform and assured her she was making the right decision. Parting was still difficult and they were both still in tears as the plane taxied on the runway.

Once the plane took off, however, and Ireland's green patchwork quilt of fields faded under the clouds, they began to get really excited about their big adventure.

London Heathrow seemed exotic to the pair who had never been further than Limerick. Despite all the promised freebies of cheap travel, Ali had always worked too hard and long ever to fit a trip in. All colours and cultures intermingled in the bustling airport that seemed the size of a small city and the girls were amazed that they had to bus it between terminals. Soon after they were on the Qantas flight to Singapore where they would stay for two nights before heading to Sydney where Trisha's brother would meet them.

On the second flight they were lucky enough to have four seats between them so they took off their shoes and tucked their feet up under them and settled in for the ten-hour flight. Trisha then told Ali that Mick had told Ben about her trip Down Under and she had been shocked. Ali tried to feign disinterest.

"I don't know why," she said icily. "He seems to have got on with his life from what I hear. Why can't I get on with mine!"

"Well," said Trisha carefully choosing her words in the minefield that was the subject of Ben's forthcoming nuptials, "he kind of had to, didn't he? Get on with his life, I mean. Ali, you know he tried for a solid year to get back with you and you wouldn't even talk to him. You know he wouldn't be marrying Karen if you'd given him a chance."

"And I'm very happy for them both," snapped Ali. "They're two of a kind. Anyway, he didn't even bother to turn up at my father's funeral."

"He was in London that week . . ." offered Trish weakly.

"Yes, no doubt picking wedding dresses with bloody Karen!"

Trish saw tears dancing in Ali's eyes. Obviously the impending wedding was still hurting Ali a great deal.

Trisha wondered why Ali never gave Ben another chance when she obviously loved him so much, but then again she had never suffered the pain Ali had so couldn't really judge her friend. She decided to change the subject and tried cheering Ali up with tales of the mammoth load of rashers and sausages that her mother had tried to pack into Trisha's suitcase.

"Honestly, half of Buckley's butchers were in me case. I tried to convince her there was no point. The Aussies won't let any foreign food into their country, but she hid a big load of it in me undies no less. Me knickers were full of tinfoil-wrapped sausages! I had to take it out and give it to Mick for his Mum. Mam wouldn't sleep at the thought of poor Dermot missin' out on his black and white puddin'!"

Ali laughed despite herself. Trish could always cheer

her up. She glanced out the window at the fluffy clouds below, and was happy at the distance she was putting between herself and Ben. If she were a whole hemisphere away from his wedding maybe it wouldn't hurt so much. "Anyway," she decided, "I'm not going to ruin Trisha's trip by moping. I'm going to finally put Ben Murphy behind me and find another man or preferably men and have lots of fun forgetting him."

Hours later the bleary-eyed girls awoke to the captain announcing they were landing in Singapore in ten minutes.

"Jeez!" said Trish. "I can't believe we've only travelled half way. Thank God we're getting off. I feel like I've spent half my life on this plane!"

They were almost too tired to be excited but the Singapore air was sweet and heavy and exotic smells assailed their nostrils as they disembarked. They joined the multinational throng heading for the luggage collection and hastily got their cases before heading outside where a hot breeze washed over them like a warm hairdryer. Almost instantly they felt the humidity. Little lights twinkled in the palm trees and the dark sky was littered with stars. That was the only litter they saw. The street was so clean you could eat your dinner from it. It was so different to dear old dirty Dublin.

A sign on a coach said Orchid Plaza and they knew that was for their hotel. They clambered aboard and were thankful for the lovely air conditioning as the coach sped them down Raffles Avenue towards their hotel. The city was vibrant and busy even at 11pm The many high-rise hotels that were glittering in the moonlight almost, but not quite, obscured the bay. It was stunning. Ten minutes later they were speeding to the 18th floor of their impossibly posh hotel. The view from their room was spectacular, but they were so high up they felt a bit light-headed. Neither had been higher than the third floor of a building before.

Trish dived onto her bed and announced sleep was her top priority. Ali agreed and they promptly collapsed, too exhausted even to undress, and slept fully clothed for the next eleven hours straight.

"Get up!" yelled Trish excitedly. "Ali, get up for God's sake. You don't want to miss a minute of this place. You can sleep for the rest of your life but not today – for today we shop!"

She jumped up and down on Ali's bed until she was awoken from glorious slumber; she then bullied her into the shower to wake her up for the exhausting shopping trip she had planned for today.

After a breakfast of exotic fruit and croissants they caught a courtesy bus to the city centre for sightseeing and shopping. The coolness of the hotel air conditioning hadn't prepared them for the humid 35-degree heat that almost slapped them in the face as soon as they stepped outside.

"I'm sweatin'," gasped Trish after an hour and they headed for the sanctuary of the famous Raffles Hotel where they sipped iced tea in the grand lobby and gasped at the sheer opulence of the place. Later they shopped in some of the many shopping centres before jet-lag took over once again and they headed back to their hotel.

They were very impressed with Singapore, this large

bustling city and the friendliness of the people, but it was so hot and humid they decided to just have dinner at the hotel and have an early night so they would be fresh for the final leg to Sydney. They had a beautiful meal of nasi goreng and a few glasses of wine before crashing out on their beds and raiding the mini-bar of a bottle of champagne. They drifted off to sleep eventually, excited that Australia was next.

Chapter 13

"Look, Trish. It's Sydney!" Ali screeched excitedly. Sure enough, there it was in all its glory. The plane banked to the left and set against the vivid blue sky was the trademark Coat Hanger Bridge and the famous Sydney Opera House. They were really here. Ali's heart leapt; she couldn't believe they were actually here in Australia at last. They squeezed each other with delight, almost beside themselves with excitement.

Dermot was there in Arrivals to greet them. He was looking totally Australian in board shorts, long hair and killer tan. Only the loud Dub "Howiyas!" gave him away. He hugged them both awkwardly in the typical Irish fashion and led them outside with their copious cases to his battered FJ Holden.

The warmth just enveloped them. It was hot but not sticky and humid like Singapore. Dermot informed them it was cool at 23 degrees. Dermot caught up on the family gossip as they sped towards the house he shared at

Manley Beach. The house was a large white wooden one with front veranda and stained-glass windows. It was quite unlike anything they had ever seen. He showed them to their room, which was large and airy at the front of the house. Through the side entrance of the house next door across the hilly street they could glimpse a patch of blue, which Dermot informed them was the bay where they could catch a water taxi to the city. They dropped their cases and fell into bed exhausted after their flight and promptly fell asleep until dusk.

"Girls, the lads are home and just dyin' to meet you. Come on. Wake up. I've got a barbie on!" Dermot was knocking on the door. The girls scrambled up, unsure where they were and what time it was.

"This jetlag is a real killer," announced Trish noting the large bags under her eyes.

"I wonder if any of them are beauts?" giggled Ali as she tried vainly to smooth her wayward curls. They went into the lounge room to meet the lads.

There was Paul McNamara known as 'macker' who was a chef like Dermot and from Ballyfermot, Terry from Skerries who was a butcher and Barry from Sutton who worked at the Sydney Hilton as a barman. They were all good crack as Trish commented later "but no oil paintings!" which was just as well as they all became fast friends without any strings.

After a delicious barbie of marinated chicken and lamb koftas the lads took them out on a tour of Sydney, which took in the Rocks area, Chinatown and the red light area known as Kings Cross. They finished up on Bondi, the world-famous beach, just as night fell and the many lights of the bay twinkled as a gentle breeze fanned their faces. This shook off the cobwebs, so they hit Kitty O'Shea's for a few beers and had a grand old singsong until the early hours. Trish and Ali were on such a high they felt that they might never come down.

Australia was just what the girls needed at this point in their lives. It was so different to Ireland, carefree, laid-back and sunny. It was a totally different world. Quite apart from all of that it was a new and exciting experience to be living away from home, on their own. They spent the first two weeks as tourists, visiting all the hotspots and sunbathing on Manly beach or Bondi. But after a fortnight of feeling like pampered princesses (being cooked culinary masterpieces by Dermot every night who was anxious to show off his newly enhanced chef's skills), they decided they'd better get jobs to support their trip and, as Trish quipped, "I need to get up off my arse which is taking up more of Bondi every time I go there!"

Trish managed to get a great casual job in David Jones, the prestigious department store, but Ali wasn't so lucky. Eventually Dermot got her a job at the Hilton as a kitchen hand. The work was long, hot and gritty but the buzz from working in a top class international hotel was amazing. There was such a melting pot of cultures. She made friends with people from all over the world.

First she made friends with Wannie, her trainer from Nigeria, who was the darkest person she had ever met. His face was lit up by his wonderful smile of beautiful white teeth. He was also the gentlest person she had ever encountered and he showed her the ropes and kept her out of the way of the cranky and highly-strung German chefs. Then she made friends with Rose, a tiny Filipino, who was head of the housemaids and through her she met Mary, a fellow Dub from Dundrum, who was over on a year out from uni.

But the funniest and most camp was David, a screaming queen, whose charm and acerbic wit had Ali in stitches for most of the day. He was the head of banqueting and flawless at his job in fine dining. But when the uniform came off he carried a black leather handbag everywhere, which held his Carmen rollers for his blond hairdo, a tinted moisturiser, mascara and a skimpy white vest to show of his well-toned pecs. If he hadn't been so overtly gay Ali could have been in love. He was truly model material. Ali settled for being a good mate of his and his barman boyfriend, Derek.

The Hilton was a hotbed of romance both heterosexual and otherwise and Ali had to close her open-mouthed gape more than once in order not to show up her sheltered upbringing. One thing was for sure – she knew the Gresham Hotel was never like this. The gossip of who was bedding who kept Ali enthralled and appalled at the same time. She'd never felt so small-town before. It made all her own dramas seem insignificant, which was exactly what she needed. She absolutely loved it.

Meanwhile Trisha was up to her armpits in perfumes at the cosmetics counter spraying scent onto old grand dames, while a live pianist played on a large black Steinway. David Jones, or 'DJ's' as the staff called it, was a classy store much like Brown Thomas in Dublin. Trish had to wear a uniform of black and white and the staff sometimes seemed even more posh then the already well-heeled clientele. It was a far cry from Roche's but just as exhausting. Trisha was well liked, her Dublin accent seemed exotic down under and she was very popular. She polished up her appearance in tune with the glamorous store and looked quite amazing with the entirely free expensive make-up and her hair scooped up into a classic chignon. Her golden skin flourished under the Sydney sun much to Ali's chagrin when her own face really did resemble an explosion in a freckle factory, as Damien had always said.

Chapter 14

Within a month both girls had changed so much without even noticing. Ireland seemed a long way off. Mick wrote and phoned every week and for a while after hearing from him Trish would be a bit melancholy and lovesick but would soon perk up when Dermot or one of the lads suggested a night out.

Dermot knew so many people and they usually met up with large bunches of Irish and English people at the Irish and English bars. So much so that sometimes they felt they were still at home.

One night they decided to venture off the beaten track and try to meet up with some true blue Aussie natives and went off to a bar in the Rocks area to see a band play. They found a lively beer garden where an Aussie rock band was blaring out a cover of a Cold Chisel number and Irish favourite, Ke Sahn. They got a jug of beer and sat down. Then the heavens opened in true tropical Aussie style and they were drenched in minutes from head to foot. They grabbed the beer and headed inside to the bar and found a couple of stools to perch on. That's when Trisha noticed a few good-looking guys with closely cropped hair having a laugh and a few beers sitting behind them. She and Ali both felt like a couple of drowned rats with their damp straggly hair and wet tee shirts.

"Don't look now," whispered Trisha, "but there's a load of hunks just behind you . . ."

"Huh?" grunted Ali, desperately trying to gather her wayward curls into a topknot.

"Behind you, there are four or five fellas. At least two look like George Michael and one is the split of Mel Gibson. I tell ya, if I wasn't engaged, I could be in love!"

Ali glanced behind her. Trish was right. They were drop-dead gorgeous, every last one of them.

"Just play it cool," hissed Trish. "Keep on yapping and drinking your beer. Don't let them see we've noticed them!"

Ali spluttered into her beer laughing.

"Are you kidding, Trish? Here we are like two scalded cats, not an ounce of make-up between us. Our hair is like rats' tails and you want to play it cool?"

Trisha feigned annoyance but then had to laugh too.

Just then, George Michael appeared beside them at the bar. He ordered a round of drinks for his friends and struck up a conversation with Trish. But Ali was drawn to the quiet guy in the corner. The dark-haired blue-eyed Mel Gibson look-alike with the dazzling smile. He was tanned and muscular and kept glancing over. George Michael apparently had Irish lineage despite a Greek-sounding name and was having a deep discussion with Trisha about granny's Irish roots in County Cork when Mel Gibson motioned Ali over. She simply smiled and sipped her beer – she wasn't going anywhere. Eventually he drifted up to the bar with the rest of his friends and they all got chatting. Apparently they were all police officers from Brisbane down in Sydney for a seminar. George Michael who was half Greek, a quarter Irish and quarter Australian was called Alex Triantafillou. Mel Gibson quietly introduced himself as Simon Hempnel. He shook Ali's hand while gazing at her intently with his beautiful blue eyes. Ali and Trisha couldn't help exchanging grins and so they spent the rest of the evening basking in such antipodean beauty and getting well and truly blotto.

The next morning Ali woke with a thumping hangover.

"Oh God, turn off the light, Trisha, will you?" she groaned.

"I can't turn off the goddam sun," snapped Trish feeling equally delicate.

"God! Does it always have to be so bloody bright all the time? Isn't there ever the odd dull cloudy day so a person can endure a hangover in peace!" They both laughed.

"Oh, Trish, don't make me laugh. It makes my head hurt twice as much. Never again let me touch Bundaberg rum, will you?"

"It was a brilliant night though, wasn't it?" said Trisha, as she fetched Ali a welcome can of ice-cold Coke.

"Yeah," agreed Ali, "from what I can piece together. I hate myself for getting drunk though."

"Look," said Trisha. "You hardly ever do. Just because you have the odd night on the tear doesn't mean you're turning into an alcoholic."

"Hmm . . . I suppose not," said Ali reluctantly, instantly picturing her father and wincing at the memory. She had a total paranoia about inheriting his weakness for alcohol. She knew it could be genetic. "Anyway, did you end up kissing George Michael?"

"You mean Alex, yeah! Felt a bit guilty, though it was kinda fun."

"Well, I thought you'd both decided all bets were off between you and Mick for the year."

"We did. It's just it still feels a bit like cheating. I love him so much you know. It just feels weird. The thought of him kissing anyone else makes my blood boil . . . anyway how about you and Mel Gibson. You two looked pretty 'full on' as they say over here!"

"Oh, Trish, he was so nice. It's a pity they live in Brisbane. They'll be going back in a few days."

"But Brisbane is on our itinerary isn't it? And if it wasn't it sure is now, if that's what the male population look like."

"Yeah, bloody gorgeous, aren't they!"

They both laughed again. "What are we like!"

Just then the phone rang. It was Simon. Ali was surprised.

"Oh, my God!" she squealed, putting her hand over the receiver. "Obviously he hasn't heard of the standard five day waiting period rule between phone calls! What will I say?"

"That's just in the rule book of the Dublin blokes," replied Trisha. "Just talk to him – go on!"

A crimson Ali was then invited along with Trish for a scenic drive along the coast with Simon and Alex. Ali tried to beg off with a severe hangover but Simon insisted the fresh air would do them both good and said he'd call at 2pm sharp.

"Well, he's keen!" Remarked Trisha.

"And so is Alex by the sound of things!" warned Ali. "God, we've somehow got to make ourselves somewhat human-looking by 2 o'clock."

"It'll take until 2pm the year 2000 to make me feel normal," moaned Trish. "Tell you what – let's have another two hours' sleep followed by a dirty big fry. After that we'll have a nice hot shower and we'll feel brand new."

"Yeah," agreed Ali and hopped back into bed. Soon they were both sound asleep despite sunshine blazing into their room.

The afternoon arrived all too soon and eventually the girls did feel better, after their greasy fry and lengthy showers. They did their best to cover up the bags under their eyes with make-up, but both still felt tired. Ali was tired and nervous.

"Look," said Trish, changing her shorts for the third time, "you'd no problem communicating last night. Anyway, I'll be with you, and if it's really crap or they turn out to be creeps we can pull the old migraine routine and come straight home, OK?"

"OK."

Ali was appeased. It was great when Trish took the lead in these situations. She was sure that if Simon had asked her out alone she would have refused. Even though she liked him, her confidence was nil.

The guys rang the bell promptly at two o'clock and both looked clean-cut and handsome and like they hadn't touched a drop of alcohol the night before.

Both girls were struck dumb by the wonderful soft-top bright pink Beetle car, which Alex had hired. They climbed aboard meekly and sped off down the coast with the sun glittering off the vivid blue Botany Bay. The boys took them sightseeing along the coast and then down to Doyle's on the beach for a wonderful meal of fish and chips that Doyle's were famous for. They then went for a long walk on the beach and witnessed a splendid sunset. Simon kissed Ali gently just once along the shore with the sound of crashing waves in the background and then clasped her hand tightly as they walked along the perfect white sand. She hadn't remembered a time when she had felt so happy since Ben. The guys dropped them off at 9pm, exhausted but exhilarated. They had both been perfect gentlemen and wonderful company. Even Trish found it hard to resist the charms of the George Michael look-alike that she had enjoyed the attention of so much.

"God, they are just so gorgeous!" exploded Trisha when they were safely indoors and out of earshot.

"Agreed!" grinned Ali. "Almost too good to be true."

"Wasn't it a fabulous day?" continued Trisha. "I mean, when were we last treated like queens? I could get used to this."

"Yeah, me too," replied Ali dreamily, thinking of Simon's soft kiss and his large brown hands fiddling with her hair. She couldn't bear the thought of not seeing him again.

"They're going back tomorrow, y'know," she sighed. "Simon asked me if we were going to stop in Brisbane on our way to Cairns."

"I hope you said yes," replied a worried Trish.

"Yes, I did. If that's OK."

"Yes," frowned Trish. "It very much is as a matter of fact. Alex is quite dishy and I really like him. Am I a total cow? I mean for liking someone so soon? How can I like this Alex guy – even if he is edible? I mean I love Mick so much . . ." her voice trailed off. She looked so pained, Ali felt sorry for her.

"You're not a cow," she soothed. "You came to Australia to do some mad girly things and that includes kissing a few frogs before you marry the prince!"

"Yeah," laughed Trisha as she put the kettle on for a cuppa. "Except Alex is like no frog I know!"

They both fell about the place laughing and spent the rest of the evening reminiscing about their day, before falling into bed exhausted and happy. Ali lay awake for a very long time thinking that coming to Australia was the best move she had ever made. She and Trish would really have fun here. She just knew it.

Eventually, Ben popped into her head as he did most nights, whether she wanted him to or not. He had a habit of cropping up regularly in her dreams, and so unfortunately did the awful Karen. She wondered how the wedding plans were going and finding herself teary-eyed again switched her thoughts to the lovely Simon. Perhaps at last here was someone who could make her forget Ben once and for all.

She was going to throw herself into a new relationship she decided, it was time to finally forget Ben and all the heartache and move on. She finally drifted off to sleep with the memory of Simon's soft lips and lemony smell and wondered if she would ever see him again.

Chapter 15

Meanwhile in Dublin, Isabel Murphy was looking out at her perfectly manicured lawn on a beautiful cloudless morning. The lawn that had been carefully cultivated by Flanagan, the gardener, had a sea of baby white rose trees that were almost in bloom.

It was a scant three weeks to the wedding and the timing should be exactly right. Isabel had left nothing to chance. She had managed to persuade Kate and Des, Karen's parents, that they should hold the wedding at San Etienne.

After all, the huge long garden was perfectly suited to house a large marquee tent and Isabel did so love to organise and plan events. Karen's parents simply had to foot the bill. And there was no expense to be spared for the Kennedys' only daughter.

A jazz quartet had been booked; the Berkeley Court Hotel was catering the food and supplying wine waiters; everything was in place. Yet Isabel felt uneasy, somewhat dissatisfied.

It was Ben, she decided wistfully as she cut her croissant absent-mindedly. He was so quiet, so remote. Not at all like an excited bridegroom to be. She fervently hoped he wasn't getting cold feet, just pre-wedding jitters. She knew men didn't enter into the excitement of weddings in the same way as women, but this seemed different. Ben didn't seem to express any interest whatsoever in any of the planning or details including his honeymoon, which was most odd. Isabel knew her son. Something was indeed troubling him. She hoped it wasn't that awful O'Neill girl. Honestly, she still seemed to have some pull over him.

He'd been a bit down ever since she left for Australia. Isabel had thanked her lucky stars when she'd heard the news. Mars wasn't far enough away for that one. "God!" she thought exasperatedly to herself. "Half a world away and she still causes problems."

Well, nothing was going to stand in the way of this wedding.

Her jaw set in its familiar determined line. She rose slowly as she drained her coffee and went to the telephone. She needed time to organise some diversions for Ben. She didn't want him to have time to think. Ben was going to be married to Karen if she had to drag him up the aisle herself.

As she dialled Kate Kennedy's number she viewed herself dispassionately in the long hall mirror.

"Not bad at all," she murmured half to herself.

The surgeon had worked wonders; no one had noticed the slight scarring around her earlobes. She had taken off to Monte Carlo for a week after the surgery until the swelling had receded. She looked ten years younger. Her new hairstyle of a feathered bob helped confuse people into thinking that was why she looked so fresh. Not even Ben had guessed.

He would think she was an idiot for resorting to plastic surgery just for a wedding. But it was much more than that.

Recently, Isabel Murphy had felt herself get old and all the gym workouts and designer clothes couldn't overcome her deep depression over her ageing face.

This facelift had given her a new lease on life. The last time she had surgery her nerves had bested her at the last minute and she had just settled for an upper eye lift. It had helped for a few years but not like this.

She felt absolutely wonderful! Why, she even noticed John actually looking at her again like he hadn't done in years.

That's why this wedding was doubly important to her. It had to be now when she looked her best. The pictures were bound to make the *Irish Tatler*. Ben would not ruin this dream for her.

She smiled. After all, frowning made her look ancient.

A few sessions on a tanning machine would top up her already golden skin.

"Kate!" she exclaimed when the phone was answered by Karen's mother. "We simply must get together for a cappuccino this morning. No. Nothing wrong exactly, I think my boy has a few wedding nerves. Yes. Right, I'll see you about 10.30 am at Jury's coffee dock."

She was sure Kate would have a few ideas. After all she'd managed to marry off three sons of her own.

Suddenly feeling a lot chirpier she raced upstairs to get ready for her coffee morning, wondering if Kate would notice how well she was looking.

Later that day Ben sat in the Bailey having a quiet pint with Mick.

He made no excuses to his friend. Mick was well aware Ben made extra time for him in order to keep up to date with Ali's whereabouts and actions as regaled to Mick through copious letters from Trish.

"So they're having a ball then?" he asked evenly, eyeing Mick.

"Yep," said Mick morosely, resigned to the fact it would be a year before he'd see Trisha again. He had secretly hoped she would hate Australia and be home within three months, but so far she absolutely loved it, and despite missing him she couldn't keep the enthusiasm from her letters.

They both supped their pints in silence for a moment.

"God! What are we like?" laughed Ben at last.

"Two eejits if you ask me," frowned Mick, failing to see the joke. His intended was half a hemisphere away meeting tall Aussie surfers. He might never get her back.

"It's all right for you, Murphy," he spat. "You've got your girl. You're getting married in three weeks."

"Am I indeed?" replied Ben mercurially.

"Now, don't start."

Mick was irritated by Ben's flippancy. He was a

straight arrow, always had been. He couldn't understand Ben for the life of him.

Mick had always known what he wanted and went for it. Ben just seemed to let events carry him along, until it was too late.

"You can't go messing that girl around. Not at this late stage."

He eyed Ben for a reaction. Ben hung his head.

"I just don't know if this is the right decision, that's all. How can I marry Karen if I still have these huge feelings for Ali?"

"OK," allowed Mick. "But you and Ali haven't been together in years. You're only holding onto the dream of what you had, the idea of her. You're seeing it all through rose-coloured specs, Ben. We all remember our first love!"

"Yes," replied Ben softly, "and you've still got yours, so don't lecture me about it, OK. I've enough pressure on me already."

He downed the rest of his pint and stood up to leave.

"Ben!" said Mick urgently as he grabbed his friend's sleeve. "Please don't do anything stupid."

"Don't worry. I won't," said Ben grimly. "Not anything stupid anyway." And with that he left.

Mick drained the rest of his pint wondering what the hell his friend had meant. Ben was going to do something. Mick could feel it. But there was no point in trying to talk to Ben.

He'd have to figure it out for himself. Mick felt half-responsible.

He probably shouldn't tell Ben so much about Ali.

Ben's face when Mick had told him Ali had met an

125

Aussie policeman had been a black cloud. Mick hadn't known how deep the feelings still were. The guy was getting married for God's sake. Maybe it was the wrong decision after all if he could still get so jealous over an ex he hadn't dated in four years.

"Thank God for Trish," sighed Mick taking out the recent photo Trish had sent of herself and Ali that was taken at the Sydney Opera House. She looked golden and carefree and so beautiful that he felt so much like hopping on a plane this minute and swooping her back to Ireland. Instead he would wait for her.

He'd wait forever if he had to, as long as she came back and was his. He placed the photo back into his denim jacket and went back to work. Someone had to do the long hard graft if their dream home was to become a reality, and Mick had worked twelve-hour days since Trish left so he'd have enough money to start building as soon as she got back. He couldn't wait to see her face when he told her they had enough for the wedding and the house. He just wanted her to be happy. Happy and contented, and with him. He felt infinitely luckier then Ben with his posh background and doctor's career and the obligatory BMW. Ben seemed to have it all but he didn't, Mick realised.

"I do," he said out loud as he strolled down a sunny Grafton Street. "I have it all. A great job, the girl of my dreams and the plans for my dream home in me pocket. What could be better?"

He'd ring Trish tonight and let her know how much he loved her.

He didn't know yet if he'd tell her about Ben's

apparent cold feet towards the wedding. Maybe he'd wait and see. If Ali was getting over Ben he didn't see why he should upset her at this stage. No, he'd keep quiet on that for the moment.

Let sleeping dogs lie.

Chapter 16

A week after the girls had said goodbye to their gorgeous policemen they had chucked their jobs in Sydney and informed Dermot they were off to Queensland. Sydney was turning cold anyhow in July, and they'd heard Queensland was hot and sunny all year round.

Dermot grinned at the news and then asked: "Yeah? And what's the names of these bozos anyway?"

He wasn't fooled for a moment, but insisted they take the address of his Kiwi mate's sister, Marci, who might be able to put them up for a couple of nights 'til they got settled. He'd become quite the big protective brother towards Trisha, something he'd never aspired to back home and even gave her a large embarrassed hug goodbye which brought a tear to her eye as they set off for the bus station. Trisha noticed Ali was unusually quiet. After forty minutes of looking at Ali stare unseeing out the window, she knew she would have to ask.

"What's up, Ali?" she ventured.

Ali tore her eyes away from the window as endless brown land sped by.

"Oh, I dunno. It's nothing really, and everything. Ben's getting married two weeks from today and I just feel a bit . . ." Her voice trailed away as tears stung her eyes. She blinked in vain as a large tear escaped down her cheek.

"Oh shit," said Trisha. "I clean forgot. I'm such an idiot!" She hugged her friend fiercely. "How do you feel, as if I need to ask? It must be awful for you."

"I feel like shite actually," smiled Ali weakly. "I thought I was over him. I sort of am, really. It's just today it finally dawned on me that there's no hope now of us ever getting back together. And it just hit me like a ton of bricks, that's all. Stupid, I know."

Trish was taken aback by the sudden admittance. She had guessed Ali still had feelings but hadn't realised how strong they appeared to be, after all this time.

"But, Ali, if you felt like this, why wouldn't you take him back, all the times he tried. You said you were over him."

"Yeah, I know, and to all intents and purposes I am. I mean we're rushing off to Brisbane so I can be with Simon, aren't we? It's just that Ben was my first love and I feel a bit empty and sad that he now loves someone else more than me."

More tears erupted.

"Well, that's open to debate," thought Trish but decided to keep that one to herself for the moment. Instead she asked, "And how do you feel about Simon?"

"Oh, I like him a lot." Ali brightened. "Trisha, when I kiss Simon I feel butterflies, for the first time in years, I actually feel something. He's kind and he's sweet. I really enjoyed being with him. And I want so badly to see him again."

As long as it's not on the rebound, Trisha thought. Suddenly she missed Mick so much, Mick's big strong loving arms and the lush green grasses of Ireland. She stared herself now at the large brown open space and felt very homesick. Australia, she decided, could be a very lonely place.

Ben, at that very minute, was lying awake in his large bed in Rathmines staring at the ceiling. It was no good – he couldn't sleep. He looked at the clock radio, which blinked 3.05am to him. I wonder what time it is in Sydney now or Brisbane. Or wherever the hell Ali was now. Ben had been lying awake for hours and had come to a decision. He was not going through with the wedding to Karen. All the doubts that had nagged him were very real. He loved her but never felt the passion, the heart-stopping ache that he had felt for Ali – an ache that had never dissipated. But he did love Karen enough to know he could never be the husband she wanted or deserved.

"How did I ever let it get this far?" he berated himself angrily. "I am such an idiot! Now I'll break her heart by calling it all off. They'll all think me such a coward. But I'll be an even bigger coward if I go through with this just because I'm afraid of people's reactions. It'll be worse if we get married and then split up."

It was such a mess. There were only two weeks to go and Karen had spoken of little else. She was living this wedding. She must have guessed something was amiss because he hadn't slept with her in weeks and she hadn't stayed over at his flat in months. But she seemed so consumed with all the wedding preparations that she had seemingly failed to notice his coolness. It didn't matter now.

"I'll call up to see Karen first thing in the morning," he thought. "Then I'll tell my parents. God! Mum will go ape! Just as well I'll be leaving town. Still, Africa needs good medics. If something good can come from this it will be the work I can do for the poor people of Mozambique. Médecins Sans Frontières was an excellent organisation and Charlie Quinn had been chasing him for a year to sign up.

Yesterday, he had said yes finally, and then signed up for a year. It was something he always wanted to do. He also knew that he was running away; away from Karen, away from himself, away from thoughts of Ali. He needed to focus on something else for a change, and Africa should do it. He had a vision of Isabel's face when he told her. He was terrified.

"God, I'd face those bloody rhinos quicker than my mother!" he thought mirthlessly. "This is going to be the most difficult thing I ever have to do."

Across town, Isabel was having the most wonderful dream. In it she was swathed in cream silk and was basking in glorious sunlight at a garden wedding. Ben and Karen were resplendent in all their wedding finery, and everyone was telling her what a fantastic job she had done. She snuggled deeper into her pink Laura Ashley eiderdown and slept on, oblivious to the nightmare that was about to unfold around her.

"What do you mean call it off?" Karen exploded into loud sobs. She could not believe her ears. The icing was already on the cake and gifts had started to arrive by the sackload and here was an apparently insane Ben calmly telling her the wedding was to be cancelled. She noted, despite her mounting hysteria, that he had used the words 'cancelled' and not the less devastating 'postponed'. Karen's sobbing became even more high-pitched and was accompanied by various expletives. Her mother came rushing in to see what on earth was the matter. Ben was standing in the middle of the room looking at his feet while Karen was wailing loudly on the sofa. She then flew to her mother and sobbed relentlessly.

"Ben?" Kate Kennedy looked for some kind of an explanation.

"I'm very sorry, Mrs Kennedy, but I've just told Karen that I can't marry her." He looked agonised. "I'm sorry I left it so late but I've been in doubt for a number of weeks now and I know it's not just pre-wedding jitters. Karen deserves better and . . ."

"Yes, she most certainly does!" shouted Karen's mother, enraged. "She does deserve better than this. How could you? And at this late stage too! Why did you ever ask her to marry you in the first place, if you didn't mean it?"

"Well," Ben began, but how could he tell her he never actually proposed to Karen at all. He just responded to an ultimatum from Karen last Christmas that he marry her within six months or lose her for good. It didn't really matter now. None of it did. He couldn't hurt her any more than he already had.

"I am so sorry, Mrs Kennedy. Really I am. But I figure it's better to make the break now rather than later. I have also told Karen that I'm to take a job in Africa. I'll be leaving in a couple of weeks. I will telephone all the family and friends to explain, and I'll send the gifts back. It's the least I can do."

"You damn well will!" replied Kate Kennedy hotly. She had never heard the like. The brass cheek of him, waltzing in here, ruining her daughter's life and then hopping off to the continent to escape all the strange looks and sniggers. Her daughter would have to suffer them. She felt like slapping his smug face.

"You can take us straight over to your mother's house now. I'm sure she'll have a lot to say about this!" said Kate Kennedy tartly.

"I feel I need to tell my mother alone, if that's OK," said Ben firmly. "It'll be a shock to her too. Perhaps you could come over later and see her then." He hoped she'd agree. It would be difficult enough to tell Isabel when he was alone. But with a tearful Karen and mother in tow, it didn't bear thinking about . . .

"Let him go," said Karen at last, her beautiful eyes full of hate. "Let him piss off to hell, as far as I'm concerned. Go on. Get out! Just get out of my sight. You disgust me!" and with that she broke into more uncontrollable sobbing.

Ben left quickly. He felt like an absolute shit and realised he really was one. Karen for all her faults really loved him and he had just stamped all over her. He was never straight with her from day one and let her pursue him and even win him. But he never once had the guts to tell her openly that he would never feel as deeply as she did. He had never felt so low in all his life as he drove to Sandymount to confront his mother. By the time he got to his parents' house he had realised he just wasn't hurting

Karen by his decision. His mother would also be deeply hurt by the shame of his actions, but he knew a divorce would cause even more shame in the family so he took a couple of deep breaths and turned his key in the door and went in to face the music.

Isabel was breakfasting in the newly constructed conservatory, which yielded an excellent view of the just budding white rose trees and the perfectly manicured lawn. Ben saw that his mother looked rather small and almost girlish, dressed only in a white towelling robe with her hair tied back. Unaware of her surgery, he simply noticed she looked fresh and serene, unaware he was about to destroy all her dreams.

Isabel's face lit up when she saw her son stride in, but when she saw his expression the smile froze on her face.

"Ben, whatever brings you here at this early hour?"

Ben sat down glumly and exhaled. "Mum, this is probably the worst thing you'll hear all year. In fact you won't want to hear it, but . . ." his voice trailed away, his courage deserting him.

"Oh, spit it out, Benjamin!" his mother barked impatiently. "You always did procrastinate!"

"I'm not getting married, Mother," he almost shouted. "There will be no wedding. Period. Karen and her mother know all about it and any minute now they'll be bursting in here to tell you what an absolute bastard I am, so you can compare notes."

He shuffled in his seat unable to leave but not wanting to stay.

"Oh Benjamin, but why? Karen is such a lovely girl. She loves you so much. She is the right girl for you."

His mother wasn't shouting at all. She was gripping his two hands in hers and almost in tears. She was sad but there was no expected explosion of rage.

"Mum, she is the right girl for *you*. She never really was the right girl for me. I just went along with it all! I seemed to make everybody happy, even all this wedding malarkey – it was all about me and around me but it was never anything to do with me. I've realised I can't live a lie any more. Marriage is too serious for that."

His hands covered his eyes but she spied approaching tears.

"What will you do?" Isabel said kindly.

She spoke calmly – not wanting to corner him but inside she wanted to hit her son, the bloody ungrateful little sod. All the hard work she had done the past few weeks. She was thinking fast, staying calm. This was still salvageable. She would call a meeting with Karen and her parents and they'd thrash it all out. Her wayward son would see sense.

"Now, Ben," she said firmly, "I want you to think this all through. Karen is a good girl and she loves you to bits. You're just feeling nervous and have a classic case of cold feet. God! Even your father had a touch of the jitters before our wedding. And look at us! Don't be too hasty . . ."

"Mum! Don't you see?" interrupted Ben as he stood up angrily, all six feet two of him. "I am going to Africa in two weeks' time and I'm going for a year. I need to get away from all of this and sort myself out. Your precious wedding is off and that is final!"

"You're *what*?" All hope lost, Isabel finally exploded. "You have the nerve to walk in here, land this big bombshell on me that you're cancelling the wedding that I've worked my fingers to the bone for, and now you're off to Africa leaving me to pick up the pieces? I can't believe you are bringing such shame on the family and just running away from it all. It's just too much, Benjamin. It really is!" The tears started to flow. "Just you bloody wait 'til I telephone your father. He'll be arriving in work about now. He'll have something to say about this! I just can't cope with all this on my own."

"I'm telling Dad myself, Mother, and I'm also going to telephone all the guests and return the gifts personally. In fact I'm going to start now, so I guess I'll see you later."

With that Ben strode off out of the house leaving Isabel sitting in the now defunct conservatory overlooking the superfluous carpeted lawn.

She just sat there dumbfounded, letting the awful reality sink in.

The awful shame of it all. A single tear slid down her newly lifted face. All the hard work and preparation she had slaved over and all for nothing. She didn't even hear the doorbell ring. Suddenly Karen and Kate Kennedy were standing before her with tearful and angry faces. Isabel decided this was just too much to endure. She would never, ever forgive her son. Never.

The following day Mick got a cryptic message on his pager. "Wedding off – flying soon to Africa. Will call soon." He wondered what the hell was going on. Obviously Ben had done something drastic and called the whole thing off.

But at the time Mick was up to his armpits in a burst water main and his errant friend would have to wait.

Chapter 17

Brisbane was a beautiful city. It had clean wide tree-lined streets and a smallish city centre that reminded the girls a little bit of Dublin. It was altogether more homely and laid back than hectic Sydney and they liked it immediately.

They contacted Dermot's friend's sister, Marci, who lived in leafy St Lucia. Marci happened to be splitting up from her long-term boyfriend that very week and offered to share her house with them. The girls didn't hesitate. It was a large Queenslander-style house up on stilts and had a lovely view of the city.

Marci was interminably cheerful despite catching her boyfriend of four years in bed with a 50-year-old woman and abruptly ending their relationship. Her enthusiasm was infectious and the girls couldn't help liking her. She in return told the girls they were just what she needed to help her reel in a replacement man.

Marci was plain-looking and wore large horn-rimmed glasses that made her look stern, but had a model girl figure and stunning legs. Trish resolved inwardly that the specs would have to go if Marci was going to net a new beau.

After they moved in, Marci's ex had collected his belongings, which Marci had placed carefully on the front lawn.

"I hate the bastard but I just couldn't ruin his stereo. It's too nice," Marci had explained and then took them on an evening drive around Brisbane, city-sightseeing, so she wouldn't be there when Josh arrived.

They drove across the Storey Bridge in Marci's fancy FJ Holden Commodore.

The view from the large Coat Hanger Bridge showed off the city's glittering skyline of skyscrapers that were lit up in the dusk.

Then they drove to Mount Cootha, which overlooked the whole city and bay area with fabulous views. The suburbs seemed to go on forever. Lights twinkled for miles and miles.

Australia was really vast. Ali looked down over the suburbs and wondered where Simon was. She smiled at the memory of him. It was the first time she had ever thought of any man before she thought of Ben.

She was happy about that.

A balmy breeze swept over them as the crickets made their noisy song and they sipped cappuccinos in the Cootha Cafe. Tomorrow, after they had gone job-hunting, she would contact Simon. She hoped he hadn't forgotten her already.

Eventually they drove home along the Brisbane River along Coronation Drive back to St Lucia with Marci chattering all the way. They'd heard her life story by now and realised they would become fast friends. She was kind and uncomplicated and endlessly generous.

Before going to bed Trish and Ali both agreed they had been very lucky so far with the people they had met and the ease at which they had found themselves friends.

"Let's hope we're as lucky on the jobs front," smiled Trish as they undressed for bed.

"Yeah, maybe David Jones has a branch here for you, though I doubt if I'll go back to the Hilton," mused Ali. "I wonder if we'll be as lucky on the bloke front too. I was thinking of contacting Simon soon."

"And I was wondering when you'd get around to that!" smiled Trisha.

"Yeah," grinned Ali in return. "Wonder if Brisbane's finest has forgotten me yet. I'll give him a ring tomorrow. Do you want me to mention you for Alex?"

Trisha frowned.

"Better not Ali. I mean I like him, but I don't want to get too serious about anyone. If he wants to go out with you and Simon as a foursome, as friends, well that's OK, but I can't take it any further than that, I've decided."

"Fair enough, Trish. I know you love Mick. It's fine. I just don't want to leave you home alone like Cinders, y'know."

"I know," smiled Trisha, hopping onto her bed. "I doubt if I'll get much time to be lonely with Marci around. And I thought I was a motor mouth!"

Ali laughed. "Yeah, but she's really sweet, isn't she!"

"Yeah. She's so bloody cheerful. Can you imagine us if we'd broken up with our guy this week? We'd be all tears and tantrums. And here's Marci, polishing his records on the lawn, not dancin' on them! Any more laid-back and she'd fall over."

The next morning Ali contacted Simon.

He sounded so relieved.

"I'd thought you'd forgotten me," he blurted out. "Can I see you today?"

"Yes," she replied. She and Trisha were going into the city to register with some job agencies. "Where will we meet? I'm not sure I know my way around yet. I'm going to Brook St Bureau on Queen St."

"Great!" replied Simon. "The General Post Office is right across the street on Queen. You can't miss it. I'll meet you there at 12.30, OK?"

She agreed and instantly got butterflies. What if she didn't feel the same when she saw him? What if he wasn't as nice?

Trish saw the look. "Don't get carried away. It's only lunch, Ali. And don't forget, if you're not enjoying it just make your excuses and leave. I'll be looking in the shops and we can arrange to come home together, if you like."

"Thanks, Trish! You're a star. And how did you know?"

"That you were nervous? Can read you like a book, O'Neill, that's how. Now come on, gotta make yourself beautiful for the nice policeman!"

A few hours later Ali met Simon as arranged.

She need not have worried.

He looked so handsome in his uniform. Her heart did backflips.

He had a bunch of flowers for her and had scooped her

up, swung her around and kissed her right then and there. She was embarrassed and pleased in equal measures.

Then Simon took her for a nice lunch of steamed garlic prawns with a few glasses of Australian wine at Fridays which overlooked the Brisbane River. She told him all about Marci and their new place and he told her a little about his part of Brisbane.

Then he asked if she could see him that evening. But she declined.

She really didn't want to leave Trish alone twice in one day and besides – she had an interview tomorrow for a temping job and wanted an early night. He quietly accepted it and promised to call her later in the week, kissed her softly and went back to work.

Ali, feeling light-headed and happy after the wine, met up with Trish in the Queen St Mall and regaled her with all the gory details.

"You should have gone out with him tonight," Trish insisted.

"No. I want to stay in and watch *Rebecca* with you like we planned. Besides. I haven't a thing to wear to interview tomorrow, and I have to get organised tonight."

"OK," agreed Trish. "Then let's get some crisps and chocolate and we'll introduce Marci to our girlie feasts."

That night Trish and Ali were stuffing their faces and painting their toenails. Marci already had a date with someone new and had gone out.

Then the phone rang.

"That might be Mick!" squealed Trish and dashed for the phone.

Ali was laughing at her. She looked comical, her hair in rollers and chocolate all down her chin.

But after a moment of looking at Trisha's face change, she knew something awful had happened. Trish just kept nodding silently as a look of terror crossed her face.

Ali jumped up and stood beside her friend.

"Oh, my God!" said Trish.

"What, what?" mouthed Ali frantically.

Trish put down the phone slowly.

"It's Mick," she said quietly, her face ashen. "He's had a serious accident. He was in a trench repairing a water main when it collapsed on him. He's in intensive care. Oh, my God. I have to go home! I have to be with him. Oh, Ali, what am I going to do? If anything happens to him I'll never forgive myself!"

With that she burst into tears.

Ali tried to calm her down and gave her a stiff shot of Marci's whiskey. She was sure she wouldn't mind.

"Now what are his injuries? Did they tell you?"

"Em, yeah, he's got a fractured skull, internal injuries and a broken thigh. Oh, and I think his pelvis is fractured too. Poor Mick."

"Don't worry. He'll be fine, Trish," Ali soothed her friend. She had to be the strong one for once. "Now, I'll ring the airlines tomorrow and we'll get you on the first flight. They're usually very good with this sort of thing."

Trish nodded mutely – she appeared to be in another world.

After two more whiskeys, Ali led Trisha, pale and stricken, into the bedroom and put her to bed, but neither of them got much sleep.

Ali could hear muffled sobs coming from the other bed all night, and she hardly slept herself. Apart from worrying about her friend and her fiancé she was worried about herself. Now she would be truly alone, half a world away from home. This trip was all going drastically wrong.

A day and a half later, Trish boarded a Qantas flight to London.

Amidst her angst over Mick's condition, Trish still found time to worry about Ali.

"You poor cow!" she said tearfully as they hugged each other goodbye. "I'm abandoning you to the bloody marsupials!"

"No, you're not," replied Ali fiercely. "I'll be back in Dublin in eight months, annoying the hell out of you again. You don't get rid of me that easily. Sure, aren't I your chief bridesmaid?"

Trish managed a weak smile.

"Sure, aren't you me only bloody bridesmaid!"

"Well then. You get on that plane and get Mick back to health. By the time I get there, you and him will be fighting over the new wallpaper!"

They hugged again. As Trish went through passport control it occurred to Ali that they had almost never been apart since they were three years old.

She realised how lucky she was to have such a friend and how much she would miss her.

Trish sat on eggshells through the seemingly interminably long flight back to London. She felt like physically pushing the jet forward with her bare hands to get her home quicker to her Mick. Tears pricked her eyes every time she pictured his sweet face.

"I'm a right gobshite," she thought miserably, as the air steward kindly gave her a warm blanket and dimmed the lights for the night flight. "I leave the most precious thing I have in the world and look what happens. I almost lose him. One thing is for certain. I will never leave him again."

She didn't sleep a wink and barely concealed her impatience at the two-hour stopover in Singapore. The place that had held such magic for her four months earlier now seemed chaotic and stifling. She boarded the next leg of the trip almost in frustrated tears. Her emotions were getting the better of her.

After what seemed like aeons but in reality was about 22 hours Trish finally reached London. She almost ran through the long tunnel from Terminal Four to Terminal One and when she saw the Aer Lingus logo at check-in her heart leapt. She was almost home. Two hours later the plane circled over the blanket of forty shades of green. Never was the saying more true.

Ireland really was the greenest place on earth.

She even smiled at the dark grey foreboding clouds that buffeted the plane as it descended. Below her was Mick and all her family – she couldn't wait to see them all.

Her Mum, Dad and almost all her siblings were crowded into the Arrivals hall anxious to see her. She hadn't realised how much she had missed them over the four months.

"I've got to see Mick straight away," she whispered urgently to her mother, after kisses and hellos.

"Your Da is ready to take you there right away," said her Mum quietly. "And I'll have a dirty big fry-up for you when you get back to number twelve. Now, don't be too worried about Mick. He's a strong lad. He'll be fine now you're here to see him back to health."

Trish grabbed her mother and kissed her again.

"Oh, Mum, you really are the best."

Her father then whisked her off to the Mater hospital, speeding all the way. Then, when they finally arrived at the front door, suddenly Trish was weak at the knees.

Her courage was deserting her. What if Mick was so injured he couldn't recognise her? Trisha's heart thumped. Her father led her inside the doorway and up to ICU, holding her hand firmly.

"Now, Patricia," her father said crisply as he held her by the shoulders outside Mick's room.

"Mick needs you now. Be strong for him. Go on, love. In you go."

As soon as she saw him she knew. She knew she would never be parted from him ever again. Her heart did somersaults.

She took in the black curly mop of hair, the velvet brown eyes. The wide infectious grin.

She didn't see all the tubes or the bandages, just her Mick.

She burst into tears and placed her head gently on his chest, a tear slid down his own cheek.

"Now will you marry me?" he whispered hoarsely.

"Just try and stop me," whispered Trish in reply touching his bruised hand. "Just anyone try and stop me."

By the time Trish and her father left the hospital she

had been made aware by the doctors that Mick's injuries, although not life-threatening, would take a long time to heal. He had a fractured skull, damaged spleen, broken pelvis and thigh and some internal tissue damage. But he had been incredibly lucky to escape with his life. Time would heal him. Trish felt relieved and finally happy to be heading for her small cramped little house in Drumcondra in her father's battered old Volkswagen.

A couple of hours later after a slap-up Dublin fry, she telephoned Ali to tell her the good news about Mick's improving condition.

"I'm sorry, Ali. I feel I've let you down, but you know I had to come home."

"Don't worry about me," said Ali a little too brightly, "I'll be fine. I'll miss you heaps, you know that. But in any case, now I have less competition for all the gorgeous blokes. But just promise me one thing, Trish, that you'll write to me, OK!"

"Every week," Trish promised. "And I'll phone whenever I can, OK?"

Trish put down the phone and suddenly felt jetlag overcome her. Whew!

What an emotional rollercoaster of a day, she reflected, sadness and happiness side-by-side. She fell thankfully into bed, exhausted. Snuggled up in her narrow little bed with all the familiar sounds and smells of home she soundly slept the sleep of the contented.

Chapter 18

Suddenly adrift without Trisha, Ali fell into the frequent company of Simon.

He wanted to see her every day, and she felt very alone so readily agreed.

Ali managed to get a temping office job filing in one of the high-rise towers in Brisbane's golden mile business district.

She started work at a huge Queensland building contractors and was happy to have busy days filing all the office invoices and memos.

The staff were quite friendly and made her feel welcome, but she still missed Trisha dreadfully. It was so important to have someone who knew you inside out, someone you could sound your ideas or moans out to. Someone who knew how many sugars you took in your coffee or who understood your Dublin slang. Ali had to modify her vocabulary in order to be understood at the office, which was fine all day, but she craved another Irish person to relax with in the evenings.

Marci, being a New Zealander, was also culturally different and although Simon was sweet and attentive, he couldn't replace Trish as a confidante. It just wasn't the same.

Brisbane had lost a bit of its lustre for Ali since Trish had gone home. So Simon tried to cheer her up and took her for long drives down the coast to Surfers' Paradise. It was a fabulous place, full of white sandy beaches and beautiful people. Ali was in awe of all the perfect leggy blondes with minuscule bikinis and even more perfect tans.

She felt pale and skinny beside them but Simon only seemed to have eyes for her. He took her to Fisherman's Wharf for lunch or they simply had fish and chips on the beach. He was so sweet and affectionate she could feel herself falling for him.

"I never met anyone like you before." he had said softly one evening when he dropped her home. "You are so fragile and gentle. I just want to protect you."

It almost sounded twee, but when he held her face between his two large brown hands and kissed her first softly then passionately, she almost felt her heart melt.

Simon was so different to Ben. Quiet in nature, slightly intense but he showered her with affection, unlike Ben.

Ben was loving in his own way but pragmatic and not given to too many expressions of romance. Ali wondered if this had made her a bit unsure of him. Simon brought her flowers often, insisted on collecting her from work and made her the centre of his universe. If she hadn't felt so all-at-sea when Trisha left, it might have been a bit too all encompassing – but now she abandoned herself to being wooed and enjoyed it.

He even took her to dinner with his parents. They were German immigrants who spoke in heavily accented English and adored their only son. Rudi and Magda welcomed Ali into their tiny Queenslander home with open arms and spoke proudly of their son.

Rudi had framed pictures everywhere of Simon in uniform and as a cadet. He spoke of Simon's bravery at being a hero during a bungled armed robbery, which had left him, injured in hospital and resulted in him being deskbound, removed from active duty.

"You never told me that story Simon?" Ali queried. "It must have been terrifying."

Simon blushed profusely. "Oh, not really – I mean, we're trained to expect that sort of thing. It's just not the same that's all, not actually being on the streets any more, catching the crims."

He looked wistful.

"Well, I for one am glad," Ali replied touching his hand. "At least I don't have to worry about you being safe."

"Me also," added Magda, crossing herself. "I hef many sleepless nights over my leibling."

She tickled his chin.

"Mum!"

Simon was embarrassed but he laughed anyway.

"Hef some more cake, Ellie," insisted Magda, passing Ali a huge slice of home-made Black Forest Gateau. "You're so skinny. We hef to fatten you up a little, ya?"

Ali laughed. They were really sweet people. Simon was lucky to have them and she told him so on the ride home.

"Yeah, I know," he agreed. "They have such faith in me. I'd hate to let them down."

"But you haven't have you? They are bursting with pride over you. You're quite the hero in their eyes, and mine, come to think of it."

"Is that so?" he grinned, his beautiful white teeth lighting up his handsome face.

"Yes," she replied and kissed him passionately.

"Ali!" Simon gasped. "I think I'm falling in love with you!"

Butterflies fluttered in her stomach.

"Come inside for a coffee," she whispered huskily into his ear.

She fancied him something rotten. It might not be love just yet but she felt she was falling for him. This was the first time in years she'd felt anything as deep as she had for Ben and by now Ben was married and on his honeymoon in the Adriatic.

Time to truly put the past behind her, once and for all.

"Thought you'd never ask!" grinned a delighted Simon and he scooped her up and carried her indoors.

They never made it to coffee.

Back in Dublin, Mick was on the mend. He was removed from ICU after a week and placed on an ordinary ward. His broken pelvis and fractured skull would mean months in hospital, but although recovery would be slow he was making good progress.

He was lying in bed dozing one morning, trying to

drown out the noisy hospital sounds when someone
pinched his toe.

He looked up annoyed to find Ben standing over him
with a wide grin.

"So, there you are, you old reprobate! They couldn't
kill you off. Rumour has it you fought a drain and the
drain won!"

"Ben!" Mick was stunned, suddenly awake. "What are
you doing here?"

"I work here, dopey, or had you forgotten?"

"But aren't you supposed to be . . ."

"Oh yeah, right now I'm supposed to be on my
honeymoon in Sicily. Funny that, isn't it? I'd forgotten all
about it until now. You gave us quite a scare, y 'know."

"I did?" gasped Mick. "Never mind about me! What's
the story with you? Did you not . . . ?"

"Afraid not, me old mate."

Ben grimaced and then pulled up a chair and sat down
wearily.

"Now, don't give me another lecture. I just couldn't
bear that, especially now I've burnt the midnight oil,
coming up to look in on you when you were asleep in
ICU all last week. I just couldn't marry Karen, Mick. I
never really wanted to. I just got so caught up in what
everybody else wanted for me that I started to believe
I wanted it for myself. But it's not what I want, not
really."

"Or is it rather, not what you want, but who you want,
Ben?"

Ben shrugged.

"Maybe, maybe not. I think it's all a little too late for all

151

that now. I just want to be a good doctor. Africa needs good doctors."

"Africa?" Mick was surprised.

"Yeah, Mick, Africa. Today was my last shift at the Mater. Tomorrow I'm off to Mozambique to work for Médecins Sans Frontières.That's why I'm here actually, to say goodbye. I've been trying to find a time when Trisha's not here to come and see you, I just can't face anyone right now. I'm sure you can understand. Everyone has so many questions."

Mick eyed his friend closely.

"Ben, you know you and me are good mates, and I'll support you no matter what, but you can't run away from this. You can't run away from yourself. Your problems will find a way to come with you. Africa won't solve everything."

"I know," Ben fiddled with Mick's bed chart noting that Mick's blood pressure was still quite high. "But at least I can do some good there, and forget about myself for a while anyway. I'm sick to death of thinking about myself, y'know. Sorry. Here I am, rabbiting on about all my troubles and woes and look at you. You've been through a hell of a lot. You were one lucky plumber to escape with your life."

"Who are you telling!"

Mick was in a bit too much pain to feel very lucky at the moment – but knew he would soon.

"So, how long are you going for?"

"A year."

"Just as bloody well it's not for much longer – you're going to be my groomsman, aren't you, when I marry

Trish? I'm not letting her out of my sight again, and God willing, I'll marry her within eighteen months, if all goes well, and I'd like you to be there."

"Wouldn't miss it for the world, me old mate. Now, I'd better head off before I wear you out any further. You just rest now and get better. I'll write as often as I can, OK?"

He touched Mick's shoulder and was gone, his white coat flurrying after him.

Mick couldn't quite believe it.

At least for once he'd have some interesting news for Trisha when she arrived this afternoon.

He'd never be able to figure Ben Murphy out as long as he lived, that was for sure.

Ali woke up beside a sleeping Simon. His bronzed back stretched languidly beside her, his large muscled arm draped protectively across her. He was so beautiful. She marvelled at his perfect physique and felt a sudden rush of affection for him. He had been so tender and patient with her, it being her first time.

She had almost forgotten it had been less than perfect, but rather clumsy and a bit painful. She knew it would get better. Most people would admit their first time had been less than great.

She stifled a giggle.

"I wonder if I look any different," she thought as she hopped up and looked in the mirror. "Wonder if I look like a loose woman?"

No. She just looked all red and blotchy.

"God! I must have a shower before he wakes up and sees what an ugly hag he's with."

Simon had pronounced her beautiful and swept her away with his passion and she didn't regret it. It was exactly what she needed to move out of the past and into her future.

She felt quite exhilarated.

She had a shower, washed her hair and felt a hundred times better by the time Simon woke.

"Come here," he insisted, nuzzling her neck. "Mmmm, you smell so sexy and fresh."

"And you've got to go home to change. Aren't you on duty this weekend?"

"Nope," he smiled lazily. "I have a surprise for you. Remember I was telling you about the Great Barrier Reef and how heart-stoppingly wonderful it is?"

Ali nodded.

"Well, you and I, my dear, are off there this weekend. It's only a twelve-hour drive, so if we set off soon we should be at Mackay by nightfall. The reef is only a short distance from there. I am going to show you the time of your life!"

"Oh Simon!" Ali squealed and squeezed him almost half to death. "That is just the best news. Give me thirty minutes to pack a weekend bag. I can't believe it. All the times I've booked people in the travel shop to go there I never actually believed I'd ever make it there myself. You have just made me feel like the luckiest girl alive!"

"I'm the lucky one," he whispered and kissed her gently. "Now, hurry up, Ali, 'cos we've got a long drive ahead!"

Meanwhile in Dublin, Mick was breaking the news of Ben's aborted wedding to an incredulous Trisha.

"He what?" she screeched in amazement

"He called off the wedding," repeated Mick, "for good. And now he's gone off to Africa for a year to do medicine. Left the whole lot behind him."

"I don't believe it. Really I don't! My God, poor Karen! After all the trouble she went to snare Ben. She must feel awful. I feel sorry for her. Even though she did the dirty on Ali, no one deserves that." Then Trisha started to giggle. "I've just thought, Mick. Isabel Murphy. She must be dying from embarrassment. It meant so much to her that Ben would marry the right sort of girl How truly awful for her, and how truly deserving. Ali would be delighted to hear that news."

"Do you think you should tell her?" cautioned Mick.

"Why not? I'm her best friend, after all. If the shoe were on the other foot I'd expect her to tell me. I doubt she'd ever forgive me if I didn't and she found out. Which she will, eventually."

"Hmm," frowned Mick. "It's just that she seems to be enjoying herself at the moment, putting the past behind her. She even seems to like that Aussie bloke, Simon. Don't you think by you telling her that Ben is now free; it'll confuse her all over again?"

"Maybe," agreed Trish, considering the possibility. "But if he's gone to Africa for a year, it can't do much harm. She won't come rushing home, if he's not here, will she? – Anyway, I can't lie to her. You know that. Wonder what time it is in Brisbane now? I'll have to telephone her as soon as I get home tonight."

As good as her word, as soon as she got in the door of her tiny house Trisha dialled Ali's number in Brisbane.

She just couldn't wait to hear her friend's reaction to the shocking news.

But the number just rang out.

"Damn," she thought. "I'll just have to ring back later."

Right at that very minute, Ali and Simon were happily speeding up the Bruce Highway to Mackey for the most romantic weekend they would ever enjoy together.

Chapter 19

Ali stared at the blue line on the indicator. Her heart sank. That was the second pregnancy kit she had tried and both had given the same result.

Positive.

How could it be?

How could she be pregnant?

She had slept with Simon a total of two times before they had used protection. She couldn't be that unlucky, could she?

She sat in the toilet for ages, staring at the blue line, willing it to disappear but it didn't.

"Jeez, mate, are you going to hog the dunny all day?"

It was Marci. She sounded frustrated.

"I got to get to work, come on! Surely you're beautiful enough by now! Some of us plain sheilas need all the help we can get and I gotta wash my greasy hair."

"Sorry, Marci," replied Ali, stifling a sob.

She opened the bathroom door and silently handed Marcie the vial.

Marci stared at it for a full minute.

"You're kidding, Ali! No way, you're pregnant?"

"I'm afraid so," replied Ali, tears welling up in her eyes and spilling over onto her cheeks. She suddenly felt weak, her legs turned to jelly.

Marci sat her down.

"I'm 24 carat pregnant, all right. Up the duff. I just can't believe I am such an idiot. I wait until I'm 23 to sleep with someone and I get pregnant almost straight away!"

Marcie was amazed.

"You mean you were 23 the first time you . . . I can't believe that. Jeez, you Irish sheilas are pretty slow starters. I won't begin to tell you how old I was when I first got laid."

Ali couldn't help herself. She had to laugh through her tears.

Marci's heart was really in the right place.

"Look, Ali, you have some serious decisions ahead. How long are you overdue?"

Ali wiped her tears away with her sleeve, "Um, about two weeks or so," she sniffed.

"Well, it's not too late, y'know if you don't want to go through with it, the pregnancy, I mean."

"Of course I'm going through with it," said Ali fiercely. "There is no question about it. It's just not how I pictured it. I never saw myself being an unmarried mother at 23. Pregnant by a guy I don't really love and hardly know, and half a world away from everything I find familiar. It's a disaster."

Fresh tears erupted.

Marci was all at sea. She didn't know how to cope.

"Oh, I'm so sorry, Ali. I'm sure you really miss Trisha right now, and your poor Mum isn't even around. Sod work! I'll just have to be late today. You just relax there while I make you a nice cuppa tea and we can talk this over. Old wanker Thompson won't be too amused at me being late again, but you're more important any day. So you just sit back there on the sofa. I'll have your tea in a few ticks."

"Thanks, Marci," replied Ali softly. "You're an angel. I'm just in a bit of shock that's all. It's going to take a bit of time to sink in."

Marci put on the kettle and took the Tim Tam biscuits out of the fridge.

The sun was streaming in the kitchen window and *Good Morning, Australia* was on the TV. Marci's lazy black cat was curled up in a ball in her favourite spot snoozing. Everything seemed normal, but it all looked a bit surreal to Ali.

She guessed nothing would ever be quite the same again.

She would never be the same again.

Already she had changed. This baby was growing inside her.

For a moment she was glad her mother wasn't around to see this. Then she felt horribly guilty. Her mother would have been a tower of strength. She'd have loved this baby.

A grandchild she'd never see.

A sharp loneliness filled her.

This was a time when you needed your mother the most.

She wished Trisha were here. It might never have happened if she had been.

That was stupid, she knew, thinking like that. It was all her own fault. She knew it. But it didn't make it any easier.

She suddenly thought of Simon.

How would he take the news? She hoped he'd be happy.

But what if he wasn't? What if he thought she was just out to trap him? They were only together five months now, hardly a lifetime.

She wasn't even sure if she wanted to be connected to him for a lifetime, but now she was. Through this baby, she would be.

Always.

She suddenly thought of Ben. A familiar ache emerged.

"It's funny but I always thought I'd have my baby with him," she mused to herself. "Stupid. Stupid Ali, you just never learn, do you?"

Trisha had eventually told her, when she had got back from those four glorious days on the North Queensland Coast that Ben had called off the wedding. At first she had been elated.

He hadn't married Karen. He was waiting for her. But then Trish told her he had simply headed off to Africa for a year.

When he had done that without even writing to her, even a postcard to tell her, she had been deflated.

She wasn't sorry for Karen. She couldn't be.

The relationship had been built on a tissue of lies, so it

was only a matter of time before it floundered, that she knew. But she never dreamt it would end like that.

But he was still lost to her. Still getting on with his life, without her.

No Karen in the way. But it had made no difference. So she had ploughed all her emotion into Simon instead.

Now look where she was.

"Simon will be delighted!"

Marci interrupted her thoughts. She placed a mug of hot tea and two Tim Tams biscuits into Ali's hands.

"What?"

"Yes," continued Marcie brightly. "I reckon he's dead keen to get a rock on your finger already, and this'll just do the trick."

Ali winced.

"That's kind of what I'm afraid of."

"So when are you gonna tell him?"

"I don't know."

Ali was unsure if she ever would.

"I suppose when I get my own head around the news myself, whenever that will be." And there it was.

A few days later she met Simon for lunch.

It was a steaming hot December day. Ali thought she'd pass out from the heat, so suggested they meet at Fridays so she at least could enjoy a cool breeze from the Brisbane River.

The outdoor brasserie was packed with lunch-time office workers.

Glasses clinked and people chatted animatedly and amiably, the weekend buzz lifting the collective mood.

Simon was quiet. He stared out at the boat taxis criss-crossing the river. He wasn't smiling.

"Are you sure?" he said at last.

He wasn't looking at her, but concentrating on fiddling with his drink.

Her heart sank.

"Yes, I'm sure."

More silence.

He appeared stunned. She had only just got past stunned herself.

But his amazement irked her. Had he been in her bed at all?

Did he know the facts of life? It did take two to make a baby!

She felt like screaming all this out to him, right now and turning on her heels and running right away from him. But she didn't. She would remain calm and talk this out rationally.

"God!" He was ashen, "What are we going to do?"

He finally looked at her.

She took a deep breath.

"Well, I've had a few days to get used to the idea, and I really want this baby. It's not the best planning ever, and it's not how I saw my life going, six thousand miles away from home and pregnant at 23. But I will understand if you don't want to get involved.

"No, no, I do want to be with you," Simon interrupted gravely "It's just such a shock, y'know. I'm still taking it in."

"Yes," quipped Ali with more than a tinge of sarcasm. "Funny that. Imagine sex resulting in babies. It is quite shocking isn't it?"

She issued a fake smile, but Simon took it to be

genuine because he suddenly grabbed her and gave her a huge bear hug and a kiss.

"It'll be OK," he smiled at last. "At least we both know we're very fertile!"

"Yes," Ali retorted glumly. "Two chances we took. What absolute idiots we are!"

Simon took her hand.

"I love you and we'll get through this. Now first we'll make an appointment with your GP. You do have one I take it . . ."

Ali nodded.

"OK, then we'll take it from there. It'll all be fine. Don't worry, Ali – I'm right with you."

Ali leaned on his shoulder. She really cared about Simon, but there were so many big questions.

She knew it was way too soon into the relationship for the pressure of a baby and she was also scared about the fact that they were both from opposite sides of the globe. She couldn't picture Simon settling in Dublin and much as she liked Australia it just wasn't home. She couldn't see herself staying here forever.

She definitely didn't feel like marrying him, especially just for the baby.

What a bloody awful mess!

But she was glad too. Glad a real baby was growing inside her.

Her baby.

It made her strong. She'd withstand anything. This baby would be hers and no one would ever take it away from her.

"I'll stand by you." Simon interrupted her racing mind.

"I will be the father of this baby no matter what happens. I love you, Ali."

"Oh Simon," Ali gave him a huge hug, "I love you too."

For a minute she almost believed it.

Ali called Trisha that evening to tell her the news.

Trisha was understandably shocked and more than that was very concerned by the bright happy air Ali had adopted.

It worried Trisha even more than if Ali had been down and tearful. She knew her friend well enough to know that when Ali was really worried she did her best to hide it.

"Are you OK, ducks?"

"Yeah, fine. Simon is standing by me, whatever that means. Fancy, I'll have a little bit of Australia to keep forever!"

"Oh Ali, I wish I was there. I feel so awful now, having to fly home and leave you alone out there, especially now. I feel so guilty!"

"Trisha, don't be such a wuss. You know Mick needed you. He was seriously ill! Anyway, I doubt if you could have kept the pair of us from the bedroom! I'm a big girl now, able to make my own mistakes. And the proof is in the pudding. Literally."

She laughed hollowly.

"Fair enough." Trisha was not appeased, but what could she do?

"Funny I have to make such big ones though, mistakes I mean."

"Yeah, your timing is crap," admitted Trisha. "Will they let you fly home in advanced pregnancy? It is a long haul flight."

"God! I never thought of that. I was so caught up in the pregnancy being real that I haven't even considered the birth or coming home! I suppose I'll have to discuss it with my GP and Simon, of course. God, this is getting so complicated . . ."

"I'm sorry, Ali. I didn't mean to worry you. It just popped into my head."

"No, you're right. I have to consider everything. Look I'll telephone you tonight after I see the GP, then I'll have a better idea of due dates and flying risks and all that. So I'll call you later. OK. Now, don't worry!"

"Yeah, right!" replied Trish, knowing she would do little else.

If Mick O'Toole wasn't still so fragile and in hospital, she'd be on the next Qantas flight to Brisbane to bring her friend back home where she belonged, Simon or no Simon. This was the absolute worst news ever. Ali alone back home with a baby in tow, or worse still, stuck out there in Australia, raising a child with someone she really didn't love. Either way it would change Ali's life forever.

Trisha somehow felt responsible and told Mick as much that evening when she broke the news to him in hospital.

"I can't believe she even slept with this Simon guy, y'know, Mick. She's so shy. I think she was still upset over Ben Murphy getting married. That's why she did it. God, he's got a lot to answer for."

"Now, steady on," replied Mick, nonplussed. "You can't hold him responsible. Ali's a big girl now."

"Yeah, she said that too. I'm sorry. I'm not blaming Ben as such but I can't help thinking if he'd never planned the stupid wedding in the first place, Ali wouldn't be in this predicament."

"Ifs and ands . . ." said Mick, kissing Trisha's soft fresh hair. "They're not going to change anything. Look, when this baby arrives, It'll be loved, won't it? Isn't that the most important thing?"

Trisha sighed. "Yeah, I know."

She snuggled closely into Mick's chest, feeling his heart thump reassuringly beneath her head.

"I just feel guilty. Here we are planning our dream home, and our wedding. We're so lucky. Ali has had this terribly unlucky life; nothing seems to go right for her, not even now. She hasn't even got her mother to rely on."

"She has you." Mick kissed her forehead. "And I can't think of a better friend than you. Look, if worst comes to worst, we'll have a fair few spare rooms in the new house before our own rugrats come along. Ali can always come and stay with us, if you like."

"Really? Oh, Mick, you are the best. She's in a heap y'know."

"When is she due home?" Mick asked, knowing the house wouldn't be ready for ages, now that he was laid up.

"She's due back in five months and she's almost two months now, so I suppose she'd be seven months by then. She'd probably have to travel sooner, to be on the safe side. She said that Simon would come over for the birth and she talked about her getting residency there afterwards, or something. It's all very up in the air. I didn't want to upset her too much by asking constant questions. I doubt if she's considered all the complications. She seems shell-shocked."

"Then all we can do is wait. Wait until she decides what to do and then we'll offer our help. At least this baby will be something of her own that she can love. It'll be fine, Trisha. Just you wait and see."

"Mmm," Trisha murmured, unconvinced.

She knew this whole situation was more than Ali could handle alone.

She just hoped her friend would come home soon where they could face the next scary few months together.

Chapter 20

Ali was perched on the balcony of her new apartment, roasting her rounded tummy in the hot spring sunshine. The apartment Simon had found for them both was ideal. It was still in leafy St Lucia close by to Marci's place and had a fine view of the Brisbane River and Mount Cootha.

It was lush, green and quiet, which Ali loved. It made her feel more at home.

She was indolent and happy and growing fatter by the minute. After the initial awful first three months of constant morning-noon-and-night sickness, She suddenly emerged newly energised and well in her second trimester.

Simon had been wonderful.

She wasn't sure if it had been her hormones or just her nesting instinct – but she sometimes felt herself falling for the father of her unborn child. Simon was solicitous and caring most of the time since he had seen that first scan at sixteen weeks and was amazed by this little being wriggling around inside Ali. He had tears in his eyes and had whispered "thank you" when the radiologist had momentarily left the room. It seemed to become real for him after that. He then decided they should move in together so he could spend more time with Ali and "my boy" as he termed the foetus.

Ali tried to insist the baby's sex was uncertain, "It could just as well be a girl," she kept saying but Simon was adamant the baby kicked like a front row forward and had to be male.

Ali felt a bit guilty leaving her housemate Marci in the lurch. But Marci, ever cheery, piped up that she had forgiven the errant Joshua, who had dumped his older lover when she tired of his motorbike, and he was moving back in.

So the timing for once was good and Ali was free to move out and still retain Marci as a friend.

Now Ali was basking in the sun, like a lazy cat, dozing in the heat.

She craved afternoon naps now that she was almost six months pregnant.

She wondered if she would be fit for the long-haul flight home in a few weeks and was seeing her gynaecologist the following day for a health check. Simon had assured her he could obtain a few months' leave of absence to accompany her home to Dublin and be with her for the birth. After that they hoped to get her and the baby residency, but it was as far as they had discussed.

Simon was a bit vague about the future, and Ali didn't want to feel as if she was cornering him into some sort of proposal or life-long commitment.

Right now they were happy and she didn't want to worry unnecessarily and shoot her blood pressure up – it had been a little higher than normal on her last two visits and the doctor had cautioned her to take it easy. That was why she was off sick from work and snoozing all afternoon in the sun lounger.

Just then the phone rang. Ali almost let it ring out. It took her so long to get up these days with her new awkward shape. She decided to answer in case it was Trisha or one of her brothers calling from Dublin.

She reluctantly rose and went indoors to lift the receiver, her eyes still adjusting to the different light after being outside.

"Hello, would Simon be there, please?"

It was a female voice, high-pitched and girlie, and unfamiliar.

Ali was still a bit disoriented, after being in the hot sun.

"No, he's not here at the moment. Who is speaking, please?"

"Sorry!" the girl blurted out. "I think I've got the wrong number," and rang off before Ali could say any more.

Ali still held the dead receiver. That was odd. It could hardly be a wrong number if the girl asked for Simon by name. It didn't sound like it was any of his female work colleagues either as she knew most of them at least by their voices.

She felt a familiar sinking feeling.

That sick knotted ache in the bottom of her stomach that she had felt after Ben's betrayal years ago. It felt like yesterday.

Simon couldn't be cheating on her, could he?

The thought swirled around her head.

Why not?

Ben had, and she hadn't been fat and pregnant either.

Her confidence, which was never good, had wavered even more with her advancing bump and unreliable irritated skin that had broken out in red patches.

As she lowered herself once more onto the sun-chair she deeply regretted ever rising to take the call. Her sunny mood evaporated as she fretted over the mysterious caller and remembered with fresh pain her earlier betrayal by Ben. It had hurt so much. She never wanted to experience anything like that again.

She decided not to confront Simon, just in case. She was meeting Terri Church for lunch tomorrow before her hospital appointment and she'd pick Terri's brain about Simon.

Terri was engaged to Simon's best friend, Dave. She and Ali had met frequently at various police events and became good friends. Ali liked Terri, who was straight-forward and direct and very down-to-earth. Dave told Terri everything, according to Terri, so she should know if Simon was playing around, and Ali knew she was direct enough to tell her if she was aware of anything.

Ali was quiet that night with Simon, pleading a headache and going to bed early, leaving him watching the football alone, but she couldn't sleep and tossed and turned all night. Worries danced about her mind so much it drove her crazy. When Simon finally came to bed she feigned sleep and lay for hours willing the night away until daybreak and the eventual lunch when she would see Terri and find out what was going on, or at least put her mind at rest. All this worry would do her and the baby no good.

Terri was waiting for an exhausted Ali in the air-conditioned cool of the Sheraton lounge. After all Ali's fretting and restless night, she had finally fallen asleep near dawn and as a result overslept and had a mad dash to the train station and was late.

She arrived hot and flushed and envied Terri's cool demeanour, glamorous cropped blonde hair and immaculate business suit.

Terri was an accountant for Price Waterhouse with a large expense account and so could treat her friend to an expensive lunch at the Sheraton. It meant Ali didn't have to trudge around the city in the hot midday sunshine, as the Sheraton Hotel was over the main central station.

"Wow! You're blooming!" beamed Terri at Ali. They hadn't seen each other in a few weeks and Ali's sudden expansion both surprised and pleased her and shocked others.

"Yeah, I'm like the side of a house!" quipped Ali as she sat down heavily. She was so tired after the four-minute walk from the station, she vowed to rest as soon as she got home from her hospital appointment.

Terri giggled. She loved Dublin phrases. Stuff that Ali just felt natural with – sounded exotic to Terri.

"And what are we having for lunch then?" enquired Terri. "Nothing weird like pumpkin and ice cream, I hope."

"No," smiled Ali. "I got over that one months ago, but I've a big yearning for good old corned beef and cabbage, y'know."

"Yuck!" screeched Terri in mock disgust. "Fraid you're outta luck there, darl. It'll have to be Moreton Bay bugs or the lobster thermidor – will that suffice?"

Ali laughed. Terri was a tonic.

They ordered lunch and Ali waited until they'd had a good old gossip about the other policemen's wives that they knew, before she broached the subject of the mystery caller. Many of the guys and police – women that they knew at Roma Street were on their second or third marriages. The force was not conducive to secure relationships it seemed, and Terri and Ali were in turn enthralled and appalled by the entire goings-on.

"Speaking of cheating . . ." Ali began lightly, "I had a bit of a mystery woman caller myself, yesterday."

"Really?" Terri was wide-eyed.

"Yes," said Ali, trying to keep the emotion from her voice. "Some woman called. She asked for Simon by name and then tried to pass it all off as a wrong number."

Terri's face darkened.

Ali picked up on it immediately.

"Is there something you know, Terri? Please if there is, tell me. Woman to woman – I need honesty right now. Is Simon playing around?"

Terri frowned. "I don't think so, Ali, but there is something I feel you should know."

"What?" Ali's face drained. She knew she didn't want to hear this, whatever it was.

"Well . . ." Terri began slowly. 'Simon has been known in the past to take a, let's say, very friendly interest in the female rookie cops. He's dated quite a few in the past."

"So," Ali said testily, "what's wrong with that?"

173

"The point is," said Terri evenly, "he has done so while already in serious relationships. In fact it cost him one. He was almost engaged to Leanne when he cheated on her."

Ali shuddered.

"There's one more thing, Ali," Terri continued. "Has Simon ever told you why he's deskbound at the station?"

"Yes," replied Ali, feeling a knot form in her stomach. "He was taken off active duty eighteen months ago when he was injured by a suspect and was hospitalised, wasn't he?"

"Not quite," said Terri grimly. "He was hospitalised all right. But after he'd almost killed one of the suspects. He'd beaten the guy so badly. The other suspect dragged Simon off and that's when Simon got injured. Dave says Simon has a fierce temper when riled, and that's why he is deskbound. There was an internal investigation and Simon was taken off active duty. Ali, I'm sorry. Simon has always been a perfect gentleman when I have been in his company, but he does have that element to his personality, and I feel you ought to know. It's important you're aware of it, that's all."

Ali felt her world shift again. Suddenly she felt like she hardly knew Simon at all. Tears sprang into her eyes.

"Oh shit." groaned Terri. "Now I've made you all weepy!"

"It's OK," snuffled Ali. "Hormones, you know."

"I'm sure there's nothing to it Ali, but you're better off armed with knowledge than blissfully ignorant. How are things between you both anyway?"

"Terrific," said Ali flatly, hardly believing it now. "He

has been super really, but it's early days. I mean, I'm not even sure if I love him or just need him to be my partner for this baby. I'm so mixed up and now this!"

"Well," said Terri, smiling as she grabbed both Ali's hands in hers, "I am here for you any time you need me, day or night. OK? This baby is yours, Ali. No matter what happens between you and Simon. It'll be the best thing that's ever happened to you. Soon, you'll be home in Ireland, surrounded by all your family and friends, and you'll have this precious little baby too. Just hang onto that."

"Thanks, Terri." Ali sniffed and downed her frothy cappuccino. "I'm just a bit scared. I should never have got pregnant so soon into this relationship. I'm such an eejit. It's impossible!"

Tears erupted again and this time splashed down Ali's face unabated.

Terri, unruffled as ever, wiped them away and spoke to Ali in a calm soothing manner.

"Shh, shh, Ali. Calm down now. Listen, you are young, fit and having a beautiful baby. That's all. If Simon is meant for you, he'll be there for you, but right now all you have to do is look after yourself and that precious baby inside you. Just focus on Ali for now, OK? Don't worry so much about the future. You will worry yourself sick and that's no good for you or the little bubs. Now just sit there, while I order us both an enormous pavlova and we'll both get fat together, OK!"

Ali laughed despite herself.

"Thanks, Terri. You're a real mate."

"Oh, yeah?" grinned Terri with relief, now that the

crisis had passed. "And will you still say that when ya can't squeeze into your size eight Levis, after all these gooey desserts I keep foisting on ya?"

"Yes!" Ali insisted. "No worries then!" replied Terri in her best 'Strine and gave Ali a huge hug. "What else are sheilas for?"

Chapter 21

Trisha and Mick were standing on the concrete slab that was the foundation of their new dream bungalow. They almost had to pinch themselves to feel it was real. Mick had been released from hospital over a month ago, but was still recovering and on crutches. Trisha had learned to drive through sheer necessity while Mick was laid up and as a result Mick's van sported three new dents, but despite Trisha's dodgy driving they were mobile and at least could go out and check the site as it developed.

"Trisha, grab the champagne from the van, will you? We've got to celebrate this new ground!"

"Isn't it just great?" squealed Trisha with delight. "I can hardly believe we've got this far, with your accident and everything that's happened."

"Yeah," agreed Mick, the brown eyes twinkling under the unruly mop of black curls. "Just imagine in a couple of months' time this will actually look like a house."

He hobbled around the concrete, gesticulating with his crutches. "Here will be the utility room, and here will be the kitchen. And over here, my dear, will be our boudoir, so come here and give us a kiss, will ya?"

Trish went to him, champers in hand and they kissed passionately.

"It's a shame I'm still a wounded soldier, or we could have christened the spot!" Mick quipped.

"Go way, ya big lug!" Trisha blushed with embarrassment and pleasure. "Just as well you can't chase me then, isn't it!" And she ran off into the field chased by a hobbling Mick.

They drank the champagne out of plastic cups in the van as the soft rain began to fall.

"We are so lucky," Trisha said at last.

"That we are," said Mick softly.

They were both thinking of the events of the past few months and how different things could have been. Now all their dreams were coming true.

Trisha's mind drifted onto Ali.

She wondered how her friend was and felt so guilty that somehow things never seemed to be easy for her. She fervently wished that Ali's life would turn out better after this baby. It would make all this easier to enjoy.

The soft rain then turned into torrents and they had to head for home. Trisha nervously guiding the little van through the sheets of rain back towards the airport and then onto Drumcondra, back to her little redbrick house with all its noise and family bustle.

Trisha never felt luckier then she did right now.

Isabel was sitting in her beautiful conservatory watching

the torrents of rain spill onto the roof and down the glass panes obscuring her luscious garden. The carefully groomed roses had long since bloomed and died over the summer. Now she sat with a letter in her hand from Ben in Mozambique. Tears filled her eyes.

It could all have been so different if only he had gone through with the wedding to Karen. She might even be looking forward to some grandchildren by now. God knows her daughters didn't appear to be in any rush to spoil their figures.

In the letter Ben sounded happy, contented.

He was doing good work and making a difference, he said.

He certainly made a difference here, she thought wryly.

None of her friends guessed when she boasted of him mending children in Africa that she was really very disappointed in him – disappointed and lonely. No one realised how empty her life had become since Ben had left.

He had always been her baby but now despite the bridge club and the ladies' meetings she had a huge void in her day. But she never for one moment apportioned herself any blame for the fact that Ben was now thousands of miles away. It simply never occurred to her that she was in any way at fault. It was Ben. He was always so contrary, or so she had told her husband and John never did have the temerity to tell her otherwise.

After she had read the letter again she rose slowly and poured herself a large Scotch. It was almost three pm, she told herself, almost evening.

Not too early to have a drink. After all, she needed something to get her through the next six months and then Ben would be home.

Just right now, six months seemed a very long time indeed.

Ali looked at the clock. It was after eight pm and Simon wasn't home yet. She had tried to call him at work after her doctor's appointment, but Kerrie the receptionist said that he had left early. That had been at four pm and she had needed to talk to him about her doctor's warnings that if her already elevated blood pressure didn't settle down he was taking her into hospital for a rest. She had been anxious and fretful and needed some reassurance from Simon but he was nowhere to be found.

Now she sat anxiously out on the patio staring at the moon and willing his car to come up the drive.

Where could he be?

She tried to focus her thoughts and remain calm. Just because he was late didn't mean he was playing around. There could be a simple explanation, a few beers with the lads, perhaps. Funny how he couldn't get any time off to come to the hospital with her, but he had time to go to the pub. She alternately fumed and fretted.

Suddenly his headlights swung into the long drive. He was home!

"Stay calm, Ali," she told herself. "Don't pounce on him as soon as he arrives in the door. No vicious accusations. Just see what he has to say first."

She ran to the door.

Simon had a stony face.

"Before you say anything, I went for a few drinks with the guys, ok?"

His tone was belligerent. He swayed slightly.

"OK," she said flatly and turned on her heel. "Your dinner, or rather what's left of it, is in the microwave!" she shouted behind her as she walked towards the bedroom.

She didn't want a confrontation, not now that he was obviously drunk. Years of living with an alcoholic had taught her the futility of arguing with an addled brain.

Simon followed her into the bedroom.

"What's your problem?" he roared.

Ali was shocked by his aggressive tone.

"You could have at least had the decency to telephone me and say you'd be late, Simon. I had the dinner ready since six o'clock."

"I didn't realise you had me on a stopwatch," Simon snarled and walked out slamming the bedroom door behind him.

Ali felt scared and miserable.

What brought on all this aggression? She hated the way he had spoken to her. His tone had been so vicious. It brought back old and horrible memories of her childhood. Of her father and his aggressive tone to her mother.

But she was not her mother and she would not put up with this sort of behaviour.

Her heart was still beating wildly as she heard him clatter about the kitchen noisily. Ali protectively patted her stomach. There was no way this baby was going to suffer as she did.

A steely resolve began to form inside her. All the horrible memories of her father mistreating her mother boiled to the surface. She would not lead her life that way. If Simon was going to be like this he could forget it.

Suddenly she realised how far from ideal her situation really was. She was isolated, far away from home, and dependent on the father of her unborn child for everything. She had no means of support for herself.

She sighed deeply.

At least she had her return ticket to Ireland.

And she had Trisha.

She knew one phone call and Trisha would be there for her straightaway. But still Ali felt uneasy for the rest of the evening, worrying for both her and the baby's future.

Simon never came to bed but she eventually heard him snoring from the lounge, so he had obviously passed out on the sofa.

What if life with Simon was not going to be wonderful and safe after all, she thought, as she vainly tried to drift off to sleep.

She was prepared to go it alone with the baby and leave him and go back to Ireland, but for some reason the idea chilled her.

She didn't think Simon would let go of her so easy, or let go of the baby, and he would also have rights as the baby's father.

Her mind swirled about with turmoil, until, finally exhausted, she fitfully slept.

Two weeks later . . .

"I don't like it." Dr Martyn Stone was staring at Ali's medical report. "I don't like it at all."

He frowned and looked up at Ali. His clear blue eyes narrowed.

"Ali, I'm afraid you're not to fit to fly anywhere. In fact, your blood pressure is still quite high, so I'm going to take you into hospital for a few days, until it settles."

He then saw Ali's look of horror.

"Look, I have to think of you and baby and the well-being of you both. It would be dangerous in my opinion for you to travel anywhere until some time after delivery. This baby is going to be born right here in Australia."

Ali gulped. Her heart sank. She so wanted to have this baby at home in Dublin surrounded by her friends and family and all that was familiar. Especially now that Simon had become increasingly irrational and absent over the past few weeks. He seemed to have lost any interest in her whatsoever, and he had missed all the birthing classes. She gathered from his obtuse comments about her increasing size that he didn't find pregnancy or her very attractive.

He had been spending a lot of time out with his mates and she had felt increasingly fragile and tearful. Right now, when she needed him the most, he just wasn't there for her. She felt ungainly and unloved and right now just wanted to board a plane home and never see him again, but she couldn't. She was now stuck here until after the baby was born and dependent on Simon.

She felt helpless and hated it.

"I know you're disappointed," Dr Stone interrupted her racing mind. "But I have to think of you and your baby's health. That's more important at the moment. Now, your visa expires soon, doesn't it?"

"Yes," Ali replied, alarmed, now blanching at the thought of being an illegal immigrant to boot.

"Now, don't worry," the medic assured her crisply.

Dr Stone was nothing if not efficient.

"I can issue a letter to the relevant authorities advising of your condition. It shouldn't be a problem. Now go and telephone your other half and get him to bring in all the necessary items for a few days, because I'm getting Sister Taylor to take you straight up to Ward B for a good rest. Don't you worry, we'll get you back into shape."

He eyed her increasing girth and allowed himself a small smile. "Well, blood pressure-wise at least!"

With that he called the nurse to assist her and was gone. He was a strange one, Dr Stone, Ali mused. Stone by name and stone by nature she'd overheard the nurses say when he was out of earshot. He was brusque and had little bedside manner but he had an excellent reputation and she knew he had her best interests at heart.

Ali telephoned Simon to tell him the news and he sounded genuinely concerned, albeit a little late. He assured her he'd be there within a couple of hours with everything she needed and then Nurse Taylor whisked her off in a wheelchair to Ward B.

The ward was bright and cheerful with pale yellow walls and tasteful prints dotted around them. It looked more like a hotel then a hospital and unlike anything Ali had ever experienced in Dublin.

A beautiful girl with long blonde curly hair and big blue-green eyes sat in the bed opposite.

"I see they got you too!" she quipped at Ali smilingly and within minutes they had swapped blood counts and morning-sickness stories, bonding in the way that only pregnant women do.

The beautiful girl was called Nadine and was due two weeks after Ali.

Ali was amazed at Nadine's polite bump, fabulous skin and deep tan that accentuated her aquamarine eyes and white even teeth. She simply glowed.

Ali couldn't help feeling a little jealous. After all this girl was looking like a model, while Ali felt like a big spotty freckly lump. She couldn't help admitting as much to Nadine, who promptly lifted up her nightie to reveal wide red angry marks that ran like train tracks up her torso.

"Stretch marks," she announced with a strained voice. "I'll never be able to wear a bikini again."

With that she tumbled out her tale of dating her boyfriend Scott for two years when she had fallen pregnant by accident. First Scott pressurised her into having an abortion and then promptly moved out of their apartment when she wouldn't. "He simply said he wasn't ready to be a father and packed his bags," sniffed Nadine, fresh tears emerging at the memory. He walked out then and there. That was five months ago and I haven't seen him since. He has telephoned twice to see how I am! Can you imagine? Well, he doesn't deserve to be the father of this baby, I have decided. He has lost his chance. I'm making a life for my baby and me, on our own."

Ali admired Nadine's fortitude. She was determined to succeed despite the disappearing Scott. Ali felt she should admit her doubts about Simon yet didn't. She couldn't really fathom why, except that to admit them would give her doubts credence. They were having a good old heart-to-heart when Simon blustered in, laden with a bulging overnight bag and a huge bouquet of flowers.

Ali felt a pang of guilt. How could she have doubted him. He kissed her effusively and she saw Nadine visibly wince, so she got Simon to pull the dividing curtain around her bed while she changed into her bedclothes and they had a little privacy.

Simon appeared genuinely worried about her.

"I'm so sorry," he said contritely. "I should have been paying more attention to you, Ali. But blokes get a little left behind in all the pregnancy business and we feel a bit like a third wheel. I'm sorry if I made you miserable. I just didn't realise."

Ali's heart melted. He was so cute eating humble pie she forgave him his distance of the past few weeks immediately and heaved a huge sigh of relief. She didn't want to face this pregnancy alone like Nadine. Pregnancy was really tough even when you had a partner to support you. Imagine what it must be like for Nadine.

Ali began to see a silver lining in the cloud. Maybe this blip in her health was for the best if it brought her and Simon closer together.

After an hour of cosseting Simon left with a promise to return that evening. Ali drew the curtain back and was introduced to two other 'cell mates' as Nadine termed them.

Jo who was aboriginal, 28 and seven months pregnant with twins and Elaine, who at 42 was expecting her first baby.

Jo explained that her waters had broken the previous

week and although she wasn't in labour she would have to remain in hospital until the babies were born in case of infection. Ali at first felt slightly better on seeing Jo's girth but as she was carrying two babies, at least she had good reason to resemble Santa in her red satin pyjamas and told Jo as much.

Jo laughed so much she almost fell off the bed and her huge rotund stomach shook violently, causing the rest of the women to guffaw loudly.

Elaine, who was reed-thin, had red hair and a nervous disposition, said she was worried because she had had severe nausea since week eight and at 24 weeks had lost over a stone in weight off an already thin frame. She told Ali to eat up and not to worry as at least the baby was growing as it should, whereas she was on a drip and hospitalised, having failed to even keep water down.

Ali felt better already, knowing other women had difficult and worrying pregnancies and she wasn't alone in feeling fat, weepy and unloved. In fact she hadn't laughed as hard since Trisha left.

She resolved to take all the girls' telephone numbers when she was released so they could bolster each other up at home.

The camaraderie was so good she almost forgot she was in hospital on medical grounds and felt more like she was on a Girl Guide Camp Out.

How sad am I she thought, giggling, later on that evening. To get some fun I have to go to hospital!

Chapter 22

After a few days Ali's blood pressure dropped sufficiently for Dr Stone to allow her home. "To complete bed rest, mind," he warned sternly. "The next time I take you in, I'm not letting you back out until after delivery!"

Ali nodded emphatically. She would say anything to placate him. She was enjoying the company of the girls in Ward B a lot but had got little actual sleep with all the 24-hour hustle and bustle of a busy maternity hospital. She simply longed for her own quiet dark bedroom.

She left the hospital with copious flowers and all the girls' telephone numbers and promised to visit them all on her next appointment date. Nadine was hoping to be released soon and they intended to meet for lunch. Simon took Ali home to a sparkling clean apartment and a fabulous roast dinner cooked by him and his mother. He was solicitous and caring. Ali felt a lot happier with this new attitude and hoped it would continue.

There were numerous messages on her answer

machine from Trisha and her brothers, even one from Auntie Evelyn.

Obviously they were all worried about her, so after her slap-up meal, she decided to telephone Trisha and the family and tell them the bad news. She would not be home until after the baby was born.

Just as she sat down to telephone Ireland the phone trilled. It was Trisha.

"Oh, Trisha," she said softly, suddenly tearful at the sound of her friend's voice.

"Are you OK?" Trisha was alarmed. Perhaps something was wrong with the baby.

"No, sorry. I'm OK. It's just that I won't be coming home after all, not until after the baby arrives anyhow. My blood pressure is up and it's too dangerous to take a long-haul flight."

Trisha was bitterly disappointed and a little scared. She didn't trust Simon, not after what Ali had told her, and she certainly didn't feel Ali could depend on him. Yet she was half a world away from everyone and everything she knew. Trisha felt she should be with her and said as much.

"No! No. You can't, Trish!" replied Ali fiercely, when Trisha said she would take the next flight. "You've got a house mid-structure, a fiancé only on the mend from his accident and a wedding to plan! Besides, I'm not due for another two and a half months. You'd never get Miss Ratchett to give you all that time off work. I'm fine really."

"If you're totally sure," said Trish doubtfully, picturing Ratchett's scowling face.

She had been less than pleased to see Trisha sashay

back into Roche's and get her job back from the manager, Mr Foley, and Trish knew she'd lose the job for good if she went off again.

Old Ratchett face would see to that, but Ali was worth it.

"I'm totally sure," Ali insisted, though inside she felt like screaming to her friend. "OK! Get here as soon as possible."

But she couldn't do it. What kind of friend would she be if she tore Trisha away from Mick when he needed her and the whole new life she was planning? No, Ali would have to stand up on her own two feet and get through this and remain strong. After all, she was about to become a mother. She had to be independent and resilient if she was to succeed for this baby.

"And how is the big S coping?" Trisha enquired sarcastically.

She called Simon that a lot lately, Ali noticed.

The big S, it sounded like the big shit, which is exactly what Trish believed Simon acted like, most of the time.

"He has been really supportive actually. I think he got a bit of a fright."

"Good!" replied Trisha unconvinced. "Just make sure he looks after you or else he'll have me to answer to. You tell him that from me!"

"I will," smiled Ali, feeling Trisha's fierce love through the annoyance. She knew Trisha meant every word.

Ali changed the subject deliberately.

"Any word from himself?"

Trisha knew this to be code word for Ben.

"Yeah," replied Trish guardedly. She gave Ali only

little snippets of information on Ben, as she knew it was still a minefield of emotion to her friend. "He is still in Mozambique. He wrote to Mick a few weeks ago. He seems happy there, doing a lot of good work, apparently, but according to Mick he is constantly hot and dreaming for a pint of Guinness."

"I know how he feels," laughed Ali, then she dared ask the question she had been dying to ask for simply ages. "Did Mick tell him about me and my . . . dilemma?"

"Yes, months ago," admitted Trish. "And he hasn't asked about you since. I think he is in shock, to be honest."

"Yeah well, he missed his chance," said Ali bitterly.

"Ouch!" thought Trisha. Obviously, this still hit a raw nerve with her friend so she moved on to tell Ali all about the new house and the horrible time she was having with the builders. "Honestly Ali, the work is so slow I think we'll be coming back off our honeymoon to a caravan on the site!"

Ali laughed heartily.

"Seriously!" Trish was now on a roll. "They average about seven bricks and twenty-one coffee breaks in an hour and as soon as a spit drops from the sky, they down tools and go off to the pub for the rest of the day. It's a right pain in the arse, I can tell you. Oh sorry! I'm a right selfish cow, blathering on about all my inconsequential problems when you're stuck halfway across the world under strict bed-rest orders. I'll shut up."

"Ye will not," Ali insisted. "This is the best laugh I've had in ages. Besides, I'm only delighted to focus on someone else's problems for a change. It takes my mind off me own."

They spent another ten minutes chatting and having a good old gossip. It was so great to talk to someone who understood you completely.

Eventually Ali rang off and spent the next hour on the phone assuring her three brothers that she was OK and after that she phoned Aunt Evelyn, who was most concerned and even invited Ali to stay at her house, when she arrived back in Dublin.

Finally, exhausted and worn out from talking she climbed into bed and watched TV. Soon Simon came to join her. He stroked her hair as they watched *Hey Hey, it's Saturday* but even as she watched the TV screen she was miles away, thousands of miles away.

She was suddenly feeling so homesick she could almost taste it.

She just wanted to be back in Dublin, walking down Grafton Street on a miserable March day or walking up Howth Head with a bag of steaming fish and chips, or even sitting on her own dismal number sixteen bus.

It was strange the things you missed. You even missed things you had previously hated. For instance that awful hazy rain that was so fine you didn't need an umbrella, yet it wet you just the same as a downpour.

Ali always hated that, yet she yearned for some hazy rain after six months of constant sunshine.

She never thought sunshine would irritate her, but now it did.

Her thoughts then drifted to her brothers and their quiet acceptance of her situation. They just expressed concern and worry for her future.

She felt she had let them down. She knew she had let herself down. It was something she would have to deal with.

One thing was certain, however. She would love this baby with all her heart, despite its awkward start.

She patted her tummy lovingly as Simon laughed along to Darryl Sommer's jokes. It wouldn't be long before they would both be parents to this baby. The thought scared and excited her. She snuggled into Simon almost to block out her own doubts. He kissed her forehead and smiled at her.

"It's nice you're actually having the baby here now. In Australia, I mean," said Simon suddenly.

"Yeah?" Ali was quizzical. "Why is that?"

"Well, I know you wanted to go home, but now the baby will be a true blue Australian when it's born here, won't it? And you might never want to go back to Ireland after it gets here."

Ali felt a chill at the back of her neck.

"Ireland will always be my home, Simon," she began, a little testily.

"I know, I know, I'm not saying anything bad about your home. It's just, well, it'll be nice that the baby will call Australia home, that's all."

Panic engulfed Ali.

Simon seemed to think that Australia was the only option for her to bring up this baby, whereas although she really liked Australia, and had considered residency when Simon suggested it, it never occurred to her that Simon was expecting her to raise the baby there permanently.

Ali knew she could never just turn her back on her friends and family in Ireland – she wasn't even sure if she felt she and Simon were permanent yet.

What a mess, she admitted finally to herself. How the hell am I ever going to get out of this one?

Chapter 23

The next few weeks passed uneventfully. Ali's blood pressure settled down as she took things easier and tried not to get stressed out.

The baby was very active, and feeling her baby kick inside her made Ali focus on the positive side of things. Soon she would have her very own baby to love.

The thought scared her a little but overwhelmingly she was looking forward to motherhood.

She and Nadine whom she'd met in hospital met often for decaf cappuccinos in Indooropilly Shopping Centre, where they traded gory antenatal stories and endlessly examined their love lives. Nadine still hadn't seen the wayward Scott, though he had telephoned a few times to enquire about Nadine's health.

"The absolute nerve of him!" Nadine fumed to Ali over the phone. "It was like as if I had a bad cold or something and he wanted to see if I was over it. No mention of the actual baby and his plans to be in its life or anything so mundane. He talked more about the surf in Kirra Beach!"

"What did you tell him?" asked Ali, feeling she could do with some of Nadine's strong backbone.

"I told him he didn't deserve to be the father of this baby if he wouldn't be around me when I needed him most. I'm now having this baby without him so that's the way it'll stay. He needn't come running back in a few years after he's had his wild time and think he can parent this child and mess up its life. If I have to go it alone then so be it, permanently."

"Good for you!" concurred Ali.

She admired Nadine's tenacity.

Nadine had accepted the fact that she was going it alone, and didn't falter. Her mother was to be her birthing partner and she had already planned to go back to college and part-time work when the baby was born.

Ali began to develop a steely resolve of her own – after listening to Nadine. She began to form her own idea, that if Simon was not going to be a willing father or faithful partner she would go it alone too.

She knew that after the baby was born the situation would be so much more complicated with the issue of residence of the child.

Simon had rights as the baby's father. Ali dared not think of the consequences if there was a custody battle. The place of the child's birth was important. It had a bearing on where it had to be raised.

Ali couldn't bear the idea of being split up from Simon, yet having to raise the child alone in Australia, because a court decided it was the child's primary place of residence . . .

She knew now it was important to get back to Ireland as soon as possible after the baby was born. Simon tried to avoid the issue whenever Ali tried to raise the issue and she didn't want to make him too suspicious and guess her motives. Even though she wondered at his reluctance to discuss the matter, she had never promised him that she would stay in Australia permanently and he knew that.

Always have a plan B, Nadine had said emphatically. So Ali began to form one in her mind in case the worst happened. She began to save a little of the housekeeping money each week, so she would have some emergency cash if she needed it. Now that her ticket was about to be out-of-date, she felt stuck. At least if Simon decided the whole situation was too much to handle, she would have some emergency money to get a flight home.

But she knew she would have to box clever. She had seen Simon's temper and didn't want to ever witness it again, so she knew her doubts and ideas would have to be surreptitious.

He could never know.

Deciding that, gave Ali a little feeling of power over her own destiny.

And she liked it. She liked it a lot . . .

Three weeks later . . .

Ali felt she was blooming. She was having a last burst of energy which some women experience in late pregnancy. She had given the apartment an entire spring-clean and had set off afterwards into the city to buy some last minute Babygros. She toyed with the idea of surprising Simon for lunch as the train pulled into Roma Street Station just across the street from Police Headquarters where Simon worked. She almost didn't do it but she pushed back her doubts and decided to get off anyway. As she neared the large entrance of the police station she spotted Simon on the huge granite steps of the imposing building.

He appeared to be fixing the collar of an attractive female colleague's uniform.

They were laughing.

There was just something so intimate in the way they seemed together.

She couldn't put her finger on it exactly but she felt distinctly uncomfortable witnessing them. They looked like a couple.

She almost walked away but couldn't. Instead she stood transfixed to the spot.

The girl was tall, slim and not unattractive with short cropped black hair. She was still laughing. So was Simon. That was until he spotted Ali.

Then he appeared to get flustered, but perhaps she was imagining it.

He leapt down the steps towards her.

"Ali! What are you doing here?" The surprise was evident in his voice.

"I thought I'd drop by for lunch."

She tried to keep her voice steady and light. Don't get hysterical she warned herself inwardly, "That's not a problem is it?" Her look was quizzical.

"Not at all! It's great, actually," Simon beamed. A little overdone, Ali mused.

"Ali, come and meet Jodie, my workmate"

"Hi, Jodie."

Ali forced herself to smile. She remained at the bottom of the steps looking up at Jodie. Her poor legs couldn't carry her up to the top, where the lithe Jodie was standing.

Jodie came down gracefully and shook Ali's hand, smiling brightly.

"Ali, I've heard all about you. Pleased to meet you."

"Jodie," Ali replied deadpan. "I've heard nothing about you. Pleased to meet you too."

They all laughed. Ali hadn't meant it to be funny.

Jodie eyed Ali's enormous bump.

"When is the baby due?" her voice seemed flat all of a sudden. She tore her eyes from Ali's stomach and glanced at Simon. It appeared to be a fleeting look of disgust.

"A few weeks," replied Ali. "But I'm sure Simon had already filled you in."

"Uh. No, not really," mumbled Jodie, distinctly unimpressed.

"Anyway, Si, I must go. All the best with the baby too, Ali. It's nice to meet you. See you later."

And with that she was gone. Bounding up the big granite steps in twos.

Ali momentarily wished she could just walk up them without needing a ten-minute rest afterwards, when Simon clasped her hand and led her away.

"It's great to see you, honey, but I just wish you'd phone ahead. You just caught me there."

"Obviously." Ali replied, quick as a flash. "You never

mentioned Jodie before, or the fact that she is so attractive, in an angular sort of way."

She tried to sound light and conversational, but inside she felt really low. Her earlier chirpiness had evaporated.

"Ali, there are a lot of women in the office. I can't describe every one of them. Anyway, Jodie's been dating a guy for over a year. She's practically engaged. Now. Where would you like to eat, the Pier or the Queen St Mall?"

He hailed a cab.

"I'm sorry," Ali said biting her lip as the cab sped towards the city centre. "I'm just so huge and pregnant. It's tough enough without seeing you with all these slim attractive women, when I feel so horrible."

"You are beautiful, Alison," said Simon kissing her nose. "You're about to have a baby in a few weeks. Of course you're big. But you'll get your figure back in no time afterwards, won't you?"

Ali didn't reply – she was looking out the window and thinking this is all so wrong. It wasn't supposed to be like this. She should be happy, expecting a baby with someone she loved – but that was just it – she didn't love Simon.

The revelation suddenly hit her like a slap.

She didn't love him at all.

She suddenly felt sad and weary, sad for her and Simon and their unborn child. She had such an unhappy childhood she never wanted to foist one on her unborn baby. She felt a deep pity for both of them – all of them – she looked across at Simon and felt a twinge of remorse.

How could she tell him this now?

In a way perhaps it would be better if he were having an affair, then she could hate him and feel justified for leaving. But now she was crystal clear she would leave him. She could not live a life of doubt and just settle for marrying a man like Simon even if it was for their unborn child. She was leaving him, she decided and going home to raise her baby. That was definite. How she would do it was another thing. She felt suddenly apprehensive. She knew instinctively it would not be easy and she would have to be very careful.

She must not reveal her feelings now.

She would have to wait, wait until the baby was born and she regained all her strength, then she would tell him.

She deeply feared his response, but she decided in that cab on a sunny summer's day in Brisbane that her future would be different.

It would hold love and promise and she would live happily ever after.

The fact that she had made a decision within herself strengthened her.

She filed her ideas away, and resolved to be calm and serene and have this baby first; she could act later. But she would no longer fret over Simon's perceived infidelities or careless affection, because she was in charge of her own destiny.

She smiled as he held her hand and chatted inanely as they went to lunch.

She wondered idly if the lithe Jodie was spitting chips back at Police HQ waiting to give Simon a piece of her mind. Jodie's face had said it all. She knew of Ali's existence but Ali was sure she knew nothing of the baby's.

It mattered little anyhow; Jodie could have him all she liked.

Soon.

Chapter 24

"It's a girl!" yelped Trisha in delight as she danced across the cluttered kitchen. "Mam, it's a girl! Ali's given birth to a little girl and they're both fine. I am so happy for her, I could explode."

"That's great, love," replied Mrs Costello absent-mindedly, peeling spuds for her large brood. She didn't think it was so great for Ali to be facing motherhood all alone in the world. It was hard enough when you had a good husband to stand by you, but Ali, well, that Aussie Guard didn't seem much gyp and she was an orphan to boot. Life would not get any easier for poor Alison O'Neill, of that she was sure. She said a silent prayer that none of her own would end up single and pregnant, and tried to be enthusiastic while Trisha raved on about the baby's weight and Ali's delight.

Trisha and Ali had been both in tears as they talked.

Trisha was so relieved for her friend that the labour was over and the baby was safe and healthy.

Ali was so happy and relieved to speak to someone from home after all she had endured. She decided to admit to Trisha that Simon had been nowhere to be found when she went into labour and she had spent the first four hours in hospital alone.

By the time he made it, Ali was in such deep labour that she was unable to question him about his mysterious disappearance, but it stuck in her mind.

His duty had finished when she had called the station in early labour, and Kirsty, the receptionist, had told her he had already left.

He never explained when he finally showed up, where he was or who told him the news. She planned to question him in depth and in private later.

"Is she gorgeous?" Trisha asked.

"Beautiful!" Ali confirmed laughing through her tears. "And she's got a mop of black hair and Simon's sallow skin. Thank the lord! Freckles shouldn't be a problem!"

"Trust you to think of that at a time like this!" exclaimed Trisha laughing. Then she added, "When are you coming home?"

She just couldn't help herself asking the question.

"Well, not tomorrow," Ali joked. "Seriously, I dunno really, I'll talk to you about it soon. It's just a bit complicated. There's a lot to sort out."

She sounded a bit strained.

Trisha decided to drop it for the moment.

"We'll talk soon, OK. Promise?"

"Yep," replied Ali. "I promise."

Bloody Simon! thought Trisha angrily. I bet he's putting pressure on her to stay in Australia after all, but she decided not to push it. Ali had just been through a traumatic twelve-hour labour; now was not the time.

"I'm so happy for you. I wish I could just hop on a plane and be there for you!"

"You are here for me," said Ali catching a sob escape from her throat. "You are the best friend a girl could ever have. And the best godmother."

"Really?" Now Trisha erupted into fresh tears. "Oh Ali, I'm delighted. I'll be the best godmother. I swear!"

"And tell Mick he's godfather, OK."

"Right so! He'll be thrilled. Thanks, Ali,"

"I'd better go, the baby needs a feed now. The nurse has just brought her in."

"What are you going to call her?" asked Trisha, suddenly remembering.

"Emma, Emma Joan O'Neill," Ali said emphatically.

"That's really lovely," replied Trisha and meant it. "Your Mum would be proud."

"I hope to make her proud one day." Ali said quietly, "Anyway, I'll talk to you soon."

With that she was gone.

Trisha felt a bit perturbed by the last comment and the strained tone when she had asked Ali about returning home to Ireland. She decided to talk to Mick about it when they went for a quiet drink in Fagan's later on that evening.

"I don't know, Mick. There's something odd going on. Something I just can't put my finger on. Ali seemed really vague when I asked her about coming home, yet I know she's just dying to."

"Maybe she feels under pressure from Simon and his family," replied Mick, ever practical. "Surely they wouldn't want her to hotfoot it back to Dublin as soon as the baby is born? They are involved with this baby too."

'That's exactly what I think too," said Trish resignedly as she sipped her glass of Harp. "And that scares me. He is a cop after all, with connections. She'll have to be careful. But reading between the lines he has been a less than enthusiastic father for the past few months. Do you know he couldn't be found for over four hours when Ali went into labour?"

"What?" Mick was aghast. That kind of behaviour was incomprehensible to him. "And where was he?"

"I don't know," frowned Trish. "He wasn't on duty, but my theory is, he's playing around on Ali. He hasn't treated her right in months. I'm really worried about her. I wish I was there with her."

"Look," said Mick, fearing Trisha would take a notion and insist on flying off half way around the world again, "all we can do is be supportive and be there for her in any way we can. Has she still got her return ticket home?"

"No," offered Trisha dejectedly. "If only she had. It expired a couple a months ago"

"Well, we'll send her the money then. At least she'll have a ticket home and the freedom to decide what to do for herself. She won't have the worry of finding the money hanging over her."

"Oh, Mick, you really are the best!" exclaimed Trisha, delighted. "I'll get the money out of the bank during the week and I'll call her with the news. She'll be over the moon. At least now I won't have to worry so much."

"Nor me either," smiled Mick, planting a kiss on her forehead. But for different reasons he admitted quietly to himself. I'm never letting go of this one again.

Meanwhile Ali was ensconced in the Mater Mothers, snuggling into her new baby. She was shellshocked after a hard labour but deliriously happy with this new perfect little person that lay asleep in her arms. She could barely believe the fierce love that overwhelmed her for her child. Simon appeared happy with his new daughter, although she knew that secretly he was disappointed that Emma was not the son he'd longed for.

Ali didn't care right now – she didn't care that he had been late and flustered when he'd finally arrived into the labour ward, short on excuses.

It would keep. She planned to question him at a later time. All she knew now was whatever way the cards fell – she would do her absolute best for her child. There was no way her child would ever live the life she had lived.

She cuddled Emma's soft downy face to hers and uttered a promise to her new baby that she would protect and love her whatever the cost. A new strength emerged inside her, primal and all encompassing.

She had lost her fear.

She had finally grown up.

Ben sat looking out the window with a silly grin spreading across his deeply tanned face. The nearer the plane got to Ireland, the greyer and darker the clouds got. He chuckled to himself thinking, "Never did I think I'd see the day when these dark foreboding clouds would actually make me happy."

Much like the way he never thought he would tire of an endless blue sky or the bright hot sun – but he had. Now these dark grey clouds signified home, Ireland. He just couldn't wait! Cool dark skies, really green grass and a decent pint of the black stuff.

His heart leapt. He was finally going home.

Thinking of the heat he had left behind, his mind drifted onto Ali. He wondered how she had coped with the Australian heat. Did she like the relentless blue skies of Queensland or did she sometimes, like him, crave a cool wet moody Dublin day like he'd done so many times in Mozambique? He wondered if she had given birth to her baby yet and had she considered marrying the father.

A sudden fear gripped him. She could be lost to him forever.

Perhaps she already was.

"You fool Murphy!" he berated himself. "If your brain was a bit higher up than in your trousers, you might still have the girl."

Still, he had hope yet.

She had to come home some time and if she didn't bring the Aussie cop with her he might still have a chance.

The baby didn't matter insofar as he would love it just like it was his own. It would be Ali's after all. He tried to imagine her pregnant and couldn't. He could only remember those vivid green eyes and that tumbling copper hair.

"More wine, sir?" the pretty air-hostess interrupted his reverie.

He found her soft Irish lilt uplifting.

"I certainly will." he smiled widely, proffering his glass.

He was truly coming home.

And he couldn't wait . . .

Chapter 25

Three months later

Simon was late again.

Not an hour late or even two, but four hours late this time.

Ali looked out the window yet again onto the dark silent street. No sign of him. If only he would call and say he would be late.

She hated this. When he eventually did arrive he would invariably be surly or drunk or both. Now since Emma had arrived, the late nights out and silent belligerence had become the norm. Ali wasn't sure why – she knew she was tired and preoccupied with Emma, but she was exhausted, like any new mother. The baby needed her attention.

She did her best to look good when Simon arrived home and always had a nice meal ready. She tried to be animated and interested in his day. But despite this he didn't seem in the least bit interested in Ali or anything she had to say. His eyes would glaze over as she tried to tell him about her and Emma's day as if he couldn't wait to retreat to the football on TV.

She went into the kitchen and checked on the once appetising meal that sat in a congealed lump on the plate. She tossed it into the bin.

Just then she heard a car pull into the driveway. It was Simon.

"Stay calm," she told herself. "Just ask him where he was without any shouting or hysterics."

Simon staggered in the front door – the generous mouth that had once seemed so attractive was now curled into a sneer.

"Where the hell were you?" Ali exploded despite all her good intentions.

Without warning Simon slapped her full across the face.

Ali stumbled with the force of the whack. She was stunned.

"Don't," he shouted, his face just an inch way from hers, "ever ask me where I was! You're not my fucking wife!"

Ali was so shocked she just fled to the bedroom and locked the door.

She was shaking.

She couldn't quite believe what had just happened. That he had actually hit her. Her face stung to prove it. Her heart stung worse.

That was it.

It was over then and there. Her mind was finally made up. She was definitely leaving now and the sooner the better.

As she gazed as a peacefully sleeping Emma, she vowed that would be the last chance he would ever get to do that to her.

She was sad for Emma.

She wouldn't get to be in a perfect family after all, but at least she'd get to be in a happy one, even if it meant just the two of them.

After a while she was relieved to hear the sound of the TV blaring out a football match. He would fall asleep on the couch so she was safe.

She lay awake for hours with a heavy heart, feeling a failure for not being able to make it work, but it took two people to want a relationship to succeed, to make it possible. Simon obviously didn't want her.

It made her sad, but she was resolute. It was over. She was going home. It would just be a matter of time and money.

The next day Simon left for work before six am, no doubt embarrassed by his cowardly behaviour the night before.

Ali ran to the phone and called Trisha and poured her heart out to her friend who went berserk and was glad at that moment she was half a world away otherwise she'd have murdered Simon with her bare hands.

"The bastard!" she swore when her friend burst into tears as the tale unfolded. Ali got so upset, Trisha had to become calm. "Don't worry, It's OK. Guess what? Mick and I have already sent you your airfare home. You should have it in a few days. We posted it over a week ago – even before all this happened – Mick said you should have a choice about coming home, independent of any pressure. So just do what you want to do. Now you'll have the money."

"Oh Trisha, thanks. What would I do without you? And tell Mick that he's an angel. You are so lucky, y'know, having Mick in your life."

"I do know," Trisha replied grimly but decided not to dwell on it in case Ali felt even worse for her poor choice in men.

She decided to change the subject.

"Look, Ali, you will need to get Emma onto your passport. You can't leave Australia without her being put on it, but that could take a while to do. But I telephoned the Irish Embassy, and you'll need Simon's signature on the application form. You'll have to be careful. Somehow you have to get him to sign the form without knowing what he is actually signing. If that's possible."

"Don't worry," said a jubilant Ali full of resolve. There was a hardness forming inside her. "I'll think of something. Just leave it to me."

And so it began.

Firstly, Ali watched the mail delivery closely so she could intercept the money Mick and Trish sent her. She then lodged it into a separate bank account at the ANZ Bank, an account she had opened when she first arrived but that Simon knew nothing about. She then applied for Emma to be added to her passport at the Irish embassy in Canberra. The form duly arrived days later and Simon was required to sign it.

Luckily enough the form was lengthy, verbose and in both Irish and English, so she hoped Simon wouldn't scan it too closely.

She was nervous the entire day trying to get her story straight.

She had decided to tell Simon that they both had to sign the form to register Emma's birth with the Irish authorities, and hoped for the best.

By the time he arrived home she was a bundle of nerves and almost couldn't go through with it, but then she reminded herself of that hard slap and once more became resolute.

She remained calm.

It was important that he didn't suspect. She need not have worried. He barely listened, signed the form immediately and went back to watching the cricket; it couldn't have been easier. Ali was so overjoyed, that she found it difficult to contain her excitement. She was normally so subdued. So she went off to bed early pleading a headache and spent the rest of the night dizzy with excitement, making her plans.

Eight weeks later her passport arrived back from Canberra complete with Emma's name. Ali had spent every afternoon at home to check when the mail arrived. It had been difficult concealing all the subterfuge from her new friends. Terri and Nadine and Marci had been so good to her, so supportive, but she felt that afterwards it would be better that they didn't know anything, then Simon wouldn't be able to extract any information from them.

She felt really mean though, and insincere. But it was for the best.

Better for her and best for Emma.

She knew Terri had guessed Simon wasn't up to much good. She had as good as accused him herself. She had tried to warn Ali but Ali had to find out for herself. Ali instinctively felt Terri knew something major was amiss, but she refrained from mentioning it so Ali just played dumb and focused on herself. After all, Terri was married to Simon's best friend, and she couldn't be sure that Terri wouldn't let it slip. Only Trisha and Mick knew of all her plans.

They knew that she had already booked her flight, and booked through Royal Brunei Airways whose flight path was off the beaten track, through Burma, Dubai and Brunei itself.

She felt safer somehow, travelling with an obscure airline rather than on Qantas or Singapore Airways in case she bumped into someone Simon knew.

The plans had to be carried out perfectly; she had to gain some time between her actually leaving and his discovering she was gone.

Ideally she wanted to be almost in London before he suspected anything.

She knew that as the father of her baby he had rights, even though now he barely expressed any interest in her or Emma. She wasn't sure how he would feel to have his daughter taken away from him. She believed deep down that he did actually love Emma, but was just too selfish to give her any of his precious time.

Part of her knew it was wrong to sweep the baby away from him, but she really felt it was necessary for her survival and Emma's happiness in the long run. Eventually when time elapsed she and Simon could discuss the future.

She would always be linked to Simon through Emma; that was the unfortunate thing. It made Ali realise how important it was to have a secure and loving relationship before ever contemplating sharing a child with someone.

The bonds were there for life and so were the scars if the relationship didn't work out and there was a child involved. Ali could have kicked herself sometimes for being so silly but then she would look at Emma and know she could never regret it, Emma was so precious. She would just have to make the best of it.

Before long she would be home in Dublin and she could start living again.

Trish and Mick stood at the top of their newly gravelled drive.

The house really looked spectacular. It was everything Trish had ever wanted or dreamt of. The high red-tiled roof set off the glistening white granite pebbledash and the large Georgian bay windows. Mick had even surprised Trish with a window seat in their bedroom, something Trish had only seen in old Hollywood movies and had longed for. The whole acre of land about the house had been seeded for grass and the driveway would eventually be lined with trees and surrounded by a picket fence. They had spent every available penny they possessed on the house and there was precious little left for furniture, but Trisha knew eventually that they would have it the way they wanted it. For now, plain calico curtains that her mother had sewn would suffice and they would get by on odd pieces of furniture they had been bestowed from various family members. Trisha didn't care – she was in seventh heaven just owning such a house as this.

"I'm afraid I can't spare any dosh for champers this time, so you'll have to share a glass of the black stuff with me instead!" joked Mick as he hobbled from the van with a bottle of Guinness and two plastic cups.

Trisha's eyes misted over. "Oh Mick, we're going to be so happy here. I just know it!"

"Yes," agreed Mick as proud as Punch as he surveyed his handiwork.

"And we'll fill it with kids, won't we?" he grabbed Trish and gave her a cuddle.

"You bet!" laughed Trish. "Em, how do you feel about having one a bit sooner?"

Mick looked perplexed

"Sorry, I'm not with you, what do you mean?"

"Not me you silly eejit! God, no! I haven't any surprising news. I meant Ali and Emma. They'll be back in a couple of months, and I was wondering . . . well if they could stay with us for a few months until they get sorted, that is."

"Of course they can," said Mick. "I know she needs us and we'll be there for her, But, I would like to start our married life on our own, so she'd need to be set up on her own within the seven months to the wedding."

"Yes, of course!" exclaimed Trish, relieved that Mick had agreed at all.

She knew he couldn't wait for them to start their lives together properly after so long. They needed to be alone as a couple after all these years.

It had been difficult, them both still living at home with their parents – they just couldn't wait to be married and on their own.

216

"I promise, it'll be no more than six months, tops. Now, I wonder whom I can borrow a cot from . . ."

Mick laughed as he looked at her determined face, already decorating Emma's room in her mind. If only she knew, he was putty in her hands.

He wiped away a wayward strand of her golden hair and kissed her nose. He couldn't wait 'til they filled up a cot of their own. That would make life perfect – he just couldn't wait to start a family with Trisha.

"C'mon, let's get you out of the cold," he said at last as they took another longing look at their dream home. "Soon, we won't have to just look at this place. We'll be able to move in and make it ours."

"Yes!" Trisha said. "I can't wait."

They drove off in Mick's little van, their heads full of dreams and ideas of their new life together.

Simon rolled over and grabbed a cigarette. He almost never smoked but after really good sex he always felt like one and Jodie was so good in the sack, he just had to have one of hers. He knew she disliked him smoking in the bedroom but it never stopped him.

"Do you have to?" Jodie muttered, displeased.

"Sorry," he replied, not meaning it.

She decided to change the subject, as he was in one of his weird moods.

"You were so intense today, Simon. What's the matter? Little wifey not up to the task any more?"

'No. I'm not, if you must know," Simon muttered.

"Why?" Jodie was genuinely surprised. Simon was always on call in the bedroom.

"I'm just not ready for all this serious commitment stuff. I mean, I love little Emma, I really do, and I'm really fond of Ali. It's just that it drives me nuts to have this instant family foisted on me. I'm just not ready, you know?"

Jodie didn't know. She felt like telling him to grow up. It took two people to make a baby and it was about time Simon faced up to his responsibilities as a father. But she thought better of it.

Jodie had seen his legendary temper and she had no intention of being on the receiving end of it. She also couldn't give a fig for his girlfriend.

She liked him in bed and would suit herself.

"Poor Simon," she murmured silkily, kissing him passionately. "There now – put out that damn cigarette and I'll make you feel a whole lot better!"

Chapter 26

At last the day had finally arrived. The day Ali would escape from Simon and finally go home to Dublin with her treasured bundle. It was October 10th 1985. Ali felt so nervous she could feel her stomach do somersaults as soon as she opened her eyes from a fitful night's sleep. But she knew it was important she didn't deviate one jot from her usual subdued demeanour in case Simon suspected something. She was to drop him off at the train station for 7.15am, as it was Friday and he'd be going for his usual booze-up with his mates after his shift. This meant she had the car but she had decided not to use it but would catch a cab to the airport for her 10.15am check-in.

Simon was his usual dour self. She chatted amiably as she usually did, but her insides felt like liquid jelly, and her brain swirled around with anxious fears.

"I might take a trip down the coast with Nadine today,

to see her Mum. It'd be nice to get the babies out in the fresh air at the beach." She heard her voice utter the words and marvelled at how outwardly calm she seemed.

"Hope you're not planning on taking my car," Simon snapped. Concerned as always with just his possessions.

"Nope,"she replied steadily not wanting a row. "Nadine's collecting us."

"Fine," Simon muttered staring out the window.

They had reached the station. He got out and neglected to even give her a cursory kiss. All such affection had gradually dissolved, but yet he kissed and cuddled Emma so affectionately that Ali almost winced. She felt so cruel; she was about to take his daughter away.

Then her resolve returned when Simon uttered the usual lines. "Don't wait up. I don't know what time I'll be back, could be all hours."

"OK," she said unsmilingly, not that it mattered now, but that had become the familiar catchphrase of the past six weeks as he had been home less and less.

"See ya," she called to his back as he sprinted up the station steps.

He didn't even look back.

"Don't know what time I'll be back either," Ali whispered smilingly, as she drove off back to the apartment.

She had decided weeks ago that she would travel light and take only a few essentials of her own and Emma's.

She was going to leave Simon a note to explain they'd decided to stay a couple of days at Coolangatta with Nadine's mum, so he wouldn't suspect straightaway.

She needed as much time as possible before he discovered she was gone.

She wanted to be safely back home in Dublin, before there was the remotest hint of her escape.

She knew Simon didn't know where Trisha lived or even Trisha's last name, so she would be difficult to find.

Eventually she knew he would find her and they would sort it all out, but she wanted to do it on her home ground where she had support and she needed to establish Ireland as Emma's main place of residence so she wouldn't have to live in Australia alone with her child.

She sped home and when she reached the apartment she pulled out her neatly packed backpack from under the bed where it had been ready for days. She then got together Emma's bag and buggy and grabbed the passport and tickets from their hidey-hole in the freezer. Her heart thumped wildly. She took several deep breaths and steadied her hand before writing the deliberately casual note to Simon about staying over at Nadine's parents. She had earlier asked Nadine to cover for her if necessary.

"No need to explain," Nadine had said kindly. "I'm sure you have your reasons. You are much too good for him anyway."

Ali hoped this plan would give her several extra precious hours.

She then phoned a cab and caught it to the city where she got out and caught another one to the airport just to be on the safe side.

When she finally arrived at the airport her legs were shaking so badly she feared they wouldn't carry her to the check-in desk.

"Just stay calm," she told herself, knowing if she appeared nervous that she would attract attention.

Emma began to whimper. Poor mite, Ali realised in all the fuss and bustle she had forgotten to give the baby her morning feed so sat down and fed Emma while her nerves calmed. Ten minutes later she checked in with a newly relaxed exterior. The check-in clerk was friendly enough and said how cute Emma was, but she still spent an age poring over Ali's passport and visa extension.

At last she seemed satisfied and gave Ali her boarding card and advised her that they even had a bassinet booked for Emma.

"Enjoy your flight," she beamed finally.

Ali had never heard more beautiful words uttered. But she knew the real test would be passport control. One more hurdle and she could finally breathe easy again.

The man at passport control was burly and unsmiling. He looked as if he loved his job and disliked people. Ali's heart lurched.

He perused her passport over and over and then suddenly gave a grim smile and stamped it 'Exited Australia 10/10/85'. Ali unsmilingly took back her passport and slowly put it away in order not to appear as anxious as she felt. She had just pushed Emma a few feet away when she heard the burly guy call out "Excuse me. Excuse me! Madam with the baby."

She froze. My God, I'm sunk. Her mind raced as she slowly turned around.

"Miss, I'm sorry, but you dropped the baby's bunny rabbit. I'm sure she'd miss it as soon as she got on the plane." He smiled and handed her Emma's blue bunny that she absolutely loved.

"Oh, thanks!" She gasped so relieved that she almost kissed him. "Thanks so much."

"No worries," he replied and this time gave a genuine smile. "Enjoy your trip."

"Thanks! I'm sure I will."

A few minutes later she was in Duty Free. She now felt so elated all her senses were heightened. The perfume smelled sweeter, and the lights were brighter.

Everything seemed so much better. The fog of being under Simon's depressive influence lifted. Ali felt truly alive. And free. Well, almost. She had to cross half a world first. But in a little over 24 hours she would be landing in Dublin. Home. Tears pricked her eyes and she hugged Emma tightly as they boarded the plane.

The flight was endless. Ali couldn't believe how long and how difficult it would be to take that trip with a baby in tow. On the way over, she and Trish had slept for a while, watched a movie, then had a few drinks and following that they had experienced that lovely stopover in Singapore.

Now, she found it incredible that she was returning to Ireland a little over a year and a half later with her own child.

Although Emma was a very placid baby, the incredibly long flight tried her patience. Not to mention Ali's.

First the plane stopped in Darwin, then Rangoon and onto Brunei.

By the time they had reached Brunei, Ali could have

gleefully leapt from the plane into the sea, she was that dog-tired. Yet they were less than half way there. Although Emma was a terrific baby, it was extremely tiring and wearing trying to occupy and pacify her in that tiny little seat for hours on end. Everyone else was exhausted themselves so she had little help from anyone, including the stewardesses. On the next leg from Dubai Ali managed to get some fractured sleep when Emma did and she felt entirely better upon waking when the Captain announced they were less then two hours out of London Heathrow.

Ali's spirits suddenly soared.

Only a few hours left to go.

She looked out over the green carpet below that was Bavaria and imagined the green fields of Ireland that she would see soon. For the first time in months, relief spread over her and she cried quietly, looking out that window, for all the unhappiness and trauma she had experienced.

But it was all now behind her; the future was for her and Emma.

A new calmness emerged within Ali at that moment.

She would succeed and provide Emma with the happiest little home she could afford.

The whole Simon experience had taught her to face fear and do it anyway. Everything else would be so much easier than what she had just been through.

She glanced at a sleeping Emma, all cosy in her bassinet. She looked so much like Simon, the same jet-black hair and sallow skin.

She hoped someday that Emma would understand what she had had to do.

She wondered how Simon was. Had he bothered to

check if she had really gone down the coast with Nadine? Or had he fallen in the door, too plastered to care? If he emerged the next day with one of his legendary hangovers, it might be quite a while before his brain got into gear and his suspicions were aroused.

Simon, had in fact, arrived home a few hours earlier, bleary-eyed and drunk in the early hours. He had crept into the apartment quietly and headed straight for the laundry to put his lipstick-stained shirt into the washing machine.

He might be pissed but he wasn't a complete idiot. Bloody Jodie. She was always planting evidence, hoping that he would get caught out by Ali. But the stupid cow never appeared to notice or even care.

He laughed quietly to himself.

Women were such gullible idiots.

As he lurched drunkenly towards the bedroom, he was surprised to see the bed was empty and there was a short note from Ali explaining that she had decided after all to go down the coast for a couple of days with Nadine and the babies.

"Stupid tart," he smarted. "I could have spent the night with Jodie after all!"

He collapsed in a heap on the bed and was soon loudly asleep, totally unaware that Ali and his child were almost half a world away from him already.

Chapter 27

"It's her! There she is! Ali! Ali!" Trisha exclaimed in the bustling Arrivals Hall. People milled about as she pushed through towards Ali, who was pushing Emma in her buggy while trying to tug her bag and looking around her anxiously. The two friends fell on each other as their emotions spilled out into tearful laughter.

Mick stood back a little embarrassed and eventually took Emma and steered both of them towards the car park. Dublin was freezing cold on an October evening, but Ali hardly seemed to notice. She was chatting animatedly to Trisha as they cooed over Emma. Mick smiled to himself. They were like long-lost twins reunited after decades apart. He knew he was in for a late night and copious cups of tea, but he was really happy for Trisha who sparkled when her friend was around and he was happy to have Emma around too. She really was a cute little baby. He was alarmed by Ali's appearance, however. She was thinner than ever and looked somewhat older and a lot wiser. He could tell that it hadn't been an easy time.

As they headed out of the airport towards the Naul, Ali was amazed by the colour of Dublin after a year and eight months of Aussie bright blue skies.

Everybody looked pale and rugged up against the elements, rushing home to get out of the cold biting wind.

It seemed strange yet familiar after all this time to be back home. She marvelled at the dark green grass and grey foreboding skies and felt so happy she could almost burst.

Over tea in Trisha's spectacular kitchen, Ali regaled both Mick and Trisha with tales of her life with Simon both before and after Emma. They both agreed she was much better off without him. Mick felt incensed that a man would intimidate a lovely girl like Ali and then neglect both her and his own baby so badly.

Ali admitted she was more than a little afraid Simon would follow her and try to take Emma simply because he hated to lose. Both Mick and Trisha reassured her.

"He's got no power over you here, even if he does come," insisted Mick, still fuming, "and if he does show up, I'll certainly deal with him!"

"He won't show up," interjected Trisha. "He hasn't got my mum's address or phone number. Has he?" She then glanced at Ali worriedly.

"No, I was very careful," Ali grimaced. "Anyway, he never expressed much interest in my family. He was much too busy trying to control me!"

A few hours later after exhaustive conversations and a big traditional fry-up, jet-lag got the better of Ali, and

Trish took her and a sleeping Emma to the room she had lovingly prepared for them. It had pale lemon-painted walls with bright yellow ducks and balloons on Emma's side, which had a freshly painted cot complete with teddies and rag dolls inside.

Ali's bed had a pale lemon continental quilt that matched the curtains.

It was beautiful. Ali was bowled over. The tension that had enveloped her over the past few weeks became tears and she hugged her friend and wept. Relief and happiness emerging within, she felt very emotional.

"Do you hate it that much?" asked Trish in mock seriousness, breaking the tension.

"I love it," laughed Ali sniffing back tears. "You are such a good friend to me, you know. I am so lucky to have you."

"Rubbish," grinned Trish hugging Ali. "You would do the same for me! Now get some sleep, Emma is out for the count. You'll feel a million dollars when you wake up in the morning."

A few minutes later Ali fell into bed thankfully and slept immediately,

A deep peaceful sleep of the free . . .

In the morning when Ali first awoke she was completely disoriented. The pale yellow bedroom looked totally unfamiliar for a moment until she gathered her thoughts and remembered where she was.

She looked across at Emma who was snuffling her favourite rabbit while examining the ducks on the wall with a serious intent look on her face that immediately reminded Ali of Simon. God. Her heart suddenly turned over.

The enormity of what she had just done finally hit her. She felt awful.

Being right didn't help too much, but she had been so afraid to approach him for fear of what he might do. She had made her decision and she would abide by it now. She was, however, acutely aware of the implications.

Much as it scared her to think of it, Emma was Simon's child too. She knew sooner or later it would have to be sorted out. But for now she resolved she would get a job and look after Emma. She would make a new life for them both.

Emma looked around and seeing Ali was awake, began her early morning whimper that told Ali a nice warm bottle of milk was required immediately, and Emma would resume her sunny disposition as soon as it was demolished. Ali padded out to the enormous kitchen where Trish was already conjuring up another delicious fry. They chatted away while the milk heated and Ali stood transfixed looking at the incredibly green grass that seemed to go on for miles past the bungalow. It was so tranquil here. Trish was so lucky, Ali thought wistfully.

"I know I'm incredibly lucky," Trisha interrupted, almost reading Ali's thoughts. "It's beautiful here, isn't it?"

"Absolutely," agreed Ali feeling a little guilty of her envy.

"Your turn will come, Ali. Don't worry."

"Yeah, hope so," Ali smiled wanly.

Trish decided to lighten things up.

"Ah sure, ye never know, ye might be swanning up to Sandymount to Isabel Murphy's one of these days – Ben's still free you know."

Ali laughed.

"Can you imagine the look on the oul bat's face if I arrived – complete with baby in tow – that'd finish her off altogether!"

They both cackled with laughter.

"Oh it's so good to be home, Trish," Ali said as their giggles subsided.

"I know," agreed Trish feeling on top of the world now her friend was back. "Now, hurry up and get Emma and feed her. This breakfast will sort you out for our eight-hour shopping marathon in Grafton Street later on. You'll need all your strength."

"Right. You're on," smiled Ali, remembering all the times she pictured herself walking up Grafton Street. Today it would happen for real.

She might even pop into Maisie Carter at Carter Travel to show Emma off.

There might even be a job going. Her mind raced with possibilities.

Her grin was a mile wide by the time she got back to her bedroom.

She hugged her baby closely, thinking, "I'm home I'm really home. I can start to live again."

Chapter 28

Isabel was so happy. She had her boy back under her roof safe and sound after that dreadful year in Africa. John, her husband, had secured tenure as a consultant at a top Dublin hospital and everything was good again. Her new face-lift had taken a full ten years off her face and she hadn't felt so well in years. Her small departure from reality a few short months ago when her nerves had landed her in a private sanatorium for a few weeks was a dim bad memory. She managed to convince John it was mostly the menopause, but she was aware herself that the deep depression that had overwhelmed her was more to do with Ben. And the awful ensuing debacle of his dumping poor Karen Kennedy just weeks before the wedding, and the subsequent shame it brought on the Murphy family, and more importantly on herself that had triggered her decline.

All the careful years of being upwardly mobile and fitting in and, more importantly, being accepted by her betters had almost been stripped away.

It would have been almost easier to accept the awful O'Neill girl than go through what she had endured. But thankfully, it had all worked out beautifully. She got to brag to all her friends about Ben's fine work in Africa, and now he was home again safe under her roof her life was again complete. She was slightly concerned that he was so busy with his new position as a paediatrician at Temple Street that he expressed little interest in dating again. He seemed a little too serious, even glum. She wondered if he still harboured feelings for Karen. Though she dared not broach the subject.

Still, she smiled to herself. Ben is fine. She didn't want to begin fretting again. Who knew where it might lead?

She touched up her pale-golden bobbed hair and straightened her light-blue Chanel suit as she admired herself in the mirror. She couldn't wait to meet up with the girls for lunch at the Berkeley Court Hotel.

She was bursting to tell them her good news about John's promotion, and Ben's new job at Temple Street. She'd once again be the envy of them all rather than the pity. It really didn't get much better than this.

Karen was waking up in Brian's apartment in Ballsbridge. It was located opposite St Vincent's Hospital and she could glimpse the dark sea from the bedroom window. You could almost see Sandymount. Suddenly it made her think of Ben. She didn't like to think of Ben. It made her almost queasy. When Ben popped into her head she tried desperately to get him out. It made her fearful and angry. She hated Ben for that. She hated him for making her distrust every man's compliment and kind gesture. It made her angry that every prospective partner she had met since him had to cope with her resultant paranoia and had to jump through emotional hoops to get close to her.

Brian had.

He wasn't much to look at; in fact he was downright plain.

He was chubby and comfortable and so sincere she had grown to love him, despite herself. He had an excellent job and plenty of money and she knew that he loved her so desperately she would never have to worry again. He was besotted with her. She knew she would never love Brian the way she had loved Ben but she'd had enough of that sort of love to last her a lifetime.

No, with Brian she would be comfortable and safe. It was what she wanted. The diamond engagement ring that he had given her, however, remained in the scarlet box by her bedside.

Brian understood she would not wear it until her wedding day. Their parents would have to be content with the photographs of their elopement to Barbados.

There was no way she would ever go through the preparations of a big splashy wedding again. Brian understood and readily agreed, even though he knew there would be hell to pay with the family back home in Longford.

Karen smiled. She was lucky to have him. All that happened in the past was just a bad memory. She looked out over the dark moody sea and wondered what Ben was up to. Then she banished him from her thoughts and rose swiftly.

Must get to the aerobics class soon if she was going to

look hot in her new bikini on her honeymoon. Honeymoon. She couldn't believe it was a word she'd ever use again. But there it was. Life was good again and she was going to make the most of it. She was happy and content and she wished none of that for Ben Murphy, none of it at all.

Chapter 29

Two months later

The Christmas lights twinkled brightly in Grafton Street as Trish and Ali dashed through the heavy showers to get to Switzer's. It was five pm and already dark and freezing but Ali was still enjoying the cold weather so much it quite irritated her good friend.

"Jeez, Ali!, You must be fed up with it by now – we're like two drowned rats," Trish scowled as she pushed her bedraggled sopping hair from her freezing face. The sudden heat of the department store after the cold air outside burnished both their faces bright pink.

Ali laughed at Trisha's exasperated expression. She looked truly miserable.

"Oh, sorry, Trish, I can't explain it. I'm just enjoying an Irish Christmas again so much. I'm just so . . ."

"Yeah," interrupted Trish. "*Happy*! So ye keep saying.

Well, to tell you the truth right now I could do with a bit of Aussie sunshine to warm me bones. I'm bloody freezing. C'mon, lets grab a coffee before we have to brave the elements and go home."

They bustled to the first floor with their myriad of packages. They had been Christmas shopping for Emma, Mick and half of Dublin, or so it seemed. Ali was looking forward to this Christmas so much. She had to pinch herself to believe how lucky she had been the past few months.

A visit to Carter Travel after Ali and Emma had returned home had Maisie instantly offer Ali her old job back – as she had originally promised eighteen months earlier. Trisha's mum had kindly offered to look after Emma while Ali was at work, and after work each day Ali would meet up with Trish and Mick at the Costellos' and they'd all pile into Mick's little van and head out to the bungalow in the Naul.

Ali intended to move on as soon as she got on her feet financially – and give Trish and Mick a chance to enjoy their house to themselves, but right now she was very happy to be part of a family again. Everything had worked out really well so far.

Even Simon had accepted her decision to return home and so far hadn't expressed any interest in having custody of Emma. Ali had waited two weeks after she had returned to Ireland and made a late-night phone call to Simon after several glasses of wine to bolster her courage.

Firstly he had ranted and raved and called her all the bitches under the sun but eventually calmed down, listened to her explanation and only slammed the phone down when she told him that they had no future.

A few days later she phoned him again and eventually got him to admit that he hadn't been faithful when they were together and he wasn't yet ready for commitment or fatherhood. Ali emphasised the fact that Simon would always be Emma's father and no one would replace him.

She even suggested that later on they could perhaps get together and he could visit Dublin if he liked, but even as she uttered the words she fervently wished he would never take her up on the invitation.

She still feared he would take Emma as a form of revenge.

Ali told Simon she didn't expect any kind of monetary support for Emma and this seemed to placate him. She called him every week to give him updates on how Emma was doing until one day a Telstra message told her the phone was disconnected. A quick phone call to Terri Church revealed that Simon had in fact moved in with Jodie – his rookie policewoman – a plan he had neglected to mention in any of the telephone calls.

Ali felt at last released. Simon seemed to have moved on and now so could she. She slept much easier these days without the prospect of Simon turning up on her doorstep any day demanding custody of Emma. Ali decided to let sleeping dogs lie.

So right now, having coffee with a cranky damp Trisha, she was very happy. In fact she was contented. She'd spent most of the Christmas bonus Maisie Carter had given her on presents for Emma. In fact, she and Trish were in danger of spoiling Emma with all the clothes and toys they lavished on her. They could barely sit down now with all their bags and baggage.

"Maybe we should get a taxi home," sighed Trish eyeing their load. "Me feet are frozen solid – though when they thaw I'm sure they'll be killing me. It's a pity Mick is working in Killester otherwise I'd ask him to collect us."

"Yes, let's grab a cab. It shouldn't be too expensive between us, although I hope your Mum doesn't see us. You know how she hates wasteful expense."

"Hmm," agreed Trish, "me Ma thinks the number 16 bus is a luxury! She'll be off with the story of walking from East Wall to Cabra to see her mum with six kids in tow every Saturday. God. Maybe we should get the bus after all. Isn't guilt a great thing!"

They downed their coffee and then hurried off through the evening throng up to George's St to catch the bus.

With all the traffic it was almost seven pm by the time they reached Trisha's mother's house to collect Emma.

Mrs Costello was holding a fractious Emma who appeared to be teething.

"She was grizzly all day long, poor mite. I gave her Calpol but she still seems to have a temperature. Sooner the better you get her home to bed. If she's no better by morning I'd take her to the doctor, if I were you."

"I think she's got a tooth coming up," said Ali. "She keeps pulling her ear too. And look at those rosy cheeks. Yes, the sooner we get you to bed, Missy, the better."

Mick arrived just then and they all piled into Mick's little van and headed for the Naul. The night was bitterly cold but Emma still felt hot, and grizzled all the way. As soon as they got home Ali tried to give the baby some more Calpol but Emma threw it back up straight away.

Two hours later Emma seemed to be even worse. She

was crying incessantly and her temperature had not gone down. If anything she seemed hotter than ever. Ali was getting extremely concerned. She began to feel a rising panic.

Even the normally cool-headed Mick was very concerned.

"I think we need to take her to the hospital, Ali," he ventured.

"Oh! Would you, Mick? Thanks so much. I'm very worried about her."

Ali fought back tears.

"Sure, I'll just get the van warmed up."

"I'll get her stuff ready," Trisha said, hopping up.

Just then Emma went stiff in Ali's arm and began to shake uncontrollably.

Her eyes were rolling back in her head – she seemed to be having a convulsion.

Ali screamed in alarm and Mick came running.

"Trish, grab a blanket. Hurry!" he yelled and Trish came flying down the hallway with a large car blanket and wrapped it around Emma and led Ali and the baby to the van. Emma had stopped convulsing at this point and was limp and listless in Ali's arms. All three of them were terrified, but as the van was only a two-seater, Trisha had to stay behind.

Mick drove like a madman into town. Emma seemed to rally a bit, but was still extremely poorly. Ali and Mick didn't say a word en route.

Mick sped through amber lights and prayed that the traffic in Phibsboro wouldn't be too heavy. Ali just prayed to God over and over just to make her baby well. Nothing else mattered. A million prayers raced through her mind as tears streamed down her face unabated.

What if Emma had meningitis? It could be fatal. She kissed the baby's hot forehead through her tears and was mightily relieved to finally arrive at Temple Street Children's Hospital. Mick parked the van right outside and Ali fled into the middle of Accident and Emergency and screamed for assistance.

Soon a flurry of nurses was at Ali's side and ushered her holding an unresponsive Emma to a waiting bed.

"A doctor will be along in a second," assured a kindly nurse, patting her arm, while another nurse stripped the now more alert Emma.

"Everything will be fine. Don't worry."

Ali nodded through misty tears, the huge lump in her throat preventing her from replying.

Just then the doctor blustered in.

Ali gasped and for just one split second everything stopped. The world stopped.

"Ben!" she said, after what seemed like forever. Emma whimpered. Suddenly Ali was jolted back to reality. She looked down at her sick baby.

"Please help her! She's had some kind of a fit . . ." Ali's voice ebbed away as immediately Ben expertly examined her baby, snapping out of his own surprise, back into paediatrician mode.

He checked Emma's ears and throat and her temperature.

"Yep, thought so," he murmured, as he noted on the chart. "She's got a severe inner ear infection and a high temperature. No wonder she is so miserable, poor little thing. We'll give her a suppository, which will kill the pain and take the temperature down rapidly. Make life a lot easier for her."

"But she had a fit!" Ali was unconvinced. "Her eyes were rolling and her body was shaking."

"Yes," Ben put his hand on her shoulder comfortingly, "that's the body's way of coping with extreme high temperature. In children, it sometimes results in a fit. We'll keep her in for observation overnight, but I'm sure that's what the problem is. It's OK, Ali. I'd be worried too if I were you. It's a scary thing to witness for the first time." He then called to the nurse who was passing.

"Nurse O'Malley, please get me a 12mg codeine suppository, stat."

At last he smiled at Ali, taking her in.

The nurse arrived back with the suppository. Ali looked away as it was being administered as little Emma whimpered weakly.

"Now," said the nurse cheerfully, "we'll get you a bed in the ward sorted as soon as possible. Meanwhile, we'll keep her stripped and apply cool damp compresses to try and cool the wee babe down a bit."

Ali slowly began to exhale as she eventually calmed down a bit.

Emma seemed a little easier already, stripped off down to her nappy with a cold compress on her forehead. Ali looked at Ben who was filling out Emma's medicine chart.

In any of the thousands of times she pictured them meeting again it never ever would have been like this, but right now she was so weak with shock and worry over Emma she just couldn't focus and her well nursed anger with Ben just fell away – it just simply didn't matter any more.

"Thanks," Ali said softly, watching his face.

"No problem," he replied, but appeared to blush. "I'll come up to the ward later when everything settles here and check on you both."

He looked at Emma and gently touched a wayward curl on her forehead.

"She's beautiful," he said quietly and smiled. Ali couldn't help but smile too.

The nurse just glanced at them both and caught something. Ben recovered his professionalism and stood up swiftly.

"Right so, Mrs O'Neill," the nurse began.

"Miss O'Neill," replied Ali emphatically as Ben moved away.

"Right. There's a bed available in the children's observation ward if you'll just follow me."

Ali scooped up Emma and followed Nurse O'Malley to the door unaware that Ben watched her from the doorway until she disappeared from view.

Ali got Emma settled into the narrow cot bed in the observation ward when Mick re-appeared.

"Oh, Mick! I'm sorry. I forgot all about you!"

"That's no problem," smiled Mick. "It takes ages to find parking around here anyway. How is she?"

"She's a little better, actually. Her temperature has started to drop. Apparently she had an inner ear infection. According to Ben that is!"

Mick blushed to his fingertips.

"Uh oh, I hoped he wouldn't be on duty. I'm sorry, Ali,

for not telling you that he worked here . . . guess it never came up." His brown eyes pleaded for mercy.

"Don't worry Mick. It's OK. I'm not going to bite your head off. It doesn't matter any more, does it?" She cuddled Emma closer and sniffed her baby's neck.

"No, don't suppose it does. Kids put it all into perspective, don't they? Can't wait to have an armful of me own."

"I know," said Ali, "and you'll make a great dad too," she added, meaning it. "Now, go home and tell Trisha everything's OK here and Emma is on the mend. I've decided to stay the night here. I'll call you in the morning."

"OK." said Mick standing up, suddenly weary.

"Thanks Mick. Thanks for everything."

Ali gave him a warm hug.

"No problem, and I'll see you, me lady, tomorrow." He gave Emma a huge kiss and was gone.

A few hours later Emma's temperature had returned to normal and she was sleeping soundly. Ali cuddled her close for ages until she put her down and then settled into the chair for what would be a long night. The lights were dimmed in the ward but several ill children cried out constantly and it was still a hive of activity. Ali had nothing but admiration for the people who cared for sick children. Ben had impressed her too with his caring demeanour, and the nurses were wonderful. Ali was lost in thought mulling over the events of the past few hours and wondering when you could ever stop worrying about your child when suddenly Ben was beside her.

"How is everything?" he asked softly, checking Emma's chart.

"She's much better now, thanks," Ali replied, suddenly conscious of what state she must be in, all dishevelled and eyes puffy from crying. "You were obviously right. I was just so worried when she had that fit."

Her voice trailed away and she bit her lip, fresh tears stung her eyes.

Suddenly, Ben pulled her to him and held her tightly. She smelled him again for the first time in years, that lemony citrus smell that she had missed so much. She had longed for him for such a long time and now he was here. She found herself instinctively putting her arms around him and sobbing into his white-coated shoulder.

"C'mon," he said at last. "I'll take you for a cup of coffee. The night staff are really good here. I'll just talk to Marie and make sure she takes good care of her for a few minutes." He checked with the night nurse and then took Ali down to the staff cafeteria for a cup of coffee.

Over the polystyrene cups they suddenly became a bit shy – it had been so long and so much had happened to each of them. Ali had forgotten how good he looked. The cornflower-blue eyes looked even bluer with the remains of his African tan and he had his hair cropped short, which really suited him. He looked older, but more handsome for the slight edge of world-weariness that had crept into his face. Her heart still skipped a beat whenever he looked at her. She hoped it wasn't obvious but she was still as smitten as she had been the first moment she saw him, all those years before.

He was now looking at her intently as she sipped her coffee and she found herself smiling, despite herself.

"I never would have imagined you ever treating my

child as a patient, Ben. It looks like all those years of studying paid off. You are a very good doctor. I am impressed. Thanks for fixing Emma."

"I never thought I would ever see you again," he said tightly, "and yet here you are. I have missed you so much. It's almost like a dream having you here in front of me."

Ali didn't reply – she wasn't sure what to say so she drank more coffee instead, which was truly awful.

"I'm sorry y'know. For everything." He looked at his coffee as he apologised. It was excruciating and Ali was too emotional to discuss their entire break-up right now, so she said instead, "I know and some day we'll talk about it, but not right now, OK?"

"OK." He seemed a little relieved.

Then his hand touched hers.

A bolt of electricity passed between them.

All the years just washed away and it was just Ben and Ali, just like they were sitting on the number three bus out to Sandymount, hands clasped together.

"So," he asked staring into her eyes. "How have you been?"

Ali smiled.

"Oh, where do I begin?" She rolled her eyes heavenwards. "Let me see, world trips, babies, silly mistakes – I've done the lot – and you, how have you been?"

"Similar. Silly mistakes, abandoned weddings, world trips, no babies though – not yet at least."

Ali laughed. She noticed Ben's lips looked so inviting she had to restrain herself from leaping over the table at him to devour them.

Ben laughed too. That loud hearty laugh that she

loved so much. It brought out the kid in him, that sixteen-year-old boy she had fallen in love with.

"So," he said looking down at her tiny hand held in his big one, "no big Aussie guy for me to beat up then?"

She knew that question would emerge sooner or later.

"No. It didn't work out. I thought you'd have known about that. I thought Mick kept you up-to-date."

"Well," he admitted, "he used to – but I would get so bloody-minded and we would disagree over you and everything else, so we decided to limit ourselves to safe macho conversations like football and the price of a pint of the black stuff. Anyway he's a lousy writer and I've only been back from Africa a few months. Mick's been very busy with the new house too. I haven't even seen it yet."

"Yes, you must! It's beautiful. I'm staying with them at the moment, a sort of endless house guest that never goes home," Ali enthused, then instantly regretted it. He'd think she was dying to get him over there.

"Emma is a beautiful baby, though I'm sure you know."

"Yes," Ali smiled. "She is, isn't she?"

"Can I see you?" he said out of nowhere, the blue eyes piercing her very soul. "I mean, is there any chance I could take you to dinner some time – even just as friends so we could talk about it all. I'd really like to do that. I know I behaved like a complete shit and I want to sort it all out."

Ali paused.

"Yes, OK, there is a chance, Ben. I would like that very much."

He grinned widely, relief spreading over his face. Then he suddenly looked at his watch.

"God, I have to do rounds. I should have been there ten minutes ago. I'll just take you back to the ward – then I'm afraid I'll have to rush off. If I don't get to see you later, in case it gets hectic – I'll call you, OK. I have Mick's number."

They walked slowly back to the children's ward in silence, their hands locked together. Then he bent down slowly and his lips brushed hers softly and she got to smell him once again. It was like coming home.

"Goodnight," Ben whispered and was gone in a flurry of white coat.

Ali clambered into the narrow cot bed beside a peaceful Emma and cuddled in.

"Oh, Emma," she whispered to her baby kissing her damp cheek, "this has been the worst day and the best day."

She lay there for ages listening to her baby breathe and marvelled at what had gone before. It was all like a dream. She felt on a high as she finally drifted off to sleep.

The next morning Emma was once again her bright and sunny self, gurgling happily and climbing all over Ali excitedly. Ali felt like such a fraud with her bouncing baby among all the sick children – although, it had been a different story the night before. It had all seemed surreal, including her time with Ben at the cafeteria. At seven am, the morning registrar, a sweet gentle Kuwaiti doctor, gave Emma her release. Ali telephoned Mick and Trisha with the good news and a mere hour and a half later, Ali and Mick were speeding towards Swords with an ebullient Emma.

"So you saw himself afterwards then?" Mick asked, as

the van raced through St Margaret's out past the back road to the airport.

Ali was watching an Aer Lingus jet lumbering up the runway and barely making it into the bright blue sky, for once not wishing that she were on it.

"Don't tell me, Mick O'Toole, that Ben Murphy has been on the phone to you already!"

Mick chuckled.

"The very same, and he phoned at six am no less. He started off by telling me he was phoning to let us know that Emma was fighting fit again but really he was bursting to tell me that himself and yourself had a good chat and were on the way to being friends again."

"And they say women are the great gossips? Honestly, Mick, you men leave us in the shade. I haven't even dreamed of telling Trisha yet, at least until me first cuppa tea has gone down . . . Is there any point in me telling her now, if Ben has got there already?"

Ali was smiling.

It looked like a beautiful day was dawning in Dublin, a bright Christmassy day, and Ali had just got the best Christmas present ever, her daughter was in her arms and Ben was back in her life. She really couldn't ask for more.

Chapter 30

Six months later

The day was spectacular. The June sky was a flawless blue. The forecast was for fine hot and sunny weather. It was Trisha's wedding day.

Ali pinched her.

"Ow!" said Trisha perplexed, "What was that for?"

"So you'll always remember this moment. This moment on your wedding day when we sat here in your bedroom, getting you ready. This fantastic day, the best day of your life."

"Ye big sap!" Trisha blustered, pleased and embarrassed. She hugged her friend.

"Now, come on. Let's get cracking. We don't want to be too late, or they'll all feck off to the pub!"

Trisha looked amazing, Ali thought. Almost ethereal in a stunning creation of cream silk dress with a pale cream-and-gold embroidered fitted bodice.

Her golden hair was simply twisted around baby cream roses and fell onto her bronzed shoulders. She looked breathtaking – but was the usual Trisha, wisecracking and joking all through the morning. Only Ali knew it covered up her nerves.

Emma looked divine in a matching ballerina style dress. And although Ali was unsure of her carrying out her flower-girl duties as a tottering seventeen-month-old, so far she was relishing her duties.

Ali was even sure she looked divine herself. In her simple pale-gold sheath and her own auburn curls twisted round with baby roses, she couldn't wait for Ben to see her.

"Oh, no! All the old bats off the road are in the hallway. They've come in for a drink, I'll have to go down and give them all a twirl. Ali, are ye nearly ready?"

"Yes, Trish, go on down. I want to fix Emma's hair and put on my lipstick. I'll follow you down in a moment."

As she checked herself in the mirror and Trish constantly called her, she admired her image and wondered over the news Ben had to tell her. She hoped he was going to propose. It would be just wonderful on this beautiful wedding day if he were going to ask her to be his bride. She'd get what she always craved. To live happily ever after like they did in the fairytales.

She knew it sounded silly, even crass, but that was what she wanted. After all her turmoil, her miserable childhood, she really wanted Ben to be the Prince and make her life a happy one. She never told anyone this because she knew life wasn't a fairytale, but Trish had managed to get herself one – surely Ali deserved the same happiness?

Trish yelled up one more time to tell her the cars had arrived and Ali knew she really had to go this time. Her heart gave a little jolt when she pictured Ben's face when he saw her come up the aisle. Hopefully it would make him want her so much he'd propose before the wedding meal!

She grinned at herself in the mirror and fled downstairs.

"Girls, girls, get into the car now." Mr Costello fussed as Ali and Emma clambered into the wedding car. He and Trish followed in an open-topped limousine and they set off towards Griffith Avenue to the church.

The tree-lined avenue was perfectly coifed in lush trees that glimpsed through the hot sunshine. It was a fairytale setting.

Mick was waiting anxiously at the top of the aisle, flanked by his brother John and Ben. They all looked smart in navy-and-grey evening suits with gold cravats. Ali looked up the aisle on the long church and saw it was packed with the two large families that were delighted to see these two soulmates pledge their love. Also present were Ali's three brothers, who were regarded by the Costellos as part of the family. Louis stood proud and tall – dressed in his full Navy uniform; along with his girlfriend Jill. Damien and Kevin were also there with their partners and she felt rather proud of them all. They had turned out all right, despite all their setbacks. Ali felt happy and sad too.

Nothing would ever be the same for her and Trish.

She felt a sense of loss, as Trish became the most important person in another's life. Even though Ali had known this moment would come for years, it still came as a bit of a shock.

Ben had only eyes for Ali. He spotted her at the end of the church peeking in. She looked stunning in that gold dress. His heart sank. She looked so beautiful; how could he ever tell her he was about to leave. She would probably never forgive him, but this opportunity he had been given to head his own medical team in Mozambique for another stint would be a brilliant challenge and would cement his career. He had already agreed to go but couldn't face telling Ali 'til after the wedding. He fervently hoped she would wait for him, but he was afraid of losing her. Maybe she would understand. He certainly hoped so . . .

Here Comes The Bride began and everyone looked around to see a stunning Trisha glide up the aisle on her father's arm followed by a beautiful Ali and a tottering Emma. Mick almost burst with pride as he saw his bride come towards him – soon they would be man and wife.

Simon sat nervously in Departures. He had never been overseas before but he just had to try and get Ali back. He had been so miserable without her and Emma the past eight months, especially since his relationship with Jodie had broken up. He realised what a fool he had been. He wasn't sure what reception he would get in Dublin but he had to try and find them. He had the name of that Travel Agent place that Terri had let slip. Carter Travel, yes that was it, and he'd go to Dublin and find Ali and beg her to take him back.

The last call came for his Qantas flight direct from Brisbane to London.

He made his way quickly though the departure gate clutching a large koala bear for Emma.

In his breast pocket nestled a glittering diamond ring he hoped Ali would accept.

He'd find her and tell her he loved her and couldn't live without her.

Soon it would all happen. Soon.

Chapter 31

It had been a really splendid day. The wedding was a complete success and there wasn't a dry eye in the house when Trisha and Mick took to the floor for their wedding dance. They were a handsome couple. Mick looked so dark, handsome and debonair in his morning suit, and Trisha so fair and looking beautiful in her cream tulle gown that swished as she turned around on the floor. They swirled around and kissed to INXS's *Never tear us apart*.

All too soon it was time for them to leave for their honeymoon. Trish now looked amazing in a short cream suit that she had bought in the new Design Centre on Stephen's Green and Ali had wept into Trisha's hair and held onto her for the longest time before she left. It was the end of an era and she felt maudlin. It was the end of Trisha's old life and the start of a new one. A life where Mick would be her number one partner instead of Ali.

It was a bitter-sweet time for Ali. She was so happy for

Trisha, but sad that their terrible twosome days were over, and were a thing of the past.

Still, Ali had Ben back in her life now. He had been wonderful all day, romantic and attentive. She couldn't wait for him to propose to her. It would have to be soon, or so she fervently hoped. He had said he had something important to discuss and had booked them an overnight room at the hotel, so they could have some time alone.

Emma, who was exhausted, was taken home by a teary-eyed Mrs Costello so Ali could have Ben all to herself. She was giddy with anticipation and flew up to the room to change clothes. After a day of being all pinned up and ladylike, she desperately needed to let her hair down and relax. She changed into a cool long silk dress in sapphire blue, which really suited her colouring. She shook her hair free into wayward curls and sprayed herself with Miss Dior and then examined herself in the mirror.

Not bad, she grinned. Then she dimmed the lights and drew back the large heavy drapes to open a window. The lights of Howth sparkled. It was a lovely view. She hoped later that she and Ben would watch it together over champagne. She felt butterflies in her stomach at the thought. "Calm down, O'Neill," she berated herself. "Don't lose your nerve now!"

She headed back downstairs to the reception room. To Ben and her future. Oliver, Ben's old flatmate, was sitting on a couch in the lobby earnestly listening as one of Trisha's rather inebriated uncles launched into a long diatribe. He caught Ali's eye as she passed and winked, an almost imperceptible smile crossing his face.

That was typical of Oliver, Ali mused. He would

endure any bore rather than tell them to go away. He was such a nice guy.

That was one of the nice things about being back in Ben's life. She had caught up with the old crowd: Oliver, Joey and Derek. They had all blossomed into earnest responsible grown-ups, with decent jobs and even a couple of fiancées. All except Oliver, who apparently was too busy to meet Miss Right. Derek was still a loveable oaf, all the years of pizza had caught up with him and he was rotund and bearded but otherwise unchanged. He had met and fallen in love with Melanie, a Galway hippy, who loved him deeply and somehow found him deep and meaningful. Joey, true to form, had acquired a glamorous blonde from Artane whose ambition was only exceeded by her jewellery and they were due to be married in a few months' time.

Ali had been surprised that Oliver was still single. Of them all, he was without doubt the sweetest, and most attractive.

But he had a seriousness and intensity that put off some people.

Those serious green eyes and square jaw that often set and made him look a bit moody didn't help. But Ali knew he was a kind and sincere guy who ran deep. When they had met up again he had kissed Ali shyly and quipped, "He still doesn't deserve you." Oliver had been there when Ben had broken her heart and he obviously hadn't forgotten it either. That warmed Ali to him. She felt he was a kindred spirit.

Now, she smiled brightly at him and rejoined the wedding reception.

She found Ben sitting quietly in a corner nursing a pint of Guinness while most of the wedding guests were up dancing to Bruce Springsteen's *Dancing in the Dark*.

"Penny for your thoughts?" Ali enquired as she sat down.

Ben smiled a little and took her hand.

"Ali . . ." he began but was drowned out by Bruce belting out his song. "Sorry," he almost roared. "Can we go somewhere a bit quieter, maybe back to the room?"

Ali was a bit disappointed. She felt good in her new outfit, and just wanted to have some fun and dance a little before they left. But Ben seemed so serious she thought better of arguing the point and just nodded in agreement.

"Ali, I have something to tell you and if I don't do it now, I might just lose my nerve," Ben blurted out as they reached the room.

Ali was taken aback. She noticed he had said 'tell' and not 'ask'.

She didn't like the nervous tone of voice or his agitated manner. It didn't seem like it was going to be a proposal. She tried to focus on the glittering lights of Howth Hill and waited.

Ben cleared his throat. "Ali, firstly I want you to know that I love you. The past six months since you've been back in my life have been wonderful. Really. But . . ."

"There it is," interrupted Ali, laughing hollowly, "that big 'But' word."

She was incredulous. He was breaking up with her or something. Whatever it was, this was not a proposal and she didn't want to hear it.

"Please, Ali," Ben searched her eyes for understanding, "let me finish! This is difficult enough."

257

"OK," she replied quietly, "go on."

"I'm going back to Africa. This time I'm leading the team and it is something I need to do. It should be only six months, but it might be for a year. It will make such a difference to my career when I get back. I'm hoping that you'll wait for me."

Ali was stunned. He was going off again! First he had left Karen and now he was leaving her. Why hadn't he been straight all along? Obviously, he had known for quite a while. All those promises about never letting her out of his sight again, now here he was talking about moving out of her life for what could be a year. She was devastated. How could she have got it so wrong?

She remained silent, a huge lump formed in her throat and she fought back tears while staring at the blinking lights of Dublin.

"Please say something, Ali." Ben tried to take her hand.

She noticed absently that his cravat had come undone and his shirt revealed a tiny expanse of tanned hairy chest. She still found him irresistible and felt like clinging to that chest and begging him to stay.

"Don't!" she said fiercely, pulling away. She couldn't tell him that she had been expecting him to ask her to be his wife. Not now. She felt like a complete fool.

"I can't believe you are going away, Ben, after all we have been through – I'm sorry, I just can't. You're just leaving me."

"Ali, I am not leaving you," Ben protested, his cornflower blue eyes pleading. "I hoped you would support me in this."

"I'm sorry, but I can't. I just can't," Ali cried and fled the room. She needed to put some distance between them and fled downstairs, through reception and blindly ran outside into the car park where she dissolved into angry tears. Suddenly Oliver was beside her.

"Ali!" he exclaimed gripping her by the shoulders. "Are you all right?"

"No, Oliver, I am far from all right! Did you know Ben was going back to Africa? I am such an idiot. I thought when he said he'd something to say to me, that he was about to propose. What kind of an idiot gets it so wrong? He's going off for a year and we just . . ." She could find no more words and Oliver put his strong arms around her while she cried as if her heart would break.

"He's the bloody idiot!" Oliver blazed, his green eyes flinty with anger. "I told you before, Ali. Ben is not good enough for you. He's basically selfish. He only considers Ben in the long run. I'm sorry to say this but you were better off without him. He didn't deserve a second chance."

Suddenly Ben was there, pulling Oliver off Ali.

"Get away from her!" he roared to Oliver. "What the hell do you think you're playing at?"

"Some could ask you the same thing," Oliver retorted hotly.

"Ali," Ben was now trying to grab Ali himself. "Ali, please come back inside. We can't just leave it like this."

"I don't think I have anything more to say," Ali replied sadly, pulling her arm free. "Oliver, would you take me home?"

"Sure," replied Oliver, glaring at Ben as he took Ali's elbow and ushered her away.

Soon they were speeding down the coast road in Oliver's sleek BMW.

Ali was too stripped of any emotion to talk, so Oliver put on a *Sade* tape and they sped in silence towards Trisha's house in Swords.

Within an hour Ali was roaming around the large bungalow alone. With Emma staying at the Costellos' for the night she had no one.

Oliver had offered to stay but she felt far beyond conversation.

She ran herself a hot bath and sank deep into the steaming water and tried to make sense of the whole thing. One thing was for sure. From now on Ali would depend on herself and no one else. If she was to find happiness, it had to come from within. She resolved to find herself a new dream, and one that didn't have a Prince Charming to stuff it all up. Things were going to have to change.

Chapter 32

Trisha and Mick were lounging across sunbeds on the terrace of their honeymoon suite at the Sol Paradiso in Lanzarote. The hotel was truly luxurious; Mick had spared no expense. They had spent the first two days lazing around their suite, which had a large bedroom complete with a huge king-size bed that was raised up on a dais.

The bedroom had French doors leading onto a fabulous sun terrace, which overlooked the flawless blue sea. Trisha felt like she was in heaven. Thick fluffy towelling robes were provided and the maid even turned down their bedclothes at night. Trisha had also sampled the beauty salon and enjoyed being pampered with a soothing massage that left her feeling like she was walking on air. At night they had dinner served in their room and watched the twinkling lights of Puerto del Carmen while they quaffed champagne and made slow sensual love afterwards. It was bliss. Trisha had never been happier.

"Wonder what they're up to in Dublin now?" Trisha

mused as she lay on her sunlounger. It was the first time she had thought of home.

"Probably up to their arses in rain," Mick laughed, turning over.

"No, silly. I was really wondering if Ali had got her proposal from Ben."

"You're not serious are you?" retorted Mick, suddenly all ears.

"Well, she seems to think that's what he wants to discuss with her. He said it was very important, and was going to talk to her after our wedding."

Mick sighed deeply. "I hope she's not disappointed, love. Ben was telling me recently he had an offer to go back to Africa for another stint."

"Surely not!" said Trisha, alarmed at the thought. "Was he serious?"

"Dunno. But you know Ben. He's a lovely guy but he's so ambitious. I have a feeling his career will always take precedence."

"Hmmm," Trisha was now concerned. "I hope he doesn't let her down. She's been so happy lately. I think she had plans of moving in together and being a proper family, her, Ben and Emma."

"He does love Emma, though," Mick reflected. "That's never going to be a problem."

"Yeah, I'd miss them if they go," Trisha said, slapping on some more sunscreen. It was really hot today.

"Sure, won't we be havin' one of our own soon," Mick ventured. Now was his opportunity to discuss what had been on his mind for some time. He wanted kids straight away and there was no time like the present.

"Do you really mean that, straightaway I mean. Can we afford to live on one wage?" Trisha was delighted. She just couldn't wait to grow fat and pregnant and finally quit her much-hated job at Roche's.

"Yeah, why not?" replied Mick. "I'm sure we can. Anyway, if they were anything like little Emma I'd have ten of them –"

"Hold your horses there, sunshine. I'm the one doing the having, so let's have one first and see how it goes, OK."

"Right!" said Mick hopping up of his bed to give Trisha a huge kiss.

"Might as well get some practice in," he whispered as he lifted Trish up off the sunlounger in one swift motion and carried her into the bedroom.

Trisha melted into his arms and all thoughts of Dublin and Ali were soon banished from her mind as she revelled in the passion of her suddenly ardent new husband.

Meanwhile in Dublin, it was raining. It had been raining for an entire day, not helping Ali's dismal mood. She looked out the window dejectedly in Carter Travel and sighed loudly.

"Jeez, Ali, will ye cheer up for God's sake? Ye'd curdle milk with that face!" Maisie Carter exclaimed. Ali had sighed about once every ten seconds since Maisie had arrived to help out with the month-end accounts and Maisie was convinced it was putting off the customers.

"Sorry," sighed Ali, yet again. "I know I'm a real misery guts. But I just can't help it. And don't tell me he's not worth it, 'cos I already know that. I just miss Trisha so much. I feel a bit low. I need something exciting to happen to get me out of this mood."

"Well, go make us both a nice coffee, and I'll tally the month-end figures, OK." Maisie was solicitous. She needed Ali at her best right now.

"Would you?" Ali was delighted; her head was in no mood for figures today. She went into the tiny kitchen at the back to make them a brew.

Just then Maisie spotted a very handsome man enter the shop. He approached Jennifer, the new receptionist. Jennifer pointed towards Maisie, and the Mel Gibson lookalike strode towards her. Maisie fleetingly thought about how good he would look without all that raingear before regaining her composure.

"Yes, can I help you?" she said in her sweetest tone.

"Certainly hope so," he drawled in an unmistakeable Australian twang. "I'm looking for an Ali O'Neill. She used to work here."

"And you are?" Maisie asked, already guessing the answer.

"Simon," the handsome Aussie answered somewhat guardedly.

"Hold on a second. I'll be right back." Maisie blushed as she rose abruptly from her chair. She went into the tiny kitchen where she found Ali, stuffing herself with chocolate biscuits.

"You did say you wanted something exciting to happen, Ali. Well, it's standing just outside and looks divine. It also answers to the name of Simon."

Ali almost choked on her biscuit. "What?" she screeched.

"Yep," Maisie smiled. "In the flesh no less. What shall I tell him?"

Ali's mind raced. This was all too much: she wasn't sure if she wanted to see him or not, but she did extend an invitation and he was Emma's father.

"I'll be out in a minute," she said at last and checked her pasty complexion in the mirror, unsure why, but for some reason she wanted to look good.

There he was. All six foot three of him, looking tanned and incredibly handsome but somewhat incongruous in arctic style raingear. Ali's heart did a little somersault. He was still extremely attractive, but she was very wary of him. She knew, after all, his appalling track record.

"Ali," he said awkwardly, leaning over for a kiss but seeming to change his mind. "I'm glad I found you. It was a long shot that you still worked here." He smiled, exposing those white even teeth.

"What are you doing here?" she asked as evenly as possible, hoping she didn't sound as alarmed as she felt.

"Look," Simon said quietly, "can we go somewhere to talk. There's a lot I need to say."

Ali glanced at Maisie who nodded profusely. "Go on," she said, grinning. "I'm sure the number-crunching can wait."

"Thanks, Maisie." Ali gave her a frazzled look and grabbed her coat.

She took him quickly to Mary Rose's at the Powerscourt Townhouse Centre, where they sold cappuccino. Over the frothy coffees they were suddenly both shy and exchanged pleasantries about the weather and Simon's plane trip before they dared discuss more serious matters, like Emma.

Ali was first to broach the subject.

"Are you here to see Emma?" she asked directly. Her

heart was thumping. She fervently hoped it was just a visit, and he wasn't going to inform her he was fighting for custody.

"Emma, yes of course, I can't wait to see her, but I'm also here to see you."

Ali blanched visibly.

"Ali," he took her small pale hand in his large brown one, "I have not been able to keep you out of my mind the past few months. I was such a pig to you. And I am so sorry for the way I treated you. I just wasn't ready for all that commitment at the time."

"And now you are?" Ali interrupted, acidly.

"Yes, now I am. I know you might not believe me but I've done a lot of growing up recently. I guess you had to leave me before I realised what I had. Both you and Emma. I miss the two of you so much. I know I didn't treat you right."

"You can say that again," Ali hissed, bad memories flooding back.

"I know," Simon insisted. "I have a lot of making up to do. But I'd like you to give me another chance. I really believe you and me, and Emma, we could be a family – a real family. Please, just wait a minute . . . I flew all this way because I just had to do this in person." He fished beneath his multitude of jackets and took out a small black velvet box. "I love you, Alison," he announced, opening the box. A solitaire diamond glistened brightly at her. "Will you marry me?"

Ali was stunned and completely lost for words.

Simon closed the box.

"I know this it a bit of a shock. Just please don't say no yet, until at least you have given it some thought."

Ali looked at his handsome face. He looked so sincere and earnest. She would have dearly loved this offer, if he had made it a year ago, but now, so much had happened between them, much of it bad, she just couldn't consider it. But she knew she would have to tread carefully. As Simon was Emma's father and could make things difficult for her with child custody, she would have to be conciliatory.

"I'll think about it." she lied.

"Good." He smiled at last, and seemed to visibly relax.

"Now, I really must get back," she said lightly.

"Yes, sorry."

They rose to leave. The rain had stopped and a glimpse of sun battered its way through the black ominous clouds.

"At last!" exclaimed Simon. "I've only been here a day or so, but that's the first time I've seen the sun since I left Australia."

"What's seldom is wonderful," laughed Ali, despite herself. "You don't come to Ireland for the weather."

They walked slowly back to Carter Travel. Ali found out that he was staying at the Mont Clare Hotel and she told him she would telephone him later on to arrange a visit with Emma. She didn't want him out in Swords, in case things became complicated. It would be better to meet him on neutral territory for the moment. She would have to ask Maisie for some time off to take Emma to see him, as she wouldn't consider the concept of unsupervised access.

She had taken Emma from him. How did she know he wasn't here to do the same? It felt awful to be so distrustful, but she been burnt too many times. In some ways it was better that Trish wasn't here. She would hit the roof knowing Simon was back. Ali would have a bit of time to sort the whole thing out and get the situation settled before Trisha and Mick returned. And this morning she had thought her life was complicated! It had reached an all-time high in a roller-coaster of emotions this afternoon.

She said goodbye to Simon and watched him stride away purposely. He always strode, like a man on a mission. She knew this mission would not be successful for him, but she would have to find a diplomatic way of letting him down.

She went back into Carter Travel to be quizzed by an inquisitive Maisie who was enthralled by any kind of gossip.

"Sit down there immediately, Ali," she gushed. "Now, Jennifer, hold all our calls. I want to hear every gory detail."

Ali regaled the whole story to Maisie, who oohed and ahhed at every turn.

"How romantic!" she said when Ali had finished. "He is such a dish, Ali. How could you resist?"

Ali hadn't told Maisie the whole story about Simon, but she did now, leaving nothing out. And combined with her recent experience with Ben, men didn't seem all that trustworthy to Ali.

"Do be careful, Ali," Maisie advised. "Keep the relationship cordial, at all costs. It will be better for you, but particularly Emma in the long run. You can say you are involved with Ben and have moved on. He doesn't need to know about the latest glitch in your relationship."

Ali winced. Is that how people saw it? Another glitch in a long line of glitches? She really wondered at her taste in men. Did she attract men who would hurt her in one way or another? Was there something missing in her, deep down that kept her failing at relationships? Trish seemed to have no problems, but Ali, well, it was one long problem after another. She found it even harder to concentrate for the rest of the day, so promised Maisie she would be fresh and determined tomorrow to finish the month-end accounts so she could take the rest of the week off. She would spend some time with Simon and Emma, and she would break it to him gently that she would not accept his proposal.

On the bus home to Drumcondra to collect Emma, Ali conjured up little scenarios of how she could hurt Ben by telling him Simon was back in her life and wanted to marry her. It would force his hand – make him choose between her and a step up the career ladder.

She would love to see the look on Ben's face if he knew there was a rival for her affections. The competitor in him would emerge. She remembered his angry face when he had seen her in Oliver's arms.

Poor Oliver. She should ring him and apologise. She had been almost rude to the poor guy after he had left the entire wedding to drive her home, and she hadn't even offered him a coffee. She resolved to telephone him later and explain. He had been a real friend when she needed one.

She sorely missed Trisha right now, but this one she would have to sort on her own. It was about time she stood up on her own two feet anyhow. Now was as good a time as any. The new Ali would be an independent woman, who would lean on no one, especially men.

Chapter 33

Ben dialled Ali's number again. This was his sixth attempt and there was no reply. He was sure she was at home; she never went out after work during the week and left Emma, especially now that Mick and Trish were away. He considered driving over there. What if she wasn't there, after he had travelled all that distance? Then he suddenly thought of Oliver.

Maybe Ali was with him. Ben knew Oliver well enough to know when he was smitten, and he was definitely smitten with Ali. Ben wondered why he hadn't noticed it before, but then again Oliver had always been on Ali's side. He remembered how angry Oliver had been when Ben had slept with Karen. God, had he carried a torch for her all this time? Ben had often wondered how Oliver met girls all the time but none of them lasted more than a few weeks. But Oliver had always been so deep and serious. Ben hadn't liked to ask. Furiously, he now dialled Oliver's number.

"Hello," Oliver sounded his usual serious self.

"Hi, Oliver," Ben said sheepishly. "Look mate, I'm sorry about the other night, getting angry with you, I mean. I was just so upset. Ali and I had a big fight and you, well let's say – you were just in the wrong place at the wrong time. No hard feelings, OK?"

"It's not me you should be apologising to," said Oliver tersely. "It's Ali."

"Well, that's just it, Oliver. I can't get her at home. There's no one answering the phone. And I don't think she'd appreciate me trying to discuss it in her workplace, do you?"

Ben didn't know why, but he felt a little bit annoyed.

"Look, Ben. It's none of my business. You are very good at wrecking your relationships all on your own, so just leave me out of it, OK!" Oliver then slammed down the phone, thinking to himself, the nerve of that guy. He should have been down on one knee the following day at Ali's door bedecked in flowers and abject apology. It was a prime example of how arrogant Ben was that he felt he could just drop a bombshell on his girlfriend, almost assault his best friend, and then think a few apologetic words would smooth everything over.

Oliver knew if he were lucky enough to have Ali, he would never let her go. But that wasn't ever likely to happen because Ali could see no further than Ben, never could. Still, maybe she needed a friend? Oliver could be there for her at least. He resolved to call her up in work the following day and suggest lunch. He hoped in one sense she wouldn't forgive Ben. He deserved a good shock to shake him up a bit, but he doubted it.

Ali loved Ben. She always had. There was no point in

getting any hopes up. She would never get to know he had loved her for years.

It would always go unnoticed. He'd never told anyone about it and he was sure he never would. That's just the way it was. He went back to his glass of Merlot and ready-made meal for one. But somehow he had lost his appetite. Stuff you, Ben, he thought, pushing his plate away angrily. You really are a selfish bastard. And I for one am going to tell you that in no uncertain terms the next time I see you. You can be sure of that!

Ali was out to dinner with Simon. She'd booked dinner for three at Captain America's. Emma fired her French fries around and squirted her sippy cup of juice all over her dinner but Ali was thankful she was being such a madam. It gave both her and Simon a focus, to distract them from the unanswered proposal. Ali knew she couldn't stall forever, but right now they were both enjoying their daughter so much, they were happy. Simon guffawed at every little turn Emma put on. He found her hilarious.

Ali couldn't help noticing how much alike they were – Simon and Emma – they were clones of each other. The same bright blue eyes, jet-black hair and sallow skin. Her heart wrenched when she saw that, because she knew deep down there was no future for them as a family. And they all would lose out as a result of that, but mainly Emma and Simon were the losers. How would it ever work? With Simon from another hemisphere it was never going to be easy.

She wondered what he expected if she had accepted his proposal. Did he think she would just up sticks and move back to Brisbane?

Or was he planning a move to Ireland? She couldn't imagine an Aussie police officer mingling with the more sedate Garda Siochana. She hadn't raised any of these issues in case it gave him some false hope that she was even considering his offer, but despite everything she didn't want to hurt him. He clearly seemed enamoured with Emma now and she knew he would find it hard to say goodbye, so she just simmered inwardly and carried on playing happy families for the moment.

She'd wait for Simon to raise the subject. As it turned out she didn't have to wait long. While waiting for dessert, he pounced.

"Isn't it great? Us all being together I mean?"

"Hmm." Ali was noncommittal. She could not help thinking that he never thought it was so great all those nights he had left Ali and their newborn daughter to get drunk with his mates or spend time in Jodie's bed.

"It could be like this all the time, y'know," he continued. "You, me and little Emma. Have you thought any more about my proposal?"

"I've thought about little else," Ali admitted. "But, I am sorry Simon, the answer will have to be no because I am involved with someone else. Actually, it's Ben."

"I see," said Simon in measured tones. "Your ex. I thought he went off and married some other sheila."

"Well, it got cancelled. The wedding, I mean. He never got married."

Simon looked crestfallen.

"I suppose I don't need to ask if it's serious, 'cos it obviously is." He looked hopefully at her.

"Yes," she said as nicely as possible, "it is. But Simon,

there are so many issues with us. Take location for instance. It's so difficult. Either you or I would always be far from home. I doubt if I could live in Australia, much as I love it, without my family and friends. And there is the issue of trust. I still feel hurt about what you did with Jodie on me. You didn't just cheat on me that time. You cheated on our daughter. You robbed me of the trust I had in you. It destroyed us, literally. I just don't think we could ever put it back together again, much as I would like to, especially for Emma. She is going to need her dad."

"I know!" he said miserably, staring down at his cheesecake. "I know I'm a bloody idiot. I just feel I should be a father for her. I thought if we gave it our best shot at one more try it could work."

"You love her a lot, don't you?" Ali replied.

Despite everything, she still felt a shred of affection for him. She supposed she always would.

"Yes," he said sadly, his eyes filling up. "How could you not love her? My mum really misses her too."

"And what was your plan?" Ali enquired, curiosity finally getting the better of her, "If I had accepted your proposal, I mean."

"Well, I thought we'd go back to Brisbane. I have bought a block of land not too far from my parents and I'd hoped we'd build a house. You could go to work and Mum would just love to look after Emma."

He obviously had it all worked out. She would still be the one giving everything up. He wasn't moving halfway across the world for her but she was expected to do it for him. But she swallowed her indignation. There was little point in making him suffer any more.

Deep down she breathed a huge sigh of relief. She had made the right choice and he seemed to take it well. At least he finally took responsibility for the whole sorry debacle.

"It's just that she'll never really get to know me. That's what hurts the most," He said clasping Emma's tiny hand into his. Emma rewarded him with a lump of ice cream over his face.

"That's not true!" insisted Ali. "I work in a travel shop, remember. I can get flights Down Under for peanuts. I'll make it my business that we will get to see you once a year. Either we'll go to you or we can bring you here. And in the meantime you can call, or send videos and Emma and I will do the same. I can assure you, there will only be one dad for Emma and that will be you."

"Do you mean that?" Simon asked, apparently relieved. "I would really appreciate being part of her life, Ali. That's all I want really. And you, of course," he added. "But I kinda knew I'd blown that chance before I got here."

"It's OK." smiled Ali, relief flooding though her. He did appear to have changed, after all, she mused. "It's all in the past. Sure, didn't we get a beautiful child from what we had. That's all that matters now. We can still be good parents for her. It's all for the best that we can get on and still remain friends."

"Yeah," he smiled, grabbing her hand. "We can. Thanks, Ali. I mean it. Now, are you going to fiddle with that cheesecake forever or am I going to have to finish it for you?"

Ali laughed and passed the dessert over. He really was

a funny one, she thought, but was totally glad it had gone so well and he had accepted that she had moved on. The awkward moment had passed, everything was out in the open and they had survived. Emma was hers, for keeps. For the first time since Trisha's wedding her heart was lifted and she finally felt everything was going to be OK, after all. Ben she could sort out later.

The following day Ben appeared at Carter Travel. It was twenty past nine and Maisie and Ali had barely swallowed their first cup of coffee for the day when he appeared in the doorway.

"What's that perfume you wear, Ali?" Maisie quipped, quick as a flash when Ben strode in. "I could sure as hell use some of it. Talk about men beating a path to your door!" She laughed as she quickly disappeared into the back office.

"What did she mean?" Ben enquired a mite suspiciously.

"You're not the first visitor I've had this week, that's all," replied Ali unsmilingly. "Now, what is it you want, Ben? Would you like me to book you a flight to Africa perhaps?"

"Ali, please don't be like that. We really have to talk. Perhaps I didn't make myself very clear last week. Can I take you out for coffee, or maybe we could have some lunch later? I've been trying to get you at home all week, but you weren't there. Please, I am miserable without you."

Ali looked directly into the cornflower-blue eyes that were pleading their best. He looked good, dammit. He always looked so good. But right now she was very angry with him.

"Number one, I don't think there is anything to discuss. Two, I've just had coffee, and I plan a working lunch today, and let's see: oh, number three – yes I was out all week. I have been spending time with Emma's father who flew in from Brisbane a few days ago and proposed to me."

Ben was open-mouthed with shock.

"Simon?" he almost screeched.

"Yes," replied Ali casually, totally enjoying Ben's discomfort. "Funny thing that, someone actually wants to marry me."

"You're not seriously considering it?" Ben was incandescent with rage by now.

"And why not?" Ali asked innocently. "I am after all, a free agent – as of last Saturday."

"So that's it, is it?" He was turning a really nice shade of deep crimson by now. His blue eyes blazed.

"I wasn't the one who was opting out, Ben." She hissed back venomously. "You were. So if it's every woman for herself, well I have to consider my future and that of my daughter."

"Ali." Ben tried to calm down. He could see he was getting nowhere and the situation looked increasingly dangerous. "Please don't go accepting Simon's proposal to get revenge on me. We can sort it out, if you just give me a chance to explain."

"Don't flatter yourself, Ben," Ali replied acidly. "Now, please leave. I have work to do too. It may not be the earth-shattering career yours is, but it's important to me nonetheless."

She busily played at her keyboard until she heard the door slam and he was gone.

Maisie reappeared.

"Remind me never to get on the bad side of you," she murmured darkly while proffering another coffee and two chocolate biscuits

"You heard that?" Ali blushed.

"Every knife-wielding word," Maisie intoned, plonking her ample frame down heavily.

"Too much?" Ali was regretting it a little bit already.

"Well, let's just say, if Ben wasn't worried before, he certainly will be now. Can I ask you something, Ali, Do you want him back?"

"I don't know, Maisie," Ali replied dejectedly looking out of the window and down the street where Ben had gone. "Right now, I honestly don't know. If you had asked me that question three weeks ago, or even a week ago I would have always seen myself and Ben together forever – but now I don't know. I just can't accept the fact that he doesn't seem to love me as much as I love him. I would marry him tomorrow, Maisie, but Ben, well he doesn't seem to feel the same way. And I'm not prepared to get myself hurt any more."

"And who can blame you?" Maisie rubbed Ali's shoulder in a motherly way. "Just be very sure that you know what you want and what you don't want before you make your decision. Anyhow, it wouldn't hurt to hear his side of the story, would it?"

"Suppose not," Ali sniffed, sipping her coffee. "Next time he calls, if he calls after today, I'll give him a chance."

Ben roamed around Grafton Street in a stupor. He couldn't believe his ears. Ali's ex was back in town and he had proposed to her. And she was considering marrying that idiot! Ben was stunned by Ali's horrible attitude to him. Anyone would think he had done something awful to her. All he had done was take another job in Africa to further his career and earn better money for the future – their future together.

He then stopped himself dead in his tracks. He loved Ali, but could he seriously see himself marrying her? He knew his mother would absolutely hate the idea, and she would never come round, but what did he feel himself deep inside? It wasn't a question he had ever asked himself. The whole idea of marriage was anathema to him since the whole Karen debacle, and he supposed he was a bit commitment-phobic.

Maybe Ali had a point.

That Aussie guy seemed to find it easy enough to propose. Ben couldn't do it even when he felt threatened with losing Ali. He knew he would have to sort out his own feelings and attitudes to marriage before he approached Ali again. She deeply wanted a commitment from him, he realised that now. And he had to be sure he wanted the whole kit and caboodle too, before he'd call her again. Maybe she was right. Perhaps Africa was a kind of escape.

All these thoughts milled around his head as he walked towards Temple Street and his next twelve-hour shift. At least in half an hour he could immerse himself in the problems and injuries of others and forget his own miniscule ones. For when he walked through that hospital door he could at least remember how fortunate and lucky he was and he could forget himself for a while. Ben

Murphy was becoming a boring subject. He was well and truly sick of himself.

The honeymoon was almost over. Trisha packed their suitcases on their last night and they dressed up in their going-away outfits for their last night in Puerto del Carmen. Mick had booked a famous seafood restaurant overlooking the sea and they intended to savour every last moment of their last sunset before flying back to dark old dirty Dublin and the reality of everyday life.

"I could get used to this life," Trisha said aloud to herself while slathering on copious amounts of after-sun oil onto her sun-soaked skin.

Always sallow, her skin had turned into a deep golden colour while her hair was a glistening pale blonde. She looked fabulous. Pulling on her cream suit, she felt that it looked so much better than two weeks ago, although it was a fair bit tighter than before. Too much of this good life makes you fat too; she then remonstrated with herself. Must get back on that diet first thing Monday. Unless, well, her period was almost a week late, she hadn't told Mick – there wasn't any point until there was something to tell. She had stopped taking the Pill three months ago now.

Perhaps she was pregnant. She almost hugged herself with glee. Mick would be the happiest man in Ireland if that were the case. She was also a bit afraid to get excited because at the back of her mind lay that awful memory of when she had miscarried a few years ago. She had never told a soul, though she often felt like spilling the beans to Ali or Mick. But she just couldn't bring herself to say the words. She felt they might judge her, or be angry that she hadn't confided in them at the time. So she simply kept it to herself. It lay there at the back of her mind, mostly hidden.

It was so important to Mick that they have children – Trisha fervently hoped she would not have a problem. All of her sisters were very fertile, almost too much so, so she didn't fret too much. Still, Trisha couldn't wait to fall pregnant and see Mick's face when she told him the good news.

Now she patted her rounded tummy and slicked on some hot pink lipstick before joining Mick who had gone to reception to book a cab.

"You look divine," he breathed while kissing her hungrily on the lips in the middle of reception, which was thronging with people.

"Oh Mick, behave!" Trisha laughed prising herself free, half pleased, half embarrassed.

"It's all legal and above board to kiss my beautiful wife in public, eh José?" he winked conspiratorially at the duty manager.

"Si, Senor Mick," agreed José, admiring the view.

"The taxi's here," Trisha exclaimed, thankful to escape the extra attention. Within minutes they were at Alberto's, and were whisked in by the maître d' to the pre-booked terrace table overlooking the entire bay. The sun was dropping over the horizon, casting glittering rays on the sea. The sky was a fabulous bright orange. Mick and Trisha were stunned into silence by the magnificent view. A soft breeze blew as the glasses of other diners clinked over the romantic candlelight.Trish had never been happier. She wished to freeze this moment and make it last forever.

Mick ordered a bottle of Moët et Chandon champagne to celebrate their last night and they ordered garlic-fried squid for starters followed by lobster thermidor for their main course. After the sun went down and the breeze became cooler the waiters came out to the terrace and lit the four large braziers, which soon burnt orange and added more than heat to the ambience.

But by the time dessert arrived Trisha was in the grip of a severe abdominal cramp. She knew although she had eaten too much that it wasn't just sharp indigestion. It was that unmistakeable ache that warned of her period. She went to the toilet as soon as she could and saw the familiar crimson stain and was crushed. Tears pricked her eyes as she made a makeshift pad from toilet tissue. "Damn! Damn! Damn!" She protested to the mirror while wiping away escaping tears. She was not pregnant after all. A rising panic engulfed her. What if she could never have children? It was too awful to contemplate. She also realised worry and stress were the two things that almost guaranteed failure in the baby-making process. She scrambled through her make-up bag and repaired her eyes with fresh mascara and gave herself the brightest smile. Mick mustn't know. She was so glad she hadn't told him that she had thought she might be pregnant. He would have been devastated.

So she resolved to keep it to herself and try harder next month.

When she returned to her seat she was her usual bright cheery self.

Mick never guessed at the heavy heart that lay beneath the gaiety.

By the time they fell into bed that night exhausted, she was glad she was going home tomorrow. She needed Ali right now, and she couldn't wait to unburden herself to her friend. I hope her news is happier than mine she mused as she drifted off to sleep – suddenly Trisha couldn't wait to get home.

Ali had taken the day off work to welcome back home Trisha and Mick. She had risen early and caught a bus to Drumcondra to leave Emma with Mrs Costello to mind. She knew she would get precious little housework done with Emma around the house; she was a one-baby demolition derby. She wanted the house gleaming for them when they arrived at noon and she intended to have a huge Dublin fry ready for them too. She felt it was the least she could do. It wouldn't hurt either to have a bit of time to fill them in on all the latest developments in her love life. Two weeks was a long time, or at least it was how it seemed these days in the life of Ali O'Neill. How was she going to explain one proposal and one break-up, but not from the person Trisha had expected it from? She also fervently wished she had taken the driving lessons she had long promised herself so she could get about more with Emma and could have collected the newlyweds from the airport. As it was, it took ages to get back to the Naul from Drumcondra, so she hadn't much time to clean up. She vowed to take driving lessons the following week. It was all part of the new and improved independent Alison O'Neill. She was determined to change and she would. She used her determination now to scrub the kitchen floor tiles 'til they shone and soon the house was like a new pin. She had just placed the sausages and rashers under the grill when she heard the taxi pull into the gravel driveway.

She flew to the doorway and saw Trisha emerge from the cab a bronzed blonde goddess. She looked amazing. Ali was dumbstruck. Trisha's blue eyes gleamed out of golden skin and under a thatch of white blonde hair. She had never looked better. Ali even felt a tinge of envy. Trisha was beautiful and blissfully happy. Mick looked extremely handsome too – in fact he looked totally Spanish with his dark eyes, dark hair and killer tan.

The girls fell on each other giggling like they hadn't seen each other in decades and Mick was left like an afterthought to struggle indoors with the myriad of bags. If he was irritated he didn't show it. By the time he made it into the kitchen, the fry smelled so appetising and Ali placed a much longed-for mug of tea into his hand, he was smiling. Ali and Trish were gossiping about the honeymoon with Trisha regaling Ali with the tales of sumptuous luxury that they had enjoyed.

Ali felt a little bit guilty that Mick was being left out and she tried to include him in their conversation. After all, he and Trisha were newly-weds. She would have to fit in with them, but she thought she felt a frisson of disappointment on his face when Mick saw her fling open the front door. She felt that as he had enjoyed Trisha to himself for a fortnight, maybe now he was reluctant to share her. She resolved to make herself scarce this evening so they could have some "newly-wed couple" time together.

After enjoying the tasty meal Mick pushed his plate away and excused himself.

"Do you mind, Trisha, if I go for a lie-down for an hour or two?" he said quietly. "I'm bushwhacked."

"Sure," Trish replied easily, dying to get Ali alone to get the real gossip. "I'll join you in a little while, OK?" She pecked his check and topped up her tea and settled down for a good chinwag.

Mick slipped from the room unnoticed and went to lie down alone in his big king-size bed. He tossed the pillows down angrily. He couldn't believe it. He had wanted so much to carry Trisha over the threshold.

But Ali had ruined it all, by being there and commandeering his new wife as soon as they had arrived. Trisha hadn't even noticed that they hadn't carried out the tradition. Mick felt jealous and he hated that emotion, but he couldn't help it. He had shared Trisha for so long, now he really just wanted her to himself. He couldn't help wishing that Ali would find a place and move out so he and Trisha could start their own married life together, but on their own. He loved little Emma being around but soon they would have a child of their own.

He tossed and turned angrily in the bed, unable to settle. He would have to say something to Trisha later but knew he would have to tread carefully. Still, he didn't want to feel like an outsider in his own home and that was exactly how he felt at this minute. He heard laughter coming from the kitchen and felt even more miserable. Mick knew Ali and Trisha were as thick as thieves and this was not going to be easy. But they had agreed all those months ago, before Ali came back from Australia that Ali staying with them was only going to be a temporary measure, and right now Mick felt that temporary arrangement was going to have to come to an abrupt end.

Meanwhile Trisha was agog in the kitchen with all Ali's latest developments.

"God!" she exclaimed. "I can't believe all this has happened in just two weeks. There was I lying on me sun-bed, thinking nothing much would be happening in dreary old Dublin, and there you were, going through all that on your own. What are you going to do now?"

Ali put her cup down and frowned.

"I think I'm going to let Ben go. Permanently. Look, Trish. If he had wanted what I did, then he would have proposed. Instead he's going off again. I know it's a noble cause and I applaud him for what he is doing but I can't help feeling he is still running away. As soon as anyone gets close he seems to back off a bit. If he was really serious about our relationship, he would discuss our future plans first. But Ben didn't do that. I want him so much, but I'm afraid he doesn't seem to feel as strongly, and I need that, Trisha. I need someone that's committed, to Emma and me – 100 per cent – all the way. Otherwise in the end, they'll cheat like Simon and Ben both did. I can't have any of that in my life again. I'd rather be alone."

Trisha gave her friend a huge hug.

"You know something, Alison O'Neill? That's the most sensible thing I have ever heard you say. You are right. You deserve better and you should expect better. That Ben Murphy should be down on his knees begging you to marry him. He was so lucky you gave him another chance. You don't need to hang around waiting on him to decide if you're good enough to be his wife. You're dead right."

"I'm going to start doing things for Emma and me," intoned Ali with a steely look of determination in her green eyes. "It's time I started to make a life for us both."

"What do you mean?" Trisha enquired, amazed at this new, tougher Ali.

"I mean I am going to build a proper career for myself. I'm going to ensure a real future for Emma and me. A secure future that won't need a man to complete it."

"You know Mick and I are here for you both," said Trisha gravely, her blue eyes misting over. "We will help you in any way we can."

"Thanks," Ali smiled. "You've both done so much already. But right now, I think there's a lonely groom waiting up in the boudoir. And I think he needs you to himself right now. I'm going to make myself scarce this evening. I'm off out soon to collect Emma from your mum's and then we're going out with Simon for dinner and maybe even to a movie. Hope she likes the *Breakfast Club*."

"Right so," said Trish, rising. She hadn't missed Mick's forlorn face when he had gone off to bed alone. She just always felt she needed to give Ali some attention too. Men were such babies when it came to themselves – always wanting to be the centre of attention. "I'll go and join him for a siesta. Do you know what? I'll be falling asleep in Roche's tomorrow around 2pm. We got so used to our little nap in the afternoon in Lanzarote that I don't know how I'll do without it!"

"Well, enjoy it while you can," laughed Ali, "for tomorrow, you work."

"Please don't remind me," grimaced Trisha. "You know I really need to find another job soon. I'm getting so stale there. I need a fresh challenge."

"You and me both," sighed Ali. "I love Carter Travel, and Maisie has been so good to me but I often wish it was my own business. I practically run the place as it is."

"Mmmm," murmured Trisha pensively. "Y'know you could start up your own business Ali, if you really wanted to. You still have that money left to you from your parents' house. And you really want a proper career for yourself. You could open up your own travel agency. Why don't you look into it? It can't do any harm."

Ali looked at her friend in amazement.

"You know, Trish, you are absolutely right. There is no harm in me investigating the possibility. But there are so many things to think about. Oliver is a financial adviser. I could ask him for some advice. Wouldn't it be wonderful? I could secure a decent future for me and Emma."

Trisha smiled briefly and looked out the window at the vast green expanse before her.

"Yeah, and if only I could get pregnant as soon as possible, I could leave my rotten job forever and take care of someone else's future."

"Are you trying already?"

Ali was surprised. The icing was barely dry on the wedding cake.

"Yes," sighed Trisha downcast. "I have been for three months actually. No luck so far. Me sisters only have to glance at their husbands and they're booking into Holles Street Hospital."

"Yes, but Trisha, three months is no time at all. It can take up to a year."

Trisha thought for a minute. Should she now tell her friend about that miscarriage that had occurred all those years ago? No. She couldn't – Ali would never understand why she hadn't confided in her at the time. Nor would Mick. She had held the secret for so long, she would have to keep on being silent. It was too late now. They would never understand.

"Yeah, you're right," she said at last, tidying up the dishes so Ali wouldn't see the tears dancing in her eyes. "I'd better get going so, and keep on practising making babies. Who knows? We may get it right soon."

"Go on," urged Ali, shooing her away from the breakfast table. "Go join your husband. I'll look after these."

Trisha sloped off wearily towards the bedroom. But her friend hardly noticed her anxious mood.

Ali's mind was already racing with the possible plans for her new business that had already formed in her mind. She might finally be on the road to happiness. If she dared enough to dream it true.

Chapter 34

Isabel was having a rare lunch with her husband.

He was seldom home during the day. But inexplicably his golf date with the boys was cancelled and he was at a loose end.

Isabel had had Mrs Mulvanney create a nice cold buffet lunch, which she had carefully laid out on the patio. They were lunching on fresh crusty bread and cold meat salad, enjoying the late summer sunshine.

Isabel watched John carve up his lunch robustly and fork it quickly into his mouth. Her husband had never changed – she smiled. He had always bolted his food as a young man and here he was, thirty years later, still the same. All that had altered was the mop of curly hair, now almost white and the blue eyes crinkled with lines. But he was still essentially the man she had fallen in love with and still loved. She hadn't told him she loved him in over fifteen years, but she was sure he knew.

"I bumped into Kate Kennedy the other day, with a very pregnant Karen in tow," she told him.

John looked up from his meal; Isabel had broken the companionable silence. He looked up askance, not willing to open up that particular can of worms again. He could feel a tirade coming on, and silently cursed his golf buddies for letting him down today of all days.

"They were in Blackrock Shopping Centre, shopping for baby clothes. I felt so envious, John. There they were as happy as Larry, laden down with bags of Babygros from Next. I still feel ill when I think of Ben letting that poor girl down."

"But she's happily married now, isn't she?" John cut across her. He didn't want her to go dragging that debacle up again.

"Oh yes. I suppose. She married some businessman from Longford. She seems to be happy, to have got over Ben. I'm just saying that it could have been our grandchild we were looking forward to, that's all. Heaven knows I'll be waiting forever for bloody Una and Penny to spoil their figures. I mean, our Una's nearly thirty-two, for heaven's sake. Their house is like something out of Vogue, and how many skiing trips a year do they need? And as for Penny, she and Brendan live totally separate lives. Don't be surprised if that marriage doesn't last the pace. And Ben, well, I can't see him ever getting married at all, at this rate."

"He might if you didn't keep sticking your oar in," John replied briskly, then immediately regretted it.

"What the hell is that supposed to mean?" Isabel hissed venomously.

"Oh, don't get your feathers all ruffled, mother hen,"

soothed John , anxious to placate. "I just mean you get a bit involved with his partners, that's all."

"I care about his happiness, if that's what you mean," she snapped back. "I knew Karen was good for him and I knew that the O'Neill girl wasn't. And she proved herself, didn't she, coming back from Australia with another man's child? I knew she was no good the moment I laid eyes on her. And I stayed right out of it when he got back with her six months ago. Against my better judgement, I might add; but I let him get on with it, and now he's off back to Africa for another year. So he obviously doesn't feel all that happy about raising another man's child. I just wish he would find a nice girl and settle down."

John put down his knife and fork and poured himself another cup of tea.

"All we do is raise them and send them on their way, Isabel. We can't erase their mistakes or live their lives for them. We just have to be here for them, and hope for the best."

"I suppose you're right," she sniffed and touched his knee. "I just want what's best for them all, you do know that, don't you? I do love them all, and you too of course, even though I don't always show it."

He smiled widely, his blue eyes crinkling and for a brief second, to Isabel he looked almost 30 again.

"Of course, I do, my dear. Of course, I do. And I love you too, you silly old duck."

And they sat in quiet silence sipping their tea on the patio for a long time, reading the newspapers. Isabel had not remembered being this content in a long time. John had seemed to be away somewhere for a while but now he was back to her and she was glad.

Karen patted her formidable bump as she sat down to watch another home-birth video. At almost six months pregnant she absolutely glowed with health. It had not been planned. She and Brian were only back from their beachside wedding in Tobago when she had fallen ill with some awful virus that they had blamed on the airline food.

After throwing up for three days, she finally called a doctor and discovered the wonderful news. Brian was ecstatic and actually cried when she told him about the baby. Now he was looking for sites around the Wicklow Hills to build a dream home for them all. The apartment would never accommodate a child's pram and all the associated paraphernalia. Karen couldn't wait as the nesting instinct had already kicked in.

The baby kicked suddenly causing Karen to wince and laugh at the same time. This had to be a boy, she mused. It kicked like a footballer. She thought briefly about her chance meeting with Isabel Murphy at Blackrock the other day.

Isabel had frozen when she had discovered Karen's obvious bump, which was more accentuated by her slender frame. Kate and Isabel had drifted apart after the disastrous ending to Ben and Karen's proposed wedding. Karen's mother never quite forgave the Murphys, so Isabel hadn't known Karen was pregnant. When they bumped into her they had been shopping for hours and were carrying copious bags of baby clothes. Kate left

Isabel in no doubt at how happy Karen was and what a successful marriage she had made.

She also pointedly inquired as to Ben's welfare and Karen had smirked inwardly as Isabel blushed and admitted he had been seeing Ali O'Neill again. But hurriedly followed on by telling them that he was off back to Africa for another medical stint.

"Getting cold feet again?" Karen had enquired icily.

Karen couldn't help the frisson of joy that passed through her at Isabel's pained expression that greeted that barb. But Karen had listened for years about Ben's fantastic success and achievements, with little about his weaknesses. She couldn't resist a swipe at him.

"Not quite," Isabel had replied evenly instead, addressing Kate. "He obviously hasn't met the right girl yet. Right for him in any case." She added, now looking at Karen, "You were always the right girl for me."

Karen felt awful then. It really wasn't Isabel's fault Ben was such a weak treacherous lout. Karen really was over it, although she nursed a deep hatred of Ben and would always carry that wound. Still, Brian had more than made up for it, with his endless devotion. She had been able to love again. She had a new life inside her and it wasn't right to enjoy such negative feelings when she was so happy. "I'm sorry, Isabel. That was uncalled for."

"It's quite all right," Isabel said with a tight smile. "You do have a point, Karen. He is a deep worry to me. But I am so happy for you, and you too, Kate. It must be wonderful, expecting the first grandchild."

"Yes," lied Kate, who really wasn't sure she was ready for the title of grandmother. All those years of gym workouts to remain the perfect size ten, and the face-lift that made her look almost thirty-five again, and now here she was, about to be Granny Kennedy. She really wished Karen had waited another three or four years at least, but she was loath to ever let anyone else know her ambivalent feelings – especially Isabel bloody Murphy.

"We really must meet up for coffee," gushed Isabel now, seizing the opportunity. She had been too embarrassed to telephone before, but she had missed Kate and Des's company badly over the intervening years.

"Yes, why don't you give me a call soon," Kate Kennedy replied, inwardly deciding she would have to change her telephone number.

Being friends ever again with any of the Murphy clan was not an option. But she found the need to remain at least civil.

"Now Karen," she quickly said. "We really must plough on. We still have the cot bumper to buy yet. See you soon, Isabel. Bye."

And with that she led Karen swiftly away by the arm.

"The nerve of that woman," she muttered under her breath.

"It's OK, Mum." Karen replied, steering them both towards the coffee shop. "I'm glad she met us. She can regret at leisure that she isn't a grandmother to this baby. I know for a fact she is dying for Una or Penny to have children, and obviously Ben is never going to settle down. Here we are shopping for my baby. She is the loser, not me. I reckon I had a lucky escape."

"You know, Karen. You are absolutely right. Now, you

sit yourself down right there and rest your feet. I'm going to toss the diet in today and find the biggest, most fattening chocolate cake there is for us both. We are going to celebrate."

"Yes!" Karen exclaimed triumphantly. Her mother seldom let a cake past her lips. She and Kate had become so close lately. Since her pregnancy, they had become very close again. She was so lucky to have what she had, a wonderful husband, doting parents and a baby on the way. As she put down the myriad of teeny baby items she realised that she had never felt happier.

Ben came out of the Molesworth Street Passport office. He had renewed his passport and now needed to get another work visa from the Mozambique Embassy. He couldn't help it, but he got so excited at the thought of returning to Africa. It gave him quite a buzz. There he felt needed, successful and in charge. Unlike in his personal life, where he often felt he was all at sea and in turmoil. Perhaps that's why he was so eager to return. He still hadn't sorted out anything with Ali. She was still so angry. She refused to even see him. But he still had time. There were three weeks left before he had to go. He felt deep down that she would calm down and see his side of things.

He knew she loved him passionately, but the re-emergence of Emma's father disturbed him deeply. If only he hadn't reared his ugly Aussie head, things would be a lot simpler. Well, he couldn't change things now. All he could do was hope she would see sense. Either way he wasn't going to let Ali blackmail him into staying, just as

Karen had tried to blackmail him into marriage, and his mother tried to control his entire life. He was going to do what he wanted regardless. If Ali couldn't handle it, well, she obviously wasn't going to make a good doctor's wife in any case. Women could be such a pain sometimes. He would never be able to figure them out.

He headed towards Ballsbridge with a new-found vengeance.

Ali's head was full of dreams and plans and she couldn't wait to explore them with Oliver. At least he could give her a realistic view on the viability of her idea to have her own travel agency. She knew there would be huge hurdles to overcome, but if there was even the slightest chance that she could make it, she wanted to give it a try.

She decided that she would telephone Oliver at home, that evening when he would be more relaxed away from the office and she'd give him brief details and perhaps arrange a lunch with him to discuss the matter further. They both worked in town so it shouldn't be too much trouble. She decided she wouldn't confide in anyone else yet, in case it all came to nothing. Simon was due to fly out within the week, and Ben well, he could take a flying leap back to Africa for all the difference it would make to her. So it would only be herself she had to worry about in a few weeks, herself, her baby and her new dream.

She almost hugged herself in anticipation as she walked down the country lane to catch the bus into Swords and onto Drumcondra to collect little Emma. Even a few hours without her made Ali ache with missing her lovely baby smell and those cute dimpled cheeks – she couldn't wait to hold her and kiss her again. Emma was by far the best thing she ever had done. She hoped this new proposed venture would be the next.

Chapter 35

"Hi, Oliver, It's Ali."

Oliver's heart leapt.

"Hi, Ali. How are you?"

"Fine. Oliver, could you meet me for lunch sometime this week? There are a few things I need to discuss with you. Things that require your expert opinion."

"Sure, that's no problem," Oliver replied slowly, his heart crashing back down to earth. It was a business matter, that's all. Don't be an idiot, Johnston. She needs financial advice, not you personally. "How about today?"

"Oh, Oliver that would be great. Say about 12.30. Is Mary Rose's at the Powerscourt Townhouse Centre OK?"

"That's fine, by me. See you there." Oliver put down the receiver, perturbed. Now what kind of financial advice would Ali need from him, he wondered. Whatever it was, he hoped she had made a decision regarding Ben and he hoped she had seen sense and decided to write him off as a bad debt. Oliver then jumped up and checked his briefcase for his electric shaver and a posh tie. Even if she hadn't the foggiest idea that he loved her, he would still look his best. He glanced at his watch: it was a quarter to ten. In just over two and a half hours he would be having lunch with Ali O'Neill, and he simply couldn't wait.

Oliver spotted Ali sipping a coffee in the corner of Mary Rose's restaurant, which was situated in the centre of the emporium.

The sun bounced off her beautiful auburn hair, and as she sat alone clad entirely in black she looked like a girl except for her crimson-stained lips. She saw him and then smiled shyly, watching him approach.

"Hi, Ali. Have you ordered?" he asked, which was something he had rehearsed asking on the way over.

"No, I haven't, not yet. I thought I'd wait for you."

Oliver blushed at that response and cursed inwardly, hoping she wouldn't notice.

"The lasagne and salad looks good," Ali said looking up from the menu and Oliver agreed.

"I'll have it too."

Oliver ordered for them both and sat back down.

"Right, Ali, what can I do for you?"

Ali told Oliver then of her ideas and plans for setting up her own travel agency.

"I have some money left to me from my parents," she explained.

"It's about £14,000. I'm not sure if that's enough."

"It should be, if you intend to leasehold a premises." He went on to explain the pitfalls: most new businesses folded within the first four years and she should find a niche market, in an area which needed a travel shop.

"Swords is perfect," Ali assured Oliver. 'The closest travel shop is in Drumcondra."

"You're really keen on this idea," marvelled Oliver, suddenly seeing Ali in a new light. "I can see you've done your homework. There aren't many women with their own travel shop."

"Well, there's one," smiled Ali. "Gillian Bowler. She's my inspiration. Look what she has done with Budget Travel. I'd like to have a quirky feel to my business, find an angle, perhaps long-haul trips for the under 30's."

"Well, there you are. That's the kind of thinking that's needed. Next you need to draw up a business plan that you can take to a bank manager and I can help you draw one up that will impress him. Then you have to seek some suitable premises. There are a lot of hurdles to climb, but in essence I think it's an excellent idea. You've got money behind you and a good idea. Couple that with your experience and sheer determination and you should succeed."

"Determination I have," said Ali with a glint in her eye, "in bucket loads."

"Me too," replied Oliver and they both laughed.

Ali really enjoyed Oliver's company. He was direct and honest and didn't have a duplicitous bone in his body. That didn't endear him to everyone but Ali liked his honesty. After all the deception she had endured, it made a refreshing change.

"So," Oliver heard himself ask, despite his intent not to. "Have you heard from the Doc?" It was a nickname that he had given Ben years ago.

"Yes, in a way," Ali replied briskly. "He has attempted to put his case, but I haven't been able to listen yet. I'm still far too emotional to deal with him, Oliver. And Emma's father is over at the moment and I'm busy dealing with him as well. It's just not a great time."

Oliver's heart sank. She had another man in her life too. What hope would he ever have?

"And Emma's father, are you thinking of going back to him?" He tried to make the words sound light, but he was sure she could hear the tension in his voice.

"Oh no, that's over. Simon cheated on me too, Oliver. I guess my taste in men is not so great." She gave a hollow laugh. "Now you can see my frustration with Ben. I'm a little low on understanding. I just want someone who is committed to me and to Emma, one hundred per cent. That's what it'll take. But so far there's been no one who can last the pace." She made a feeble joke of it but Oliver saw through it.

"You will meet someone who will treat you right and who deserves you, Ali. Just wait and see. Don't settle for anything less than what you want."

Her pale hand was so close to his he almost touched it, but didn't and just then their lunch arrived. Suddenly the moment was gone.

All too soon it was almost a quarter to two.

"Yipes. I'd better hightail it back to Carter Travel. Maisie is on one of her sojourns to Cairo and the other pair can wreak havoc with the bookings when they are left unattended. Sorry, Oliver. I really must dash. Can I give you a call in the week, when I research the business plan and we could go over it then?"

"Yes, please do," replied Oliver. "And maybe next time you could come over to my place. I'll cook you dinner and we'll discuss it all at length."

Ali was slightly taken aback but decided not to read too much into it.

She was a novice at this business stuff – perhaps it was quite normal to discuss business in the adviser's home over dinner. Oliver was a friend after all.

"That would be lovely," she smiled in return. "Perhaps next week. Simon, Emma's dad, is leaving on Friday. So this week's a bit hectic. Is that OK?"

"That's perfectly fine," Oliver beamed, rising. "Here, I'll walk back with you. It's time I got back to the grindstone myself."

They had just walked through the archway out of the centre which led to Johnston Court when they bumped straight into Ben who was walking in.

"Ali, Oliver?" he mumbled, nonplussed. He eyed Oliver darkly.

"Hello, Ben." Ali was civil, if a bit icy.

"I've being trying in vain to call you Ali, we really need to talk."

"Yes, and we will," replied Ali evenly. "Next week would be better for me."

"Yes, well, OK. Shall I call you?" He glared at Oliver, who smiled back all innocence.

"Yes, please do. Now I really must go."

She walked off, barely containing a grin. Leaving Ben looking after her and Oliver following in her wake, Ali felt great. Ben could do with a bit of insecurity. She knew he would be smitten with jealousy.

"I don't think he was too pleased," remarked Oliver as they came out onto Grafton Street at Frends.

"Good," smiled Ali. "It serves him right. Ben thinks

I'm on a little string that he can reel in whenever he wants. Well, the string is broken, and I'm off the hook. I've got a business to get off the ground. Ben Murphy will just have to wait his turn for a change."

"Good for you," Oliver replied, grinning. "It hasn't happened often enough. Ben is very used to getting his own way. He's not too used to the NO word."

"Well," said Ali acidly, "he'd better get used to it, because he'll be hearing that word from me quite a lot over the next few weeks."

Oliver watched her green eyes darken with anger. She looked so beautiful – he would do just about anything for her, except tell her how he felt. He decided to remain silent. After all, Ben was his friend and he wasn't going to add fuel to the fire. If he ever won Ali's affections, and that he seriously doubted, he would do so honestly.

He left Ali at the door of Carter Travel and headed back to Fitzwilliam Square, his head full of Ali O'Neill for the remainder of the day.

Ben walked around The Powerscourt Centre in a dazed rage. What the hell was Ali doing with Oliver Johnston? Surely Oliver hadn't being seeing Ali since the wedding? Oliver had refused to answer him properly in that phone call. He fumed as he wandered around aimlessly forgetting what he had come in for. Oliver had looked at him like he was the cat who'd got the cream. Ali was still obviously furious with him. She wouldn't even look him in the eye. Still, he realised he would have to tread carefully. Ali would need to be calm before he had any chance of her listening to and understanding his position.

He would play it her way and try to win her back, but what hope did he have when he would be out of the country in a couple of weeks and Oliver Johnston and that bloody Aussie could charm their way into her heart, as much as they pleased? He began to regret his decision, and realised it could cost him this relationship. Damn. Why was everything always so complicated? He had sincerely never believed Ali would leave him, especially over a career decision. He suddenly remembered why he had came into the centre and he headed for Pia Bang. It was his mother's birthday on Saturday and he was going to get her a voucher for the exclusive boutique. At least, he mused wryly, I'll be in one woman's good books for a few days.

Ali regaled Trisha with all the day's events when she reached home that evening.

"Wow, I can't believe it – Ali O'Neill with her own business. It'll be so fantastic."

"Well, it's early days yet. It might not happen, but I'll do my best to make it happen. It's all thanks to you in anyway, Trisha. You gave me the idea. Oliver says I have to draw up a business plan to impress the bank and he is going to help me. I'm young and female. It just makes it a little more difficult."

"Mick can help you there too," assured Trisha. "He went through all kinds of hoops and hurdles when he set up on his own. But once you get the bank manager behind you, it'll all fall into place."

"I'm going to check out Swords village for some premises. I'm going to try for a shop that has living accommodation above it so Emma and I also have a place to live."

Trisha waited a moment before replying. Mick had made it plain to her yesterday that he wanted Ali and Emma to move out sooner rather than later. He had shared her for long enough, he had said.

Six months had been the agreed term and he wanted them to begin their married life on their own, just like every other couple. Ali had been right after all. She had noticed Mick's dismay when she was at the bungalow to greet them from their honeymoon. Trisha had appealed to Mick's better nature to give Ali another few months, but here was an opportunity for Ali to make the move herself. Trisha might not need to have that talk she dreaded, after all.

"Well," she began, "it would be good for Emma and you to have your own place. But we have loved having you here."

"I know," agreed Ali. "You and Mick have been my salvation. I'm sorry I've been so slow to move on but it felt so nice to be here and part of a family. I have loved it so much, but you need to be a family now and I need to make a life for us on our own. It's about time I got on with my own life – it'll be really exciting, won't it? Living above my own shop."

"Why don't I drive us around Swords on Saturday and we'll have a look around to see what's available?"

"That would be great. Simon is leaving Friday evening, so Saturday I shall be totally free. It feels good y'know, being on my own and having to answer to no one or consider a partner's feelings."

"Do you really feel like that?" Trisha was unsure.

"Yes, I do. If Ben was still in the picture I would be reluctant to move into my own place, because I'd be hoping we'd be moving in together. I'd be less inclined to get this business together because I'd be focusing on marriage and more babies. This I am doing for myself. All the rest can wait."

"So you've closed the door on a relationship with Ben, then?"

Trisha just could not believe Ali could forget Ben. She had loved him for over ten years now – from girl to woman. He had been a constant love in her life.

"I didn't close the door," Ali said indignantly. "Ben did. He can't commit to anyone, Trisha. Look at what he did to Karen. I'm going to live my own life. I'm not putting it on hold until the moment he realises I am good enough for him. Maybe he's not good enough for me, as Oliver says."

"Oliver does have a point," Trish admitted. "You're right. Make your own plans. If Ben is right for you he'll fit into them eventually."

"Right," smiled Ali, happy to have Trisha on side. "What time is Mick home? I need to pick his brains about drawing up the business plan."

"He should be home about 8pm, or thereabouts. Let's have a glass of wine to celebrate your new business proposal."

"Any excuse," laughed Ali and they sat in Trisha's kitchen drinking red wine and making grand plans while Emma played happily on the floor below them. Things were about to change again, Trisha mused, watching Emma play with her doll and pram.

She'd miss Ali and Emma. Hopefully by the time they

leave I will be pregnant myself, she mused. It will give me an interest. She had her whole house perfect and could do her job at Roche's with her eyes closed. She really needed something to occupy her and excite her. A baby was what she and Mick wanted more than anything. Hopefully it would happen soon.

It was Friday, the day Simon would return to Brisbane. Ali was feeling a bit sad. It was sad for Simon and for Emma that he was leaving. She knew it would be difficult for him to part with Emma. They'd had such a good time together over the past four weeks. She couldn't imagine being separated from Emma for more that a few hours so she knew this would really hurt Simon, but it couldn't be helped. All she could do was remain positive and promise lots of photos and a return visit as soon as possible. They decided to spend the day with Emma in Bray. They would take the DART there from the city, take Emma to the beach and then onto the fairground rides.

The day was sunny and warm so it helped lighten the mood. Emma seemed amazed by the beach. She loved the crashing waves and all the stones that littered the strand, most of which she tried to cram into her buggy. Then she had her first ever candyfloss and copious rides on the carousel. Simon was drinking in every moment, Ali noticed and several times her eyes brimmed with tears for him, but she couldn't let him see her weaken, because she knew he would pressurise her to try again. They headed back on the train to Dublin at 4pm to collect Simon's bags and then they headed for the airport for his 6.30pm check in.

"It feels weird leaving you both behind," Simon said

sadly over coffee. He had checked his bags in and they had a bit of time left.

"I know," admitted Ali. "It's going to be so difficult for Emma. She has really enjoyed having you around."

"But not you, eh?" His eyes glistened with tears.

"Yes, me too." She took his large brown hand in hers. "But we both know it wouldn't work. I promise I will send you a video of us both at Christmas, and you can call her every day. She knows you now. We'll take a picture out of Daddy every night and I'll make sure she doesn't forget you. I'll be in Brisbane with her this time next year. Focus on that, OK?"

"Right so," he replied. "I'm sorry, Ali. I know I stuffed up."

"It doesn't matter now, Simon – only Emma matters now, and we need to do what's best for her."

"I'll send you some maintenance money soon," he said earnestly.

"You don't have to," Ali interrupted.

"I want to," Simon replied. "She's my little girl, aren't you, darling?"

He tickled Emma under the chin and was rewarded with peals of laughter. "It's the least I can do."

They finished up their coffees, as it was time to leave. Simon gave Emma the longest hug and dozens of kisses before he went though passport control. He squeezed Ali's hand tightly and kissed her cheek. She could feel the wet tears touch her skin and she hugged him tightly in return. He moved away and went through the doors looking back and waving as long as he could, until he disappeared from view. Emma, watching him go, had called out "Dada, Dada," and Ali couldn't help the tears, which spilled freely onto her face. It was very sad to see him go and they both waved for the longest time. Then Ali went to find a taxi to take her home feeling emotionally exhausted but also relieved. Simon was gone and she was now alone and free to focus on her own life, unhindered.

Chapter 36

Trish was telling Mick all of Ali's latest news. How the bank manager had warmed to Ali's business proposal and was prepared to finance her. It was in no small way due to Mick and Oliver who helped Ali draft it, spending long hours helping her with all the costing and analysis.

Ali and Trish had already scouted around and found a suitable building for long-term lease in Swords village, which had a small two-bedroom flat above it. The premises were centrally located but very run-down which made the price attractive, but it needed a lot of work.

"So it's looking good so far. I'm really happy for her, Mick," said Trisha.

"Yes, so am I," smiled Mick back. "But I'm even happier for us. Soon we'll have this place to ourselves at last."

"I didn't realise my friend was such a burden to you," snapped Trisha, piqued.

She felt so irritable tonight, even Mick sipping his tea had grated on her nerves so much, Trisha just really wanted to be alone. She had just got yet another period that afternoon, despite her and Mick making love almost every night. She was on tenterhooks that he would ask her about it soon and she'd have to endure the disappointed look on his face. Deep down she knew she might have to see a doctor about this difficulty in conceiving. Her earlier miscarriage weighed heavily on her mind, but she couldn't face telling Mick. Not now. He hated secrets and it would really hurt him that she had concealed something so serious for all these years.

"Sorry. You know I didn't mean it like that," Mick replied wearily.

He had grown used to his new wife's ever-changing moods lately. She really hadn't been herself since the honeymoon. He reckoned that perhaps Ali moving on had unsettled her a bit, and on top of that they were having no luck in the baby-production department. Funny, he had always thought they would strike lucky straightaway. He watched Trisha's terse expression recede and decided to change the subject. "I wonder how Ben and Ali are getting on? They should be at the restaurant by now. I'd love to be a fly on the wall."

"Me too," said Trisha agreeably. "I just hope they end things on a peaceful note before he goes. I'd hate to see them enemies. Ali seemed calm when she left. I doubt if it would do any good if she had to deal with opening up a new business and nursing a broken heart at the same time."

"Yeah, it's going to be tough enough. Still, we'll all help out. Oliver and myself and the rest of the gang will get stuck in with the renovation. It'll do Ali good to have something so challenging to focus on. Ben's due to fly out in a few days."

"I got my period today," Trisha blurted out suddenly. She looked totally miserable and close to tears.

"I see," said Mick evenly, anxious not to seem too dismayed. Last month Trisha took it badly that he showed such disappointment. "And how do you feel?"

"Pretty rotten," she managed a weak smile. "We'll have to try harder."

"That sounds pretty good to me," enthused Mick. "Maybe you've been working too hard at Roche's. It's pretty hectic being Acting Deputy Manager, isn't it?"

"I'm fine," Trisha replied tersely, rising. "My job has nothing to do with it. It just takes time for some couples to fall pregnant, that's all. Now I think I'll go check on Emma. She's getting a couple of back teeth and she was grizzly when Ali put her to bed."

With that she swept from the room.

Mick felt uncomfortable. He wished dearly Trisha would get pregnant for both their sakes. He really wanted a baby but Trisha seemed to be more and more uptight about the situation as time progressed. He was getting tired of walking around on eggshells the whole time. Trisha seemed to have lost her happy-go-lucky attitude lately.

He resolved to have a chat with Ali about it and maybe even Trisha's mum, anything that would give him a better insight on how to approach the subject. This was not how he had planned to start their married life. They had always had such an easy relationship. He dearly hoped that wouldn't change. He sipped his tea alone in the perfect kitchen and wondered if Trisha would mind if he slipped down to the pub for a pint. He felt too agitated to stay here and stew over their problems.

Ben and Ali were having dinner in an intimate restaurant called Quo Vadis, on Suffolk Street, where they could be assured of peace and quiet to discuss their relationship. Ali felt really nervous, like she was on a first date.

She gulped her red wine quickly and fiddled with the stem of the glass. They had been making polite conversation while scanning the menu and she dreaded the moment when they would have to face the fact that their love affair was almost over. She watched his strong handsome face examine the menu as if it were a terminal patient. He looks as nervous as I do, she mused and stifled a giggle.

Ben looked up quizzically and smiled.

"What?" he asked, catching her giggles.

"What are we like?" Ali laughed. "We're like two strangers on a blind date that's going nowhere."

"Thank God. I thought I was the only one. I feel so nervous my hands are shaking holding the menu."

"Have more wine," Ali replied mischievously. "It works for me."

"Let's enjoy dinner first and then talk. Is that OK with you?"

"Fine," Ali agreed, looking into those intense blue eyes. He still made her heart do back-flips. That was something she felt would never cease. But it still didn't make for a real relationship. The past two weeks Ali had calmed down and talked to Ben often on the phone, until her anger had dissipated. But Ali still felt hurt that instead of choosing her he had chosen to move a continent away, without even consulting her. It was something that made her ache deep inside – she didn't feel that they could get past it. She always remembered Maisie Carter telling her that when men said they didn't want to get married, they really meant they didn't want to get married to *you*.

She felt Ben loved her, but just not enough.

Now she chose her usual crab while Ben had the beef. Old habits died hard and they chatted amiably about Ali's proposed business plan and Emma turning the terrible two soon. Ali felt maudlin after three glasses of red wine and by dessert she was wishing he would get down on one knee and propose. She could forgive him anything if he just did that, but of course he didn't.

Instead Ben launched into what Ali surmised was a heavily rehearsed speech about how much she meant to him, but how much good he could do in Africa and how he hoped when he got back, they could take up where they left off and see how things went. He finished with, "I never ever intended to hurt you, Ali. Please believe that."

"I do believe that," Ali sighed, feeling her cheeks, which were burning with annoyance and too much wine. "I believe you felt it was in your interest career-wise and an exciting prospect running your own medical team. But what saddens me is you never even considered discussing it with me. We are on such different wavelengths. I believed you were about to propose to me, Ben, not tell me you were leaving."

"Ali, if I were ready for marriage, you would be the girl I would choose, but in all honesty I'm not ready again for all that . . . stuff."

"The word is commitment, Ben. It's OK – you can say it

without catching anything. You are not ready for commitment, am I right?"

"Yes, I guess that is what I am saying, but it doesn't change how I feel for you," he protested lamely.

"Oh, but it does change how I feel for you, Ben. I have loved you for the longest time, and I'd go across the world with you or marry you in a heartbeat, but if you don't feel the same, well, I think it's probably best if we finish it now before you go. That way we can both be free. If in a year's time you feel like calling me, then please do, but I refuse to put my life on hold while you wait and ponder how you feel about commitment."

"Is that your final word on it then?" Ben looked a bit stunned.

He seemed unable to react. Ali thought he hadn't ever believed she would end it. He had always thought good old reliable Ali loves me so much she'd wait forever. Well, he was wrong.

"Yes, I believe it is," she replied sadly, and the trouble was, she was telling the truth. She just never expected to feel so empty, so vanquished by what happened.

"Can you take me home, Ben?" she asked him quietly.

"Sure," he replied softly and summoned the waiter for the bill.

Soon they were walking silently up Grafton Street not holding hands or touching. The summer sun was still up and all the Spanish students were yelling loudly as they spilled happily down the street. Couples seemed to be entwined everywhere, whereas Ali and Ben walked together but alone. Too much had been said and done and it couldn't be undone. Ali had never felt so alone. It was over. She now knew in her heart that they no longer had a future. It was finally over. They walked silently to the car park and when they reached his gleaming Volkswagen Polo, Ben opened the passenger door for her and suddenly swooped down and kissed her. It was a kiss of such passion and longing that Ali was powerless to resist and found herself kissing him back. Then wordlessly he let her go and went around the car and got in, quickly firing up the engine. Ali sat and looked at Ben whose jaw had set in a strong determined expression.

"Ben . . ." Ali began, not sure of what she was going to say.

"Not now, Ali." Ben interrupted gruffly as he quickly reversed.

So they sat in uncomfortable silence as they sped towards Swords.

"Is it OK if I write?" Ben finally asked as they neared the Naul.

"I'd like that very much," Ali replied. There was no point parting on bad terms.

When they reached Trisha's house, Ben swerved into the gravel drive and stopped the car just inside the gate.

"I still love you, Ali. I just want you to know that."

"I do. I know that, Ben." She wanted to say "And I love you" but she couldn't. It wouldn't make any difference, so she said instead, "Be safe. Take care of yourself, OK?" and kissed him chastely on the cheek.

"I will." His blue eyes looked into hers penetratingly for a moment then looked away. "Guess it's goodbye, so."

Ali opened the door of that car and got out.

"Goodbye, Ben." And she walked away up the crunchy

gravel drive and didn't look back. She could feel his eyes follow her every step.

When she got to the door she heard the car start and looked back but Ben was staring straight ahead and he didn't look back or wave.

Suddenly he was gone, out of her life and off to his future.

It was over. She had to move on.

Trisha was curled up on the couch alone, watching of all things the *Late Late Show,* which was odd because she hated Gay Byrne.

"You're early," she said, throwing down the cushion she had been cuddling.

"Yep. Doesn't take too long to say goodbye." Ali said flippantly as she flopped down on the couch beside Trish.

"Isn't *Miami Vice* on? I thought you hated this."

"I wasn't really watching," Trish replied wearily. "But enough of that. How did it all go?"

"Well," Ali began, "it was all very civilised. There was no shouting or roaring, but the ending was the same. Ben isn't ready for commitment and he felt I should understand him and support him while he makes up his mind whether I am good enough, which I'm not prepared to do. So it's over."

Trisha looked at Ali for traces of tears. There were none.

"You seem very together about it all."

"I am, Trisha. Honestly, I just can't sit around for a year wanting him and waiting for him knowing he may walk away. It's better if we end it now and I can carry on and focus on my life and Emma's. I'm not putting my life on hold for a year, just in case he decides he wants to marry me."

"Point taken," Trish agreed. "You are right. Still. It can't have been easy."

"No, it wasn't," Ali said, slowly rising. "I'm going to make some tea. Do you want some?"

"Love some," Trish replied jumping up too. "I'll join you in the kitchen."

"Where's Mick?" Ali enquired over tea and toast.

"Gone to the pub," said Trish too brightly. "Bored rigid with his menstrual wife."

"Oh, I'm sorry Trish. No luck again?"

"No. And I think I'm beginning to drive Mick away. I've been so moody the poor fella doesn't know which way to talk to me without getting his head bit off."

"I'm sure he'll never go off you," Ali assured her. "But why is it so important to you to get pregnant straight away? You know it can take up to twelve months. You've only been trying for a few months now."

"Well, there's something else that has me worried. It's something that happened a long time ago and I never told a soul, not even Mick or you. And it's something I wanted to tell you for years but I just couldn't." She looked out the window dreamily.

"So what is it?" Ali asked alarmed.

"I had a miscarriage, years ago, that time, the time I was a few weeks late. Remember, when I was seventeen?"

"Oh, Trish!" Ali was shocked. "But why didn't you say something? I could have helped. You mean you went through all that trauma on your own."

"Yes," said Trish reliving the awful memory of that Sunday. "I just closed my mind to it. I was so ashamed. I didn't tell Mick because I thought he'd finish with me. I don't know why I thought that but I did. I was just a silly kid."

"Exactly," said Ali firmly. "Which is why you shouldn't be beating yourself up over it now. You had an awful experience and you dealt with it alone at seventeen. There's no one to blame."

"Yes, but Ali, I should have confided in you, my best friend in the world, and in Mick. It was his baby too. That's why I am so uptight about getting pregnant. I'm worried there may be a problem. If I miscarried once I can miscarry again, and what about if we go to a doctor? They are going to ask me my full medical history. Mick will find out."

"You have to tell him, Trish. You didn't tell him before but you have to tell him now, before this secret comes out another way."

Trish poured another cup of tea and had yet another slice of toast.

"Mick and I have never had any secrets, except this one. He always prides himself on honesty and he thinks I am the same. I'm not sure he would forgive me, that's all."

"He might be mad for a bit, but I'm sure he'll come round eventually. I really feel you should tell him, Trisha, sooner rather than later."

"There's one thing for sure," Trisha muttered darkly.

"What?" Ali looked alarmed. What would her friend surprise her with next?

"We're a right pair of eejits!"

Ali laughed and so did Trish. They laughed for longer than they felt it, but at least it helped a bit.

Chapter 37

Oliver drove his sleek BMW into the car park of Charles Nesbitt's Solicitor-at-Law in Swords village. He was accompanying Ali to sign the deeds on her new premises. She would be the new leaseholder of the shop on seventeen Main Street in an hour's time.

He had seen a lot of Ali the past few weeks, helping her with her business plan and the financial forecasts and projections for the coming year. Oliver had witnessed her blossom as she grasped the intricate details of running her own business and he felt deep down that she would be a successful businesswoman in the long run.

Ben had left for Africa weeks ago and Ali seemed totally together and Oliver hadn't seen any signs of a broken heart or even depression. He hadn't known that Ali had thrown herself into her new venture in order not to even think of Ben and to that extent she had largely succeeded.

"You really have to learn to drive," he admonished

her as she ran pink-faced from the ever more delayed Swords bus.

"Are you offering to teach me?" Ali laughed, eyeing his glistening car, which was his pride and joy.

"I might," Oliver grinned in return, "after you learnt the basics. Anyway, are you feeling excited?"

"I didn't sleep a wink," Ali admitted. "Oliver, I am doing the right thing, aren't I?"

"Yes, you are," assured Oliver, patting her arm in a brotherly fashion. "Now, we've been over this. You have done the sums and you have the finance. All you need now are the clients, and off you go. I have told you I'll take three holidays a year until you make some money and I'll rope in as many business colleagues as I can muster for Spanish golf trips, so don't fret."

Ali laughed. "OK. OK. Take me to your leader. I'll sign my life away."

They went upstairs to the tiny offices of Charles Nesbitt. He was an old college friend of Oliver's and had done all the legal work for Ali regarding the lease and registration of her business.

Charles had all the documentation ready and he explained all the details to Ali before signing and within an hour she was holding two Yale keys that signified she was in business.

She came out onto the street back into the crisp September air and let out a large whoop of delight.

Her excitement was so infectious, Oliver found himself whooping too and lifting her up and swinging her around.

"Hope he always makes ye that happy, love,"

murmured an old woman as she passed with her heavy load of shopping.

Ali laughed, embarrassed as Oliver let her down.

"Let's go to number seventeen right now. I just have to put these keys in the lock and open the door to my new business."

"Lead the way, Miss O'Neill," Oliver said taking her arm as they walked the short distance to Ali's new shop. The 'for lease' sign had a new 'leased' sticker over it, which made Ali's heart skip a beat. This really was happening. She couldn't quite believe it still wasn't just a pipe dream.

Ali turned the key in the lock and they walked inside.

"I feel like I should have carried you over the threshold or something," Oliver remarked casually.

Ali blushed furiously. "That's just after a wedding, Oliver, but thanks anyhow."

The shop had a large bay window and had high airy ceilings, but other than that it was a nightmare, Oliver thought with dismay. Bright orange swirled carpet that had seen years of traffic, wallpaper with bright gold embossed stripes, and the doors into the office behind were paint-chipped and full of dry rot. There was a lot of work that needed to be done.

"Strange décor for an optician's, though I suppose most of their clientele were lucky enough to be short-sighted," Oliver quipped, as they viewed the back room which had an even more lurid crimson-flocked wallpaper.

"I've got my work cut out, I'll admit. But it's got the basics, large airy rooms and a great window. Do you want to see the upstairs flat?"

"Sure," said Oliver who was very unsure if he wanted to

endure any more design nightmares. But he was pleasantly surprised.

Obviously someone had lived above the shop and cared for it a great deal. All the rooms were painted in a warm cream, and the lounge, which faced the street, had a large bay window complete with window box. It also had a real fireplace and there was a warm caramel carpet throughout. The kitchen was tiny but well appointed and the bedrooms had built-in wardrobes and were small but functional.

"Hey, this is not bad at all," Oliver was impressed, Ali could tell.

"Yes, and the best thing is, it's just big enough for Emma and me. And it's rent-free. It comes with the premises. I'd prefer a garden for Emma, of course, but she spends all day at the Costellos', so she gets to run about quite a lot. What do you think, Oliver? Did I get a bargain or what?"

"Yes, I would say you did," replied Oliver, back in financial adviser mode.

"So, can I count you in on the painting team?" Ali joked.

"I'd be delighted," replied Oliver, in earnest. Any reason to be close to Ali was good enough.

"Great," said Ali warmly, giving Oliver a huge hug. "My brother Louis and Damien, and Mick are going to help out as well. We'll have it done in no time."

"Right," said Oliver. Now it was his turn to blush. "But first things first. I'm taking you for a celebration lunch and a few glasses of champagne to celebrate. We've got the whole weekend to revamp this place, though I think we'll need a month to remove the awful wallpaper downstairs."

"Yes," replied Ali, dreamily, "but it will be a labour of love."

"I'll remind you of that when you're up to your elbows in red-flocked fluffy bits!" Oliver joked as they walked downstairs.

He had never seen Ali so happy, and he was glad to be a part of it.

Ben Murphy really did seem to be a thing of the past. And her life was taking a new and exciting turn.

Trisha's life however, had turned an unhappier corner.

She was struggling with the zip of her Roches skirt and it had just broken. She knew she had been hitting the biscuit barrel a lot more lately, due to all the worry about having babies but she hadn't realised it had become that bad. She had gained over a stone since her honeymoon and her hourglass figure was now too well padded. Getting her new car hadn't helped – she drove absolutely everywhere and had become lazy. Angry tears stung her eyes. She knew she had no one to blame for this but herself. She had been comfort-eating for months now, and this was the result. She felt deeply embarrassed at the thoughts of having to request a size eighteen uniform. She remembered how embarrassed she had been when she had to have a size sixteen a few years ago, but at least her weight had remained constant and the sixteen was very loose on her just before the wedding. Soon people would be asking her when she was due, if she wasn't careful. She cursed herself silently and vowed to go on a strict diet immediately, but right now she had to wear a plain navy skirt that she had in the wardrobe that hopefully still fitted her.

She hoped the manager wouldn't notice. The last thing she wanted was to go to work today, on Ali's special day. But she had taken off the whole weekend to help out with the painting so she couldn't call in sick today. But sick was what she felt, well and truly sick of herself. This couldn't continue. She realised she had to tell Mick and soon as this secret was eating her up inside. But she dreaded picturing the look on his face when he discovered she had held it from him for all these years. She looked at her tear-stained face in the mirror and focused on the new double chin.

"You are a stupid ugly bitch," she told her reflection, before rummaging through the wardrobe for the necessary navy skirt.

She'd try and tell Mick tonight maybe, if she could summon up the courage. But right now she really had to get a move on. She was due into work in half an hour and by the looks of it she would be dead late. Just as well she said she would drop into the office to get the staff rosters first so her late appearance on the floor wouldn't be as noticeable. The last thing she needed right now was to have to worry about holding onto her job too.

She found the necessary skirt at last which zipped up with a few complaints and she fled towards the door, hoping as she reached her car that the traffic would be kind and she wouldn't be too late. She uncharacteristically forgot to even think of Ali and her special day, as she raced towards Dublin with her mind in turmoil.

Mick was interviewing a new office assistant. His workload

had become increasingly heavier, leaving him little time to attend to invoicing and VAT returns, so he had advertised for a young person with a couple of years' office experience. Someone who wouldn't mind the draughty prefab he was based in or a set of books that were three months behind. And he had found someone. Her name was Amanda and she was barely 20 but had three years' experience in a builders' providers. She seemed to know the cash-book inside out and on top of that was quite a pretty, friendly girl who seemed enthusiastic about the job.

Mick didn't offer it to her on the spot, as he would have liked. He decided to discuss it with Trisha first. Trish had always done his books until just before the wedding when she had become too busy and she never got back to them afterwards. Now, Trisha hardly ever seemed in an approachable mood, so he had let them languish. He decided to discuss the matter with her tonight and hopefully she would be enthusiastic. He didn't know why, but he was a bit apprehensive that she might object to him hiring an attractive 20-year-old. This was why he wanted her blessing first.

Trisha arrived home a little after nine hoping that Ali and Mick would be home with something hot and tasty on the stove and lots of warm stories about their days, which she hoped had been more productive than hers. But the house was dark and cold, and she swore silently under her breath as she turned the key in the lock and checked the answer machine. There was a brief message from Mick to say he'd be late, no reason given, and a slightly intoxicated one from a happy Ali to say she was on her way, and not to worry.

Trisha was burrowing through the freezer for anything edible when she saw the lights of Mick's van pull into the drive. Irritated, she walked towards the hallway to confront him. He swayed slightly she noticed as he entered the door.

"What time do you call this?" Trisha snapped, a little more viciously than she had intended.

"I had a hard day, Trisha, so I had a couple of pints with the lads. But, I got you a chinese. I knew you'd be exhausted and hungry." He proffered a large brown steaming bag.

"If it's special chow mein, you're forgiven." Trisha smiled, contrite. She really must try to be a bit nicer. It wasn't Mick's fault she was so unhappy.

"Right so. Might I be in with a chance tonight?"

"You might, if you deliver the Chinese to the living room with a nice glass of wine."

They had just finished their Asian feast when they heard Ali come in.

Oliver was carrying a sleeping Emma to her room on tiptoe, his boots clacking on the wooden flooring in the hallway.

Trisha noted that they looked suspiciously like a couple, but she knew Ali – you could never say anything like that to her without a verbal explosion coming back your way. So she just smiled and let Ali speak.

"Oh, Trisha, it has been the most exciting day. I wish you could have been there."

"Well," said Trisha, shutting from her mind her awful day. "Tell me all about it and spare me no gory details."

In a sec," Ali explained, rising. "Ill just settle Emma in and say good night to Oliver."

"Why don't you offer him a coffee first, Ali?" Trisha ventured, to be shot back a stern look.

Within minutes they heard the door close and Ali returned.

"Oliver's gone," she said. "He said to say goodnight."

Trisha knew Ali had bundled Oliver out unceremoniously but she demurred and asked Ali to recount her important day instead, and Ali happily obliged.

The hall she said was full of paint for the shop that she and Oliver had picked this afternoon, after several glasses of champagne, she added, laughing, hoping they'd all still like it in the morning.

Trisha noticed Ali was light-hearted and excited in a way she had never seen before. But this time she was different. Confident. That was it; she was confident.

Ali had never been confident.

"So," Ali said at last, after relating her exciting day, looking a little glassy-eyed, "I'm off to bed now, so I can leave you two lovebirds alone. Just remember, Trisha. Don't tire him out too much. Mick's on paint patrol tomorrow."

"We'll be up, bright and early, won't we, Mick?" Trisha enthused.

"If I get a cuppa in bed from you, and a rasher sandwich made by Ali, I will," Mick replied, before getting a cushion hurled at him from both girls.

After Ali went to bed, Trisha decided she had summoned enough courage to tell Mick about the miscarriage. She had rehearsed a little speech in the car on the way home. She felt her heart flutter in her chest as she told him they had something important to discuss.

Mick looked concerned.

"Mick, remember years ago when we had that scare? My periods were a few weeks late and I thought I was pregnant? Well, I was."

"What?" Mick looked shocked. He stared at her, uncomprehendingly. "What do you mean?"

"That time I was late, I really was pregnant, but I lost it. When my periods arrived they were very heavy and then the baby came away in the toilet."

She winced at the memory and looked at Mick for a reaction.

"Why didn't you tell me?" he said quietly, looking at her as if he was seeing her for the first time.

"I didn't tell anyone. I was just a frightened kid. We hadn't been going out that long, and I wasn't sure how you'd react."

"How do you think I'd react? You know I would have been there for you. Do you sincerely doubt that?" Now Mick was getting angry. This was all going pear-shaped.

"No, that's not what I mean. I never told anyone, not even Ali. I was so shocked I just shut it out. I just tried to put it out of my head. I didn't want to believe it had ever happened."

"So why now?" Mick's voice was cold. "Why tell me now, after all this time?"

Trish looked into the fire and replied guiltily. "Because it may have a bearing on my medical history, if we need to see a doctor about having a baby."

"So, the only reason you are telling me this now, is because of some doctor?" Mick said, his voice dripping in disgust. "I really can't believe what I am hearing. We lost a child together seven years ago, and now you decide I can know. Trisha I can't believe you kept this from me all this time. I don't think I know who you really are any more."

He rose abruptly.

"Mick," Trisha tried, but it was no use. Mick stormed out of the room and down the hallway. She could hear the bedroom door slam.

This had not gone well, at all. Trisha knew that he would be upset, but she never guessed he would be so wounded by her admission.

She had gauged his love and support all wrong. He was instead blaming her for keeping a secret, not knowing how much it had hurt her to do so.

She sat for the longest time in the darkened front room watching the embers of the fire glow and fade, and wondered how she could repair the damage.

When she finally went to bed, they both lay like stones, seemingly acres apart and Mick never even tried to touch her. Trisha tossed and turned for hours until, exhausted, she finally slept.

Chapter 38

The next morning when Trisha awoke, the bed lay empty beside her.

As she dragged herself to the kitchen she found Ali and Mick deep in conversation over toast and tea, discussing the paint colours.

Trish decided to act as normally as possible. She didn't want Ali involved in their spat, so she asked instead. "Ali, would you like me to take care of Emma today? I'm a bit tired and I think painting is beyond my dubious DIY skills."

"Really?" Ali was delighted. "That would be a great help, Trisha. Thanks."

"I'll go get her, so," Trisha mumbled and escaped the kitchen as soon as possible. Mick didn't even raise his head, seeming as intent at studying the paint charts as if his life depended on it.

If Ali noticed anything amiss she did a good job of hiding it. She and Mick chattered on while Trisha changed a sleepy Emma and prised her from her cot for breakfast.

Within half an hour, Mick and Ali had loaded the van with the paint and rollers and were ready to leave for Swords.

"Mick, we have to talk," Trisha hissed quietly while Ali was kissing Emma goodbye.

"I don't feel like talking to you," Mick replied gruffly and slammed the van door shut.

Trisha took Emma from Ali and brightly wished her well.

"I'll have a nice roast dinner ready for you both," she said too brightly, noticing Mick's grimace. He sped from the drive like a man possessed. Ali could not have failed to notice his black mood. Trisha went back inside dejectedly and tried to forget the episode and concentrated on entertaining Emma.

She'd have to try and think of a way to get through to Mick and she had just a day to do it. Why did I open my mouth at all, she wondered as she cleared away the breakfast dishes. I' ve made a right mess of things.

Mick's mind was racing as he sped the van towards Swords. Outwardly he was half listening to Ali chattering on about paint and textures but inwardly his mind could only focus on one thing. Trisha had kept an awful secret from him for all these years. She didn't trust him enough to tell him about the loss of their baby, his baby. He was hurt to the core and couldn't see why Trisha had kept it from him all the years that had intervened.

He had never kept a single thing from her and had believed it was the same for her. What other secrets did she harbour? Had she slept with someone else in

Australia? Mick wasn't sure of anything any more – he wasn't sure of the one person he had been most sure of and there had been a seismic shift in his world.

He wasn't sure how he felt about Trisha at the moment – all he felt was anger. He needed Ben to talk to and dearly wished for Ben's advice right now. But the guy was in Africa and that was that. He needed time to digest all of this, and time away from Trisha was just what he needed. So he nodded to Ali in all the right places and vowed to take on the hardest task he encountered in the shop today. He needed something to take his mind off his troubles.

Oliver was as ever, waiting. Punctual to the point of being almost too early, he had enjoyed a coffee and croissant and had read the paper while waiting on the others to turn up.

Within minutes, Ali, Mick and Louie had arrived, laden with paint, electric wallpaper strippers and ladders.

Ali quickly introduced Oliver and Louie. Oliver was amazed that darkly Italian-looking Louie was Celtic-skinned auburn-haired Ali's little brother. Louie was carrying a lethal looking wallpaper-stripping machine and quipped, "And I know how to use it."

Everyone quickly got down to their tasks and the moistening and stripping of the awful golden wallpaper began in earnest.

Several hours later they were still only half-way through the front office when Ali was feeling so exhausted, she excused herself and went off to the deli to boost the troops with coffee and cream cakes.

By 4pm the main office was stripped bare and true to his word Oliver reminded Ali of her labour of love and she cursed the fluffy flocked wallpaper of the back office as the red fuzz stuck to her clothes. Mick carried out all the plumbing work to the downstairs bathroom and worked like a Trojan painting the window and door frames. By 6pm they all decided to decamp for the day and Mick asked Ali to telephone Trisha and ask was it OK to add another two for dinner.

Ali did so and kept quiet about how odd a request it was. He never asked her to talk to Trisha before. She had guessed there was something up with them both this morning but now realised it was a bit more serious. Trisha also sounded subdued on the phone and asked how they had all got on, not mentioning Mick directly. Ali hoped there would be no strained atmosphere when they went home.

When they arrived back at the Naul, Trisha had a beautiful roast cooking and little Emma was all freshly bathed and cosy in her fluffy pink pyjamas. Louie swooped on his niece and the kitchen was full and noisy with the bustling conversations of the workers. Oliver was all chat to Mick about the plans for the following day, and Mick was jovial in response, only Ali could tell Trisha was flustered and on edge by the constant nibbling of biscuits and the high colour in her cheeks.

They had a beautiful dinner of roast beef and all the trimmings and some nice red wine before Oliver and Louie got up to leave.

"Please stay," insisted Trisha, anxious to keep the level of gaiety in the house. "We have a spare room with two single beds. "

"Yes, please do. We'll get going all the quicker in the morning," added Mick, thankful for the distraction.

Both Louie and Oliver agreed, thankful to stay on and have a few more glasses of good wine.

Ali breathed a sigh of relief. Whatever seemed to be going on between Trish and Mick, it would have to wait 'til after tomorrow. And perhaps by then it would all have blown over.

Ali relaxed back, hardly noticing her aching shoulders, and sipped her red wine, thinking that all her favourite people were in this very room. Ben briefly shot into her mind before she dismissed him.

She watched Oliver tell Mick a funny story and noticed how handsome he looked when he smiled and the sombre expression he wore that made him look older disappeared. She saw how gentle and loving Louie was with Emma and she felt truly blessed. How lucky I am, she thought before dropping exhaustedly onto her bed. Blessed.

The next day they all felt a little sore, some in head and most in body but they were anxious to get the work done and after a huge fry cooked by Mick they set off bright and early to paint the shop. Ali thought she noticed a slight thaw between Trisha and Mick. They seemed to be on speaking terms at least, and Trisha waved them off smilingly in the frosty crisp air.

When they arrived Ali unleashed her choice of paint for the front shop, to gasps of disbelief.

"Bright yellow?" chorused both Louie and Mick.

"Yes. Bright yellow," Ali replied evenly as if to children. "The colour of the sun – I want my clients to come in here in dark dreary November and feel like they're already in Las Palmas. Wait 'til you see the carpet, if you think this is too much."

"It's yellow-and-grey candy stripes," Oliver informed sagely to more shock and outrage.

"Just bear with me," insisted Ali. "You will love it. Just wait and see."

Mick quipped they'd all have to wear sunglasses just to paint it on, while Ali retorted that he was finally getting the message.

Bright and sunny was what she was selling.

"By the way," said Oliver, intrigued, "you never did tell anyone what you were going to call it, the travel shop, I mean."

"All will be revealed on that too!" smiled Ali. "The sign-writer guy should be here by three, so you guys better get cracking on the outside paint. Oliver and I will do in here. The carpet fitter wants to fit the carpet on Monday morning."

They all set to work and by lunchtime Ali and Oliver had one complete coat of the bright yellow paint on the wall.

"I really like it," Oliver enthused, to Ali's delight. Mick and Louie had made good progress on the outside, which was a glossy black. The place was really taking shape.

By three when the sign guy arrived, Mick and Louie were painting the back office and Ali and Oliver had completed the front office, which gleamed bright and cheerfully. Ali had ordered grey desks and all-yellow office trays to complete the look.

Oliver couldn't wait to see what the sign read and raced outside to see it.

The gold lettering on the black background said simply 'Ali Travel' and in the corner was a girl genie on a magic carpet.

"Girl, you've arrived!" exclaimed Oliver, as he lifted Ali up and twirled her around. Ali was so happy she was close to tears.

"Wait," said Oliver and disappeared inside, only to return with a camera.

"I want to capture this moment," he said, and he snapped away happily at a girl covered in yellow paint, wearing old overalls with the happiest smile he had ever seen.

Ali Travel had finally arrived.

The following Monday, Ali was at the shop bright and early to await delivery of the office furniture which was due at 10 am and the carpet layer wasn't due until three pm. At twelve pm she was holding interviews for a part-time staff member and hadn't an idea where she was going to conduct them. Everything was still at such a raw stage, she was afraid the half finished appearance of the shop might put them off.

She decided to interview in the flat upstairs instead, which had at least a finished lived-in look, and where she could at least sit down on the old sofa that Mick had brought from his parents' house over the weekend.

She ran down to the shops and bought a plain cream cotton sheet, which she draped like a throw over the tired chintz sofa and also bought a pen and notepad in order to look at least a bit professional when the interviewees arrived. She had just got back when the telephone engineer arrived to set up her phone lines. Luckily Oliver had a friend in the connections department, and Ali was able to skip the waiting list.

At 12 exactly, she was ready and waiting for her prospective staff.

The first girl was rather unsuitable, and seemed more interested in the possibility of frequent foreign jaunts then a career in the travel business.

Ali marked a big no beside her name with her biro, after she left.

Then after that short interview, Helena Conway arrived and instinctively Ali knew she had hit the jackpot. Helena was in her late thirties and had several years of earlier experience in travel but was now returning to work part-time while her children attended school. She was business-like but friendly and knew her way around a travel sheet, and Ali liked her immediately. Not everyone was suited to deal with the public, but Helena, Ali felt, was. After Helena left Ali couldn't help but remember her interview all those years ago when Maisie Carter had taken a chance on her. She had felt really bad telling Maisie that she was leaving to set up her own travel agency. Ali had assured Maisie that she would not poach any clients and that her shop would be far away from town.

Maisie with characteristic generosity had waved her assurances away and remarked that she knew it was only a matter of time before Ali bloomed into a sharp business-woman. She wished Ali well, and gave her a huge hug.

Ali had replied softly, "If it hadn't been for you I would have never got here."

To which Maisie replied, "Rubbish. Sure, doesn't the

cream always rise to the top? Just make sure you ask me to the opening bash. The hardest part for me is that I am going to have to replace my girl. And I'll miss living vicariously through your love life, that's for sure."

Then they had both laughed heartily, the awkward moment gone.

Ali would miss Maisie – she had almost become a surrogate mum to Ali over the years. It would feel strange without her. But Ali felt Helena was just right.

It was ages yet until the carpet fitter arrived so Ali went for a cup of coffee at a local cafe and called Trisha from there.

After she had regaled her with all her news she asked how Trisha was.

"Oh, you know," sighed Trisha. "Same shit, different day."

"It can't be that bad, is it?" Ali was alarmed. Trisha and Mick still seemed to be involved in some cold war. Ali was just so caught up in her own affairs she hadn't had time to talk to Trisha about it. "Is it because you've told him about the baby?" It finally dawned on Ali.

"Yes, and he's not all that impressed with me right now."

"Look, obviously you can't talk there but do you want me to come into town this evening and meet you for coffee so we can have a proper chat?"

"No," replied Trish. "You are so busy with the shop, and you've hardly seen Emma the past week. I've taken Wednesday off. Maybe we'll do something then, OK?"

Ali agreed reluctantly. Trish seemed very down. Not wanting to talk about it was very unlike her. But she couldn't force her friend.

The remainder of the day flew by in a stressful blur.

The carpet fitter wasn't too impressed having to haul furniture about before the carpet could be laid and took chunks out of the doors shifting them to the tiny back office. Ali was exhausted by 6pm.

Luckily enough, Mick had promised to collect Emma from Mrs Costello's on his way home. Ali hoped he would have softened a bit by now over Trisha's revelation and she hoped the atmosphere wouldn't be too bad tonight. She was so tired she'd have an early night, anyhow. She hadn't realised all the things you had to do before you opened a new business. She hoped everything would be ready for the opening in a week's time.

There was stationery to be organised and flyers to go out. The list was endless. Trish was right – she had hardly seen Emma recently. She would have to make it up to her and soon.

She dragged herself to the bus stop and couldn't help looking back to see 'Ali Travel' shine under the spotlights and wondered if she would ever tire of seeing that sign.

Trisha had also dragged herself to the bus stop, but for different reasons. She wondered if ever Mick was going to forgive her for not telling him the truth about the baby. He had barely uttered a word to her all weekend, unless he absolutely had to, and he lay like a stone on the very edge of the bed every night. She missed him. She missed his arms about her and his loving words. She was also getting a little angry with him by now. Hadn't she been punished enough? She had done what she had thought was best at the time. Mick just wasn't making any allowances for her emotional state at the time – if he didn't talk to her soon he could shag off.

She wouldn't talk to him either. Two could play that game.

But on the bus she softened again – she didn't want to fight with Mick. She just wanted him to say it would be all right and that they would clear the slate and start from here. Maybe tonight he'd be in a better mood. Thank God Ali and Emma was staying with them at the moment, as they took the attention away from the freezing atmosphere between her and Mick.

But soon Ali would be gone and what would it be like then. Trisha knew she couldn't live in a cold loveless marriage. Yet here she was only a few months as Mrs O'Toole facing exactly that.

This wasn't exactly like the married life she had imagined.

That was for sure.

Mick had collected Emma from the Costellos' and hadn't stayed for his usual cup of tea. He didn't think he could sit in that cramped little kitchen with Alice Costello and not blurt out all about Trisha and the miscarriage. He knew Trisha would never forgive him if he did that so he made his excuses and bundled little Emma into her car seat in the van. Emma smelled so sweet, of baby powder and milk, and she cuddled him tightly around the neck as he carried her to the van. His eyes smarted with unexpected tears as he imagined his own little girl hugging him. He felt as if he was feeling the grief of a parent who had just lost a child. He just couldn't explain to Trisha how he felt. She'd had years to get over it. For him it was as if it had happened yesterday and he couldn't even talk about it yet. He alternately felt sad and angry towards Trisha. And for once Mick O'Toole didn't have a plan or a design to cope with what was thrown at him. He felt all at sea, and suddenly his carefully crafted life had thrown something entirely unexpected at him, and he didn't know what to do.

He slowly drove the van towards his dream home, wanting to be anywhere else, anywhere else at all.

Chapter 39

It was, at last, the day of the official opening of Ali Travel.

Ali had finally got the shop to look as she had pictured it in her mind's eye, and only she and Oliver had seen it completed. He had helped her shift the heavy filing cabinets and desks into place. The back office had been converted into a small staff room with a table and chairs and microwave for lunches.

Oliver had helped blow up the yellow and grey balloons with Ali Travel printed on them and Ali had got matching uniforms made for herself and Helena. The champagne and canapés were all ready and laid out. Ali had framed a huge print of the Great Barrier Reef and put it on the main wall, its brilliant blue water complementing the bright yellow walls.

"Don't worry. It looks fantastic," assured Oliver. "I have to admit, I had my doubts especially with the striped carpet, but it looks very modern and avant garde."

"Praise indeed," smiled Ali. She knew Oliver wasn't

344

given to rash compliments. "I just wish everyone would just come now. I feel I just can't wait another half an hour."

She had invited anyone of any importance to her, and a few trade people as well. She was so nervous, her mouth was dry and her hands shook.

"Here," Oliver proffered a glass of champagne. "This will help calm the nerves. Do you have a tape deck? We could do with some background noise."

"Yes, there's one in the back office. I don't have any suitable music, though. Do you?"

"You know me, Ali. U2 and more U2, I'm afraid," Oliver grinned.

He was immensely proud of his Mount Temple buddies.

"I have a Beach Boys tape in my car, if that's any help," piped up Helena, who appeared at the door, looking very professional in her new uniform of yellow blouse and grey skirt, and grey matching jacket.

"Oh, Helena, that's perfect. You're an angel," Ali exclaimed, gulping another sip of champagne. Why hadn't she thought of music? She was so lucky to have Oliver here. He thought of everything.

She tidied the travel brochure display for the umpteenth time and soon the Beach Boys were blaring out and people started to arrive.

One of the first guests to come was Auntie Evelyn and the awful Mr Clarke.

"We're so proud of you, aren't we, darling?" Evelyn prompted her husband, who indeed looked impressed.

"Yes, very," he added gruffly, twiddling his cuff links and appearing to blush. "I may be able to throw some business your way, with school tours and the like."

"Great," Ali replied, not sure how great it would be to have the exacting Mr Clarke as a customer.

"Joan would be so proud of you," Evelyn added, misty-eyed.

"Thanks, Evelyn," Ali replied, patting her aunt's shoulder. "That means a lot to me."

She spied Damien and Kevin at the door and made her excuses.

Then Trisha arrived, thankfully with Mick in tow. Soon everyone was there. Maisie Carter together with her husband, and Oliver's old flatmates, Joey and Derek and their partners. The only person missing was Ben. Ali looked around the room and thought about him for a few seconds then dismissed it. He could have been here if he wanted. The champagne was flowing and the canapés seemed to have gone down a treat. After a suitable time had elapsed, Ali clinked a glass with a pen to get the crowd's attention and made a little speech.

"I would just like to thank you all for coming," she began falteringly. "It means so much to have you all here."

She looked around at all the faces of the people she loved and who had helped her so much. Trisha and Mick, who had rescued her, her brothers who had always loved and supported her, and Mr and Mrs Costello, who had become like family, looking after Emma and her, Maisie Carter who had been her mentor and friend, and, of course, Oliver who had helped her through the last few difficult months.

"I know people always say that family is the most important thing. Well, I have discovered family doesn't always mean just blood relations. Some friends of mine here have been like family to me over the years and I would simply not be here without their help and support. You know who you are, and I won't embarrass you by naming names but I would like to raise a toast to 'Friendship', so if you all could raise your glasses." Everyone clapped and toasted friendship.

Then Oliver raised a toast to Ali Travel and Ali herself, and everyone clapped again and clinked their glasses.

Ali then made her way over to Trisha who was standing alone while Mick was talking to Oliver on the other side of the room.

"I can't believe what you've done to this place," Trish exclaimed while giving Ali a huge hug. "It looks so fantastic. I'm really sorry I've been so involved with my own problems that I haven't helped you more. It's truly amazing, what you've done. I am so proud of you." She was full of admiration for her friend.

"I know. I can't quite believe it myself. Shy little Ali, with her very own travel shop, it's like a wonderful dream. And don't apologise, Trisha. You have been the best friend anyone could have. Sure didn't you give me the idea yourself. How are things anyway, between yourself and Mick?"

"Oh, we're talking on a superficial level. But he hasn't touched me since that night. And as you have noticed, he's spending a lot of time working late. He just won't discuss anything, no matter how I approach him. So I've decided to leave him alone until he gets over it himself. I can't do any more."

"I suppose so," Ali frowned. She was so concerned for her two friends who seemed to have reached an impasse. But there was nothing she could do to help. Not this time.

Then she had an idea.

"Why don't you go to his office during the week and surprise him by taking him to lunch. You could take him up to Howth for some fish and chips, even. Anywhere different where you can be away from your normal environment would do. It might just break the ice."

Trish smiled. "Y'know that's not such a bad idea. I just might try that. I'd have to make sure he's there though."

"Well, what day does he do the wages?" Ali asked.

"Friday. He's there most of the day Friday to pay the subcontractors. Yes, that's it. Friday it is. Thanks, Ali. This might just work."

"Ssh, Trisha. Here comes Oliver," Ali whispered as she saw Oliver approach, while Mick stayed put right across the room.

Ali wasn't too sure her idea was a good one after all. She felt they needed a lot of help to overcome this, but by the way Mick was acting, he was far from in a forgiving mood.

Oliver came over with news that quite a few trade clients had taken her business card and he had quite a few bookings already through his business partners.

"It looks like you're in business," he said as Ali grinned.

"I never got to thank you properly," Ali said, as Trish moved away to speak to her mother and father who looked like fish out of water in a quiet corner.

"None needed," replied Oliver, visibly reddening.

"No, Oliver – I believe there is. You have been an absolute rock to me over the past few weeks, and I couldn't have done it without you."

"Thank you, but I was glad to help," Oliver replied, very pleased.

"Yes, it's been the best time of my life really, apart from . . ." her voice trailed off.

"Oh, yes, the errant medic. Have you missed him?" His heart was thumping waiting on the response. He knew the answer she might give would crush him. He had so enjoyed having her to himself the past few weeks that he had forgotten she was in love with someone else.

"A bit," was the eventual reply, "but there is no point in missing him, is there? He chose not to be in my life, so I've just got to get on with it." She smiled brightly and grabbed another two glasses of champagne from Helena who was passing with a tray.

"Here, Oliver, have this. I want to raise a toast to you, for being my best mate the past few weeks. And to thank you I have booked us a very posh dinner for next week at The Sea Urchin."

"Wow." Oliver was impressed, and touched. "Mind you, don't go blowing the first month's profits in that place. The seafood is first-class, or so I've heard, but it's a bit pricey."

"You are worth it," Ali replied smiling coquettishly. "Anyhow, I saved hundreds having you as my Financial Adviser cum Furniture Mover and Painter."

"I suppose if you put it like that, you can count me in." Oliver's glass clinked hers and they both laughed.

It had been a truly successful evening. Ali was so happy and contented that Ben receded to the back dark corners of her mind where she had banished him. He wasn't going to spoil her golden moment, that was for sure.

Oliver was happy too. At least he had the girl that he loved in his life. Maybe Ali wasn't on his arm or in love with him – but he had become an important friend to her, and he was happy to have that, for the moment – who knew what the future may hold?

Trisha and Mick were unhappy and unsure what their future held.

They slowly came together as the night progressed, just in case Trisha's parents suspected anything was amiss.

Mick noticed Trisha, though glamorous in a plain black trouser suit, looked tired and strained. His heart ached with love for her but he still could not yet forgive her, though he hated himself for it. He stood close to her talking to her father, hoping she would notice he was making an effort.

Trisha felt miserable standing next to her husband, watching him chat amiably to her father like there was nothing wrong at all between them, when in reality he was shutting her out of his life. She wished to grab his hand tightly, but, afraid he might spurn her, she didn't and just nodded dreamily as her mother prattled on.

She just wanted to go home. She refused another cocktail sausage as she had scoffed almost half a dozen already, and this new trouser suit, which she bought to impress Mick was a very tight size 16. She would really have to rein herself in soon or it would have to be outsize kaftans for her.

She glanced at Ali, laughing aloud with Oliver and for once envied her friend. Ali, who was a slender size 10, with her beautiful smile and her gorgeous hair, and now, she not only had a beautiful baby girl but a new business and a fantastic career. And by the look of Oliver he seemed deeply smitten with her. Trish felt ashamed for her envy. Ali had endured such a difficult life in the past – she really deserved all the good times coming her way. Trish just wished it could be good for them both at the same time. They never seemed to have good luck together. Trish felt right now like running a mile from this place that she felt reinforced what a failure she had become. Her cheeks burned with shame over her feelings, which she could never admit to anyone and could barely admit to herself. She was jealous of her best friend, and that didn't feel good at all.

As the photographer's flashbulb popped, Ali and Oliver smiled brightly. Then they answered the questions of the journalist friend that Oliver had casually invited.

"I can't believe you did that," exclaimed Ali excitedly. She had never been in the paper before.

"You need all the publicity you can get. Jim's an old mate. He owes me a few favours. It was no problem, really."

Ali looked at Oliver in admiration. Nothing really was a problem for him, it seemed. He really was a good friend. She felt lucky to have him.

"Thanks," Ali murmured, kissing him chastely on the cheek.

He smelled nice, a delicate mix of Kouros and sandalwood soap.

"You are welcome," Oliver replied looking a bit bashful. "Now, go mingle with the suits. This is your big night and you' ve got to enjoy every last minute."

Ali lifted a bundle of newly printed Ali Travel brochures and headed for 'the suits' as Oliver termed them. He was right, this was her night and she was going to make the most of it.

This was the beginning of her new career and she was adamant it was going to be a huge success. She was going to make damn sure of that.

Chapter 40

The next evening Isabel was glancing absent-mindedly through *The Evening Herald* when she spotted something alarming in the society pages. There, large as life, smiling as brazen as the hussy she obviously was, was Alison O'Neill, clinging like a limpet to Oliver Johnston. "The common tramp!" thought Isabel crossly. "Getting her claws into Ben's best friend now, by the looks of things." She flicked quickly to the column piece and read all about the exciting new travel shop opened in Swords, owned by one Alison O'Neill, and specialising in the long-haul travel plans of the 18-35 age group.

"Well, I never," she said aloud, aghast.

"What is it?" John peered over his *Times*. He never read the *Herald*, but he knew Isabel secretly loved it despite her protestations that she only had it delivered because of its excellent TV guide.

"It's that awful O'Neill girl. She's only opened up her

own travel agency on the northside, of all places." She made the northside sound incredibly like the bowels of hell.

"Let's see," cried John. He had always liked Ali despite his wife's objections and could never fathom why Ben didn't ever propose. He had already decided he was going to cut out the photo and send it to Ben in his next letter.

"Well, I'll be damned. Looks like she's made a success of herself, after all."

John beamed as he spoke to his wife. He always got a superior feeling towards the snobbish Isabel when one of her prejudices backfired.

"And by sleeping with whom did she acquire the money to finance this deal?" asked Isabel acidly, while snatching the paper back. "No doubt some sugar daddy has been coming up with the cash while she provides a service. I do hope it's not poor Oliver Johnston she's got her hooks into this time."

"Isabel, that's an awful thing to say," retorted John – for once genuinely shocked by his wife's acerbic tongue. "She could have been our daughter-in-law, after all."

"You silly old fool," smiled Isabel malevolently. "You and I both know that I never would have let that happen."

"Yes, indeed I do," sighed her husband, "and look where Ben is now. Where has it really got you?"

"Oh, he'll find the right girl, someday," Isabel retorted back, miffed.

"Yes, but will we still be around to see it?" remarked John, stifling his own smile, and flicking his *Irish Times* loudly. "That's two nil to me, I think," he thought to himself, as he saw Isabel throw down the paper and turn on the TV – he didn't care what she thought.

He would send the article to his son and let him ponder on what he missed out on, and if Ben was jealous because Oliver Johnston seemed to have taken his place, well, all the better. He took up the discarded *Herald* and placed it inside his blazer pocket – Isabel wasn't going to win all the battles, not if he had anything to do with it.

Trisha had taken the Friday off as planned with Ali. She had soaked in a scented bath after Mick had left, defuzzed her hirsute pins and glammed herself up as much as she could without looking too over the top while visiting a prefab office on little more than a building site.

She then went to the salon in Swords for a wash and blow-dry and managed to squeeze herself into her black leather trousers, which she was sure strained considerably when she sat down. She felt good when she left the hairdresser's with a gleaming golden mane and popped in to see Ali and Helena in Ali Travel on the way, so they could give her the once-over.

The phones were ringing constantly when she arrived which was a good sign and Ali waved her into the back office, past the three awaiting customers.

After a few minutes Ali emerged.

"You look fabulous," she gushed. 'Mick will be putty in your hands."

"Do you think so?" asked Trisha, pleased.

"Of course. Now, did you set up the picnic basket and get the vino, like I said?"

"Yep, it's all stashed in the car. I just hope the rain

holds off. It looks a bit threatening out there at the moment."

"Well, you look a bit threatening in those 'come to bed with me' leathers. Sorry, Trisha, but I have to get back. We are really busy today."

"Good complaint though, isn't it?" Trisha replied, rising. "Look, I'll be off. God! I feel like I'm going on a first date. I am so nervous."

Ali gave her a huge hug.

"It'll be fine. Just take a few deep breaths and breeze in there, and don't take no for an answer."

"Right," said Trisha forcefully, now buoyed by her friend's assurances.

She ran from the travel shop to her car hoping the dark skies would hold off all downpours until after her lunch with Mick. Still, they had enjoyed plenty of picnics indoors when they were building the bungalow. She thought back to how happy they had been then.

They could be that happy again, if they both worked at it. She was going to make sure of it.

She turned on her 'Black' tape as she sped her little Micra car towards the Airport Road and hummed along to *Wonderful Life* hoping that it truly would be.

When she got to the tiny prefab office at the rear of a business park she was glad to see Mick's van parked outside. Great. Everything was going according to plan. She parked hurriedly and ran into the prefab to escape the heavy rain that had just begun to fall. Her hair would get ruined. As she tumbled through the door she was stopped dead in her tracks by the sight of Mick leaning over the desk towards a pretty blonde girl who was barely out of her teens and was giggling while gazing up at Mick like he was some sort of Adonis. Trisha took in the whole scene right up to and including the teenager's long lithe legs clad in a tiny mini, and her low-cut top.

Mick looked up, stunned.

"Oh, Trisha, I wasn't expecting you."

"Obviously," retorted Trisha, her voice dripping with disgust as she eyed the girl suspiciously. "Who is this?"

"Sorry, this is Amanda, my new assistant. Amanda, this is my wife, Trisha."

"Looks like I'm not the only one able to keep a secret." flashed Trisha and stormed out of the tiny office. The rain was now pelting down and she made a frantic dash to her car, followed closely by an anxious Mick. She managed to get into the car and lock the door by the time he reached her.

"Trisha, Trisha! It's not what it seems – please open the door. I want to talk to you."

"Well, that makes a bloody change!" yelled Trisha through the window. '"Maybe now I don't want to talk to you."

The deluge was now soaking Mick and rain ran down his face – but Trisha didn't care. She fired up the engine and drove off at speed, heading for God knows where. She couldn't believe what she had just witnessed. Mick had already replaced her, and with someone barely out of knee socks. If his assistant had been hired with entirely innocent intentions, why had he not told her? It was as if he had deliberately withheld the information to hurt her, and it had succeeded. She felt like such an idiot. She glanced at the carefully prepared picnic lunch and swore. Where the hell could she go now?

She was too ashamed to go back and tell Ali what had transpired and she couldn't face going back to that large empty bungalow on her own, so she turned the car towards Drumcondra. She might go and see her mother, or else she'd go into town. She wasn't sure yet. She just wanted to forget this whole day ever happened. One thing was for certain. She and Mick were in a whole lot of deeper trouble then she had anticipated. Now she wasn't sure if he was a person she knew. Old reliable Mick might not be all he seemed.

She burned with anger and shame over the possibility that he might be interested in someone else. It had never ever crossed her mind that Mick would look beyond her, but now it did, and it made Trisha very uncomfortable indeed. Suddenly their problems were a lot larger than having or not having babies. She decided as she neared Drumcondra that she would indeed call into her mum and would pour her heart out to her. She needed strong advice on preventing her marriage from unravelling any more than it had, and she knew her mum was the very person to give it to her.

Mick was livid. He never wanted Trisha to find out he had hired Amanda that way but now she had and it looked very bad indeed. But after that initial confession by Trisha and the ensuing coldness between them, mainly on his part, there had never been an opportunity to tell her, and now she suspected the worst. He was the first to admit, he had been flattered by Amanda's obvious fawning over him. And she was a beautiful girl, if a little immature. But he would never cheat on Trisha, surely she would realise that. He had felt ignored and unloved lately and wallowed in Amanda's adoring attentions which appeared a little more than professional, but that's all it was, a little harmless flirtation. If Trisha now considered him a cheat as well as a heartless man who would have dumped her if she had been pregnant, then he wondered what he was doing in this relationship. It seemed he couldn't win.

He really needed some advice from an interested but neutral party. He couldn't talk to Ali, as she was too close to Trisha. Ben was in Africa. Oliver, he could talk to Oliver – he seemed like a nice sound guy. Mick had made Trisha so much his life, that he had lost touch with all his friends apart from Ben. He decided to give Oliver a call and arrange to meet him for a pint. This would have to be sorted out soon, as he could see things going from bad to worse for himself and Trisha. Things just couldn't go on the way they were. He called Oliver at work and arranged to meet him at 6pm in The Duke. There would be no point in trying to talk to Trisha anyhow, until she calmed down, and by the look on her face when she had thundered off, that wasn't going to be any time soon.

Alice Costello appeared to be calm as she poured a strong cup of tea for herself and a tearful Trisha, but inside she was shocked and more than a little shaken. How well you think you know your children, she thought, and every time they manage to shock you when you least expect it. She had stopped worrying the day Trisha had sailed down the aisle. She and Mick had the happiest of marriages. It was bad enough to discover they were in real trouble, but to find out your then teenage daughter had suffered a miscarriage all those years ago and then went back to her school books the following day, left her trembling.

She wasn't sure if it was that, or the fact Patricia was having sex at just seventeen, that shocked her more. But right now, she knew Trisha needed her concern and advice. The lecture, if there were to be one, would come much later.

"I doubt there's anything going on between Mick and this girl, Trisha. He mightn't have told you he hired her because the two of you haven't been getting on," she said now to Trisha, whose face was red with all the crying.

"And whose fault is that?" Trisha asked hotly, wiping her eyes angrily, mascara streaking the well made-up face.

"It's no one's fault," replied her mother gently. "Mick is in shock, love. For you this happened years ago, but for Mick, it's only been a couple of weeks. He's probably grieving the loss of his child, as well as being annoyed with you for keeping this from him. You must remember this was his baby too."

"Oh, God, I had never even thought of it like that, Mam. You are right. I feel so awful. I was so upset that he wasn't comforting me that I forgot I should comfort him. I feel like such an eejit. But what now, where do we go from here?"

"You both need to sit down and talk about it. You need to hear his feelings without flying off the handle and he needs to understand why you did what you did, but you also need to listen, and Trisha, I know you, you're my daughter, and I'm here to tell ye', listening was never one of your best qualities. You are so used to Mick being the big softie and being there for you, that you haven't realised you have to be there for him, at least until he comes to terms with the whole thing, which I might add, has come as a great shock to me too."

Trisha looked at her mother, who looked tired and a little bit old.

She had been selfish to just land this on her mum after all these years, just to make herself feel better. Her mother was right.

Trisha would have to be a bit more understanding of others, especially her husband. She hoped it wasn't too late. That Amanda looked like a right fox circling her prey. She felt better already, and sipped her tea gratefully after she had given her mother a huge hug.

"Thanks, Mam, and sorry for landing this on you so suddenly. I do realise it was very selfish of me."

"Go on out of that," smiled her mother, embarrassed by the open display of affection. "Isn't that what I'm here for?"

Later that evening, Oliver met up with Mick in The Duke. Oliver had been perturbed by the terse phone call from Mick that afternoon, requesting to meet. Oliver knew it was urgent by Mick's tone so he decided to wait to find out what the matter was, as he had never socialised with Mick before, except when Ali and Trisha were involved. He hoped it wasn't anything to do with Ali wanting him out of her life. Even though he was not her boyfriend he hoped he wasn't being dumped. Maybe she had discovered his feelings and it had scared her off. A myriad of situations ran through his mind as Mick went to the bar and ordered the pints.

"Well, I'll cut to the chase," said Mick as he sat down.

"Oliver, I need your advice. I feel my marriage is falling apart and as Ben is away, I need another impartial bloke's advice on what to do to save it. You seem like a sensible guy and you know Trisha, so I was hoping you could help."

He looked at Oliver steadily. Oliver looked back in amazement.

But he could see Mick was deadly serious. He didn't know Mick well enough to make a facile joke so he, feeling like Marjorie Proops, asked, "What seems to be the problem between you?"

Mick poured out his heart to Oliver over the next two pints. Leaving nothing out and ending with Trisha storming off after eyeing up the delectable Amanda.

"Is that it?" Oliver asked when Mick finished the sorry tale. "You have no ulterior motive in hiring this girl?"

Mick searched his conscience.

"Well, maybe I was trying to make her a little bit jealous, I suppose."

"You idiot. That was your second mistake." Oliver was nothing if not a straight talker.

"What was my first?" Mick was surprised by that comment.

"Your first mistake was not taking her into your arms after she had told you and sharing your sorrow with her over your baby. Together. The questions about why she didn't tell you should have taken second place. You also didn't make any allowances for the state she was in at the time. The girl was probably terrified. She told no one, Mick. That explains a lot. Sure you had a right to be a bit miffed that so long had elapsed before she told you, but not to punish her like you have. She loves you. I wish I was so lucky."

Mick felt ashamed. Oliver was right. He had behaved like a spoilt child. Trisha's secret must have been a terrible cross to bear for all those years. He felt like running home right now and telling her how sorry he was, but it would be a bit unfair to Oliver to rush out now, after dragging him out on a horrible night like this.

"You're right, Oliver. I'm an idiot. I'll make it up to her."

"Well, make sure you do," Oliver's green eyes were flinty.

"Tell me, are you always this backward in coming forward?" Mick enquired, grinning. Oliver didn't pussyfoot around.

"Yes," replied Oliver, smiling himself, "except when it comes to matters of my own heart, that is."

"Ali, right?" Mick asked, sipping his pint.

Oliver was aghast. "Is it that obvious?"

"Not to everyone, no. But Trisha and I agree on one thing. You two are made for each other. All you have to do is make Ali realise it too."

"And what would be your sage advice on how to approach this?"

Oliver was all ears.

"Well. Ali has been let down a lot, as you know, and even though Ben is my mate, he has hurt her badly too many times. Just be there for her as you have been, as a good friend. That's just what she needs. Take it really slowly. Eventually she'll realise you are there, you'll see. I've known her for years, Oliver. Don't crowd her and you'll win her over."

"Thanks." Oliver felt more hopeful that he had in a while.

He was going out to dinner with Ali tomorrow night. He was going to try and ask her out then, but now he would wait, as Mick advised. He had waited all this time, another bit longer couldn't hurt.

"You better go home after this," Oliver said as Mick neared the end of his second pint. "You don't need another reason for Trisha to stay mad at you."

"Do you mind? Cheers, mate." Mick grabbed his coat and rose to his feet. "And Oliver?"

Oliver looked up. "Yeah?"

"Thanks. Thanks a lot, mate. You really made me see things much clearer. I owe you one."

"I'll hold you to that," grinned Oliver. "Now go home to your gorgeous wife. Pity me going home to a ready-made meal for one and the *Late Late Show*."

Mick laughed. Oliver was right. He was lucky, lucky enough to have a beautiful wife who loved him and wanted nothing more than to have his child. He would make it up to her, soon.

For the first time in weeks he got into his van to go home with a light heart. Things would be different. He'd let Trisha see that she was the most important person in the world to him.

Trisha and Ali were home just five minutes when Mick arrived home, complete with a large Chinese takeaway and the biggest bunch of flowers Ali had ever seen. He planted a huge kiss on Trisha's cheek and whispered in her ear that he was sorry and could they talk later. Trisha, for once, bit her lip and graciously nodded and they all sat down to their

Chinese feast while Emma played happily about their feet.

For the first time in ages harmony reigned in the O'Toole household and Ali felt a flood of relief. Trisha had told her the entire story in the car on the way home from the Costellos' and she had been unsure where Mick had gone, but Ali had received a call earlier on from Oliver telling her that Mick was meeting him so she had guessed Oliver's no nonsense advice had done the trick. Good old Oliver. He really was a nice guy. She was quite looking forward to her meal at the Sea Urchin tomorrow night.

Ali couldn't wait to tell him about what a successful week she had enjoyed at the travel shop – but right now, she was happy her friends seemed to be over the worst of their problems for the moment.

"I think this calls for a nice bottle of wine, don't you?" She smiled at Trisha, who was happily tucking into her chow mein.

"Yes, I do," replied Mick and Trisha together and they all laughed.

"Do you think this is a good time to ask if you two could baby-sit tomorrow night?" asked Ali, remembering her date.

"I don't see why not," replied Mick, looking at Trisha. "We've nothing planned, have we love?"

"No," said Trisha looking back at him tenderly. "We're just sitting in with a nice bottle of Merlot and a video, if that suits you, Mick."

"It suits me just fine," said Mick, grinning widely.

"Right, that's sorted so, Ali. You go and enjoy yourself. "We'd love to mind Emma."

And it was sorted, thought Ali. Thank God.

She intended moving into the flat next week, but had hesitated because she didn't feel she could leave Trisha alone to her unhappy home life, but now that everything seemed to be improving she could move out. It was time she and Emma had their own place. She loved living with her best friend, but it really was time to move on.

It would be the first home for Ali and Emma on their own.

While Ali was a little bit afraid of the prospect of being out there alone, she also wanted to create her new life, and that meant standing up on her own two feet and going it alone, just her and Emma.

Chapter 41

"This is really nice. Thanks for inviting me. You really didn't have to."

Oliver was taking in the sumptuous surroundings of The Sea Urchin, the priciest and some said best seafood restaurant in County Dublin. It was perched on the hill of Howth with million-dollar views and a price list to match. Ali had never been here before either, but had envied people who could afford such luxury. She had promised herself that she would go there if she ever got her business off the ground and thanks to Oliver she had. So it was only right and fitting that he be her guest.

"I did have to, Oliver. It was largely due to you that I got the confidence to reach for my dream and achieve it. It's only a posh fish dinner. You can return the favour some time if you like."

Oliver smiled but remained silent. Play it cool, he thought, just like Mick had advised. Don't appear too keen.

Ali hoped she hadn't offended Oliver by offering to

take him here. She knew he was a proud man. He just seemed a bit quiet tonight. Ali had earlier surprised herself by sweeping into town and buying a sexy off-the-shoulder black dress to impress him.

After she had left Switzers with the outfit and some new perfume she had realised she wanted to look nice for Oliver.

It rather made her smile instead of becoming alarmed. It signalled at least that there was life after Ben. She had been living like a nun over the past six months since he had left. It was about time she started to have some fun again.

"Are you OK?" she asked at last. Oliver was studying the menu like for an exam.

"Yes, fine. The prices are a bit steep, to say the least."

"If that's all that's worrying you then don't. Just enjoy yourself, Oliver. It's all taken care of."

"OK. And how was the first week of trading?" Oliver decided to keep the talk mainly on a business track. That way was safest.

He wouldn't blunder out about how amazing she looked in that black dress or how much he had longed for this evening.

Ali regaled him with of tales about how busy they were and how she and Helena were exhausted at the end of every day. Helena had ended up working a few days until 5.30pm to help Ali out. But if it continued she would need to hire another staff member.

Then Ali told him about her plans to move into the flat above the shop.

"I could help you move your bits and pieces, if you

like," Oliver offered. He liked to be indispensable, as Ali had termed it.

"That would be great, if you wouldn't mind. I'd appreciate it," Ali smiled. He really did have lovely eyes, she thought.

"How do you feel about moving out on your own?" Oliver asked despite himself. He hadn't meant to – because he knew soon after he would follow with a question about Ben, and that was too forward. But he needed to know did she still miss him as awfully as she had in the first few months since Ben Murphy's departure.

"Oh, a bit scared, but excited. I know there'll be a lot of quiet nights when Emma is in bed and I'll be rattling around on my own, but Trisha and Mick need their space. I'm really excited about putting my stamp on the place though, and doing up Emma's room, just for her."

"Any regrets?" Oliver felt it was the most tactful of enquiries.

It meant she didn't have to mention the Ben word if she didn't want to.

"No." Ali shook her head, vehemently. "None, Oliver. It's taken me the past six months to feel a bit better about what happened with Ben, but now I feel that it obviously wasn't meant to be. What happened to my mother taught me several things, one of which was you just can't hang around waiting for life to happen. You have to get on with it. I'm happier now than I've been in a very long time. I'll always have a love for Ben. But that doesn't mean I'll never be capable of falling in love with anyone else again."

Oliver lowered his gaze. If he had stayed looking at Ali he would have confessed his love for her. Right then and there. But now wasn't the time – instead he replied, "Well said. I admire you, Ali. You have taken whatever life has thrown at you and survived. And look at you now. I'm sure your mother would be really proud of you."

Ali smiled. He was very sweet.

"Yes, Oliver. I do believe she would be."

The evening passed enjoyably. The Sea Urchin lived up to its famous name and the food was indeed divine. Ali had the chilli crab while Oliver had a sizzling Thai seafood curry. They both had a lime cheesecake for dessert, and a few bottles of wine.

Afterwards, Ali convinced Oliver that she wanted to walk up the rest of the long laborious and very steep hill up to the summit, where Dublin looked spectacular on the clear frosty November night.

Ali had spent a lot of time on that summit with Ben. It was her favourite part of Dublin. She always left there serene and calmed by the scenery. It felt a bit strange, coming up here with someone else.

Oliver longed to grab her hand, and walk with her like a couple but he didn't.

After a few minutes of taking in the twinkling lights, Ali dismissed her ghosts and stood next to Oliver who was sitting on the wall, breathing into his frozen hands.

"It's freezing isn't it?" asked Ali, the wine was keeping her warm enough, but her face and hands were very cold.

"Yes," replied Oliver, "but look at the view. It's worth the odd bit of frostbite. Ali, would you like my coat? Come here and I'll warm you up a bit."

Ali moved in closer, and Oliver rubbed her hands with his and then rubbed her back. She then moved closer still, into his chest, and he caressed her hair gently. Suddenly he took her face in his hands and slowly kissed her full on the lips, so gently and carefully as if she was made of glass. It was the softest, gentlest kiss Ali had ever felt and she felt her head go dizzy. Suddenly Oliver pulled away, saying, "I am sorry, Ali. I hadn't meant to do that. It's just you look so beautiful up here in this beautiful place, I couldn't resist."

"Oliver," Ali replied looking into his handsome face. "It's quite all right. I really enjoyed that. In fact, I'd very much like it if you kissed me again."

Oliver took her into his arms and kissed her once more, just as gently but this time with more passion and Ali really did feel her legs go weak.

Maybe it was too much wine, but she felt that same way she had with Ben, but somehow it still felt different. Oliver was different. He had been a wonderful friend and now it seemed he might want to be something more. Ali was pleased about that, but she was also a little bit wary. She needed time to get over Ben, and didn't want to fall for Oliver on the rebound, or just because she couldn't face living on her own. She would have to give this some thought. But right now, it was only a kiss. OK, two kisses. Let's not run away with yourself, O'Neill, she berated herself.

"Shall we go?" she said at last, breaking the silence.

"Yes, I don't want Mick to think I'm taking advantage of his baby-sitting duties," Oliver quipped as they made their way back down to the village for a taxi.

They caught a cab back to Swords where Oliver dropped Ali off with a soft kiss and a promise to help Ali move. He deliberately didn't pressurise her for a date in case he blew it, but he sailed home in that cab reliving every delicious moment of what had been for him, simply the best evening he had ever had.

Ali crept into the house, seeing no lights on. Trisha and Mick must have gone to bed early. She would loved to have told Trisha that Oliver had kissed her and endlessly dissected it over copious cups of coffee, but it would have to wait. So she clambered into her warm bed and tried to make sense of it all herself. But all she could think about was his warm velvety skin and that soft mouth. She soon fell asleep, and for the first time in months didn't dream of Ben Murphy.

Ben Murphy was re-reading the letter his father had sent him. In it was the newspaper clipping of Ali looking suspiciously close to his former friend, Oliver Johnston. Ali looked amazing in the black and white photo, her smile wide and happy, snuggled in close to that traitor, Oliver. Some friend he turned out to be. Ben had burned when he first saw the photo and hadn't really calmed down yet. He guessed he still felt jealous and proprietorial over Ali, even though he had no right to, especially now. He was also surprised Ali had opened a travel shop of her own. It certainly hadn't been something she had ever expressed the wish to do when she had been around him.

"Still checking out your ex, I see," Susie Kendall was peering over his shoulder.

"Nothing's changed since I last looked," replied Ben lightly. It wouldn't do to let Susie know he was feeling a bit jealous.

"If I didn't know better, I'd say you still carried a torch for her," said Susie playfully as she wrapped her arms tightly around his chest.

"Susie, how could you?" replied Ben in jest, pulling her onto his lap. "You know I only have a huge torch for you, my love!"

"As the Bishop said to the actress," giggled Susie, kissing Ben on the neck.

"Seriously, though, Suz, it is all in the past. I love you now."

"So you said, fifteen times today, so far," grinned Susie.

And he did. He really felt he loved Susie. It had been love at first sight. Since the moment tiny Susie Kendall had walked into the Field Hospital in Beira, to be the head sister for the Triage Ben had been smitten. Susie was a no-nonsense nurse from West London.

She was a petite blonde 27-year-old, with sparkling blue eyes and a ready wit, unlike anyone Ben had ever met before. She was seemingly immune to his charms and it had taken him weeks to get her to have a coffee with him. But Ben had gradually worn her resistance down and they had become good friends and finally lovers. The one thing Ben liked about Susie was the fact she always kept him guessing. He never quite knew where he stood with her. He had declared his love abundantly, and Susie would just smile enigmatically at him and declare him mad with dengue fever. She never once had said she loved him, and now he had received this letter and she had noticed it had obviously unhinged him. He was afraid it would scare her off even more, something he didn't want.

Ben now stroked her short hair and wondered if she loved him, and if so, why she couldn't admit to it. It drove him crazy sometimes, just trying to figure her out.

"Well, honey, any chance of a quick shag? I'm on duty in two hours."

Suzy still shocked him sometimes.

"Why, you loose woman. I'll have you know I'm a good Irish Catholic boy, who has never heard the like before."

"Sorry, I offended your moral sensibilities. I'll re-phrase that. Would my darling like to ravish his little rosebud before tea or after?" With that Suzy ran giggling into Ben's tiny bedroom with its even tinier single bed and awaited his ravishing.

"Never a dull moment," quipped Ben as he chased after her. She really was the most amazing woman he had ever met.

And he never wanted to let her go.

Chapter 42

Trisha and Mick had arrived into Mount Carmel to have a consultation with an excellent gynaecologist – according to Trisha's GP. Dr Molloy apparently had great success with problem pregnancies and infertility. Trisha was delighted that Mick had agreed to go with her, while the possible problems with her conceiving were explored.

After that horrible few weeks, culminating in Trisha's discovery of the delectable Amanda, who had since moved on to a bigger posher office in town to Trisha's relief, she and Mick had had a heart-to-heart. They laid everything bare on the table and came away with a new respect and understanding for each other. Things since then had been a lot better; they had communicated more and discussed the past and the future and the possibility that they might never have children.

But today was the day that could decide their future.

Trisha would find out the results of some blood tests that would tell if she had polycystic ovaries or endometriosis, conditions that could make her less fertile.

Mick clasped her hand tightly as they waited for the lift to take them to the third floor to Dr Molloy's clinic. Mick appeared to be as nervous as she was.

The lift door opened and an attractive blonde woman with a tiny baby and a doting partner got out.

"Karen!" Mick exclaimed. "Is it really you?"

"Mick, hi." Karen exclaimed back. "God, it's been years. How are you?"

"Fine. This is my wife, Trisha. Trisha, this is Karen, an old friend. Is this your baby?"

"Yes," grinned Karen proudly, 'this is little Oisin, and this is my husband, Brian."

Brian shook hands quietly and then busied himself with Oisin who was loudly exercising his little lungs.

"Well done, Karen. I'm delighted for you, you know, after everything that happened."

"All in the past, Mick, all in the past," Karen replied briskly and then it dawned on Trisha who she was. Karen Kennedy. Ben's ex-girlfriend, the one who shafted Ali to get her clutches into Ben and then was left practically at the altar. Trisha took her in while smiling frostily.

"I really must go now," Karen said, slightly embarrassed by Trisha's open stare. "It was nice seeing you Mick, best of luck to you now, and you too Trisha." She smiled graciously at Trisha who smiled back and then almost kicked herself for doing so. It almost felt like a betrayal of Ali.

"Well, I never," Trisha said under her breath as they got into the lift.

"There you go," said Mick affably. Nothing ever seemed to bother him too much. "Looks like it worked out for Karen after all. She looks a lot happier than she ever did with Ben, and the baby is really cute. I'm glad it worked out for her in the end."

"Is that so?" bristled Trisha. "It's a pity she wasn't so kind-hearted to Ali all those years ago."

"Yes, and didn't she pay a high price for it," replied Mick gently.

"When did you meet her?" sniffed Trish, slightly mollified. "I certainly wasn't with you."

"I had to have a fitting for my groomsman's outfit, and she came in to see Ben's. I met her then. She was a nice girl, behind it all, Trish."

"You're just a sucker for a glamorous blonde, Mick O'Toole," Trish replied, rolling her eyes.

"And didn't I fall for one and marry her too?" said Mick, giving her bum a squeeze. Trish jumped and giggled as the lift door opened. Her nerves promptly returned. This was it. In a few minutes they would know if their future was going to be one long quest to have the baby they had always dreamt of.

They sat on Dr Molloy's plump sofa in the waiting room for what seemed like hours but had been in fact only twenty minutes before they were called in. A small bespectacled grandfather-type doctor peered at them both and then shook their hands profusely.

"Well, Mr and Mrs O'Toole," he began smilingly, "you

are here because you are experiencing difficulties with conception. Is that correct?" He took up the file, which contained the test results from the blood tests that Trish had had ten days earlier. "Mrs O'Toole, you have had several tests, I see. All of which came back normal, I am happy to say."

"Great!" Trisha exclaimed, relief flooding through her. Perhaps this wasn't going to be so bad, after all. Mick squeezed her hand tightly.

"There was something else that showed up, however," continued Dr Molloy, his expression suddenly serious. "Something that led me to conclude that we cannot help you."

Trisha felt her heart stop. She fought back welling tears.

"Surely, there is something you can do . . ." she began.

"What was it?" Mick interrupted, his face pale.

"I cannot help you, Patricia, if I may call you that, because you are in fact, already pregnant. About nine weeks, by my calculations."

"What?" Trisha and Mick yelled together. Trisha couldn't believe it, pregnant! All this time she had been gaining weight and feeling miserable, she had been pregnant.

"But, Doctor, I had a period last month."

"Was it light?" Dr Molloy asked over his glasses and Trisha nodded.

"Yes, sometimes this is the case. But you are pregnant, please be assured of that. Now we have to get you signed up to our ante-natal clinic and I'll hand you over to my colleague, Dr Sarah Kehoe. She handles all the normal pregnancies, which, to all extents and purposes you appear to have. She won't need to see you 'til about thirteen weeks for a scan, but you can go to your GP in the meantime for a general check-up. Now, Mr O'Toole, I suggest you take your wife for a nice lunch. It's been a bit of a shock for you both." He beamed at them both, as he escorted them out.

They left the office in stunned silence. Trisha just couldn't believe it – she had been playing out all kinds of scenarios for the past week, but never this one.

She never expected to get what she had always wanted.

How could she have missed it? It seemed such a simple explanation for all her mood swings, the tight clothes and general tiredness she had been experiencing recently, but she had put it all down to the stress, when she and Mick had been locked in battle.

"I just can't believe it," said Mick, again and again, as he hugged her tightly.

"Nor can I," replied an amazed Trisha. "If I wasn't pregnant, I'd ask you for a large brandy. I'm in such shock. Dr Molloy is right – we need to have a nice chat and then a long lunch. You better take the rest of the day off."

"Why is that?" Mick asked unnecessarily, for today he would grant her anything.

"Because, Mr O'Toole," she replied, mimicking Dr Molloy's posh voice, "we are going shopping for baby clothes. Lots and lots of baby clothes!"

"We're actually going to be parents," Mick said as they got into the car and drove away.

"Yes, I do believe we are," Trisha replied and gave his arm a squeeze. She patted the stomach that had earlier caused her much concern over its widening girth and quietly thanked the Lord above for everything. All the troubles of the past few weeks evaporated and she could now look forward to the future, their future. Everything would be OK now. She was having a baby, her very own child. Suddenly the world seemed a wonderful place again, where Trisha felt happy and hopeful again – she simply couldn't wait to tell Ali.

Ali was up to her armpits in Pooh Bear friezes that were to adorn Emma's room. It was an impossible task to do alone. Oliver had offered to help but she had refused. She felt she needed some space from him, after the kiss, or rather kisses the other night. She didn't want him to think they were an item in case they weren't. Ali wasn't sure yet. She knew she was attracted to Oliver, but she held back. After all her rashness of jumping into a relationship with Simon after Ben, which had been a bad decision, she dearly wanted to get it right this time. If it was meant to happen, it would. She knew it had to be for the right reasons. But right now she wondered at how independent she really was. It certainly didn't help that this border looked awful the way it dipped and rose like a wave across the wall.

If she ripped it off it would take half of the new pale pink paint with it. She was tempted to run downstairs to the travel shop and beg poor overworked Helena to come and help but she felt like an idiot already. She would ring Trisha tonight and see how she had got on at the hospital and casually mention that she needed another pair of hands with Emma's room. Emma's new bed looked cute with the pale yellow duvet with the pink rosebud detail. She had got curtains to match and the room looked really girly and cosy, wavy border not withstanding.

Emma had fretted the first few nights at the new flat and had cried to go home to Trisha's as she so cutely pronounced it.

Ali resisted taking Emma into her own bed as she felt lonely herself and wasn't sure if she would ever let her go. They both had to be grown up about it. Emma was little more than a baby, but what was Ali's excuse?

She tried vainly to straighten the border and failed so threw her hat at it and grabbed her coat. Stuff it for today, she decided.

She was going to collect Emma early from Mrs Costello and telephone Oliver and ask him over this evening to help her decorate. She'd even throw in dinner to sweeten the deal.

Trisha had enough on her hands with all this hospital business. She might not feel up to a girly night if the consultation had gone badly. Ali would telephone her anyway to see if she was OK.

Trisha would laugh to see Ali change her mind like the weather.

After all her protesting and insisting to Trisha last week, she had told Trisha the next morning after her date with Oliver that they had kissed and Trisha had whooped and punched the air, and then announced: "I knew it. You are made for each other."

To which Ali had protested and insisted that it all

meant little and she was taking her time and so on and so forth and yet here she was, barely five days later, unable to put up a bloody border then ringing the bloody guy to come to the rescue.

"Little Miss Independence, indeed," she said aloud to her paint-splotched face in the hall mirror. "What are we to do with you, at all?"

Oliver was in his office, staring out over the tall Georgian buildings towards the north side of the river. He was wondering when he would pluck up the courage to call Ali. He had promised to help her move but she hadn't telephoned nor had he. The silence had been deafening since last Friday. Surely she had moved in by now? He took up the telephone and almost dialled her number but lost his nerve. Damn it. Why was he playing these games and driving himself up the wall? Because you're afraid if you don't, you will lose her, Mick would have answered. And you never had her in the first place, Ben would have said.

Just then the phone trilled making him almost jump out of his chair.

"Hello," he barked impatiently.

"Oliver? Are you OK?" It was Ali. He couldn't believe it.

"Ali, hi, yes I'm fine. Just been one of those days, y'know." One of those days when I can't do any work for thinking about you, he almost added.

"Oh, I'm sorry. I was about to ask you something that would only make your day a bit worse, but if you're under pressure . . . "

"No, not at all, ask away," Oliver interrupted cheerily.

"If you're sure. I need a bit of help decorating the flat,

actually. And I don't have a great deal of time. I took today off but I was hopeless. I'll cook you dinner as a thank-you. Nothing fancy, maybe a spag bol or a pizza. Can you come?"

"Yes, I'd be delighted," Oliver beamed. "Is 6.30pm OK, and should I wear my old clothes?"

"Yes, that would be great. Thanks, Oliver, you're a mate."

With that she rang off. Oliver hoped he was a bit more than a mate, but he still was delighted she had called. One step at a time, he reminded himself, one step at a time.

Trisha and Mick were laden with bags from every baby shop and children's boutique in the city. Exhausted but happy, they stored their hoard into the car and headed for the Naul. Trish examined the tiny white knitted booties she had bought in Brown Thomas.

"Aren't these divine, Mick? I really feel like calling into our parents and just handing them these, just to see the look on their faces."

"Well, why don't we?" asked Mick. "I can tell you're just bursting to tell everybody and I'm sure Ali will know by nightfall. Let's go and see my folks first and then your mam and dad, after that we'll drop into Ali on the way home."

"That's a great idea," agreed Trisha. "I was afraid you were going to say let's wait 'til after the three month period was over, you know just in case . . ." her voice trailed off – she couldn't help but worry already about another miscarriage.

"Now, there'll be none of that," insisted Mick. "This

baby will be fine and will be kicking off those booties before you know it. Now, think positive. This baby is meant to be. I just know it. Trust me and trust in yourself. You are going to be a great mother."

He gave her hand an affectionate squeeze.

"Yeah," smiled Trisha. "You're right. I just needed that reassurance. Thanks, Mick."

She was going to be a mother, after all. She just couldn't wait to tell Ali.

Oliver couldn't help but laugh when he spotted Ali's attempt at pasting a border in Emma's room. The glue squelched out of either side and the wavy line would surely make the little girl seasick when she went to bed at night.

"Oh, Ali, I'm sorry," he guffawed while Ali glared at him in annoyance.

"I know it's hopeless, but it was the best I could do. I was on my own, you know," she protested before laughing herself. It was the worst border she had ever seen.

"That's just it. You don't have to do everything on your own," Oliver replied gently. "Just because I help you out now and again doesn't mean that I expect anything from you. I help because you are one of my dearest friends, and besides, I can't resist a damsel in distress."

"Easy now, fifties man," Ali grinned. "Can I leave you to rip it off the wall yourself, I think the pasta is ready. C'mon Emma. Let's leave Oliver in peace."

But Emma wasn't for budging; someone was tearing paper, her favourite pastime and she wanted to be involved.

"She's fine, aren't you, Emma?" Oliver said. "I need an

assistant anyhow. You can help me rip this off the wall, can't you?"

Emma smiled brightly and said to Ali, "Oliber help Emma."

"Bossy, just like her mum," Oliver quipped before getting a mock punch from Ali.

Ali went back into the kitchen after watching Oliver and Emma for a moment. He was so gentle and patient with her, totally interested in what she was doing. Even though Ben had an easy affection for Emma and indeed all children, there was a different kind of attitude from Oliver. He seemed to really like Emma and the little person she was. Ali was touched by that. And Emma who didn't take to people too easily appeared to adore Oliber, as she called him. She was becoming quite the little madam, and was losing the baby look. Ali must remember to take more photos for Simon. He was really missing her and Ali didn't want him to get any ideas about fighting for custody. Christmas was coming soon and she knew he'd feel it more then. She would have to try to get over to Brisbane next spring to see him.

It would be wonderful to see all her old friends again and get a bit of sunshine on her skin. Her thoughts then naturally drifted onto Ben. She wondered how he was enjoying the hot sun of Africa and would he re-appear in Dublin at Christmas? His six-month contract would be up soon, or would he extend it for another six months? She then dismissed him from her mind.

It didn't really matter anyhow. She had closed the book on that one. She stirred the spaghetti bolognese some more when the intercom buzzed.

Ali answered, wondering who it could be, when she

heard an excited Trisha and Mick argue over who would press the buzzer again.

"Any food in the house?" Mick piped up to Trisha trying to get him away from the microphone.

"It's us, Ali. Can we come up?"

"Of course," Ali replied looking around resignedly at the messy kitchen. It wasn't how she had pictured them seeing it, but what could she do? She frantically tried to tidy up as many of Emma's toys before they made their way up the two flights of stairs.

"Welcome," she breezed, totally forgetting Oliver was still in Emma's room.

"Sorry it's such a mess. We're trying to do Emma's room at the moment."

Just then Oliver peered into the kitchen, holding Emma who was clutching him and several pieces of stripped border tightly.

Trisha gave Ali a knowing look that said, "I'll get you later." And they all sat down around the tiny table while Ali stretched out the bolognese to feed five.

"I can't wait any longer. I've just got to say that I'm pregnant," Trisha blurted out before anyone had a chance to begin eating.

Then followed many kisses and teary hugs between the girls and hearty congratulations from Oliver to Mick and Trisha.

"I am so happy for you both," said Ali. "This calls for champers, but I haven't got any."

"I always carry a spare bottle in the car," Oliver piped up, hoping no one would think him weird. "It's for my clients," he added, "when they clinch a deal."

"Go get it, Oliver," said Trisha. "I can't have any, but for the first time in my life, I don't care!"

When he was gone Trisha grabbed Ali and quizzed her about Oliver being there.

"Are you two an item?" She was agog to know.

"No, Trisha! He's just helping me, as a friend."

"Will ye come up for air!" Trisha snorted. "You looked mighty cosy when we came in. In fact some would say you looked like a family."

"Yep," Mick nodded in agreement.

"It's OK, you know, to fall for someone else," Mick added. "You know Ben is a good friend of mine but Oliver, well Oliver is a better guy, a better guy for you, Ali. His feelings for you run deep. He is not playing around here."

Ali was surprised and a little bit pleased, but she was about to protest some more that it was too soon for a romantic entanglement when Oliver returned with Wolf Blass in hand to toast the new baby.

It was after 10pm by the time Trisha and Mick left. Emma had long since gone to bed in her new room, so there wasn't much more that could be done tonight.

"Do you want a coffee, Oliver?" Ali asked. She didn't want him to leave just yet. She was feeling all warm and affectionate towards Oliver, partly from the effects of the champagne and Mick's earlier words.

"I'd love one, thanks. But after that, I'd better head off. I have a conference in town tomorrow."

"On a Saturday?" Ali tried to hide her disappointment.

She had hoped Oliver would offer to come back to finish off Emma's room, but she couldn't be so selfish. Oliver had his own life, after all.

"I'm afraid so," Oliver grimaced. "It's an international seminar – so people just fly in for the weekend. But I am free on Sunday. If you want we could finish Emma's room and then I could take us all out for a pizza. That is if Emma likes it."

"She loves it," Ali smiled. "And so do I."

"Good, its settled then," said Oliver sipping his coffee.

Twenty minutes later he said his goodbyes and just pecked Ali on the cheek as he left. Ali, for once would have been delighted for him to make a move but he hadn't. So she went to bed alone, and tossed and turned for ages. She wasn't sure if it was because of what Mick had told her, or the way she had seen Oliver connect with Emma, or even just that the champagne had made her remember his kiss from the other night and made her want to repeat it. She wasn't sure why but if Oliver Johnston had swept her into his arms and made mad passionate love to her this very night, she would have been truly happy.

But he hadn't and now Ali realised she had to figure out her own true feelings before long. Because little by little – Oliver was growing on her and soon it would be too late – but for what? She hoped that the answer to that wasn't Ben. She really hoped that what was holding her back wasn't the faint little glimmer of hope that Ben would come running back to her at Christmas with an apology and an engagement ring, professing undying love.

Surely she wasn't that much of an idiot?

Ali fumed at her pathetic self as she tried vainly to fall asleep.

Eventually she went into Emma's room to check on her and found herself lifting the sleeping babe and

387

carrying her into her large empty double bed for company. She snuggled closely to Emma's peaceful sleeping form. Tonight, she could not sleep alone.

She lay there for the longest time, with thoughts of Oliver and Ben swirling around her head, until eventually exhausted, she fell asleep.

Chapter 43

Ali couldn't believe it. Only two weeks to Christmas. What an eventful year it had been, full of ups and downs, successes and failures! The big success had been Ali's business. It was thriving, giving Ali a feeling of self-worth that she hadn't known before.

The travel shop was doing so well she had in fact hired another full-time assistant in the form of Sarah Kelly, a young 19-year-old girl from Swords, who had taken a travel and tourism diploma and was very enthusiastic about working for Ali Travel.

In fact, Sarah had reminded Ali of herself when she had gone for the interview with Maisie for Carter Travel. Sarah had arrived with her crumpled cv in a plastic binder, and her interview suit, while spotlessly clean, was well worn. Ali related so much to that, and was impressed by Sarah's enthusiasm. Maisie must have spotted something like that in her, all those years ago. Now Ali could buy nice clothes and her bank loan for the business was well on its way to being paid off, which was almost unheard of for a first year in business. But Ali had filled a niche in the market, and the business grew from strength to strength. Ali had been taking driving lessons for the past few weeks and hoped to buy a little car soon. It would make life so much easier for herself and Emma. Although Trisha dropped Emma home most nights on her way home from work, that wouldn't continue forever, with a baby on the way.

Ali had enjoyed a few dates – if you could call two friends getting together with a chaste kiss at the end of it, a date. She and Oliver had been to dinner and the movies and all without any passion. Ali was puzzled and intrigued by it all, and eventually wondered if Oliver had gone off her as a prospective girlfriend or maybe Mick had it all wrong. Still, she preferred not to rock the boat. She got lonely often and Oliver was charming and great company. He had completed Emma's room and was now helping Ali put some character into the living room. Ali wondered would he cry off when it came time to paint her room with its large inviting double bed – a huge bed that hadn't seen any action, except for Emma's continual bouncing up and down. Emma at almost two years old was becoming a right little madam, wanting Barbie everything from Santa. Ali was meeting up with Trisha for lunch in town today to take a break from Christmas shopping. Trisha was enduring her busiest time in work while suffering the worst morning and all-day sickness that Ali had ever seen. Ali was going to try and convince Trisha to let her cook Christmas lunch for all of them.

Trisha had invited Oliver and Ali and Emma for Christmas lunch along with her parents, but Ali felt it would be all too much effort for the sickly mum-to-be. She hoped Trisha would agree to come over to the flat, or else Ali could cook everything at the bungalow where there was more room.

Ali sat waiting in Bewleys when the tired but radiant Trisha appeared.

"Sit down immediately," Ali ordered when she spotted her friend's hugely swollen feet. "I'll get the lunch for us both while you rest yourself there. What would you like?"

"Well, bubs only likes baked potatoes or fried rice at the moment, so I'll have a baked spud with cheese, and no butter, thanks."

Ali went and ordered lunch for them both. Trisha looked well but Ali fretted about her standing on her feet all day.

"You must look after yourself and the baby first," she lectured Trisha over the baked potatoes. "It's more important than anything to get enough rest."

"I know," Trisha admitted. "It's been so hectic. I don't know how long more I will be able to carry on at the current speed. It's tough being Acting Manager. You hardly get a break and there's so much involved."

"Well, Trisha, you have wanted this baby for so long and you intend to quit work anyway afterwards. Does it matter if you finish a bit earlier?"

"No, suppose not. I just feel I'd go batty, watching daytime TV and knitting booties all day. You're at work, so it wouldn't be any fun."

"It'll be less fun in hospital, believe me. I know. I've been there. It still seems like yesterday."

"Yeah. I forgot you were an expert. It must have been

awful, being so far away from home on your own, and in hospital too. I'd forgotten."

"I haven't," Ali muttered. They had really been her darkest days stranded in Australia with Simon being so cruel to her. She shuddered at the memory. "Anyway, let's change that depressing subject. Now, about Christmas, I feel you should rest, and I'll do the cooking. It was very nice of you to invite Oliver."

"Oh yeah," grinned Trisha like a Cheshire cat. "Well, he is a bit noticeable in your life, Ali. I could hardly leave him out. Is there any development on that front?" She raised an eyebrow.

Ali had been notoriously private about herself and Oliver. Trisha wasn't sure what their relationship was but she knew what she'd like it to be. Oliver was quite obviously besotted with Ali, blind Freddy could see that, but somehow there hadn't been a breakthrough. Trisha wondered if she should tell Ali that Ben might be home for Christmas as Mick had hinted at this morning. She didn't want Ali to get all built up about it in case it came to nothing, so she stopped short and said nothing until she was sure. She'd ask Mick tonight.

"We're good friends, and no, he hasn't kissed me again since that night. I told him I need time and he respects that."

"Well, I wouldn't hang about too long, Ali O'Neill, because he is too much of a good catch to last. Someone will snap him up from under your nose if you don't give him some encouragement. The man's not made of steel, you know."

"I know," Ali smiled deviously. "Actually, I've been

thinking of moving the whole thing up a notch, but I'm not sure how to, without looking like a cheap floozy."

Trisha laughed heartily. "Hardly. You're more like the ice queen than the tart with a heart."

"Thanks a bunch," frowned Ali. "Are you going to help me or not?"

Trisha then advised her of the best way to seduce Oliver without him really knowing it. It involved a sexy outfit, copious amounts of alcohol and a candlelit dinner for two. Ali felt it was all a bit obvious, but decided to give a toned-down version a try.

They also decided to have Christmas lunch at Ali's. Trisha wasn't in the mood any more to cater a huge lunch and happily accepted Ali's offer.

"I just didn't know how tired you could get," she yawned. "I could cheerfully go to bed right now."

"Don't worry," assured Ali, patting her hand. "It gets better in the second trimester. Now, take my advice. Go and see your GP and try to get a sick note. You need to rest."

"Yes, Nurse O'Neill," replied Trisha rolling her eyes up to heaven. "And you take my advice. Get Oliver Johnston into your bed before someone else does."

After Ali left Trisha back to work to walk another four hours on those poor swollen feet, she pondered Trisha's advice and decided to invite Oliver over tonight, if he was free. She went into Arnotts and bought a sexy black basque and onto the fishmonger's where she purchased some hugely expensive monkfish and prawns. She hoped Oliver was free after going to all this trouble but it was exciting planning a seduction. All she needed was her

Sade tape and a well-behaved Emma to go to bed on time. Lately she seemed to sense when Ali needed her to be compliant and did her best to be the opposite. Ali felt so guilty for all the time she spent away from her that she was very lax about bedtimes, which she knew was wrong, especially for herself. She telephoned Oliver.

"Hi, Ali." He sounded happy to hear from her.

"Oliver, sorry this is late notice but I wondered if you might be free for dinner this evening, at my place?"

"I'd love to, Ali," Oliver replied in amazement. "Any special reason?"

"No," Ali blushed furiously, glad he couldn't see her at that moment. "I'd just like to see you that's all. I've bought some monkfish and prawns and they are going to waste . . ." she added lamely.

"Who am I to turn down prawns and monkfish? I'd love to, Ali. I'll bring the wine. What time shall I be there?"

"Is 8pm OK? I'll try to get Emma down to sleep by then."

"Fine, see you then." Oliver hung up the phone.

That was strange. She never ever put Emma to bed when Oliver visited; they had always been a threesome.

"Catch yourself on, Johnston." He told himself. "Don't get carried away. Perhaps she just needs some business advice."

Still, he popped out for a haircut and splashed out on some new aftershave, just in case. He wondered if flowers were a bit presumptuous and bought a huge bunch of white lilies from a stall in Grafton Street, anyway.

The rest of the day dragged by as Oliver clock-watched endlessly, going home early to have a shower, and to change and yet he still was ready by six and paced about incessantly, willing 8pm to arrive.

Ali was frantically busy, trying out a new recipe for monkfish, mixing up a marie rose sauce for the prawns and trying to bath a cranky Emma at the same time. Her hair flew into a mad frizz from the steam in the bathroom and she despaired that she could ever look glamorous and have a culinary feast on the table by 8pm. She wished she had said 9 o'clock or even tomorrow night. She fervently wished the bath would pacify Emma and make her sleepy. Thankfully Emma was tired enough to sink into her cot bed by 7pm, so Ali could concentrate on her seductive look and the dinner for the next hour.

She lit candles and got into her little black dress and slicked on some red lipstick and put on her Sade tape quietly in the background, while she sizzled the monkfish in olive oil and coriander.

Oliver arrived at 8pm sharp with some gorgeous flowers and a bottle of wine. He looked really smart in a crisp white linen shirt and black cords. Ali noticed his newly cropped hair, which accentuated his high cheekbones and made him more handsome.

"It suits you short," Ali said admiringly, touching his hair lightly.

Oliver smiled. "Ali, you look terrific, but where's my other girlfriend?"

"Oh, Emma, she was exhausted. I'm trying to get her into proper sleep habits. I've been a bit lax."

Oliver's heart sank until he spotted the candles burning in the dimly lit kitchen.

"Something smells good. I'm starving."

"I'll dish it up in a moment," Ali said brightly. As she opened the wine, she hoped Oliver hadn't noticed how nervous she was. Her hands were shaking so much she couldn't get the corkscrew in.

"Here, let me help." Oliver was now beside her, touching her hand to retrieve the bottle. He smelled good enough to eat.

Oliver poured the wine and Ali gulped hers quickly, hoping for some sort of Dutch courage. It was because she had planned to seduce him that it all seemed so fake. She felt entirely false with him and immediately regretted her decision to do this. It simply wasn't her style. But thankfully, Oliver appeared not to notice anything was amiss and she relaxed a little as he chatted on while she dished up the starter and turned down the heat on the main course.

The meal was a great success. Oliver raved over his monkfish, and the simple cheesecake that she had made for dessert had left him speechless. He told Ali that no one had ever made a cake for him before, except his mum who died when he was six and had baked him birthday cakes before that.

He suddenly started to tell Ali all about his childhood then. The cake had evoked a happy memory, which were few apparently. His mother passed away and his father arrived home with a succession of girlfriends, none of whom were the least bit interested in a sad little boy. Oliver's father had been wealthy but became a bit of a drinker after his wife died, and the barflies he picked up were only interested in his money. Oliver just remembered the loneliness, and being left with a succession of babysitters.

"By the time he met Hilda, who straightened him out and married him, I was already in college. If only he had met her ten years sooner, I might have had a happy childhood. I hardly remember her, you know. My mother. Just her perfume and the rustle of her taffeta skirt as she kissed me goodnight before they went out."

"They went out?" Ali echoed. She was transfixed by his story – certain elements had been similar to hers, only worse, much worse. Poor Oliver. She had never guessed.

"Yes, they were returning home from the theatre. The old man had a bit too much to drink and crashed the car. He escaped with a few scratches, but Mum was killed instantly. He never really forgave himself. That's why he distanced himself from me. He felt guilty, I guess, for depriving me of a mother."

Oliver looked into the burning embers of the fire, as if he was transported back there.

"Sorry, Ali, all this over a cheesecake. I apologise. I didn't mean to unload my unhappy childhood onto you."

Ali touched his handsome face with her hand.

"Oliver, I am so glad you told me. You know that I too lost my mother. Not as early as you. But in a way my father was responsible and he was also an alcoholic, so I completely understand. You poor guy, six is so young. At least I was fifteen and even then I couldn't bear it."

"All I ever wanted was a happy family," Oliver said with a half smile. "I used to be so jealous of Ben with his happy family. It made me green with envy."

"Me too," grinned Ali, remembering. "But I'm so glad now that I never have to be part of the Murphy clan. That Isabel is a right witch."

"She's a true southside snob if there ever was one," Oliver agreed. "Do you know she is originally from the northside? Cabra, would you believe? Apparently she has spent her life distancing herself from her humble beginnings."

Ali was speechless. That bitch had looked down her nose at Ali all those years when she hadn't been born with a silver spoon at all herself. Ali laughed out loud. All those years she had tried so vainly to fit in and to be accepted by Miss High and Mighty.

And all along Isabel Murphy was no better than she.

"Did you mean it?" Oliver asked then quietly, looking at her seriously. "About being glad you're not part of the Murphy clan?"

"I most certainly did," Ali replied vehemently and suddenly kissed Oliver with a passion that surprised both him and her.

"Ali," Oliver whispered when she eventually stopped, and gasped for air, "I thought you needed time."

"I've had all the time I need, Oliver." Ali replied looking into his deep green eyes. "And right now, I need you. I want you."

She rose up slowly and taking his hand led him to her bedroom, which was lit seductively with several scented candles. New bed linen was on the huge bed, crisp and unused. She wanted tonight to be fresh and new. A new beginning, with no whispers of her past loves. No shadows of Ben.

"Are you really sure?" he asked softly as she let her hair loose from its chignon. Her long curls tumbled over her bare shoulders and he touched it as if touching gossamer.

Ali answered him with a long kiss and then she replied, "Yes."

As Oliver's lips grazed her neck and his arms held her tightly, he whispered her name again and again as he gently undressed her and they fell onto the bed and made a deep languorous love that touched Ali's soul. It was unlike anything she had ever experienced with Ben or Simon and she knew that this man genuinely loved her and would never hurt her. Ali lay for a long time after he had drifted off to sleep, marvelling at her luck and feeling like she had finally come home.

Chapter 44

Ben was lying in bed with Susie. They had made love too and it had been wonderful, as usual. Susie had been passionate and loving but as soon as it was over she was back to her usual wise-cracking, take-no-prisoners self.

She lit a cigarette and fetched them both coffee and crawled back under the sheets. They didn't have a shift until 6am so there was plenty of time.

Ben was looking at the ceiling fan whirr around, seemingly deep in thought.

"You look worried. Is everything OK, Murph?"

"Yes, it's fine. I'm just thinking about Christmas."

"I know. I can't believe it. Three whole weeks out of here. I can't wait to go shopping in London. Hopefully on a dark dreary day with fog, or better still, snow. Anything at all except hot sunshine. Never thought I'd say it but it certainly loses its appeal after six sweaty months."

"It would be even better if we could spend it together,

Susie. I could have ten days at home and spend the rest of the holiday with you."

Susie frowned, her perky little face looking adult for a moment.

"Now, Murph, we agreed no strings. We're having fun aren't we? Let's not complicate it too much. Everything seems so intense here, until we go back to our real lives, you know that. Let's not spoil it."

"Don't you love me then?" Ben was petulant. Susie seemed immune to his charms. He couldn't bear to spend Christmas without her. He had already offered to take her home to Dublin for the holiday but she had earlier refused.

"You know I do," Susie insisted, taking a deep drag on her cigarette. Why was Ben always so clingy, she wondered?

She cared a lot for him but he took everything so seriously. She knew they were having a passionate affair but a lot of medics did out here. There was precious little else to do. As soon as you went home, it ended. It was rather like a film shoot.

"Tell you what," she giggled, stubbing out her cigarette. "How about I show you how much I love you?"

With that she dived on Ben and smothered him in passionate kisses and once again they made love. Anything to keep him quiet she mused as she trailed kisses along his chest.

She'd be glad to fly home on Sunday. Ben was becoming a little bit too much, lately. She needed a rest from him.

Ben decided as they made love, that this was the girl

for him. He was hopelessly and madly in love with Susie and she was the girl he would marry. She wasn't going to get away from him and for once he didn't feel like marriage was a scary option. He could not wait to make Susie his wife. She thought that he was going to Dublin for Christmas and he was, but not before he called into her flat in Streatham. He had managed to persuade one of her friends to give him her home address; he was going to surprise her in a big way. His mother would be so happy that he had finally met the girl of his dreams and he was about to settle down.

He had written to Isabel and told her that he might bring a friend and that he had something important to tell her, just enough to make Isabel wonder, but nothing concrete. She would be so happy for him, finally settling down. He thought briefly of Ali and Karen. He had loved them both, and in a way he would always love Ali. She had been his first love. But now he had found what he had always been looking for – and he wasn't about to let it go. As he watched Susie sleep serenely, looking waiflike and so young in repose, he gently touched her soft blonde curls and kissed her forehead. She really was the most precious thing he had ever had. Just a few more days and his plan would be in action and he would be the happiest man in Ireland. He had a large amount of cash to go shopping in London, and he wondered if Susie liked diamond solitaires? He would soon see.

Ali woke up. Oliver was still lying next to her watching her with those deep intense green eyes.

"I have been wondering whether or not you would

like some breakfast and would it be cheeky of me to invade your kitchen and rustle us up some eggs and maybe some cereal for Emma?"

Ali smiled, shyly, hoping her hair wasn't like a bird's nest and she hadn't got those awful panda eyes. She suddenly felt very naked.

"Yes, that would be fantastic, Oliver. Thanks." That means I can shower and then dress hurriedly while you are busy, she thought.

Oliver kissed her gently on the lips and then swiftly rose. Ali got a good look at his naked behind and had to admit he was gorgeous without his clothes. He was tall and nicely built with the remnants of his summer tan still lingering on his back.

His bum was by far his best feature and Ali blushed about the lustful thoughts she had about him as he padded out of the bedroom. She jumped up immediately and headed for the shower, then fetched a sleepy Emma from her cot. Although it was Saturday, the travel shop still opened from 10am 'til 2pm, so Emma usually went to Trisha's for a few hours.

By the time she had washed Emma and dressed her, Oliver had scrambled eggs and toast ready for them all. He had even cut Emma's toast up into fingers.

"You'll be kept," murmured a thankful Ali, who was ravenous.

"I certainly hope so," grinned Oliver, munching a piece of toast as he served the eggs.

"Oliber, juice," complained Emma, and Ali and Oliver laughed.

"Madame usually has juice too," Ali explained.

"I do apologise, madame," Oliver replied to Emma and fetched the orange juice from the fridge.

He wiggled his eyebrows at Emma and she giggled happily.

He was so good with Emma, Ali thought. That was important to her. Trisha was right, she mused. Oliver *was* a good catch.

"Eggs OK, madame?" Oliver quipped, tea towel over his arm, pouring more tea.

"More than OK," replied Ali, with a knowing smile. "I'd say damn near perfect."

"Well, that's all right then," replied Oliver sitting down to his own breakfast. And it was.

Damn near perfect.

Chapter 45

Isabel Murphy read and then re-read Ben's cryptic letter. What did it mean she wondered? Was he bringing a female friend home or wasn't he. It sounded rather more serious than a mere flirtation. "Wait 'til you meet her, Mum. I'm sure you'll love her too." *Love her too*. Isabel echoed the words. Oh dear, she dearly hoped he wasn't traipsing around after another unsuitable female, like they all had been, before and since Karen. What was wrong with the boy? Why couldn't he settle down with a nice girl that was suitable to his class and his upwardly mobile career. Then another even more fearful thought enveloped her. What if it was a black woman, a native? Surely not? Her mind began to race before she took stock and calmed herself. She was letting things get on top of her again and that must not happen again.

She reached for one of her Valium pills. She must not get too agitated. Christmas was all planned and she was sure it would be perfect. Just let Ben arrive and enjoy seeing him. Whatever cat he dragged indoors with him, well, she would have to deal with that when the time came. Right now she had a Christmas party to plan. She had to get a move on, as she needed to go into town to get some truly wonderful table accoutrements. The Baileys and the O'Connells were coming and nothing but the best would do. Her worrisome son would have to wait.

Trisha felt her expanded stomach. She couldn't wait for the moment when she would feel her baby stirring. She also couldn't wait until this pure exhaustion and abomination for food would pass. She couldn't face another potato yet it was the only thing apart from rice that she could keep down and would make for a boring Christmas lunch. Still, maybe she'd lose a few pounds, which was always a bonus.

She wondered how Ali's seduction plan had worked with Oliver. She dearly hoped her friend would see sense and snap the man up while he was still around. Ali had endured enough losers. Trisha wanted her to be happy and settled like she was. She would never take Mick for granted again. She knew what they had was really precious. The past few weeks had taught her that. The New Year would bring new challenges and a new baby. Everything was rosy.

All except that bloody Ben was coming home for Christmas.

She had prised the information from a reluctant Mick last night in bed. He told her little, in the way that men do, but mentioned that Ben had said he had met a girl. "I bloody hope so," thought Trisha. "I hope he stays miles away from Ali. I don't want him stuffing things up for her with Oliver, just as she's getting over him." She still hadn't decided whether to mention it to Ali or not.

There might not be any need. In a few weeks he'd be gone back to Mozambique and she'd be none the wiser. She decided then to wait a while and see how Ali's budding romance with Oliver was going. If things went well between them then why spoil it? She would let things happen by themselves, and for once not interfere.

Ali and Oliver decided to take Emma off to town after Ali had closed the shop. Oliver thought she could see all the fairy lights and the Christmas window at Switzer's and BT.

Emma was amazed and enthralled by all the reindeer and moving Santa. It was magical when you saw it through a small child's eyes.

Ali had lost Oliver in the fragrance section of BT as she got carried away with all the glamorously packaged gift sets.

She spotted him from behind in the giftware section, his height and the hands running constantly through his blond curls when he was agitated, giving him away. He was talking to some woman.

Ali clasped Emma's hand tightly and smilingly tapped him on the shoulder. She was about to say something glib or amusing when her smile froze on her face as she was standing next to Isabel Murphy. She now knew the reason for Oliver's nervousness.

"Mrs Murphy, you know Ali, of course."

"Yes, Ali," replied Isabel, her eyes narrowing. The unsaid 'brazen hussy' was left dangling in the air.

"Hello, Isabel," said Ali deliberately, aware that using the familiar first name would aggravate Isabel Murphy no end. "And this is my daughter, Emma."

"Oh, isn't she such a cute little thing. Takes after her father, by the looks of it." Isabel had lost none of her venom.

"Yes, she does, actually," Ali replied airily. *Don't let the bitch see she has hit a nerve.*

"I was just telling Oliver that Ben is about to come home for the Christmas holidays and by all accounts he's bringing a special friend with him, if you know what I mean. You should call in on him over the Christmas, Oliver. I'm sure he would love to see you."

Ali felt like pulling the expensive cashmere scarf from Isabel's scrawny neck and gleefully strangling her with it.

"And what are your plans, dear?"

The question was intoned innocently enough, but Ali knew it to be code for *what poor man are you going to get your lower-class talons into this year?*

"Well, I'm very busy with my new travel business, actually. So it will be a small but family affair with relatives and close friends."

With that, Ali grabbed Oliver's hand and gazed lovingly into his eyes, before planting a smoochy kiss on his lips. Oliver grinned widely guessing her game and pulled her even closer.

"This girl," he beamed at Isabel Murphy. "Isn't she something else?"

"Something else indeed," sniffed Isabel tartly. "Well, I must be off. I have lots to do, so Merry Christmas to you both."

And with that she was gone, storming off in one of her legendary huffs, clearing the bustling crowd in an instant by barging through the melee with her copious packages brusquely.

"You are terrible, Ali O'Neill," laughed Oliver.

Ali was triumphant.

"Ah well, the old hag deserved it. I've been waiting for years to get my own back. I was polite, I can tell you. The things I could have said would have given her a heart attack."

"She was trying to needle you. Even I could see that. What about all that guff about Ben coming back? I doubt if she approves of me and you being an item."

"Tough," snapped Ali, then she softened. "Are we, are we an item?"

"You'd better believe it," Oliver replied as he gripped her hand.

He was so happy he just couldn't find the courage to ask how Ali felt about Ben coming home. But he for one wasn't too impressed. He hoped Ben wouldn't just waltz back in and expect to resume his relationship with Ali. If he did, he would find himself with a fight on his hands. And after waiting so long to have Ali in his life, Oliver wasn't about to give her up just like that.

They spent the rest of the afternoon shopping and showing Emma all the Christmas lights before Oliver swept them into the new Tex-Mex restaurant called Judge Roy Beans on Nassau Street for a meal. Oliver knew Ali to be a fan of Mexican food since her travels to Australia, and she fell on her nachos like a woman possessed.

They enjoyed several margaritas and listened to Dwight Yoakum sing his sad country songs, while Emma tackled a huge burger and buffalo fries.

After two drinks Oliver decided to broach the subject of Ben's return.

"How do you feel about Ben coming back?"

"Well, he's not coming back to me; he's coming home to spend Christmas with his family, along with his 'special friend'," Ali said obliquely, staring into her margarita.

"But what if he was, for argument's sake, coming back to you, what then?"

"He burnt his bridges last year, Oliver. There is no going back. I know it's taken me a long time to get over him, but now I have. I am happy now. I am happy within myself. I'm really glad you're in my life but I can be happy on my own. This year has taught me that I need to find happiness within me, not try and depend on someone else to make me happy or make me a whole person. God, I sound like one of those weird American talk-show hosts, but you know what I mean."

Oliver thought for a moment, and studied her earnest face, realising that she meant it.

"Yes, I think I do," he replied, touching her hand. "Just as well," he then added darkly, "because I wasn't going to give you up without a fight."

"Get back into your cave," Ali retorted, grinning. "Here am I going all 'new age' and you're going all Neanderthal on me."

"Sorry, I am suitably chastened. I guess I don't want to lose you. I know you and Ben have a lot of history and that weighs heavily."

"History," interrupted Ali, "that's all we have. It's all in the past. You never forget your first love, but some time you've got to let them go."

"I don't know," said Oliver quietly, looking at her shyly from under his dark eyelashes. "I've just got together with mine."

Ali was stunned by his admission.

"Are you saying, all these years . . . "

"Yes," finished Oliver, "all these years I have carried an Olympic sized torch for you, Ali. That's why I never settled with anyone else. I always believed you would be Ben's. I never dared hope, well, not until after Trisha's wedding. But since that night we drank that awful cheap wine from those chipped mugs in the flat in Rathmines, I have wanted you. 'Admired you from afar' as they say."

Ali was still trying to take it all in. She was amazed that Oliver had felt this way all those years, when she had simply no idea. She had been so wrapped up in Ben.

"I don't know what to say," Ali said, at last.

Just say you'll marry me, Oliver felt like blurting out, but he knew that would sound ridiculous. But he had never wanted to say anything more in his whole life.

"Just say I haven't scared you away," he said instead. He hoped it hadn't been too much.

"Quite the reverse," Ali replied enigmatically and finished off her drink. Emma had begun to growl and complain in her high chair.

"I think we'd better get this little one home." she said and they got up to leave. "Well," Ali said, putting on her coat and scarf and bundling up Emma for the cold frosty December evening, "it's been quite a day, quite a weekend, really."

"Yes," said Oliver, kissing her nose, "it has. I'll have you both home and in front of a warm fire in half an hour."

"You're on," smiled Ali. "And if you promise to light it, I might even consider you staying over again."

"I'd love to," Oliver said, happy that his admission to Ali hadn't made her turn and flee. He felt a lot more confident as they headed towards Swords. Even with the shadow of Ben's homecoming lingering over him, he now felt that Ali had put Ben finally into her past and that maybe, just maybe, Oliver would be her future. As the three of them sped along in his smart BMW he realised that it would appear to other drivers that they were a family, Mum, Dad and baby. And that was what he wanted more then anything in the world, a family of his own. Now it looked like it might just happen. This was going to be a very special Christmas for Oliver. He hoped it would be his first really happy one since he was six years old. Now that Ali and Emma were in his life he finally felt like he belonged once more.

Chapter 46

Ben felt the sharp piercing breeze as he exited Terminal 2 at Heathrow. He couldn't believe how cold he felt. Despite his warm coat and gloves that he had packed for his return, nothing could quite prepare you for a chilly four degrees after the balmy temperatures of Africa. At least it's dry, he thought, as he caught the tube into London. He had left most of his luggage in the storage room at the airport. He needed to go shopping for a diamond and didn't want to lug cases around. Besides, Ben thought, any Irishman with a large bag in London was an automatic terrorist.

He clutched Susie's address in his hand, though by now he had memorised it by heart. Soon he would surprise her and she would be the happiest girl in England. First he'd buy the ring and then the champers and he'd catch a cab to Streatham. He had rehearsed what he would say and he could picture her pretty little face when she realised what he was up to.

First he went to Goldsmiths Jewellers in The Strand and chose a perfect pear-shaped diamond solitaire. The price had been as stunning as the ring but it was the best one he could afford. He had it gift-wrapped and then went into Fortnum and Mason in Piccadilly and purchased a gift box of Moët complete with engraved flutes. He finally bought the biggest bunch of lilies he could find and caught a black cab to the address that Cindy had scribbled down for him. He was sure he looked a mess after his long flight and could do with a shave, but he was so excited that he simply couldn't wait.

It had only been three days and he felt bereft without Susie, her perky little face and her cute little figure. She was an amazing girl. It had seemed like the sun had gone in when she had left and Ben was miserable without her.

The taxi pulled up at a slightly dilapidated row of early century redbrick terraced houses that for a brief second resembled Ali's street all those years ago. But Ali was far from his mind at the moment. Ben paid the taxi and braved the even chillier night air, arms full of champagne, flowers and, of course, the diamond box that nestled in his pocket.

He rang the bell loudly, and heard music in the distance within, so thank God someone was home. He was excited but absolutely freezing.

Suddenly the large door opened and suddenly Susie appeared, clad only in a pink dressing gown with a towel wrapped around her head but still looking amazing.

Susie seemed shocked but not happy as she digested the reality that Ben was really here, standing on her doorstep.

"Ben," she half whispered, "what the hell are you doing here?"

Ben's smile froze on his face. It hadn't been what he was expecting.

"Susie, I had to see you. Can I come in? It's bloody freezing out here."

"No, you can't," Susie snapped in a worried whisper. "I never expected this, Ben. I told you we were having a bit of fun, that's all."

"But, Susie," Ben protested, "I have flown all this way to see you. I got you flowers and champers and something else that's very special, the very least you can do is make me a cup of coffee and we'll talk it over."

"We can't talk this over!" Susie hissed while pushing her left hand in front of his face. A wedding band flashed before him. "I'm married!" she spat, her little face screwed up in annoyance and fear.

"Danny and I have an open relationship when I am away, and what we don't see, we don't grieve over. But I'm back home now, and it's over between you and me, do you get it? I love Danny and I'm not going to hurt him. Now go away, Ben. Go home to Ireland. Get out of here before he comes out and finds you here."

A man's voice then emanated from inside the house.

"Susie, we need to get a move on if we're going to that party. What's keeping you at the door?"

"It's nothing love. It's just someone selling Christmas cards. It's no one." She glared at Ben and with that she closed the door on his shocked face.

He stood, stunned, for a few minutes in the doorway. He couldn't believe what had just happened. How had he not seen any of that coming? How could she have led him on all that time in Africa, when she was already married? He finally dumped the flowers in her doorway, let her explain them to the poor unsuspecting Danny, and he slowly walked away. He walked around dazed in the cold night air for what seemed like hours, trying to make sense of it all before he saw a taxi and hailed it. An hour later he found himself back at Heathrow and trying to catch a standby flight to Dublin.

He managed to catch a flight around eleven and reached Sandymount at 2am, glad that there would be no one awake to question him. He simply couldn't face it. But he hardly slept.

Susie's angry face and that wedding ring she flashed kept playing like a bad record in his mind, over and over again.

Ben had never been so disappointed and hurt in his whole life.

For a brief moment he realised that all his chickens had come home to roost. He had broken Karen's heart and then Ali's so he believed deep down that he probably deserved it, but that didn't help. He was gutted that the only girl he had ever really considered marrying and sharing the rest of his life with had cruelly broken his heart, and she hadn't even had the decency to be sorry about it. Ali would never have done anything like that to him.

He fretted over what to tell his mother about it.

All the fanfare and teasing he had bleated on about in his letters home. He really felt he would have a new fiancée to parade about. Now he wished he had stayed in

Mozambique and never come home at all. At least Susie would still be in his life and he would be blissfully ignorant of her forgotten husband tucked away in a corner of London. Now things would never be the same. In less than twelve hours his whole life had fallen apart. He lay freezing in the single bed of his youth surrounded by all his teenage paraphernalia and wondered what had happened to him over the years and what the hell was going to happen to him next.

Isabel was having her customary croissants and coffee in the conservatory when Ben appeared the next morning.

"Oh my God, when did you arrive?" she exclaimed in surprise.

"Late last night, in the early hours. Much too late to wake you," he replied, kissing her papery cheek and flopping down into a delicate wicker chair.

"You look terrible, son. I don't mean to be rude or anything. It's just that you look so exhausted and worn out. I'll call Mrs Mulvanney and get her to make you a nice fry."

"Nothing for me, Mother. I couldn't face anything. I am exhausted and a little 'tired and emotional' as they say."

Isabel was perplexed. "And your friend, is she with you?"

Ben shook his head. "No, Mother, I'm afraid the appearance of her husband put paid to my chances of having her here with me. She forgot to tell me she was already married, so there you go. You can line up whatever suitable offspring your ladies' bridge club has to offer.

417

They'll be glad to know that I'm on the market again." He grinned brightly but his eyes looked pained.

"I'm so sorry, darling. Really I am. But don't worry. The right girl will come along for you soon. Just you wait and see."

"What if the right girl, no, the right girls, have come and gone thanks to my stupidity and I've had all my chances. What then?"

"You can't turn back the clock, Ben," replied Isabel gently, inwardly alarmed that he might try to hook up with that awful O'Neill girl again. She almost felt like blurting out that she and Oliver were a couple now, but somehow it didn't feel right.

She took his brown hand instead and said, "It's so nice to have you home. We'll look after you for the next few weeks, and by the time you have to go back things will look a lot better. Now, I'm not taking no for an answer. You need a good Irish fry to cheer you up and put some of the colour back into your cheeks. You just sit there while I have Mrs Mulvanny cook it up. I'll go wake your father as well – he's dying to see you." She rose swiftly and kissed him on the top of his head just like she had done when he was a little boy and left the room.

He stared out into the lush greenness of the lawn and watched the drizzle creep down the window pane and thought it was going to be a long three weeks, but he was glad to be home.

He'd need as much support as possible if he was going to feel this bad for a while. Right now, things looked as bleak as they had last night. He opened the smartly wrapped box he had been clutching in his hand all night and unwrapped it. He had to admire the large glistening diamond ring, as it lay pristine and unwanted in its case. Tears fell unabated onto his cheeks and he finally realised what the term broken-hearted meant. He felt sad for himself and all the others that he had made feel this way in the past. Wouldn't they be glad to see him now, suffering as they had?

"What goes around comes around," he said aloud before he closed the box and wiped his tears. He had a lot of fence-mending to do and hoped he would find the courage to mend them. At least that was what he told himself. He knew that sooner or later, he would have to see Karen and apologise, but really he would have to see Ali. Soon he would see her and he would tell her how sorry he was, for all the times he had wronged her. It was the least he could do, the very least.

Chapter 47

Trish and Ali were in Trisha's large and perfect kitchen having hot chocolate and biscuits, and Ali was regaling Trish with all the latest developments regarding Oliver and herself.

Trisha was squealing with delight at every tasty morsel of information that came her way. She was delighted that finally Ali and Oliver had become an item.

"And then to top it all," Ali informed her with saucer eyes, "who do we meet in Brown Thomas – but the wicked witch of the west, Mrs Isabel Murphy herself? She almost choked when she saw Oliver and I together. I could practically see the old cow's blood pressure rising as I plonked a big smacker on Oliver's face. You would have loved it."

"And speaking of the Murphys, I have something to tell you about Ben." Trisha then blurted out, her face blushing bright crimson. She hoped Ali would not be annoyed that she hadn't already told her.

"If it's about Ben coming home, I already know – Isabel couldn't wait to throw that into the conversation. Did you know, he's bringing a 'special friend' with him?"

"A special friend?" echoed Trisha," Do you mean a girlfriend?"

"Well, I presume so. It was the way she said it. It seemed like she was someone special, special enough to take home to Ireland anyhow."

"And how do you feel about it all?" Trisha asked, hoping Ali was over him by now. She couldn't bear to see Ali or Oliver get hurt, if bloody Ben decided to show his two faces around Dublin again. She knew Ali had an eternal weakness when it came to the lousy two-timer. She had finally begun to hate Ben after his last episode. He had proven he was no better than the awful Simon, who at least didn't pretend to be a good guy.

"Well, as I told Oliver, it's over, Trisha. We're history. I will always have some affection for him, but I'm happy now. Oliver is a really good person, I feel I can trust him, and we have a lot in common. He had a similar upbringing to me. He values family and commitment and he loves Emma, and I feel I am falling in love with him. I don't want to spoil all that for someone like Ben who could never make up his mind that he loved me enough to marry me."

Trisha was relieved. "I am so glad to hear you say that. And Oliver, do you think he's the one?"

Ali was pensive. "I think he could be. I really needed to be married to Ben. I needed to be wanted. But with Oliver it's different. I feel wanted already, so marriage, well, I'm in no hurry. If it's for me it won't pass me, as my Mam would say."

421

"That's great," said a relieved Trisha and gave her friend's arm a squeeze. "I was so worried that I might have to cook at Christmas after all."

"What, you wagon," Ali retorted, and seeing Trisha giggle saw the joke.

"Oh my God," Trisha then exclaimed, looking panic-stricken.

"It's OK," Ali replied rolling her eyes. "I get the joke."

"No, Ali," Trisha gasped. "I felt the baby move. I really felt it move." She was close to tears as she held her stomach. Her baby had at last made its presence felt.

"Isn't it wonderful?" Ali sighed, remembering the first time she really felt Emma stir. It was an incredible moment.

"It's the best Christmas present I could ever have," Trisha said and she jumped up quickly. "I've got to phone Mick right now and tell him the news. He will be so chuffed. Sorry, Ali."

"Go. Go ahead," Ali replied, to her friend who was already running up the hallway. She sat in the kitchen alone, remembering her special moment and trying to get a call through to Simon to tell him. He didn't phone her back and by the time he eventually rolled in at 3am the next morning she hadn't felt like telling him any more.

She looked at Emma who was happily playing with her dolls on the kitchen floor. "I might regret Simon, but I could never regret you," she told her daughter softly under her breath.

Things obviously happened the way they were meant to, and it was meant for Ali to be given the gift of Emma. If she and Ben hadn't split up and Mick hadn't had his

422

accident, Emma might not be here at all. So there was no point in regretting things and looking back. She must look forward and embrace her future. That would be her New Year's resolution. No going back.

"How did he take it?" she enquired of a flushing Trisha who looked inordinately pleased with herself.

"Oh, sure he's over the moon. On the way to the florist's as we speak. Anyway, I'll make us a fresh cuppa and you can tell me all about Oliver and the moment your passion ran away with you."

Ali giggled. She was so lucky to have someone like Trisha.

No one quite saw the world as she did.

Chapter 48

It was Christmas morning and Isabel was up bright and early to organise the mammoth task of putting together a gourmet lunch for their friends. She had all the food organised and ready to go but that blasted Mrs Mulvanney had point blank refused to come in and give her a hand. Isabel had even offered her triple wages if she would just put in the morning, but she wouldn't budge. She had huffily informed Isabel that she couldn't miss lunch with her son and his family. How insufferable! Obviously she didn't need the money enough. Isabel would remember that next Christmas at bonus time. Now Isabel was left to cater the lunch alone. The Baileys and the O'Connells were discerning diners and expected the best. Isabel had the cooked tiger prawns that now lay chilling in the fridge, but she had never cooked duck before and felt a little frazzled.

Her mood wasn't helped by incessantly fretting over

her errant son. Ben had been in a foul mood ever since he had arrived home in Ireland and had been drinking sullenly in his room for most of the week. She fervently hoped he would put on a brave and cheery face when the guests arrived. Tessa Bailey was bringing her sweet and available daughter Ellen, who was really perfect for Ben. But Isabel had been afraid to even mention the fact to Ben in case he blew up at her. She had told John to speak to him and he had, so she hoped he would be on his best behaviour.

She had enough to worry about. It was so hot in the damn kitchen her face was bright red and her carefully coiffed hair was dampening into wispy tendrils. She regretted ever dreaming up this fancy dinner party but she hadn't realised she would have to do all the work herself and that Ben wouldn't be home happily showing off his new love. It had all gone horribly wrong. Still, the tiger prawns were simple enough, now if only her cookery book had an easier recipe for Aromatic Duck she would be OK.

She poured herself a large glass of red wine, and sipped it gratefully even though it was only 10am. It was Christmas Day after all, and she needed something to steady her nerves. She wished the day was over already, and it was all behind her. One thing was for sure, next year she would make John take her off to the Canaries for Christmas. It was the new in-thing with all her set.

She wasn't going to go through all this again, for her uninterested husband and ungrateful children. That was for sure.

It was a hot and industrious kitchen too at Ali's little flat in Swords. But the atmosphere could not have been more different. Ali had the large turkey roasting away while she and Emma danced around to Christmas carols and Oliver took endless pictures of them. Oliver had arrived early that morning with a beautiful silver chain for Ali and a huge teddy for Emma. Oliver had cooked a baked ham the night before and the cinnamon and cloves and mustards that he had spiced it up with filled the tiny kitchen with enticing aromas. When the smells had overwhelmed them both, Oliver and Ali couldn't resist cutting a few slices and had made a midnight feast of ham and pickle sandwiches, which they had eaten under the Christmas tree along with mulled wine.

Ali had then explained carefully to Oliver that she didn't want him to stay overnight as it was Christmas, and that she didn't want Emma to become confused if Oliver was to be there most mornings when she woke up.

Oliver was a little hurt by that but basically he understood what Ali meant. It still made him feel like a bit of an outsider. He wasn't sure if it was a hint that he wasn't to get too comfortable or if it was a hint that Ali wanted a more permanent relationship before she involved Emma getting too close. He already knew that Emma loved him so he could see that Ali would be worried that if everything ended between him and Ali Emma would suffer. She had already lost a father. He hoped this was the case and remained resolutely cheerful and charming, kissing Ali passionately goodnight before returning to his own cold and empty house. But it left him worried. He wanted Ali to know how important she was to him but yet he didn't want to rush her. So he put the worry to the back of his mind and arrived at her flat at

10am full of Christmas cheer and bearing appropriate presents.

"What time are Trisha and Mick arriving?" Oliver enquired idly.

"About noon," Ali replied. "They're collecting Trisha's Mum and Dad first. Do you know it's the first Christmas day in over 20 years that Mrs Costello hasn't cooked the dinner? She really deserves this break, for all she has done for Emma and me over the years. In fact I've got a little surprise for them both."

"And what little surprise have you in store for them?" Oliver enquired, whirling Emma about to Rudolph the Red-nosed Reindeer.

"I've got them two tickets to London. They went to Galway for the weekend for their honeymoon apparently and have never been out of Ireland. If I can prise Alice Costello away from her stove on Christmas Day I think that maybe I can persuade her to take an airline trip. She never takes any time for herself, that poor woman."

"That sounds like someone else I know," Oliver remarked sagely. "Maybe I can persuade you to take a few days off in the New Year and we could take a little trip ourselves."

"Oliver, that sounds like an excellent idea. Where did you have in mind?

"Paris, I thought. Have you ever been?"

"No, but it's always been on my list. Now if you promise to peel the spuds while I top and tail the carrots, you've got yourself a deal."

"That was too easy," smiled Oliver, his inner worries dampening. "Lead me to your potatoes."

Trisha and Mick arrived at 12.15pm together with an anxious Alice and an ebullient Jim, who had already sampled several cans of Guinness that his son had given him. Alice was worried about causing such a fuss and commotion by being a guest at Ali's. She was not used to being fussed upon. She kept fixing her pink twin set and fluffing her curls while demurely sipping a dry sherry.

"Mam, will ye just relax!" Trisha hissed at her nervous mother.

"Ali begged me to invite you. Now everyone else in the family is already looked after. They are all having fun, so why can't you?"

"She's right," added Jim quietly. "The poor girl has gone to a lot of trouble. Now just enjoy the day off, Alice."

Alice sipped more of her sherry, resisting the urge to jump up and put on an apron and get working. She decided she would look after little Emma while Ali and Oliver worked so at least she would be doing something useful.

Ben was staring out at Dublin Bay. The day was bright and sunny and from the living room it almost looked like summer time. The Baileys and the O'Connells had already arrived and his father was making polite golf club conversation while a daughter of one or other of them was making sheep's eyes at him from across the room.

"Benjamin?" his mother's shrill voice summoned him from the kitchen. She only called him that when she was extremely annoyed or trying to impress.

He found her confused and distracted in the steamily cluttered kitchen, food on every available surface. It didn't look like it was going too well.

"Can you pass around these canapés like a good lad, and please try to look like you're enjoying yourself. Ellen is a nice girl. You'd like her if you gave it a chance." His mother looked too frazzled and uptight for him to retort that he felt like an Indian groom about to have yet another arranged marriage thrust upon him, but he remained silent and grabbed the plate of obviously shop-bought starters and gloomily headed back to the living room. After another 10 minutes of talk about handicaps and course fees Ben simply couldn't stand another moment of it all and asked his father for the car keys.

"But Ben," his father half-heartedly protested, "you've had a drink or two today. Are you sure you're safe to drive?"

"Of course," Ben flashed a smile at the cow-like Ellen who gratefully smiled back. "I just need to get some fresh air. I won't be long. I'll be back in time for dinner."

"Here," his father hurled the keys over to him and went back to his golf talk, Ben sneaked quietly out the front door before his mother discovered he was about to escape. He made it to the Audi and sped out of the drive in seconds. If he hadn't got out of there when he did, he felt that he would have exploded.

His father's car headed for the east link bridge. He knew where he wanted to go and nothing was going to stop him.

Twenty minutes later Ben pulled up outside 'Ali Travel' in Swords. This wasn't the first time he had been here. He had stolen over a few days previously and watched the busy travel shop from a few dozen yards away but hadn't seen Ali.

Today it was closed. The smart black shop with the gold lettering and the little genie on the flying carpet was a clever look, he thought. He sat watching the place, wondering what it would be like to see Ali inside, toiling away when he spotted Ali in the window above, holding a glass of wine, while pulling up the blinds. She was laughing happily and appeared to be having some type of a party. There were other people there. Ben's heart jumped in his chest. There she was!

He couldn't believe it. Without thinking, he got out of the car, walked briskly across the road and pressed the buzzer on the large black front door.

Ali and all her guests had just sat down to lunch when the buzzer went.

"It's bound to be Louis. Oliver, would you please buzz him up. He said he'd drop in but wasn't sure what time. "Now has everybody got everything they need?"

Ali happily surveyed the table. Oliver had done a marvellous job of making it look special with his own candelabras and his expensive crystal. Everyone looked suitably impressed with the feast that lay before them. And now Louis was here to make it all perfect.

Suddenly there was a sharp knock to the living room door and then the door opened.

"Ben!" Ali was as shocked as everyone else in the room. If a pin had dropped it would have made a loud clanging noise.

Ben looked embarrassed, but he was looking only at Ali.

"I'm sorry for intruding, but someone buzzed me in. I

was wondering if I might have a word, Ali, just for a few moments. If that's possible?"

"For God's sake, Ben!" Trisha exclaimed indignantly.

"It's OK, Trisha. I'm fine," Ali reassuringly patted Trisha's arm. "I'll be back soon," she said evenly trying to ignore Oliver's stricken look. "Everybody carry on. I won't be long."

She grabbed the white angora jumper she had bought herself for Christmas and followed Ben out.

"Where to?" she said briskly as they came out onto the freezing street.

"My car is parked over there," Ben replied, pointing to the smart silver Audi. Ali need not have asked. It stuck out like a sore thumb among all the other average sedans.

Once inside the car, Ben appeared to have been struck dumb.

"I'm sorry, Ali," he said after what seemed like forever. "I hadn't expected to see you today. I didn't know that you actually lived there."

"So you have been here before?" Ali was surprised and amazed that he had taken the trouble to seek her out.

"Yes, I came over last week. My father told me how well you were doing. He sent me a newspaper article. I guess I wanted to see it for myself"

"Right," Ali said acidly. "So now we have established that I'm not already dead from a broken heart but rather, thriving instead, what did you want, exactly?"

Ben looked at her inexplicably sadly.

He seemed older, she thought, brown and handsome but yet thinner and older, somehow. It had only been six months but it had seemed like a lifetime ago. It was a lifetime ago.

"I'm sorry," he said quietly. "I have been the worst kind of fool. I didn't ever intend to hurt you. I just wanted you to know that."

"Yes, well, you did hurt me, Ben. But I'm over it as they say." She folded her arms defensively and smiled. It was more of a grimace.

Ben fished into his pocket and pulled out a brown velvet box.

He opened it and showed Ali a fabulous pear-shaped diamond that lay inside.

"Isn't this what you always wanted, Ali?" he asked, taking her hand and placing the glittering diamond into it.

"I thought I did," Ali replied, "but it's too late for that now."

"It's not too late for us. It never will be," Ben was pleading, his blue eyes watering.

"What's the matter, Ben? Did your special friend not want it then?" asked Ali.

Ben looked as if he had been slapped.

"Is it him then. Is it Oliver Johnston?" he asked finally, slamming the box shut. She had obviously hit a nerve.

"Yes, it is actually. I am in love with him, Ben. Really in love with him and he loves me. He loves me enough to stay around."

"Touché," Ben admitted. He desperately wanted to kiss her and make her love him again but he could see that it was no use – Ali was lost to him and he could see that now.

They sat in silence for a few moments.

Meanwhile all the dinner guests hadn't touched their

432

fabulous lunch. Oliver was so stricken he had Trisha peer out of the window surreptitiously and see if she could see anything. Trisha had spotted them both in the flash Audi and was reporting back on developments.

Oliver was distraught and he kept muttering, "I have lost her, I just know I have," while Mick tried to convince him otherwise.

Alice fretted about in a nervous fashion. She worried about Ali and didn't want her to throw over this nice dependable chap for that uppity Ben fellow. She worried that the dinner would be inedible by the time they all got around to eating it and resolved that she would never leave her own cosy little house again on Christmas Day. It just didn't feel right.

"That's it, I'm going down there," Oliver blasted, banging his fist onto the table and rolling up his sleeves.

Mick stood up and caught him by the arm.

"If you do you'll regret it. You have to know that she wants you. Let her decide herself. Please, Oliver. Don't interfere. I doubt if Ali will have him back."

Oliver sat down again. Mick poured everyone a glass of wine and appealed to the other diners to tuck in. Ali would be so disappointed at all her hard work being left to congeal and grow inedible. So gradually everyone except Oliver began to eat.

Ali was still in the car with a silent sullen Ben, who appeared to have been deflated by her last admission.

"I'm going back to my party, Ben. OK? Just know this. I will always have a certain type of love for you. You were incredibly important to me and six months ago I would have never believed that I could love anyone more than I

433

did you. But I do, and I don't think I realised that until this moment."

Ben fiddled with the jewellery box, flicking it open and shut.

"Well, I suppose I deserve that. I just keep on making the same mistakes all the time, don't I? I met someone, you know, in Africa. But she didn't want me, not like I wanted her, so I guess I've experienced some of what you have."

Ali looked at him incredulously and realised what a self-centred oaf he really was. Even now, it was all about him.

"Goodbye, Ben," she said, touching his hand lightly and getting out of the car before he had a chance to react.

She ran back to her door and buzzed the intercom.

"It's me. I'm freezing. Let me in," she said abruptly into the receiver.

Oliver was standing at the living-room door – pale and worried when she came back inside.

"Are you OK?" he asked, looking for some outward sign that she was still his.

"I'm fine," Ali replied. And she pulled him to her and encased in his big warm arms she snuggled deep into his chest, and said, "I've never been better."

"Is he gone?" Trisha ventured when Ali rejoined the party.

"Yes," said Ali firmly. "I think we can safely say that he is finally gone."

Oliver grinned at Mick who smiled widely and popped open the champagne.

"I think I shall raise a toast. Please raise your glasses to Ali and Oliver."

Everyone clinked their glasses and clapped as Ali and Oliver shared a passionate kiss. Everything Oliver had feared for the past few months had finally drifted away with one ten-minute encounter between Ben and Ali. He wondered what had transpired between them but he would never ask. If Ali ever wanted to tell him she would. Right now he had a Christmas to enjoy, with the woman and little girl that he hoped would be his family soon.

Everyone tucked into their Christmas lunch with renewed gusto and soon a great time was being enjoyed by them all. By the time Louis and his girlfriend arrived Ali had decided that this was her very best Christmas ever. She cuddled Emma closely to her and was thankful for all she had, and she even had a sad thought for Ben. He was truly unhappy, and she was sad about that, but it was mostly of his own doing, and she had moved on. She watched Oliver uncharacteristically doing a highland jig with a merry Mick and hoped that this man was to be part of her future. But even if he wasn't, she would still live happily ever after. She had made her own fairytale.

Chapter 49

It was New Year's Eve and Trisha and Mick were having a party.

Trisha had decided to invite all their friends around and have one last blast as she had put it, before parenthood set in.

Ali worried that Trisha was taking on too much, so she and Oliver had made a huge curry and everyone was instructed to bring a plate of nibbles so it hadn't proved too much of an onerous task. Mick had procured a barrel of Guinness so all the men were happy to attend. It had been a successful evening with everyone in high spirits and the curry going down a storm after multiple days of turkey and ham. At the countdown to midnight, Mick had called everyone out into the cold frosty night whereupon he released a huge batch of fireworks, which lit up the inky black sky. Oliver kissed Ali passionately at the stroke of twelve and then asked her the time.

"Is it 1987 yet?" he enquired seriously.

"Yes," Ali laughed. "A minute past to be exact."

"Good," Oliver replied, leading Ali by the hand indoors, into the living room where the huge Christmas tree glittered in the quiet darkness, the myriad of fairy lights giving the only romantic glow.

"I want to ask you something, now that it's officially 1987," Oliver said and proceeded to get down on one knee. "Being so beautiful and popular, Alison O'Neill, you already had two proposals in 1986, so I wanted to be the first one in this New Year, to ask you to marry me."

Ali giggled. "Are you serious, Oliver?"

Oliver took her hand. "Ali, I have never been more serious in my life. I love you. I have always loved you. I will promise to take care of you and Emma and I will always put you both first. I know you might need time to think about it and I'm not looking for a quick answer or a short engagement. You can have all the time you wish, just please say you'll consider it. Please say you'll consider being my wife."

Ali touched his face with her hand and replied, "I don't need any time, and I have considered it. I would love to be your wife, Oliver. So the answer is yes."

Oliver who had been waiting for either a hesitant no or a reluctant maybe was overwhelmed with the unexpected response and simply pulled Ali to him. The tears that welled up inside him prevented him from speaking.

"What's the matter?" Ali quipped. "Didn't get the answer you wanted?"

"Ali, this is everything I wanted. I am just so amazed that you want it too."

Ali pulled away and studied his handsome face.

"Oliver, I have never met a kinder, more decent man in my whole life. I am so lucky that I ever found you. I realise that and I am not letting you get away. Don't be amazed that I love you. That's the easiest thing I ever did."

"And the hardest?" Oliver enquired, seeing a certain kind of wistfulness in her eyes.

"The hardest thing," Ali said, "was letting myself realise that. Now this is a new year and we have a new beginning. It's just you and me and Emma. There will be no looking back and no doubts. We are together and that's the way it will stay."

Oliver kissed her gently and they sat quietly for the longest time, just looking at the twinkling Christmas tree, their arms about each other, while the party rocked on around them in the distance. Ali felt so happy and at peace. She knew at last she had travelled the journey and had reached her mysterious destination. Everything else had brought her to here. And it all mattered. It had made her who she was now, and she felt worth loving at last.

Oliver was the happiest that he had ever been. All of his life he had felt removed, a little bit to the side of life. Since he lost his mother at six years old he hadn't known real love or belonging until his father remarried a few years previously. His heart was overwhelmed that this girl, that he had loved from afar for so long but had never felt there was a chance of him having, loved him back and had chosen him over everyone else. He knew he could repair that lonely little boy that was locked away inside him and put him to rest. He would never take this girl or her daughter for granted. Emma would never grow short of love or affection.

He held the two tickets for Paris in his pocket and imagined Ali's face when she saw them. He had hoped she would say yes and he could use them. Now he would take Ali to the most romantic city in the world, where they would buy the finest diamond that he could afford.

He briefly thought of Ben and felt some regret that this was one of life's ironies. Ben who until recently was one of Oliver's best friends would have been the first person that Oliver would ordinarily call on and share the wonderful news. Ben had lost Ali and that had to have hurt, but he had lost her six months ago and while Oliver had some sadness for Ben he realised also that Ben had brought about much of his own misfortune. Oliver didn't understand why Ben was the way he was. After all he had every good start in life and had a stable background. But Ben would have to sort himself out before he could love another person properly. Oliver wished him well, despite everything.

Ben had spent the New Year with a nameless nurse that he had met in a club on Leeson Street. He somehow ended up drunkenly in bed with her at the nurses' residence in the early hours. By the time he bedded the poor girl, her face had melded into a blend of Susie, Karen and Ali. Ben felt so confused and unhappy by the time the faceless girl had fallen asleep that he had stolen from her room like a customer. He vowed to give up alcohol and change his airline ticket the very next working day so he could fly back to Africa and feel useful and alive again.

Right now he felt empty.

The furthest distance he could put between him and

this god-forsaken country, the better. He knew he would have to face Susie when she arrived back at the base hospital, if she ever came back to Beira, but he would face that if he had to. He wondered if he could ever be happy or feel fulfilled outside of his work.

At least in Mozambique you could forget who you were or how inadequate you were at relationships while you exhausted yourself saving lives. He'd face himself some other time. Right now he just needed to get away. Women were bad news for him. He idly wondered if the French Foreign Legion needed doctors as his cab sped him home towards Sandymount at 5am. It was a new year. He would have to make a new start, because it was a sure bet that he had run out of old girlfriends and relationship re-runs. He smiled grimly as he looked out of the window as a hung-over Dublin sped by.

He couldn't wait to leave this town.

Then suddenly he thought of his parents. How insulting it must be to them that he was always trying to escape them! Perhaps he needed to spend a little time with his mother and maybe she wouldn't be so clingy and needy all the time. He remembered all the hurt he had caused her in the past with Karen. All she had really wanted was the best for him, however misguided.

He resolved that after this stint in Africa, maybe he needed to take a hard cold look at himself and sort out his true feelings. Running away wasn't solving anything. He had lost Ali through his own selfishness and idiocy. Maybe the problems with women lay with him and not with them. All these thoughts muddled around his addled brain as he travelled home. Alcohol muddled the mind but sometimes cleared it and Ben realised that kissing a nameless girl you didn't even know because she reminded you of a love you threw away on the eve of a new year was just about the saddest thing you could do. And he resolved before clambering into his cold bed that this would be the last time that he would ever waste his life again. He needed to change and he would start tomorrow. It was time for a new beginning.

Trish and Mick climbed into bed wearily after 3am when the last guest had finally left in a cab still singing 'The fields of Athenry' for the fortieth time. Trish had been enthusiastic about having the party but was now glad it was all over. This pregnancy lark really played havoc with her energy levels and by 10pm when the party was at its highest and loudest, Trish just wanted everyone to go home.

"I'm glad that's all over," she sighed as she flopped heavily onto the bed.

"Me too," answered Mick, eyeing her guardedly. "I could see you were wilting early on, but you did insist."

"I know," murmured Trish. "Sometimes I think I've energy to burn, then ten minutes later I feel exhausted. But still, it was a great night. Everyone enjoyed it."

"Yes," replied Mick, "and two especially. Did you see the two lovebirds, Ali and Oliver, sneak off in the middle of the fireworks display?"

"Sure, I did not. I was too busy dishing up curry to your savage aunties. Honestly, the pair of them are the size of prize heifers and you'd swear they hadn't had a bite in weeks the way they fell upon the food. Why, what happened?"

"Well, I think Oliver was about to ask Ali a very important question," Mick replied, looking a tad sheepish.

"What?" screeched Trish, suddenly alert, and sitting up in the bed.

"Well, he didn't say exactly, but I got the impression that he was about to ask her something serious on Christmas Day. Then the bould Ben arrived and stuffed everything up, so I guessed from the way he flitted around so nervously tonight that he was going to ask her then."

Trish rolled her eyes heavenward.

"Honestly, Mick, you're like an old woman. I'm sure you're putting two and two together and making five. If Oliver proposed, Ali would have told me. Anyway, I'll phone her in the morning and ask her."

"I doubt it," Mick smiled. "Oliver has secretly asked your mother to take Emma for three days because he's sweeping Ali off to Paris for a romantic few days."

"Mam would have told me that," Trisha remarked huffily, irked that her husband seemed to know more of what was going on with her own family and friends.

"She was sworn to secrecy. If she had told you, you would have blabbed to Ali, and it had to be a big surprise. So if he hasn't proposed already, he'll probably do it up on the Eiffel Tower."

"Hmm," Trish harrumphed. "Well, I hope she doesn't fling him off then, because I think she's had her fill of men proposing for the moment. She's getting as bad as Liz Taylor."

Mick grinned, and kissed Trisha on the forehead.

"If I didn't know you better, darling, I'd say you had a touch of the green-eyed monsters about you."

"I can't help it," wailed Trisha. "Am I awful? It's just that Ali has had three proposals in a year and her life seems very exciting at the minute. I feel like a fat old whale at the moment, and my life seems very tame in comparison. Don't get me wrong, Mick. I'm very happy and content and dying for our baby to arrive. It's just that I feel that all the thrills and romance are behind me. I'm just a boring old married woman." She sniffed into his shoulder.

"Trisha, you have what Ali craves, a loving family and a partner who adores her. And if I'm not mistaken you've had a quare few admirers in the past, and I'm sure in the present too. It's just the old hormones making you feel a bit low. Don't envy Ali, she's your best friend and she has had the most horrible childhood. The grass is pretty green on your side of the fence from where I'm sitting."

Mick cuddled her tightly to take the sting from his words.

"You're right," replied a chastened Trisha. "I do feel a bit hormonal. Please forget what I said. I wonder if Oliver has asked her to marry him. They disappeared from the party very mysteriously."

Mick smiled indulgently. Trisha was amazing at the moment. One minute she was in tears, next she was in a full flight of fancy, as chirpy as can be.

He wished that this pregnancy would hurry up and deliver him a beautiful bouncing baby and his nice sane wife back. He couldn't wait until April when the coming spring would bring their new bundle – but he dare not utter his wishes to the emotional rollercoaster that was Trisha at the moment. He just hoped his nerves would hold up that long.

It was New Year's Day. Isabel woke to find the bright sun streaming into her bedroom. It was going to be a beautiful day.

Suddenly there was a sharp rap on her door and there was Ben with a breakfast tray, and a big smile on his face.

Isabel stifled her amazement as her son placed the large greasy fry in front of her and her husband.

She almost uttered the words that would have crushed his exuberance but somehow didn't. She hadn't eaten a fattening breakfast in years, but the poor fellow seemed so earnest that she ate it gratefully.

"I just thought, with it being the New Year, that I'd treat you both to breakfast in bed," Ben said cheerfully, sitting on the corner of the divan, watching them eat. John just peered over his glasses at Ben as if a stranger had inhabited his son's body, and raised his bushy eyebrows in surprise, but ate on in silence.

"Thank you, love," Isabel trilled. "It's much appreciated."

"You know, Mum. I was thinking. We didn't get a lot of time together over the Christmas, I was hoping maybe you and I could hit the sales tomorrow. I really need some new clothes. Perhaps we could take a trip into town for the day."

Isabel's eyes lit up. She now felt like her husband did, an alien form had taken over her wayward son, who had never spent any more then ten minutes with her voluntarily in the past five years.

"That would be great, Ben," she replied through munches of toast. Whatever had happened to Ben, he seemed to be over his dark mood so she wasn't going to question it, but rather enjoy the moment.

"Right, I'm back to bed for a few hours. I've got a bit of a hangover. But get me up by midday, Mum and we'll take a walk up the Vico Road. It's a beautiful day, isn't it?"

"Yes," agreed Isabel smiling, believing it. "It is."

After he left, she and John just stared at the door for a few moments wondering if that had all been real. If it hadn't been for the bacon they were chewing on they might have felt that they dreamt it.

"I don't know who he is," quipped John at last, "but I like him."

"Me too," laughed Isabel happily. "Me too."

Ali called Trisha from Dublin Airport the next morning, while Oliver was in the coffee lounge ordering breakfast.

"Trisha, you won't believe where I am now," she gushed excitedly.

"Diving naked into the forty foot?" Trisha quipped, trying not to let Ali know she knew.

"I'm at Dublin Airport. Oliver has asked me to marry him and I've accepted. We're now off to Paris for a couple of days."

Trisha squealed with delight down the line. That she didn't have to fake.

"Ali, I am so happy for you. You deserve it. I'm also a bit jealous. I've never been to Paris. Has my Mam got Emma?"

"Yes," Ali replied, "and Trisha, get Mick to promise to

take you to Paris after the baby is born and I promise I will baby-sit for you."

"It's a deal," said Trisha. "Now go and enjoy yourself. I'll get all the gossip when you get back. Give my love to Oliver."

"I sure will," purred Ali, as she put down the receiver and she would. Three days in Paris, the most romantic city in the world, with the man she dearly loved. She just couldn't wait.

Chapter 50

It was unseasonably hot for April. The sun shone relentlessly for the past two weeks and Trisha thought she would pass out from the heat. She was sorry she ever said she would help Ali to pick out bridesmaid's dresses never mind take a starring role in the wedding, which was going to be in a scant five months' time, barely four months after the baby would arrive.

Trish looked disdainfully at all the tiny gowns which looked like they were made for 12-year-olds and noted her enormous bump. She didn't ever think that was going to shrink back sufficiently to do any dress justice. Right now, it would be nice to see her feet again and even better to find a shoe in Ireland that would fit them. For the past few weeks she had hobbled around in open toe sandals or flip flops. Luckily enough the weather had been so mild that it didn't look too odd. She flopped down onto the armchair at the fitting rooms while Ali paraded a myriad of colourful dresses, none of which she liked.

"Trisha, I can see that look. Don't panic. You will be back to your old self by the time the wedding occurs, but we have to choose now, and I am not going down the aisle without you."

Trisha looked petulant. "I know. It's just I am generously proportioned at the best of times, but right now I feel like a hippo in a dress. My boobs are huge and who is to say they will disappear afterwards? I just feel I will let you down if I have to wear a marquee down the aisle."

Ali laughed and patted her friend's hand.

"That's rubbish. Even I swelled up to beached whale proportions with Emma and I never thought I'd see size 10 again, but I did. You'll be fine. Just concentrate on the baby and yourself for now, but I need to know what you like at least."

They looked at some more miniscule creations before retiring to Switzer's coffee shop for elevenses.

Trisha comforted herself by ordering the biggest gateau she could find, coupled with a large hot chocolate. Ali felt sorry for Trisha. She knew all too well how unattractive you could feel while heavily pregnant, but there was no comfort to be had until the anxiously awaited bundle arrived.

"So," Ali enquired when they had settled, "what did the doctor say at your last visit?"

"Oh, everything's fine, the old blood pressure is a little high and of course I am gaining a bit too much weight, but otherwise I am fighting fit. I'll be on fortnightly visits from now on, until the baby is due."

Ali noticed Trisha looked worried.

"You'll be grand, Trisha. Don't fret. I was a complete worry wart and all the way out in Australia too. I felt totally weird, but at least you never got to see the huge fat me. It was a scary view."

"Yes," Trisha replied cheering up a little. "You showed me that photo, remember, the one in your big knickers?"

"So there," Ali said, triumphantly. "It happens to everybody. Now, what's it going to be, the cream off-the-shoulder, or the bronze -coloured classic empire-line dress that we saw at The Design Centre?"

"If I can be keelhauled into it, I choose the bronze number," Trish replied through munches of cake. Ali realised this was going to get worse before it got better and decided that she was not going to let all these little dramas with wedding dresses and flowers and churches affect her. If she could run her own business effectively, surely organising a wedding couldn't be so difficult?

Suddenly getting wed on a sandy beach with just her and Oliver present seemed like a wonderful escape but she knew she wouldn't ever do that. After Trisha had the baby, things would get better and her only bridesmaid would hopefully jump into the fray. At least Ali had chosen her wedding dress, a beautiful deep cream fitted bodice made of guipure lace and a narrow waist followed by a full tulle skirt. She was foregoing a veil and letting her curls tumble free with just a few cream flowers in her hair.

Emma and Trisha were going to be flower girl and bridesmaid respectively and Mick was to be best man. Ben, who Oliver had always been closest to in the past, was now no longer in touch with Oliver, and thankfully he wasn't going to be back from Africa until a few weeks before the wedding. Ali felt a bit sad that the relationship between Oliver and Ben had soured, but, of course, it had to be a casualty. It was just the way things were – Ali didn't fret over Ben any more.

She sometimes thought of him with the affection with which most people remember their first love, but that was all there was now. It was just sad that he could no longer be a friend to any of them. She wondered sometimes if Mick still kept in touch with him. He never mentioned Ben, nor did Trisha. And Ali was afraid to ask in case they all thought she was still interested, which she wasn't.

"And how was Simon?" Trisha interrupted her reverie.

"Oh, yes. Sorry I said I'd tell you all the scandal. Well, it seems that he and Jodie are back together and there's a baby on the way. He sounds ecstatic by the way. Really happy, which I suppose takes the sting out of the tail for me, seeing as how I haven't been over to see him with Emma. But Oliver wants to take Emma on honeymoon and we've decided to go to Australia. That way Simon gets to see Emma and we can take a few days off on our own. Maybe we'll go see the Barrier Reef. Oliver has always wanted to go there."

"Thank God," Trisha breathed a sigh of relief. "At least with Simon settling down and getting on with his own life, it'll be a bit easier."

"Yes," Ali replied thoughtfully. "Do you know Oliver wants to meet up with Simon and put things right with the custody issue? He wants to formally adopt Emma but only if Simon is entirely comfortable with it. I know I would love it if Oliver could adopt her, then I'd know she would be truly ours, but we'll have to see. It's a delicate process."

"You know I've just realised that I am very lucky, Ali. I constantly forget you always have the threat of Simon lurking in the background with the possibility of a custody case and here I am whingeing about swollen ankles. Next time I act like a selfish bitch, please remind me."

"I will," grinned Ali, knowing this moment of wisdom was short-lived. "Now hurry up, Mrs O'Toole. We have another three shoe shops to visit before I will let you off home."

"Oh, no," groaned Trisha vowing that whatever the blasted shoes looked like she'd say she loved them, for they weren't going to fit her big canal-boat feet anyway.

"Why don't you get married in Bali, Ali? That way I can stay fat and happy in my dressing gown with my new baby until at least October."

"Trisha, that is the best idea I have heard all year," Ali gushed. "I am having so much trouble getting churches booked and dresses organised. I could just pop my dress into the case and have a stopover in Bali. We could be married in a simple low key way and just have a big party when we get back."

She looked at Trisha's crestfallen face and laughed.

"Gotcha! As if I would ever get married without you at my side! Now quit moaning and let's try to buy something today. This is probably the last time you and I get to shop before you're too big to fit in the shop doors."

After that barb, Ali ducked a sweeping blow from Trisha.

"All right, Miss Fussy Knickers, lead on," sighed Trisha.

She hadn't remembered her own wedding being such a trial. She just wished that this baby would arrive and she could get back to some semblance of normality, or whatever passed for it with a newborn. As she waddled behind her friend up Wicklow Street which looked more like the Wicklow Hills to her today she vowed she would get fit and slim after this baby arrived, so she would look amazing at her best friend's wedding.

Twenty weeks gave her an opportunity to lose 20 pounds.

She knew she could do it if she tried hard. She looked at Ali's svelte back and dainty rear and felt a stab of jealousy before dismissing it. Everyone was different and she knew she would never be a size ten. Anyway it was high treason to be jealous of her best friend so she quashed the emotion as soon as it arose.

It was just that sometimes it wasn't easy being friends with a rasher rind when you were more of a pork chop. She would get over it. She just wished she didn't feel so fretful. Being pregnant hadn't agreed too well with Trisha so far. After all the time wishing she would become pregnant she had always envisaged herself glowing and all earth-mother style, not swollen and cranky most of the time. It hadn't been the type of pregnancy depicted by the books or the TV programmes.

She hoped fervently that she'd make a better mother when the baby arrived, but she daren't admit her fears to anyone.

Not even Ali. Some things you just could not discuss.

Chapter 51

Mick and Trisha were sitting in the car at Howth Head munching on fish and chips. They had take a long walk along Howth's pretty pier hoping that the extra exercise would bring on this reluctant baby who at 12 days overdue seemed in no hurry to come into the world. Trisha was fretting at the delay and becoming more nervous and irritable as the days passed.

Mick knew, apart from being so uncomfortable that she hardly slept, Trisha was worried about the forthcoming wedding and the amount of weight she would have to lose. That hadn't stopped either of them indulging over the past few weeks and Mick had noticed that his own trousers were becoming a bit too tight from all the midnight feasts of fast food and icecream that Trish had craved.

Mick glanced at Trisha who was chomping away happily on her steamy fresh cod and couldn't resist a smile. She worried so much, but if she had seen how beautiful she looked to him right now she wouldn't care about an extra few pounds. Her skin and hair glowed and she looked truly beautiful to him, carrying their precious child.

He looked out to sea and spotted the ferry heading towards port. The day was sunny and uncharacteristically warm.

Trisha moaned softly.

"Yes, it's really good fish isn't it?" Mick asked.

Trisha moaned again. This time louder and it sounded more like a painful groan.

"Mick," she said quietly while grabbing his arm tightly, "I think I've got a contraction."

Mick's chips went up into the air and he had the car speeding towards Clontarf in minutes from sheer fear.

"Are you sure?" he asked Trisha at the traffic lights at Sutton Cross. She didn't need to answer. One look at her pale worried face told him that this was real, and they were, in fact, about to have their first baby. Mick was scared and overjoyed and anxious to be at the hospital as soon as he possibly could, so no harm would come to either his wife or baby. In forty minutes they were at the Coombe Hospital, where a calm midwife took over and agreed that indeed Trisha was in the early stages of labour but that there was going to be quite a wait as her waters hadn't even broken and that it would be hours yet.

Mick felt a rising panic. If Trisha was in such pain already, how bad was it going to get? He telephoned all the parents and then Ali and Oliver who said they'd collect Trisha's packed bag and they'd be over in an hour.

Eight hours of painful and fruitless labour later, Trisha

had to be rushed into theatre when the baby's heart showed signs of distress, for an emergency c-section. Within thirty minutes a jubilant Mick emerged complete in hospital greens to inform a nail-biting Ali and a worried Oliver that Trisha had given birth to a baby girl, and both mother and daughter were doing well.

"She's just perfect, the image of Trisha. She even has blonde hair," blurted out an exhausted Mick through happy tears.

"Can I see her?" Ali asked fighting back tears of her own. She had been so worried for her friend.

"She's in recovery at the moment. Soon they'll take her up to the ward. You can see her then. I'm going to make a few phone calls now. We've got some anxious grandparents to inform."

With that he was gone. Oliver hugged Ali close to him.

"See, I told you she would be fine. Are you OK?" He tipped her chin up so he could read her face.

She looked drained.

"I'm fine," Ali insisted, kissing Oliver softly.

"I suppose this is a bad time to say that some day I hope this will be us."

Ali grimaced at the memory of her delivery and all its pain.

"You'd be right. It is a bad time. Wait until I hold the precious little bundle and my hormones kick in. Maybe then I'll be more amenable."

They then rushed off to the flower shop to buy the pinkest teddy and nicest flowers they could find.

Soon they were allowed up to see Trisha and her new daughter.

"Oh Trisha, she's adorable," Ali insisted as she held the sleeping babe who was to be named Carli.

"Isn't she?" beamed an exhausted-looking Trisha. She had obviously been through an ordeal, and was on heavy pain-killers from the operation. Carli would not be able to room with her mother for a few days. Trisha was a little woozy from the drugs but feeling no pain at the moment and was elated.

Mick arrived back and festooned the room with pink balloons and white roses for his wife. A little while later Trisha fell asleep, and Ali and Oliver left the little family alone to bond a bit more.

"I'm just glad she's over the worst of it," Ali said, breathing a huge sigh of relief when they'd got outside.

"It's not easy, is it?" Oliver mused, in awe at the little bundle he had just seen and how worn out Trisha had seemed.

"No," Ali replied pensively. "It's scary and wonderful, but seldom easy. But when you hold them in your arms you can't help wanting to do it again."

"Thank God," Oliver said, relieved. "For a minute there I thought you had no desire to have any more children."

"It's funny. We've never discussed it. How many children would you like, Oliver, and bear in mind before answering that you'll be on the midnight shift for feeding?"

Oliver laughed. "OK. I'd love another one to start with, maybe two if possible. But I would like a sister or brother for Emma."

"That's the right answer," said Ali, kissing him on the cheek before getting into the car.

Oliver looked puzzled as he put the key into the ignition.

"You're wondering why it was the right answer, aren't you?" Ali asked.

"Yes, I suppose I am."

"Well, you could have said, "I'd like a child of my own" but you didn't, and I love you for that. You didn't specify that Emma isn't your daughter."

"But she will be," said Oliver. "She'll be as much my daughter as any more that we may have."

"And that," smiled Ali," is partly why I'm marrying you."

"Lucky old me then," replied Oliver. "For that I shall take you wherever you want for dinner."

"Home with you and our little girl, please," replied Ali, feeling incredibly lucky and fortunate. "That's where I want to be. Just at home with you."

Oliver thought now was a good time to mention his idea, an idea to buy some land together and build a dream home like Trisha and Mick had done. He could sell his place and he'd get a great price as it was in the right part of town. If Ali agreed, she could rent out her little flat above Ali Travel. He hoped she would like the idea.

"And speaking of homes, what do you think about you and me looking at some land around the Naul ourselves and maybe building a house for all these little babies we're going to make?"

Ali was amazed.

"You mean build our own place?"

"The very same. I could sell my old pile. It's a cold old place but worth a few bob. Would you mind giving up the flat? I know you love it so much."

"Oliver, I would love to build a house with you. I never dared dream of having my own bungalow on my own acreage. It would be wonderful for Emma too. Of course I love the idea."

Oliver was pleased.

"Well, tomorrow we'll take Emma out and we'll view a few blocks of land. Then we can work out the finance part when we see what's out there."

"I can't believe it!" replied Ali excitedly, her mind already full of Aga cookers and rooftop bedrooms. She couldn't believe her luck.

Everything was working out better than she had ever dreamed.

She felt she didn't deserve to be so lucky, and quashed the little negative angel on her shoulder that whispered to her that when anything was this good it never lasted.

Chapter 52

It had been sixteen weeks since Carli was born and Trish despite all her great intentions had lost only eight pounds. She had mistakenly believed her extra two stone would melt away after the birth, but it hadn't and Trisha had not envisaged the sheer exhaustion that she would encounter, which left her with precious little energy for aerobics classes or diet food. She was lucky if she got out of her pyjamas on most days during the first two months.

She now hopped off the scales dejectedly. The slinky glamorous bridesmaid's dress that Ali had selected for her would never fit, and it also had shoestring straps, which would show off her flabby arms. She could picture how horrible she would look and it was almost enough to send her scurrying towards the biscuit tin. She had told everyone that she had lost twelve pounds and she wasn't sure Ali was convinced, but she was sticking to her story. She thought she might try that Cambridge Diet, the very low calorie one that seemed to work quickly. If she did, she wouldn't tell anyone, but it seemed time for drastic measures. Trisha felt truly miserable. She knew she should be focusing on her best friend's most important day but all she could think about was her own disgraceful size. It had taken any joy out of the occasion and she felt a rising panic as the day drew nearer and she still remained 'cuddly', as Mick had termed her while trying to be supportive, and that was the unkindest cut of all. She remembered when he had called her 'sexy'. Still, she must put a brave face on it for there was to be a fitting today, and Ali had enough to worry about.

Ali was worried. She knew Trisha wasn't keen on the dress as she hadn't got back to her normal weight, but she still looked fabulous. Ali wished Trisha could see how attractive she still was. A few extra pounds couldn't change that, but she knew she would have to jolly Trisha along. There was still time to lose another few pounds before the wedding. Everything else was going according to plan. All the invitations had been sent out and the menu selected. Nothing had been left to chance. Oliver decided he was to choose the wedding rings. And everything else that needed to be done had been expertly handled by Ali. She took to the organising like an embattled general. She and Trisha were going for another traumatic fitting today. Honestly, Ali wondered, there would be more tears and tantrums from Trisha than there would be from Emma who was in full princess mode and enjoying every last minute.

Still, she mustn't fret – there was still so much to do.

Oliver was in Brooks Brothers on Dawson Street with Mick and his father, having fittings on their morning suits. Ali had chosen the colour and styles, basically the men just had to show up and try on their clothes. The suits were a deep grey with rich tapestry waistcoats and Oliver had a deep bronze-coloured cravat. Oliver's father looked immensely pleased as he saw his son dressed up in all his finery as a bridegroom. He slapped Oliver heartily on the back and whispered in a gruff voice, "Your mother would be so proud to see you now." Oliver reckoned that was the closest his father would ever come to saying "I love you" and that was OK. They had come a long way, Oliver and his father Bill. Bill would never be a demonstrative and openly loving parent, but Oliver had accepted him now. It was at last a comfortable relationship.

Oliver was happier than he had ever been.

Bill sat down heavily on the chair and took up *The Times*, and started to leaf through it.

"By the way, I was talking to John Murphy the other day at the Golf Club, Ollie, and he tells me that Ben is due back this week. Why don't you give him a call. I'm sure he would love to hear from you."

Oliver grimaced into the full-length mirror – he could see his father reflected behind him. He had his head stuck in the paper, apparently not waiting on a reply.

That was not the best news Oliver had ever heard. He was concerned Ben would try another surprise visit on Ali. Oliver didn't know why but he felt very uncomfortable with that idea.

He still felt Ali could be persuaded by Ben to take him back. Oliver grimly decided he was not going to contact Ben Murphy and he sincerely hoped that Ben wouldn't get wind of the news of Ali's impending wedding. It could very well ruin everything.

All Oliver's earlier happiness vanished and he felt the day had been soured. He fervently wished that Ali and he had decided to take off to Bali like they had discussed and got married there. Then he would have nothing to worry about. Now he would just have to wait and see.

Ben was reading his latest letter from his father. It would be the last one he would receive before he quit Beira and headed back home for good. He was tired. Burn-out was a typical reaction at the end of a long and arduous stint in Africa. Eventually your energy levels depleted and you had to leave. Ben was looking forward to going home and resuming his normal life. He eagerly awaited his father's weekly letters, which cheered him up no end. They were always witty and informative and made Ben feel like he had just been down to his local pub for half an hour.

This letter told him of his father's latest failure on the golf course and a chance meeting he had with Bill Johnston who had casually mentioned that Oliver was to be married in a few weeks. His father had joked that surely that was a hint to Ben when his peers were making the leap into wedded bliss, surely he might follow. Obviously his father had no idea that the bride was one Alison O'Neill. Ben was gutted, but he had no one to blame but himself. He could not believe deep down that Ali loved Oliver, not in the same way that she had loved him. His heart ached for all the stupid things he had done, the arrogance that made him doubt his enduring love for her. All the Karens and the Susies of the world would never come close – surely she wasn't serious about marrying boring staid old Ollie?

Ben resolved that he would go and see Ali one last time and try to persuade her that he was sorry and he still loved her. This time he would make sure that he saw her when she was alone so no pressure would be brought to bear from any of her friends or indeed her fiancé. When Ben told Ali that they were soul mates she would not deny it. He just knew she still loved him. She had even said that she would always love him.

He wished that he was leaving tomorrow now instead of next week, then he wouldn't have to endure Susie flaunting her new intern doctor under his nose. This poor chap seemed to be as besotted as Ben once was. Ben felt such an idiot that he had fallen for Susie so hard. Now he could see her for what she really was, a real man-eater. She had told everyone at the base hospital that Ben had arrived on her doorstep with an engagement ring and he had been the laughing-stock for weeks. His self-esteem and confidence had taken quite a battering and he hadn't dated anyone since. So his thoughts eventually drifted back to Ali, and Ben realised what a fool he had been. Still, it might not be too late yet, he mused as he re-read his father's letter in his hot little room. The only other noise was the whirring of the ineffectual overhead fan. Soon this would pass and he would be back home where he belonged and he hoped he could convince the woman he loved that she was still his.

Isabel and John were enjoying a rare lunch at the golf club. Isabel enjoyed it immensely when John brought her to his inner sanctum because it made her feel special. She liked all her friends to see that she still enjoyed a happy marriage. John was telling her over their coffees that he had met Bill Johnston last week and that Bill had told him Oliver was getting married soon.

"So I wrote to Ben and told him to give Ollie a call, when he gets back. They were good friends you know. Can't think why they ever fell out."

Isabel was fuming.

"They fell out," she retorted acidly, "over that awful O'Neill girl. She is the one whom Oliver has the sad misfortune to be marrying and our son had a lucky escape from. She's nothing but a common gold digger. Now you've probably dragged up the whole sorry episode again. And just when Ben was doing so well. I hope for your sake he doesn't end up stopping that blasted wedding. Why can't you leave well enough alone?"

John was bristling. Several of his acquaintances at the bar were staring at Isabel's outburst with raised eyebrows. Honestly, you couldn't bring the damn woman anywhere without her making a show of you.

"Please keep your voice down, Isabel. All I did was ask my son to contact an old friend. Stop making 'Gone with the Wind' out of it. Now drink up your coffee. I have an appointment this afternoon and I don't want to be late."

Isabel sighed resignedly. She hoped that Ben would not do anything silly and would just let Oliver get on with making the biggest mistake of his life. He had never really got that O'Neill girl out of his head, for whatever reason. She then idly wondered at what John's appointment was this afternoon. She knew his medical appointments were clear; she had checked his diary earlier. She hoped that he hadn't resumed his dalliance with that awful Marjorie from the Yacht Club. She fretted for a moment and then dismissed it. He wouldn't have brought her here today if he had been planning an illicit meeting. She must have just irritated him. She gave him her biggest fakest smile and murmured a heartfelt 'sorry' and resolved to be more demure in public in the future. After all John did have a reputation to protect.

John smiled back at the performance. She really didn't know that he could see right through that calculating little brain of hers. He managed to stop himself from glancing at his watch wishing he were anywhere else. Still, this had been a brilliant plan by Marjorie. Give Isabel a little more attention and she'll never suspect. Only another couple of hours and he would be with peaceful passionate Marjorie, who made him forget his advancing years and his shrill cold wife. He wished that Ben hadn't ruined his chances with the warm-hearted redhead.

He knew from experience that she would have made his only son very happy. But there was more than an element of his wife in Ben and that would be his downfall, and there was nothing John could do about it.

He looked out over the perfect golf course and sunny day and thought perhaps he might take Marjorie down to Wicklow for a nice drive.

"You look so peaceful, John," Isabel remarked, while regarding him gazing out over the green. "We really must do this more often."

"Yes, indeed," John lied to his wife. "That would be very nice."

Chapter 53

Ali was busy trying to get ready. Emma had spilled the entire contents of her make-up bag over the new lemon duvet, which was now covered in fake-tan powder and Emma was adorned in red lipstick over her entire face.

Ali had to clean Emma up and take the duvet cover off and she was running late.

Oliver was picking her up in twenty minutes. The Marine Hotel had phoned to say that they were dressing the room that they had booked for another wedding and did Oliver and Ali want to see it and get an idea of how it all looked. Ali was very excited, as they had only viewed the room on a cold damp March evening and today it was bright and sunny. The room had huge French doors leading onto the long garden and seafront. Ali wanted to see it at its best.

Now, she tried to remove the crimson stain from Emma's sulky face. She took Emma's lipstick-stained pink gingham dress off and replaced it with a pale lemon one.

"Now, try to keep clean. Oliver is taking us out soon."

Emma sulked on, not even the idea of the wonderful Oliver could shake her from her tantrum. She was furious at being removed from her make-up game.

Just then the bell buzzed. Damn, Ali thought. Oliver was early.

"Sorry we're not quite ready, Oliver, but come up anyway."

"Ali." It was just one word but Ali instantly knew who it was.

"Ben?" She couldn't quite believe it.

Not now, she thought her mind racing, Oliver will be here any minute. If he sees Ben here, he'll go nuts.

"Can I see you, Ali, for a few minutes?"

Ali hesitated. If she said no, he might hang around outside, which might be worse.

"OK," she said, at last. "Come up."

She waited at the top of the stairs, which Ben was bounding up in twos.

He looked good, better then he had looked the last time she had seen him. That haunted look was gone.

"You look great," he said, smiling, drinking her in.

"Ben, please tell me what you have come for. Oliver is due any time soon and I don't want a scene."

"I just want to tell you not to marry him. Oliver is not for you. Ali. You and I, we have this great history, this love that won't die. I know it and you know it. Tell me that you love him more than you loved me and I'll go away."

Ali looked at him. She still found him incredibly attractive. When she looked at him she was fifteen again. All the old memories came rushing back. She had loved him, like no other.

But that was the whole point – she *had* loved him. She now loved Oliver.

"Ben, I told you at Christmas. I love Oliver. And I have to tell you that we're still going to be married, no matter what you say. Please don't make this any more difficult than it already is."

Just then Emma came out of the kitchen and eyed Ben darkly.

"She is beautiful," Ben said, bending down to say hello. "How are you, Emma. It's been a long time."

Emma looked at him blankly then climbed up into Ali's arms.

"Where's Oliber, Mummy?"

"He's coming soon, darling," Ali said kissing her. "Ben, I think you better go."

Ben looked at Ali and tried again.

"Can we have dinner, maybe? Just as friends."

"No, Ben – we can't. I haven't the time. It's only two weeks away from my wedding. There's no point. Please go."

She walked towards the stairs and started to go down, grabbing her bag. She had to get him out of here. Ben followed silently. Ali opened the door.

"I'm sorry, Ben."

"So am I," said Ben, touching a wisp of Ali's escaping hair. "I never thought I'd lose you entirely. I always felt we would at least be friends."

"We might be, later. It's just that right now . . . "

Ben interrupted her reply with a kiss that landed gently but passionately on her. Ali pulled away.

"What the hell are you doing?" she asked Ben. Just

then she spotted Oliver across the street. He was staring open-mouthed.

It must have looked awful, Ali thought. She grabbed Emma's hand and tried to cross the street, but the traffic was busy and by the time she had got to Oliver he was already in his car and driving away. He looked devastated. Ali ran back across the busy road with Emma in her arms.

"You idiot, Ben Murphy! You may have just cost me my wedding."

Ben looked repentant.

"Ali, I'm really sorry, I didn't mean for that to happen."

"Yes you did," retorted Ali coldly, her eyes icy. "It's exactly how you meant it. You didn't want me to marry him and now it looks like you got your wish."

Oliver drove away like a madman. He could not believe what he had just witnessed. Ben kissing Ali full on the lips and the way he had touched her hair had spoken of real intimacy. Ali hadn't looked as if she minded. His mind spun and he felt physically ill. Everything he had feared so much had come to pass. Ben was back and now was taking his place in Ali's life again. Oliver had lost her, if indeed he ever had her. He drove like a man possessed towards Malahide. He needed some air and some time to think. Everything he had ever wanted was falling away from him and he didn't know how to stop it.

Ali slammed the door shut on a pleading Ben and was in hot angry tears by the time she got to the telephone to call Trisha.

"I'll be right over," Trisha had replied and gathered her

little baby and the mountainous bag of necessary baby items and got into her little car and headed for Swords.

Ben buzzed Ali relentlessly and Ali ignored him, pacing up and down until Trisha arrived, unsure of what to do. She knew she had to speak to Oliver, to try and make him believe nothing had happened, but she doubted he would believe her. Would she believe him, if the shoe were on the other foot? Not likely.

Ben buzzed again, and this time he kept his finger on the doorbell 'til Ali answered.

"What the hell do you want?" Ali roared down the intercom.

"Ali, maybe if I talk to him, tell him this was totally my fault. He might just listen to me. Where do you think he might go?"

"Wouldn't that be counter-productive? I mean you got what you wanted." Ali was crying.

Ben felt terrible. He had been such a shit.

"I want you to be happy, Ali. I didn't accept that you were happier with Oliver, but you obviously are. I know that now. If I can tell him that, maybe he'll believe me. Please!"

"Try Howth Head, where you and I used to go. He knows that's still my favourite place. He might be there. That's where Trisha and I were going to try."

"Well, you stay put for the moment – leave it to me. I'll try to fix it. Oliver and I were good friends for a long time. I think that might still count a bit."

Ali doubted it, but stayed silent.

She watched out the window as Ben got into his smart Mercedes and sped away. For a moment she thought of the waiting events manager at the hotel, waiting on a couple that might never arrive and might be cancelling their dream day altogether and she wept until Trisha arrived.

Ben found Oliver on top of Howth Head, just like Ali had said.

His friend was staring out to sea as if looking for something.

If Oliver heard Ben approach he didn't let on.

"Oliver, it was not how it looked back there. I kissed Ali without her consent. She told me that she loved you and was going to marry you and I was so jealous I kissed her, but that was it. Nothing else happened."

Oliver remained silent, his face stonily staring out into the blue.

"I lost her, Ollie. I lost her to you and it was my own damn fault. I'm here now only because she made me know that her heart will break if you call off this wedding, and deep down I want her to be happy. You make her happy, more than I ever could."

"Why did you have to spoil it all? Is there no end to your vanity?" Oliver roared, his eyes blazing. He was still very angry.

"I didn't spoil it all," Ben roared back. "Only if you let me, will it all be ruined. And when are you going to realise that you deserve to be loved, Oliver? Ali chose you. She chose you over me and Simon and every other bloke who wanted her. Now if you want to throw that all away, then you can't pin it all on me. You have to own that responsibility. Why do you think I tried? I knew if I so much as got her attention for five minutes you would throw in the towel. You're such a quitter. Always have been."

Oliver landed his best right hook square onto Ben's chin.

Ben fell down onto his bottom and sat there, stunned.

Oliver then got into his car and roared off, hopefully Ben thought, to Ali's flat.

Ben smiled ruefully while rubbing his chin. "Gotcha."

For the first time in his life he had done something for someone without anything being in it for him. He hoped Ali would come to appreciate that.

Trisha had made Ali a strong cup of tea, soothed all her friend's terrors and called the hotel to advise that the couple would be late and would call back later to re-schedule.

"You should have cancelled it altogether," Ali sniffed.

"No," Trisha replied darkly, "that's bad luck. Don't worry. Ben will sort it out. If nothing else he's got bags of charm. Oliver will be back and everything will be OK. Now just wait and see."

Trisha sounded more cheerful than she felt. She knew Oliver had a fear that Ali loved Ben more than him and seeing the kiss might just push him over the edge.

She looked out of the window anxiously while patting a grizzly Carli. She prayed that Oliver would return, or at least phone.

Ali would be a basket case if the wedding were called off at this late stage – Trisha wasn't sure if she could cope with the ensuing carnage.

Just then she saw Oliver's car pull up abruptly outside.

"Here he is," she screamed and hastily gathered all Carli's things.

"Now, I'm off. I'll leave you two in peace to sort it all out. Call me later if you can."

With that she was gone. She slammed the door shut and gave Oliver a quick wave across the street before putting Carli into the car in record time and fleeing – she didn't want to have to say anything to Oliver that might inflame the already taut situation.

She noticed he still looked tense and prayed that he wasn't back to tell her friend that their engagement was over and the wedding was off.

She looked down at the carefully grown fingernails that she had managed to resist biting for the past few months, had cultivated into long elegant talons, and sighed. They would be bitten to the quick before her friend called her later with the final verdict. She thanked God that she and Mick seemed to be in calmer waters and were now happily enjoying each other and their new little daughter. She drove towards the Naul saying a silent prayer that Ali's drama would all work out.

Oliver buzzed the intercom silently and Ali let him in without a word. She stood at the top of the stairs unsure of what awaited her. She felt her heart thump loudly under her shirt. Oliver seemed calm at least.

"Are you OK?" Ali asked, feeling it was the wrong thing to say, but what was the right thing? Did it bother you seeing my ex devour me an hour ago?

"I've been better," Oliver replied wearily.

He put his arm around Ali's waist and led her inside.

"It's OK, Ali. Ben told me what happened. He followed me. I didn't realise I was that predictable. You knew exactly where I'd be."

"I know you," said Ali softly. "And I love you. And I thought you knew me. I thought you'd trust me enough to know I would never do anything to hurt you, especially with Ben. I thought you understood me when I told you it was over."

"Well, obviously Ben didn't," Oliver retorted hotly then quickly apologised. "I'm sorry, Ali. Ben was right. I never felt I deserved you. I always wait to be abandoned, even instigate it. Somehow I knew this would happen. I actually waited for it to happen, for Ben to come back and claim you as his. But something Ben said made me hit him but also made me realise he had a point."

Ali looked at him intently. She couldn't tell by his sad expression what he was going to say next. Her knees were knocking – she hoped he wasn't going to say that it was over, whatever had Ben told him.

"What did he say?"

"He said that I was always a quitter. So I hit him. I knocked him down, because I knew he was right. I was a quitter. I was always so afraid of letting myself love someone so I'd push them away. You were the only one I didn't do that to. So I'm not quitting now. I still want to marry you, if you'll have me. I'm sorry for being such an idiot and not trusting you, despite what it may have looked like when I saw you two together."

Ali jumped up and kissed Oliver.

"Come on," she said, with a wide grin spreading across her face. She grabbed Oliver's hand and picked up Emma.

"Where are we going?" Oliver was confused.

"Have you forgotten? We've got a wedding to finalise." Ali beamed and she stepped happily down the stairs.

The sun shone brighter than ever as she opened the door onto the street. The door on the ghosts of the past had finally been shut and another one to their future finally fully opened.

It was a new day.

Chapter 54

It was Ali's Wedding Day.

The rain was bucketing down in sheets. Unusual for August but as this was Ireland, anything could happen.

Ali was unconcerned. She was sitting in Trisha's huge attic bedroom on the king-size bed, having her curls somewhat tamed and sipping on a large cool Baileys and ice.

Trisha was in a tizz, the look she had been trying to achieve somehow eluded her and she felt like a giant bronze sausage squeezed into the too tight dress. All the tummy control pants in the world couldn't disguise her large stomach.

She frowned at the mirror, holding in her stomach for three seconds until she felt like she could burst. She had lost another six pounds by sensible dieting and exercise and while she was still less than happy with her appearance, everyone else seemed to think she looked amazing.

"Trisha, you look sensational. Stop fussing about your stomach and have a drink of Baileys. It calmed your nerves before your wedding, now it's my turn. You are making me nervous with all your fussing about."

Trisha did look fantastic. Her hair was blonder from the sun of the past few weeks and her sallow skin nicely tanned. It was a shame the good spell hadn't lasted but nothing could keep Ali from feeling anything less than sunny today. Ali wondered if Trisha would ever be satisfied with her appearance. All Ali could see was a curvy beautiful woman who had fabulous skin and hair everyone envied. Yet all Trisha could focus on was her few extra pounds.

"Do I look OK, really?"

"Trisha, I want this to stop now, this obsessing about your figure. You are a beautiful woman. Stop ruining a very special day just because you feel you're not a stick-pin in that dress. I would kill for your sallow skin, but my freckles are part of me. And I'm OK about my 32b chest. Even though I'd prefer yours. I accept me so can you please accept yourself, and let's enjoy this day?"

Trisha was full of remorse and admiration at how her shy insecure friend had blossomed into a confident strong independent woman.

"Sorry, I didn't realise I was being such a pain in the arse. I won't be such a bore in future. And thanks for the compliments by the way. I guess the grass is always greener."

"Here," Ali smiled. "Drink this up and we'll get me into my dress. After that there'll be no more Baileys until the reception."

As the hairdresser finished Ali's hair and the cream tulle and lace creation was removed from its large white box, Trisha felt a lump rise to her throat.

"Do you know how absolutely proud I am of you right now?" she said while Ali stepped into the beautiful dress.

Ali looked taken aback.

"Proud of me?"

Trisha had tears dancing in her eyes and she was busy trying not to cry and ruin her perfectly applied mascara.

"Yes. You overcame so much and now you are successful, independent and strong. You are so different from that shy little Ali that always hid behind me. To tell you the truth, I'm a little bit envious of you."

Ali was amazed by that admission.

"But, Trisha, I have always envied you. Your good looks, your confidence, your happy family. I used to lie in bed wishing I was your sister and I could be part of that large loving crowd that you enjoyed around you. Then you met Mick and had this great house, wonderful marriage. I envied you for years." Ali became a bit tearful herself now. "Trisha, you have been there for me through thick and thin. I would never have made anything of myself if it hadn't been for your belief in me, and your standing by me, no matter what. I owe you such a lot."

She gave her friend a huge hug.

"What are we like!" Trisha exclaimed as the tears fell.

"Two lunatics – if anyone came in and saw us, we'd be carted off by the men in the white coats. Anyway, any more crying and we'll have to call up Madge's Make-up for emergency repairs."

Ali pulled up the dress and murmured, "Now, no torrents of tears when you see how fantastic I look in this creation."

Trisha gasped when Ali turned around and she could see how amazing Ali looked.

The lace top on the gown glanced off the shoulders but had long bell sleeves. It was fitted at the bodice and came into Ali's narrow waist, but then the cream tulle took over and the full skirt fell to the ankles where Ali wore a simple pair of cream kitten heels. She carried a tied bunch of cream tulips and roses.

And a few roses adorned her hair.

"You look beautiful!" Trish enthused.

Ali smiled.

"I know."

Jim Costello shouted up the stairs.

"The cars are here, and you'll be glad to know the rain has stopped."

"I knew it," Ali said triumphantly. "I knew the rain would clear."

"We'd better make a move," Trisha said. "Mum has Carli and Emma at the moment. If we don't get down there soon it'll all end in tears."

"OK, I don't want to be late anyhow. Poor old Oliver is nervous enough already."

"Ali, I have to ask you something?"

Ali looked quizzical.

"Fire away."

"Are you happy, with Oliver I mean?"

"What you really mean is am I happier with Oliver than I was with Ben?"

"Yes," Trisha replied slightly embarrassed, "I suppose I do."

Ali looked out of the attic window. From here you could glimpse the sea.

"Yes, I am. You probably find it hard to believe because I loved him so much. But I'm not that needy little girl any more who felt that if someone as special as Ben loved her then she might actually be someone. I love Oliver for entirely different reasons. I know we will be happy. He adds to my life, which is pretty good already. He doesn't define it, and if I had to live without him I would survive, whereas when Ben left me I felt I wanted to die, because I didn't feel special enough on my own. Oliver has been through the same thing, and he loves me for me. I can't ask for anything more than that."

Trisha touched her friend's shoulder and looked out over the green fields with the patch of blue in the distance and said softly, "I couldn't have put that better myself. Now come on. You've got a bridegroom waiting."

The sun shone partially through the grey ominous clouds as Ali's wedding car got to the church on Griffith Avenue. Thankfully the clouds cleared long enough for her to make it up the large granite steps towards her future.

At that very time, Ben sat in the conservatory that was

built for his and Karen's wedding all those years ago and sipped on an expensive brandy while watching the rain fall heavily.

It was a pity that the sun hadn't shone for Ali's big day but he felt that the rain pouring down was apt for the way he felt right now.

It was finally over and Ali was gone. He was going to have to get on with the rest of his life. He didn't however, regret what he had said to make Oliver return to her. Oliver would make her happier than he ever could. He had realised that. It was probably the one unselfish thing that he had done in years.

Isabel spotted her son looking wistfully out at the rain and wondered if she should go into him and issue some words of comfort. But she didn't. She could not muster up a falsehood that she was sorry this had happened, because she wasn't.

She had never liked that common O'Neill girl and she never would. However, seeing him sitting there looking so alone with the barest hint of grey starting to grace his hair she couldn't help wondering that if she had never interfered would he have been happier. Then she dismissed the notion before it took hold and made her feel too uncomfortable. Ben was her son. She knew best and she knew him best. There would be someone suitable for him soon.

She just knew it.

Ali stood on the altar saying her vows and a tear sprang from nowhere and splashed onto her cheek. It was a tear of happiness for she had never been happier. Oliver held her hand tightly and wiped the offending tear away, while she whispered thanks.

The priest then pronounced the pair to be husband and wife and the entire congregation burst into spontaneous applause.

Ali and Oliver laughed.

She felt sure she was going to live happily ever after.

She just knew it.

THE END